CRY FOR THE DEAD

THE FIRST BOOK IN THE ROSSI TRILOGY

Dominic G Smith

Dominic G Smith

ISBN-13: 9798722339706
ISBN-10: 1477123456

Cover design by: Art Painter
Library of Congress Control Number: 2018675309
Printed in the United States of America

Dedicated to Marian F.

My long suffering wife who has to deal with my long flights of fancy.

The first Royalty cheque belongs to you.

CONTENTS

PREFACE

Cry for the Dead is the first book in the Rossi Organised Crime thriller series.

The second book, Past Sins, due for publication 2022.

Sign up for advance chapters and special offers at;

https://www.facebook.com/dominic.smith.96387189

ONE

Jack Malone was angry. He scooped up his gambling chips from the mahogany table and walked from the private members lounge of the Glasgow Grace Riverboat Casino to the cashier's booth, more than a little bit drunk. An hour ago he'd had been mellow and happy, lusting after a young French knickered waitress until that prick Fat Tony Smith had cornered him. Now he was agitated, waiting for the machine to finish its tally. He knew he would need to let Rossi know about Smith's half arsed attempt at bribery and getting him to jump ship. But if it hadn't been for Domenico Rossi taking him under his wing in the BarL all those years ago, he would be a washed up alcoholic by now instead of just an alcoholic. Shit, truth is he'd be dead instead of wearing two grand a pop made to measure suits and downing twenty five year old Lagavulin like bottled water. Anyway, he preferred to stick to what he knew best; laundering Rossi's money from the high class brothels disguised as health spas and from the drug running. And as the only volume wholesaler of narcotics into the country, Domenico Rossi needed Jack to keep the pieces of the ever growing jigsaw he was creating firmly in place. The 'Jabba The Hut' look alike Smith was right about one thing though. He wasn't paid nearly enough. But Jack had developed ways to siphon money for himself that didn't involve betraying his boss to anyone. Work for Ian Gilmour? No bloody thanks, thought Jack. Gilmour might be trying to take over every small, tuppence halfpenny outfit in the West of Scotland on his way to becoming Mr. Big, but the guy was a sociopath and Jack intended to go nowhere near him. A ping from the tally machine announcing its completion broke Malone's reverie. Jack pocketed the receipt for his winnings, then turned unsteadily and walked towards the exit. He'd cash the chit on his next visit.

'Can I get you a Private Hire Mr. Malone?' a suited and booted doorman asked as Jack walked towards him.

Malone had driven in earlier, intending to stay for a couple of drinks and an hour on the tables. That was at nine o'clock and the Tag on his wrist now told him it had just gone three fifteen in the morning. With six, or was it seven doubles under his belt he knew he was well over the limit. But the roads would be quiet and he would be back in Bothwell in thirty minutes, tops. Plus with his tolerance levels it barely showed.

'Thanks Eddie, but not tonight. I need the car first thing in the morning and I don't fancy leaving it here overnight. Bring it around to the front would you? It's in a disabled bay in Hope Street.' He tossed him the keys. 'And get me another double of that Lagavulin while I'm waiting?' He was still angry with Smith.

The doorman hesitated. Jack looked at him with a stare that said, remember who I am.

He nodded. 'No problem Sir. I'll have it here in five.'

When the car arrived, Jack placed the now empty tumbler on a nearby table and walked slowly down the boat's boarding ramp. Stumbling around to the driver's door, he tripped, falling into the car as he opened it. He sat down with a sigh, shook his head to clear it and picked the Blue Badge off the dashboard, shoving it in the Jags glove compartment.

Back on the boat, 'Fat' Tony Smith finished puffing on his cigar and watched as Malone walked out of the casino trying his best to look sober. He reached for his phone.

'Hi, it's me,' he said. 'He didn't bite. I don't think he will. Seems to have a bit of a hard-on for our Mr Rossi.'

He waited and listened.

'Okay. I'll make the call. Yes, tonight, within the next half hour.' He finished the call and dialled another number.

'It's on. Follow him and make sure it happens before he gets home. And remember, it needs to look like an accident.' He hung up.

In his car, Malone switched on the batteries, fumbled with the seatbelt, then headed off towards the Kingston Bridge, feeling dizzy and light-headed. Reaching over, he tweaked the climate control to blow cold air onto his face and almost clipped the kerb. Shit, best not to scuff the fifteen hundred quid a piece alloys of the Jaguar SUV, he smiled to himself. At the traffic lights under the bridge, he turned right, heading up to Argyle Street, and overshot the next set slightly as they turned red. Damn! Maybe he should have taken that private hire after all, he laughed to himself again. Looking in his rear-view mirror he noted it was quiet, with only one other car behind him. Too close behind him though, headlights blazing. Stupid fucker. Still, he should be okay, the alcohol convincing him there was nothing wrong with his reflexes. Drumming his fingers on the steering wheel, he waited for the lights to change, his eyes drooping closed.

A beep of a horn brought Jack out of his half sleep. The lights had turned green. He pulled forward, keeping to the right as he crossed Argyle Street. He moved onto the M8 slip road and accelerated to build up speed before hitting the motorway proper. The car following him was close, and Jack didn't see it pull onto the motorway behind him and accelerate in the other lane to try and draw level with the Jag. Eventually Jack realised he'd travelled further than he'd intended. Even drunk, he knew if he carried on in this lane, he would end up leaving the motorway at St George's Cross, a hell of a detour and not what he wanted. He pulled to the right without indicating, taking the other car by surprise, almost clipping its front end. It blasted its horn, but slowed down enough for Jack to complete his manoeuvre. Malone shook his head, trying to clear his vision. Fuck you, Jack said to himself. No one beeps at me. His drunken bravado kicked in. Flooring the accelerator, the gearless electric motor whined in response and Jack felt the surge of power from the batteries as the Jag leapt forward with a burst of greyhound-like speed. Gripping the wheel, he pulled away.

Exiting the Charing Cross tunnel, he hit eighty before noticing the tail lights of a car coming on from the slip road on his left. Cursing, he swung the steering wheel to the right, moving himself into the overtaking lane as he approached the elevated section of the motorway. But he failed to notice the car which had beeped him had mirrored his actions and was still close behind. Suddenly, another vehicle appeared at his right-hand side, a white SUV, this time coming onto the motorway from Great Western Road. Jack glanced over. He glimpsed a dark-haired woman in the front passenger seat who looked across towards him, obviously surprised at Jack's speed. The lane they were in didn't merge with his on the motorway, but in his drunken state he thought the car was about to side swipe him. Pulling the wheel of the Jag to the left, he knew he'd overcompensated as he felt himself lose it. He swung back to the right again, his car rocking, but he did bring it under control. Then though, he heard a loud bang and felt a violent push from behind, one that swung the back end of his Jag to the right.

The right rear wing of Jack's car caught the unfortunate white SUV full on its offside front wheel. The Jag fishtailed again, its traction and lane control struggling to keep it from rolling. The driver of the SUV he had hit tried desperately to straighten his own vehicle, frantically spinning the steering wheel both ways. But he was to close to the Motorway edge kerb. He hit it hard, tumbling through the lightweight, three bar crash barrier into the gap between the opposite carriageway and the road below. The SUV somersaulted as gravity took hold, flipping upside down as it became airborne in the space between the east and westbound carriageways. Twisting as it fell, it shook its occupants, rattling them around the interior despite their seat belts, necks straining with whiplash. Finally it landed on its roof with a metal rending crash. Beneath it lay the remains of a Glasgow black cab that had been passing as it dropped from the sky. The cab's old diesel engine kept running for a few seconds, an accent to the cacophony of the crash, before giving up as its fuel flow died. Steam and water vapour rose from the mangled wreckage of both vehicles until all that could be heard were the screeching tyres of the next few cars that happened upon the scene.

Jack was oblivious to this. His Jag had stayed upright, but was fishtailing its way along the road. He had his foot on the brake, fighting for control, the ABS working overtime. Eventually he swung the wheel too far to the right and also thumped the crash barrier, coming to a stop with a thud as his airbags erupted around him. The Jag did not leave the road. It did not somersault. But it was hit again hard, from behind, moving it closer to the edge of the motorway, nearer the drop. Its wheels had become entangled in the broken crash barrier though, and it stayed on the overpass. He was dazed, but he knew he had tagged something then he himself had been rammed. Looking back between the headrests, he caught sight of two people running from a car abandoned at an angle behind him. They piled into another one that had stopped beside them before it too sped away. What the hell was happening he wondered? But he was dizzy, both from the impact and the booze. His neck was stiffening. Pushing open the driver's door, he unbuckled his seat belt, clambered from the Jag and bent over, feeling the growing pain in his shoulders from the whiplash. White powder from his exploded airbags vented out the door.

Other cars had stopped further back, their hazard lights flashing, occupants running across to the crash barrier. It was then he noticed it, about fifty metres away. A part of the rail was bent and buckled, with one section missing completely. Jack straightened up, rubbing his neck. He stumbled back up the motorway to see just what had caused the barrier to disappear. He noted a few more cars joining the jam as they exited the tunnel. Even at this early hour, the few drivers on the opposite carriageway were beginning to rubber neck and he heard a bang as someone was rear ended. Approaching the small group, some of them turned to look at him. One woman stepped back from the edge and held her hands over her mouth in shock. Some others had their mobiles out and were filming the scene below. Jack was sobering up. He was beginning to get a really bad feeling about this.

'You all right mate?' a squat, bodybuilder of a man asked him. Jack said nothing and moved to where the barrier should have been.

'For fuck's sake watch it pal,' someone else said and grabbed him by the arm to prevent him toppling over.

'Wh ....., what happened?' he mumbled. Then he looked over the edge, to the road below and felt the bile rise in his aching stomach as realisation dawned.'

'Did you lose control or something?' a young woman asked him, eyes wide and staring, voice high pitched and accusing.

'Whad'ya mean,' he slurred in reply. He wasn't as sober as he'd thought earlier, the last double whisky kicking in.

'Your car! It hit the front of that one and sent it flying over the edge.' She wrinkled her nose and stepped in a little closer. 'Holy fuck,' the woman started. 'You're absolutely gutted.'

Jack glanced back over the edge again, and the enormity of what he was seeing hit him. His legs went weak and his stomach roiled. Twenty-five-year-old Lagavulin infused vomit splashed onto the carriageway and hit his stupidly expensive shoes. People jumped back to avoid the splatter. Eyes bored into the back of his head and he turned to see everyone gathered there staring at him.

He started to walk back towards his car, but powerful arms grabbed him from behind and held him tight.

'You're going nowhere pal!' The body builder snarled.

'Shit,' Jack whispered quietly as he felt his legs give way. 'Oh, shit.'

TWO

'Is he here yet?' Domenico Rossi asked, his voice tight as Billy Jenkins opened the door to the office. Rossi stood in the enormous bay window overlooking the garden at the rear of his Pollokshields Victorian Mansion. Outside, rows of Oak and Cedar trees behind two metre high sandstone walls hid the estate from prying eyes. Bright, early morning light poured through the window of the room and lit the carefully restored details as it danced across the cast iron fireplace and intricate plasterwork of the ceiling. A dark mahogany dado rail ran around each wall, breaking up the décor between the off white paint below and subtly patterned silk wallpaper above. With its original doors, skirting and wooden floors, sanded, varnished and polished to perfection every year, it was a restored monument to the tobacco baron who had built it decades before. Very apt, Rossi often thought. He knew the drugs he helped move were infinitely more potent than those nicotine infused leaves of the nineteenth century, but as he saw it, he was simply keeping an old tradition alive. His product came from the enforced sweat dripping from new slaves. Dirt poor farmers held bondage by their poverty and the needs of Western society to somehow escape its imagined stresses, but no different from those whose subjugation had helped build this mansion in the first place.

It was also too big for him and he knew it. But it was isolated, secure at the end of a Cul-de-sac. Plus, no one got past the stairs to his inner sanctum without a personal invite. The ground floor was for business. Rooms functioned as offices. He held his strategy meetings in what had been the dining room.

The one exception was a modest living room off the main hallway where he entertained when he had to. In her more sober moments, his mother, who he had never invited to his home, berated him about his single status. But domesticity had never appealed to him. Fleeting dalliances were all he ever had or wanted. At forty-five he did not see that changing, not while he lived in Glasgow.

Jenkins, oblivious to the architecture and its history, walked into the office and sat down in one of the leather chairs at the desk. 'Bit early Dom. You know Big Ian's a late riser. He said sometime between nine and ten,' Billy glanced at his watch, 'and it's only half nine now. Anyway, it's not like you to worry about timing.'

Dom's look hardened. It frustrated him having his morning swallowed up waiting on someone who couldn't be arsed to get out of their pit early just once in a while. 'I don't know how that lazy prick has stayed in business for so long.'

Billy laughed. 'He's a slippery bastard, I'll give you that, but he can still terrify people just by looking at them. The odd beating he carries out himself doesn't hurt his reputation either.'

Dom tilted his head and stared at the stucco plaster ceiling of his office, seeking some kind of inspiration. 'Billy, I don't give a flying fuck about his reputation or if he thinks he's the hardest dickhead north of Hadrian's wall. Without me he wouldn't have any gear to sell. You'd think he'd be just a wee bit more appreciative of that fact.' He paused, took a lengthy breath and looked at Jenkins. 'I have other things on my plate today, so I need him dealt with and out of my hair, fast.'

Jenkins nodded. 'Okay, I'll make a few calls and find out where he is.'

'Thanks Billy. Sorry to be a crabbit bastard, but with the latest batch of girls arriving today, I need to double check everything.' He shook his head. 'When I visited the farm last week, it was still in a shit state. There's fifty bodies arriving and I can't have any balls ups.'

'Dom, calm down. I was there yesterday. Toilets and showers

are working, and the beds are being moved in this morning. By the time they arrive, everything will be fine. They'll only be there a few days.'

Dom sighed. 'I know, but I still want a last look with Cassie before I head off to meet them. After you rattle Big Ian's cage let the boys up there know I'll be coming early afternoon, and I want no nasty surprises. Clear?'

Billy nodded.

'Good. Now bugger off and shut the door behind you.' Dom's hands went to close the screen of the laptop sitting on his desk. 'Oh! And Billy?' Jenkins turned. 'Find out where Malone is? He was to meet me for breakfast an hour ago and then sit in on this meeting with Ian, but he hasn't shown up. It must be a full moon or something today, because everyone seems to be winding me up.'

Billy grinned. 'Got it, boss.'

Dom liked Jenkins. He'd worked for him for ten years, like his other enforcer, Marti Galbraith. They'd both known Dom's father, and Dom thought of them as surrogate uncles with sidelines as Glasgow hard men. When Billy left the room, Dom stood and stretched some tightness out of his limbs. At five feet eleven, he looked taller thanks to his lean muscled frame, honed from almost daily workouts in his private gym. He had inherited both his father's height and his dark skinned, Italian good looks. Grey hairs were kept at bay with subtle use of black rinses. Today he'd cut short his gym session as he knew he'd be busy, or at least he thought he would, so the lack of endorphins wasn't helping his mood, or that pricks like Gilmour thought they could dick him around at will. Unfortunately he needed Ian Gilmour and people like him. There weren't that many Organised Crime Groups in Scotland of any note and Gilmour ran one of the largest, covering the entire West of Scotland. But the niche Rossi had created for himself as the only importer of drugs into the country, allowed him to work in relative safety with them all. The downside was, he ran the bigger risk if he were ever caught - or betrayed.

Smoothing a crease in his Ted Baker shirt, he walked over to a framed print above the fireplace. Reaching up, his fingers found their way under the corner and pressed a small locking switch. With a soft click, the painting swung slightly out. Rossi pulled it fully open revealing a modern Chubb safe, replete with keypad and a retinal scanner. If their locks were in every prison in Britain, then Dom reckoned their safes would be pretty damned good. He keyed in his PIN and placed his right eye on the scanner. A quiet beep indicated the safe had unlocked. Dom lifted the latched handle recessed into the door, opening it fully. It contained four handguns and half a million pounds in tight bundles of two thousand each. He would need a hundred and fifty to pay the 'importer' for their latest batch of fifty girls coming in on the ferry.

The girls were mostly East European – Serbs, Croats and Romanians plus a smattering from Kazakhstan and Greece coming off a ferry from Rotterdam into Hull, but these girls weren't in the back of a lorry or container. Too risky, given the number of deaths in the past. It was simpler and safer, to get them passports, stolen, forged, occasionally legitimate, and shepherd them through immigration one at a time. If he 'lost' a few to the Border Agency that was fine. They came from dirt poor backgrounds. Their homes were slums that made the ruins of Aleppo look like a Caribbean resort. Most were uneducated and unwanted. Their families had little use for them, keeping their hopes and ambitions for their male children. Females were used for whatever generated the most income and that was the few hundred Euros they had brought from being sold to the traffickers. If he were honest though, he *was* becoming disenchanted with this side of his business and had already started feeling out potential buyers. But that could take some time, and in the meantime, business had to continue.

Dom carefully took seventy five bundles and placed them on his desk. He walked to the cupboard, retrieved a large holdall, unzipped it and placed them inside. All done, he closed and secured the safe then made sure the framed painting was flush with the wall. The money still in there would tide him over until he could get Malone to make enough small withdrawals from the many accounts he managed, to bring the float back up to its half a million.

Jack Malone? Bane of his life, but who seemed to know every underhand way of sailing close to the financial edge and still keeping things as legal. Speaking of which! He glanced at his Rolex, what the hell is Malone up to? For all his faults, Jack was always reliable, always arrived when he said he would, even if hung-over. So something was far wrong. Dom felt it in his gut, but a knock on the door interrupted his train of thought.

'Yes!' Rossi said.

It cracked open. Billy Jenkins popped his head in. 'Boss, no need for that phone call. Big Ian's here. Want me to show him in?'

'Give me a second.'

Dom zipped up the holdall, and replaced it in the cupboard. He walked back, took his Italian handmade suit jacket from the back of his chair and slipped it on. Then he stood behind his desk.

'Ok, Billy.'

Jenkins nodded and left.

A minute later the door opened. No perfunctory knock. The six foot two inch frame of Ian Gilmour forced its way through with a 'better not fuck with me' swagger.

'Dom pal, how you doing?' Ian smiled, seemingly happy enough. 'Sorry I'm late for our wee confab, but something came up this morning that needed dealt with urgently.' He winked and grinned.

Dom could only imagine what the something was. Big Ian was well known for liking the occasional lady or two if he felt good. In his early fifties, Gilmour was fitter than most twenty-five-year-old desk jockeys who went to the gym three days a week and the pub the other four. He could be an arrogant dick at times, but Rossi let that side of him slide as business was business, and Ian always paid. As normal, he was well dressed.

Tight fitting, light grey pinstripe that showed off the lean physique of another gym junkie like Dom. His hair was dyed, but Rossi doubted anyone who knew Ian would ever mention it to him. He needed those up and coming, to understand he still had what it took to mix it in the underworld he had revelled in all his adult life.

'Thanks for coming in Ian,' Dom said as he moved around the desk, hand outstretched. They shook. Firm grips, not crushing.

'Not a problem. Does me good to get up early once in a while? It's nice to see what the world looks like first thing on a summer's morning.'

Dom smiled. The fact it was nearly nine forty five and had been light for five hours, seemed to have failed to register with Ian. 'Pull up a pew and I'll get Billy to organise some coffee for us.'

Ian shook his head, his dark brown, dyed hair incongruously bouncing as though caught in a gentle breeze. 'Not for me thanks. I know we're both busy so let's get down to business. Plus, nobody makes coffee the way I like it.'

Dom smiled again. 'You still own that French Café in the West End?' he asked as Gilmour sat in a visitor's chair and he walked to his own high-backed leather one.

'Mais oui, mon Ami. Best coffee in the city.' Gilmour replied. He then leaned forward in his seat. 'But as I said, business. What are your thoughts on the recent 'changes' in the dynamics of various players in our circle of mutual acquaintances?' he smiled.

Ian did like a dramatic turn of phrase Dom thought. Shit, every tenner bag dealer in the central belt knew Ian Gilmour had successfully gotten rid of three up-and-coming toerags who Dom had done some work for in the past, quietly absorbing their dealerships into his own. What had happened to said toerags was not Dom's business, but he could make more than an educated guess?

'I have heard you've been successful with some takeovers

and management changes in a few of the smaller firms around the city. But that's none of my concern. Everyone is welcome to use my services. I'm the only one who can get quality product at the right price. And I always deliver.'

Gilmour sat back in his seat. 'That's what I like about you Rossi. You're an impartial observer in all the crap that happens in this business. That you conveniently help cause the mayhem seems to flow over you like air in a wind tunnel.'

'I don't force the powder up peoples noses Ian. Plus players come and players go. I'm a wholesaler and hope to be around for a long time yet.'

Gilmour clapped his hands and rubbed them together. 'Indeed. So, tell me. What's your biggest delivery to date?'

Dom gave a slight shake of his head. 'Ian, I can't give you that information.'

'Okay, okay,' Gilmour said, waving his hands. 'I just need to know you have the organisation behind you to go big, enormous in fact.'

Rossi was intrigued. 'I keep things close and tight. I never lose control of anything. Nothing coming into the supply chain through Scotland is too big for me.'

Gilmour nodded. 'Aye, ok. I'll need to take you at your word on that.' He paused for a few seconds. 'What if I said I was looking for a tonne of uncut coke, all delivered in a single shipment?'

Dom's facial expression didn't change, but he placed his hands on the desk in front of him and leaned in a few inches. 'Ian,' he started softly, 'not wanting to be a killjoy or anything but are you off your tits on something? A tonne! Fuck, that's over forty-five million quid wholesale plus another twelve for my services. I've known you a long time, but if you had that kind of money I doubt you'd be enjoying the gloriously unpredictable weather of a Glasgow summer.'

'I have partners,' Gilmour shrugged. 'Besides, I love this town. I'm a 'weegie.' Anyway, nothing wrong with our weather this year.'

Dom sat back. 'Ian, you'll kill the market if you pull this off. Prices will drop like an anchor.'

He shook his head. 'Not if I control the supply, and the price, which is what me and my associates have been planning to do for a while now, hence the start of the takeovers.'

'You'll also put me out of business. Unless you plan on giving away free samples at the school gates, that amount of coke will last for years. Plus, you'll be my only customer.'

'Nah,' Ian shook his head. 'You'll still have the skunk and smack suppliers to deal with and there are always new designer drugs coming out of China. I just intend to concentrate on the one that's easiest to offload. All the professionals like the white stuff.' He gave Dom a knowing smile. 'And you also have your other business to keep you busy. All those wee lassies you have slaving away for you in those big houses around the country must make you a fair whack every year?'

Dom sat back and rubbed his chin, ignoring the implied barb and wondering if Gilmour was serious about this?

'Okay Ian. I can put together a plan for you. But it might take a while to convince my suppliers about the amount. That's a lot of snow you want me to shovel, and it's never been done before, not into a wee backwater like Scotland. There are lots of risks. Keeping quiet about a shipment that size will not be easy.'

Gilmour shrugged and smoothed down a crease in his trousers. 'That's why I've come to you Dom, the best in the business,' he grinned.

Rossi breathed deeply. 'Not wanting to spoil the mood too much Ian, but I'll need my twelve million up front! There will be lots of palms needing all sorts of greasing all the way back to Colombia for a shipment this size, and everyone will want a cut.' He held up a hand as Gilmour started to answer him. 'Plus the balance, all forty-five million, will need paid in advance before I get anywhere near a tonne of uncut Charlie.'

Ian nodded, his expression calm, unperturbed. 'Don't you worry about the money. There is a condition though. Like it or not, I'll have one of my people working closely with you on this one and I mean closely. Once we agree on the principle, they'll be embedded with you and completely in the loop. It's not that I don't trust you Dom, I do, but if this goes tits up we'll all be wearing Colombian neckties very soon thereafter.' He smiled. 'And I like my tongue for other more pleasurable activities.'

Rossi was silent for a while. He drummed his fingers on the high sheen desktop, fully thinking through the implications of what Gilmour was suggesting. Twelve million was a hell of a lot of money, but Dom's reputation had been built on confidentiality. He didn't like the last part of Gilmour's conditions, but deciding how to deal with it wasn't something he would do in the next few minutes, so there was no point in arguing. Plus, he needed to talk this through with all of those who would be closest to the operation, and Jack Malone was one of them. He held the purse strings, so where the fuck was he Dom wondered again?

'Okay Ian,' he eventually said. 'Give me a couple a few days to work through the basics and sound out my source on the Continent. I'll need to plan not just the delivery but also the payment route. The Colombians will want all their cash upfront and I doubt we'll get away with a bog standard bank giro transfer, will we.' He paused for a second. 'Timescale wise. Are we talking weeks? Months?'

Gilmour leaned back in his chair. 'Around six months from now, or a wee bit longer. I have a few other 'mergers' to sort out before I'm ready to push the button.'

Dom stood up and walked around the desk before perching himself on the edge, close to Gilmour's right side, leaning in. 'This is a big one Ian, probably *the* big one. We both know that. So I'll be blunt.'

Gilmour sat back and waited, and Dom knew he was uncomfortable with someone towering over him. Good.

'If I get even a whisper of someone trying to double cross either of us or attempting to pull a fast one, then I'll pull the plug. Once the shipment's ready to leave South America, the

Colombians will want paid regardless, so you and your new-found colleagues will find themselves out a cool fifty-seven million with none of you getting a sniff of the product, no pun intended.'

Gilmour's face hardened and Dom could see the anger rising, ready to pop the safety valve on the pressure cooker that was his temper.

'I can always fly out to Colombia and cut a deal myself,' Gilmour hissed through clenched teeth.

Rossi watched him calmly then smiled and slowly shook his head. 'No, you can't Ian. You don't have the contacts or the network to pull off something this big and you know it, otherwise you wouldn't be sitting here.'

Dom was aware Ian Gilmour normally settled his disagreements with violence and terror. Gilmour wasn't a businessman, not in the modern sense. Not where a deal this game changing was concerned. Hired thugs with guns and knives usually handled his negotiations. That might work for a while, but those soldiers would eventually get caught and sent away, while grassing you up to keep their sentence light. He knew, because he'd met a few in passing during his time in the BarL.

'Ian, I respect you and your ambition, but if this isn't planned and executed with finesse, then if you're working with some bigger players in this country, those neckties you mentioned will be Union Jack's not Colombian.'

Gilmour stared at Dom, eyes flicking over Rossi's face, teeth clenched, anger bubbling under.

'Fine,' he nodded. 'But remember this Dom. I don't like failure. If I lose even a gram of this product, I won't be happy.' He waved a pointed, manicured finger at him. 'And if you fuck this up, if the cops get a hint and start asking me or any of my people awkward questions about things they shouldn't even be able to comprehend far less think are vaguely true, then I hope you also know where my talents lie?'

He stood up, pushing his chair back on its shiny metal runners. Dom mirrored him, easing himself off the desk, pulling himself up to his full five foot eleven inches. They both looked as if they were squaring off, waiting to see who would be the first idiot to swing a punch, or more likely lead off with a 'Glasgow Kiss.' Gilmour stuck out his right hand, eyes never moving from Dom's.

Rossi looked down briefly, then, smiling, reached out and shook Ian Gilmour's hand, both grips strong.

'No need for any paperwork then, is there? Rossi smirked.

Gilmour nodded and smiled back.

THREE

Dom eased the BMW eXi up to the kerb, and stepped out of the car. Milton hadn't changed in twenty five years. The only thing that had was his mother's address. This wasn't where they had lived before his fathers murder on a job gone wrong eight years ago. After that, Dom had bought her a detached villa on the outskirts of Kirkintilloch, not that far away in distance, but light years by everything else. He had even signed the deeds over to her. It hadn't lasted. Within a year she had sold the house, drank, sniffed or injected the profit from the sale, declared herself homeless and was back on the Council waiting list for somewhere else to live. So she had put *'The Milton'* as her first choice. Such was the demand she had been offered a flat within a week and happily settled in a few days later. Now here she was. So was Dom, again! Back to clear up another pile of crap caused by the dysfunctional side of his family. But he supposed that being the family of a gangland enforcer for hire meant they were all dysfunctional in some way, including himself.

He had been driving off from the farm after visiting with Cassie Hughes who looked after his girls, but had the potential for so much more, when his private mobile had rang. It had been his mother. His dumb fuck of a brother had gotten himself in some kind of trouble again, and she was begging Dom to sort it out. He resisted at first, hating the thought of getting dragged back into the mire of their lives in Milton, even temporarily, but Cassie had convinced him otherwise. So here he was while she was in Glasgow with Marti Galbraith taking delivery of the latest batch of girl's from down South.

Dom stood on the pavement staring. The council blocks had changed little. New windows. Some new roofs. A bit of re-rendering. Landscaping around the area to soften it up. But you couldn't soft landscape the people. They were still as hard as ever. Or as stupid as his brother. A few were clean and looked near normal. A flat lived in by someone who cared, at least a bit. The rest had half closed blinds, slats missing, window's almost opaque with grime. Two had been boarded up with galvanised metal shutters. None of the balconies showed any signs of life. No plants, no disposable barbeques, no table or chairs. He looked up and down the street. He had no real idea what he was searching for. Perhaps he just wanted to make sure the local Ned's hadn't clocked his car and were planning a wee joyride at his expense. Maybe he should have brought Marti with him? But it was early, three-fifteen. Plus the sun was shining, keeping the vampires in their coffins and caves. They would only come out to leech the blood and money from their neighbours after dusk had descended.

There were two older style Mercedes parked further up the street and an Audi he could see in the distance, so maybe there were some up and comers around. Probably the same ones his brother owed money to. Taking a deep breath, Dom walked to the open door of the flats. He climbed the stairs, footsteps from his leather soled shoes echoing softly off the concrete. His mother's flat was on the top floor, the fourth. He stopped in front of her door. Lifting his arm he shaped his hand into a fist, ready to knock, but it was open. The door swung inwards and then it 'gut' punched him. The smell. The scent of squalor assailed him. Rotting food, unwashed clothes, dried urine and worse. The hallway was uncarpeted, just bare, unvarnished sticky, timber floor boards. The only light disturbing the gloom came through the open doorway. This was worse than his last visit a year ago. There was a switch on the wall to his right. He flicked it, but nothing happened. Steeling himself, he walked over the threshold into the flat. The smell became thicker, overpowering. How in the name of God did people live like this? How did his family live like this? It smelled like death's waiting room. A racking cough told him someone was in there. He walked past a closed bedroom door and an open bathroom one. Much of the smell came from there. He reached over and closed it, a vain attempt to trap some of the suffocating odours.

'Mum', he called out. 'Are you there?'

More coughing. The sound of someone getting up from a chair in the living room. Next minute, a hunched shape appeared in the doorway. It was clad in what had once been a brown bathrobe, now discoloured by unknown fluids and stains. Its hair was white, matted to its head with weeks of dirt. On its feet were a pair of old leather mule slippers. It's face lined and careworn, gaunt from lack of food. This was his mother.

'So you're here at last son. Nice of you to come and see yer old maw occasionally. Come in, come in,' Cathy Rossi beckoned him forward. 'I'll no bite.' She turned to walk back into the room. She stopped. 'Mind you,' she said, 'if ye didnae bring any biscuits then yer ontae mince as I've nuthin' in fur a cup of tea.' She cackled bitterly at her own joke.

Dom felt his guts twist at the thought.

He walked into the living room. The walls were bare. No photos. No paintings. No mirrors. Cheap hardwood covered the floor. It was chipped. Some sections towards the window were missing. The balcony was strewn with rubbish. There was a charity shop reject, stained, cream leather couch and two chairs in the room. A cheap throw lay on the couch and a glass-topped mahogany veneered coffee table sat on a matted black rug. The heady smell of skunk hung in the air making a valiant but useless attempt to disguise the other odours.

His mother walked back to the couch and resumed what he guessed was her favourite position, tucked into one corner. She grabbed the throw and pulled it around herself, seemingly cold despite the heatwave. Her drug paraphernalia lay on the table together with a whisky tumbler and a half empty bottle of Smirnov. There was a chunk of the resin block still there and Dom thought it would last her a couple of days. Well, it would if the guys who owned it didn't show up!

'Are ye going to sit down then?' she asked him.

'No thanks.' His jaw worked at chewing on nothing but his bitterness. 'So where is my arsehole of a brother then? I told you the last time I came here I wasn't bailing either of you out anymore. He needs to take some responsibility.'

Cathy Rossi shook her head. 'Dom, Dom, sure he does,' she said, sarcasm dripping. 'We all know that. But you're his big brother. He looks up to you. He sees what you have and tries his best to be as successful as you've been. But he just,..... well he just disnae get the respect he deserves from people round here. They all take advantage of him.'

'Oh for fuck's sake, he's screws them over and half the time he's so bloody high he doesn't even know he's doing it.' Dom was angry. He'd been here a few minutes, but he still hadn't clapped eyes on the waste of space.

'Is he in the bedroom?'

She nodded.

Dom turned back to the hall and went to the bedroom door. His mother shuffled after him. He opened it with no perfunctory knock. The smell from inside was a physical wall. The curtains were pulled tight across the closed windows. On a single bed facing him lay a figure cocooned in a filthy quilt. The coverings trembled. Beneath them, shaking like he was on a high spin cycle, lay Luca. Dom had no idea how long he had been in here, but the stench told him he had fouled himself. There was a puddle of vomit on the only carpet he had seen in the house, right next to the plastic basin Luca had been aiming at. He was completely out of it and starting to detox. In the condition he was in, there was no point in Dom asking him questions he would only get half answers to.

He turned. 'How much does he owe and who to?' he asked her, but she merely shrugged.

He was trying hard not to gag on the competing smells assailing his nostrils and clawing at his throat. God, he had to get out of here.

'I can't handle this,' he murmured.

Brushing past his mother he headed to the front door but then stopped. A figure stood there, framed in the opening. Male. Skinny. About five-eight with cropped hair. He was on the landing. In what light there was, Dom made out a baseball cap, tracksuit bottoms, some kind of zippered puffer jacket and a pair of dark trainers. Someone young. Someone new. Someone obviously stupid.

'How long have *you* been there?' Dom asked his voice flat.

'Long enough to know you're the guy I'm looking for,' the stranger grinned. 'Mind if I come in?' he asked rhetorically.

'Phew!' he said, stepping over the threshold. 'This place needs nuked. Hope naebody's died in here, well no yet!' The grin got bigger. 'Hello Mrs Rossi. This the wan you've been telling me about?'

Dom looked at his mother, realization dawning. His face morphed into a scowl. It seemed the closed curtains around the scheme hadn't been twitching. They had no need to. He took a step towards her.

'When did you call him?' he asked. 'Before or after you begged me to help?'

His mother shrank back a little. 'It wisnae ma fault son, honest. He made me do it. He knew Luca would use the gear and no sell it on. So he said he would kneecap him and break all my fingers if I didnae phone you.'

Dom wondered if the little shit knew who he was? If he did, it implied a lack of knowledge of his capabilities.

'Now c'mon *big* man. Is that any way to talk to yer maw?' Mr. Baseball cap emphasised the 'big' with nasal tones.

Why did they all talk through their nose, Dom wondered not for the first time in his life?

'You need to keep this mad family of yours in check. Know whit I mean. And if you don't, well! It's a family debt you know. Everywan's het for it.'

Mr Baseball Cap moved further into the hall. Another shape appeared behind him in the doorway, a similar uniform, hand's behind their back. Holding a knife? This one looked even younger.

'What's your name son?' Dom asked in a low voice. The smell in the flat faded into the background as he concentrated his attention on the dealer.

The kid shook his head. 'No need for ye to know that man. All you need to do is reach into those big, deep pockets of yours and pull out the ten grand your brother owes me. Or didn't your mammy tell you it was that much?' He swaggered up the hall towards Dom. His backup man stayed in the doorway.

Dom folded his arms. 'Now you and I both know if my brother had ten grand's worth of drugs on him he'd be dead, not in there shaking in his pit.' Dom stepped a little closer to Mr Baseball Cap. 'So tell me the actual amount before I literally drop you in the shit.' He glanced at the closed bathroom door. Mr Baseball Cap didn't catch it.

'Don't piss me about, ya prick. I told ye whit ah want!' His fists balled by his sides.

'And what should you get?' Dom said. 'I reckon you gave him five hundred quid's worth of gear. If he had cut and sold it, well, it would have been worth about fifteen hundred or two grand, tops.' Dom held up his hand as Mr Baseball Cap went to speak. 'Let me finish before you commit yourself.'

They stared at each other, Dom with an amused look on his face. Mr Baseball Cap just angry.

'So, you would make two grand less your initial capital outlay of course.' Dom could see confusion in Mr Baseball Caps eyes. 'Meaning your profit would be fifteen hundred. Three hundred percent for a couple of day's 'loan' of some gear. Now, even before the big crash, banks were never that generous.'

'Ten fucking grand or nobody walks out of here, got it.'

Dom looked to the heavens, shook his head then stared at the boy. 'Do you know who I am, son, do you really know?'

The local dealer thrust his head and chest forward and took

another step towards Dom. 'Aye, I know who you are. You're the fucking rich businessman brother of the prick lying in there with my gear in his veins.' Dom noticed the nasal tones had left him. 'You're fucking mother dobbed you in when I found out the two of them had wasted everything I'd given them.'

Businessman? Dom glanced at his mother, wondering just what she had told this low life. 'Yeh,' Dom sighed. 'She has a habit of wasting things she gets.'

'So stop dicking about.' The dealer's voice had gone up an octave. 'Either give me the cash or the keys to that car of yours out there.'

Mr Baseball Cap reached inside his puffer jacket with his right hand and pulled out a large kitchen knife. Straight from a butcher's block by the look of it. He stepped closer to Dom, knife waving in front of him until the two of them were only feet apart, just outside the closed bathroom door.

'Money. Now?' he shouted.

Dom threw his hands up as if in surrender. 'Fine, fine. I need to reach inside my jacket to get it. Okay?'

The dealer looked nervous, but he nodded.

Dom brought his left hand down as if going to his inside pocket. He slipped it inside his jacket then whipped it out just as quickly, and open handed, hit the thug's wrist, pushing the knife hand into the corridor wall. Even though Dom was a second Dan black belt in Shotokan Karate he opted instead for his favourite move, affectionately called 'a boot in the baws.'

His left leg moved forwards a few inches. Without conscious thought, he executed a low Maegeri. His right leg flew out, just below waist height, made contact, then immediately snapped back. It caught Mr Baseball Cap square in the groin. With years of training behind him, it was not a gentle tap. The dealer's testicles took the full brunt of Dom's pulled back toes. He doubled over, clutching himself, gasping, the knife falling as hot pain seared through his midriff. Dom grabbed the unlucky dealer by the ears and brought his head down fast. He drove the knee of his left leg hard under his chin. The baseball cap flew off. Dom heard a crack as something broke. A jaw or a chin? He wasn't sure. Shifting his grip to the unfortunate dealer's hair, Dom turned and kicked the bathroom door open. The smell the second time around was no better than before, but Dom ignored it. He calmly pulled Mr Baseball Cap through and pushed him face first into the shit filled toilet bowl. Grabbing the flush handle he jerked it down. Faeces laden water swirled around the bowl and over the dealers face.

Leaving him there, he wheeled back around fully expecting the backup to be there. But he only saw his mother standing in the hall with a shocked look on her face. He turned and grabbed the dealer by the back of his jacket, hauling him from the toilet, faecal matter dripping from his head and neck. Frog marching him to the door of the flat, he pushed him down the stairs, watching for a second until his tumbling body reached the half landing with a thud. Then he stormed back into the hallway, wet with faeces stained water, towards his mother. She had backed up, near the bedroom door, pressed against the wall, worried about what was coming next. A glance inside showed Luca still lay on the bed, trying to raise his head, wondering what the noise was about.

Dom pulled his wallet from his back hip pocket. He grabbed all the cash he had in it and threw it at the woman who had given birth to him. 'That's it,' he snarled. 'That's it all. We're finished. You're a fucking disgrace. Him as well. Ever since dad died all you've done is wallow in self pity. I'm sick of both of you.' He leaned forward, pointing at her with an index finger. 'Do what you want with the money. Pay off that scummy bastard who had his head in your toilet or piss off and spend it on more dope and smack. I don't care.' He ran his hands through his hair. 'I've tried to help you for the last time. It ends here.'

They looked at each other for a second. No love left between them. A mother's instinct dulled by drugs. A son's love destroyed by her selfishness.

'I'm done. Completely'

'That's right,' she screamed. 'That's right. Do what you always do, run away. Leave us here with fuck all. If your father was still here he'd skin you alive for this.'

'If my father was still here, you wouldn't be in this mess,' he shouted at her, spittle flying from his mouth.

She was crying now. Aching sobs wrenching her body. She slumped to her knees. 'I told him not to work for that bastard Gilmour, I told him. I knew he'd get himself killed, I just knew it.'

Dom stood there, wondering if he had heard her properly. 'Wh .... What did you say?' he stuttered.

'I asked him to stop fucking working, begged him. But it didnae do any good,' she sobbed. 'Every time wan ae thae bastards snapped their fingers he just went running.'

'Who did he go running to the last time?' Dom whispered.

'What?'

He towered menacingly over her. 'Who did you say he worked for that last time?' he asked her again.

She looked up at him, tears and snot running down her face. He knew he should have felt something. Pity? Sorrow? But all he felt was a growing anger at what she had just told him.

'It was some guy called Gilmour, Ian Gilmour. I met him a few times when he came tae the auld house tae pick yer da up when they went on a job.'

'Did he go with him on the night he died?'

She pulled herself up using the wall as purchase and shook her head. 'Naw. He went away on his own. Said he was doing a solo.'

Dom stepped closer. 'But you're sure it was Gilmour? Ian Gilmour?'

His mother nodded.

'Then why the fuck didn't you tell me about this before now?' he raged

She looked at him as if he were stupid and shook her head. 'It........, it never seemed important. He was dead, so who cared who did it. It widnae bring him back.'

Dom looked at her, some of his anger and despair at what she had become fading. His father had been her rock. Without him she was adrift, rudderless, but he knew there was little more he could do to help her, or Luca. He glanced again into the bedroom. Luca had fallen back onto the vomit covered pillow, breathing heavily. He could sense his mother staring at him, but Dom Rossi turned his back on them both and walked out past the still unconscious dealer, into the hot, sticky Glasgow air, sick to his stomach.

Glasgow! He was sick of the place and all it's backstabbing.

Gilmour! Ian fucking Gilmour had ordered a hit on his father.

FOUR

The door of Cassie's Tesla Five closed with a dull thud. Locking the car, she placed the keys in her handbag, slipped it over her shoulder and walked through the five hundred space visitor car park. She glanced at her watch. It was twelve thirty-five. Her visit slot was one till two. Billy had been told to be early, to clear security. How long could that take she wondered?

So this was Barlinnie. Except it wasn't. This was HMP Glasgow, a modern concrete and glass edifice with five-point-two metre high grey walls abutting the main building, and built in the shadow of the listed Grade A Provan Gasometers. But to everyone in Glasgow it was still the *BarL*, as it seemed you could take the con out of the jail but not the jail out of the con. For some messed up reason, Glaswegians were proud of Barlinnie. Perhaps because a hell of a lot of them had been in there at one time or another. And she was only here because this was where Jack Malone had been placed on remand.

When he'd failed to turn up for the meeting with Dom and Gilmour, some discreet enquiries elicited information he'd been arrested. The stupid bastard had been drunk and crashed his car on the Charing Cross overpass killing seven people, including a family of five. He had not been bailed. Lawyers, retained by Rossi, had visited Malone in police custody then followed through when he went to court for a committal hearing. The news had been twofold. The solicitor told Dom they had kept him in prison and he wasn't getting bail anytime soon, if ever. He also informed Dom Malone had asked to speak with Rossi urgently. Something to do with the accounts. Both she and Dom knew Malone was needed to navigate a clear path through the plethora of software tracking the company cash. But Dom still had access to the system and working capital, so he couldn't quite understand the urgent concern? But Rossi had asked her to visit the creep anyway, mainly because she was an unknown, not in the system.

Cassie had never been in a prison. Never convicted or arrested. She had visited no one in jail, did not need to be near one. But now, as she walked across the brick pavior, car park, she almost wondered if she'd arrived at the right place. The main building was four office block storeys high, the entrance vestibule wrapped in ten metre high, glazed, curtain walling. Laminated timber columns edged out and down the building. They angled out at the top, tapering as they swept down the facade to ground level. Strange at first sight, but designed she supposed, to make it difficult to climb up and over. There were splashes of colour dotted around the edge of a large canopy, emblazoned with the words *HMP & YOI Glasgow* picked out in large bronze letters, reflecting the harsh, midday sun. To her left, a large bi-fold vehicle gate punctured the clean lines of the black and red granite rain screen that eventually butted onto the plain grey, reinforced concrete wall of the main prison.

She stepped inside. A dark grey barrier mat guided her towards a timber teak finished reception desk with an off grey Corian composite worktop. High end Italian ceramic tiles ran off the mat and wrapped around the rest of the vestibule. A roof light, four storeys above her allowed in a flood of light, illuminating the entrance. This, she thought, was upper end office accommodation in the middle of Glasgow, not a bloody jail. She stopped before the desk and looked around. Suspended from the ceiling were two brushed satin, metal signs. One said *Official Visitors & Staff,* the other *Prisoner Visits.* She guessed that one would be hers. Here we go, she thought.

'Yes madam, can I help you,' the bored male officer on desk duty asked her as she walked up.

'It's Ms,' she replied, emphasising the 's.' He seemed oblivious to her sarcasm.

'Same question. Can I help you?'

Cassie nodded. 'I have an appointment to see a prisoner on remand. Jack Malone.'

He asked her name and checked her appointment time. He looked at her driving licence. He took her photograph with a cheap, dodgy looking camera linked to a PC she could not see behind the desk. A printer whirred somewhere under the counter, and a pass eventually appeared on the worktop. Her face, her name. He looked at her.

'Wear this at all times please and make sure you return it when you leave.'

Picking it up, she hung the lanyard around her neck.

'Empty your pockets and place everything in a locker over there,' he pointed, 'including your handbag, and any electronic devices. You can keep your jacket if you want. You'll need a pound coin,' he added. 'Everything else into this tray, watch, jacket, bracelets, necklace.' He pointed to a grey plastic tray to his right.

Bloody hell, she thought. Should've just turned up naked wearing a pair of shoes. She scrambled in her handbag for a pound coin, before dumping everything he had mentioned into the locker and taking the key. She put her jacket and watch into the fairly grubby, plastic tray.

He pointed to her neck, then her hands. Cassie looked confused.

'The key, and the Pass. In the tray.'

Her watch and jacket were X-Rayed together with their bloody key and ID badge. Then she walked through a metal detector. It beeped, so she had to go back, take off her shoes, try again. They were X-Rayed. She walked through. It beeped, again. A female officer walked from behind the desk and swept a metal detecting wand over her. It beeped, at her back.

'You must have a bloody big bra strap for this to go off,' she said.

Cassie was wearing a sheer blouse, partly see through, so it was obvious she had nothing else metallic there. A false positive. They let her go through. Worse than fucking flying she thought, as she collected her stuff and walked into the waiting area. Multicoloured metal airport chairs sat in rows around the room bolted securely to the floor. It was empty apart from her. She'd been told on the phone Malone could have one ninety minute visit once a week. She'd heard enough from Billy Jenkins to know she would probably need to wait. Prisons operated in their own time zone. There was a table with some dog eared magazines and two snack dispensers in one corner. A large fifty inch monitor was on one wall displaying a welcome message from the Governor and some other stuff about Prison Rules and how you could contact the Family Liaison Officer, whoever the fuck that was. She sighed knowing she could be here for a while. A large, clear glass screen separated the waiting room from the entrance vestibule. She sat facing it, watching the comings and goings of a prison, watching the desk officer's work, amazed at how busy it was.

Every few minutes more people would arrive, sometimes alone, often in groups. Who were they she wondered, as they were processed and moved through to the other side, the staff side? What did they do? How many people did it take to keep two thousand people locked up every day? She glanced at her watch. It was half one. Forty five minutes had passed with no sign of anyone coming for her. She was getting bored and became lost in thought about moving the girls around tomorrow when a figure leaving from the staff side caught her eye. There was something vaguely familiar about him. He was about five feet five inches, slightly heavy around the waist. Probably early fifties, but he still had his own hair, fairly thick but greying. His suit was also dark grey, marking him as management.

The man turned and joked with the officers as he showed them a chain attached to his belt, he then turned to walk to the exit. A woman in her mid-twenties wearing a tight fitting dark blue trouser suit came in, saw him and stopped to have a conversation. Cassie hated that feeling where you half recognised a face, but couldn't remember where because it was out of context. She was sure she had seen him before, but in a different environment. As the woman walked away, the man turned and blatantly stared after her, the visible panty line on her trousers sending his imagination into obvious overdrive. Hers to if she were honest. Just then Cassie heard a door open behind her. A female officer stood there, looked around the waiting room then her eyes stopped on her.

'Hughes?' she asked.

Cassie stood up.

'This way,' she told her.

They went through the door into a corridor, then through another two doors. Each time the officer pressed a button on a call plate at the side of the door. She gave her name and looked into what Cassie took to be a camera before the doors were unlocked remotely with a click and she opened them. When they entered the Visits Room, it was empty. Two other officers sat behind a desk on the wall to her left. The room itself was large. Glass topped tables were laid out in a neat pattern with four comfortable looking padded chairs around each one. The room was brightly painted in an assortment of pastel colours. The ceiling was high, at least six metres at its lowest point Cassie guessed, with three vertical north lights running the width of the room. An enormous picture window was to her right. Open vertical blinds hung down in front of it from the ceiling to the floor. It gave a view onto a garden. There were outdoor tables and chairs plus a high metal fence around the perimeter, topped with razor wire. In the far left corner there was a children's play area with a TV showing a cartoon. This surprised her. Kid's in a prison? But then again, families had to visit. Modern carpet tiles covered the floor. Cassie shook her head, amazed at it all. Shit, she had been in worse hotels.

She looked at the female escort officer. 'Where do I sit?' she asked.

'Anywhere you like,' the woman replied with a shrug.

Cassie picked a table in the middle of the room as far away

from the officers as she could get without seeming suspicious. Eventually a door opened on the far wall. Jack Malone appeared, escorted by another officer. He looked tired. Tough, Cassie thought. She found it hard to be sympathetic. Malone spotted her and walked over. He was wearing a green tee shirt and a pair of blue denims. He had a pair of black brogues on his feet, not what Cassie imagined regulation prison gear would be like. These looked like his own clothes.

He sat in the seat opposite, hands folded on his lap, looking down. Hope you're feeling guilty you bastard, Cassie thought. Although Dom had asked her to work with Malone, she didn't like him. He was a sleazeball. His visits to the brothels had become more frequent over the last year and he always picked the youngest, least curvaceous girl he could find. Given half a chance, Cassie knew Malone would happily bed anything over the age of twelve. His face looked gaunt close up. He hadn't shaved this morning, giving him a dark, haunted appearance.

'Well Jack,' she said. 'Looks like you've fucked up good and proper this time.'

He said nothing, merely raising his eyes towards her, a scowl on his face. Cassie noticed he was unconsciously grinding his teeth.

She sighed. 'You wanted this meeting Jack, so let's get to it. What do you want?'

He smirked, and this time looked her directly in the eye. 'Thanks for coming Cassie. Not even that bitch of a wife could make the time.'

'Jack why the hell am I here?' Cassie asked frustration clear in her voice.

'You're all heart Cassie. No wonder you can't keep a girlfriend any longer than a couple of months.'

Cassie leaned forward. 'Listen you stupid dickhead, I'm the one who'll be walking out of here at the end of this, not you, so stop trying to be a smart arse and tell me why I'm wasting my time in this place?'

'Finished?' Malone asked.

She just glared.

'It's simple. I need to be leaving His Majesty's Pleasure within the next two weeks. No ifs, no buts.'

She shook her head. 'It won't happen Jack. Not a snowball in hells chance. Seven people died including three kids, killed by a pissed up driver! Not exactly conducive to any judge who might even have a smidgen of sympathy.'

'Okay then Cassie, here's the wee problem you and Dom will have in exactly fifteen days if I'm still stuck in this dump.'

'I'm all ears.'

'It's about the server software controlling the accounts?'

'What about it?'

He smirked. 'It's set up so the master password changes every sixty days. If I don't update it and create a new one, then everything's locked, databases, spreadsheets, accounting software, the works.'

Cassie shrugged, seemingly unconcerned. 'So what? Dom has the same level of access you do. I'm pretty sure he can create a new password?'

'Well, if he knew the existing one, then yes, he could.'

Cassie paused for a second. 'What do you mean if he knew the existing one? Why wouldn't he know it?'

Malone's face broke into a wide smile. 'Because Rossi needed someone with lots of IT know how to get everything up and running securely. Someone with intimate knowledge of all the shitty little businesses we bought, all the fake holding companies we had set up, all the offshore bank accounts where we had squirreled our millions away. Someone who had degrees in law and IT.'

'Yeh, I know Jack. That was you,' Cassie stated, frustration evident in her voice.

'That's right. His most trusted lieutenant. But given the business we're in, well it wouldn't take much for Dom to decide that maybe I wasn't worth having around, especially when it was all but automated. So I took a few precautions.'

'Jack, don't be a complete idiot. Give me the password and I promise, Dom will look after your wife, and you too when you get out.'

'I'll give you it right now Cassie, no strings attached, but it won't do you any good.'

'And why would that be? Don't you think Dom can type?'

'Look into my eyes Cassie.'

'What?'

'My eyes. What do you see?'

Cassie sat back again. 'They look pretty vacant to me Jack. Lot's of alcoholic blood vessels in there. Bit yellow too.'

'Maybe Cassie, maybe, but the computer sees something a lot more meaningful when I stare into its iris scanner in the server room. No, what it sees is the second part of the access password, the equally important part.'

Shit she thought! The bastard *had* set up an insurance policy. When the password expired, Dom couldn't get into his own systems without him. A thought occurred to her. 'So what's to stop Dom from making a copy of all the files that don't need your iris scan? He can do that himself. You know he can.'

Jack chuckled. 'Ah, but I haven't told you the clever part.'

Cassie stayed silent, waiting for him to continue. She knew Malone was enjoying his brief moment of triumph.

'Ten days before the master password changes, the system sends an automated file to every bank where our businesses deposit money. It's a warning. A red flag. It indicates to them that maybe someone is trying to hack the company's accounts. So what do they do? That's right they put a 'hold' on them. No withdrawals. I need to set up new login ID's and passwords before they can be accessed again.'

'So the accounts are in limbo,' she hissed, realising what this would mean for Dom and his operation.

'Exactly. You can still make deposits, but withdrawals are a no-no.'

She shook her head and looked at Malone, sitting there all smug, a stupid grin on his face. 'Why?' It was all she could think to ask. 'If you had died we would have lost everything.

What's stopping me from organising a hit on you and getting your eyes posted to me?' She shrugged. 'Seems a pretty straightforward solution.'

'If I had died do you think I would have cared about what happened to all of you? As for 'borrowing' my eyes, I don't think you'll do that Cassie. It would be a bit—inelegant. Plus, it wouldn't work. There's a temperature and movement sensor built into the iris scanner. My eye needs to be alive for it to work.'

Cassie was getting angry. 'Jack, you can't just walk you out of here with me. Shit, when I think of what I had to go through to get in for this visit, I hate to think what I'll get when I leave. Plus, you don't exactly look fit enough to be climbing any walls.'

Malone shrugged. 'Not my problem Cassie. There's fuck all I can do in here. You and Dom need to organise something. Just let me know the where and the when and I'll be ready.'

'Jack your nuts if you think we can pull this off.' She looked around for the prison officers, then lowered her voice to a whisper. 'When the fuck was the last time anyone escaped from a prison?'

He shrugged. 'I have no idea and I don't care. The problem's all yours. You just need to figure out a way.'

She sat back, angry and frustrated. There was nothing else she could do here, she knew that. 'I'll speak with Dom. To say he'll be pissed would be the understatement of the decade.'

'Fine,' Malone said. 'You do that while I head back to my *cave* and the luxury of cold soggy chips with my dinner.' She noticed him drumming his fingers on the table.

'There's one other thing Dom needs to know.'

'Which is?'

'I didn't end up here by accident. In fact, I shouldn't be here at all, I should be dead.'

'What the fuck are you babbling on about?'

Malone leaned forward. '*Fat* Tony Smith was in the Casino the night of the accident. He tried to tap me. Get me to jump ship. He told me Gilmour was expanding, intending taking over everything, Dom's operation included.'

'Go on,' Cassie whispered.

'I told him to piss off, that Dom and I were in business together and if Rossi was out of the equation then everyone's supply of gear would dry up.' He shrugged. 'Then I got up and left. Next thing I know, this fucking Range Rover's trying to force me off the road. Yes I was pissed, but I've been pissed before and always managed to drive.' He looked her straight in the eye. 'Gilmour sanctioned having me taken out. That's what caused the accident.'

Cassie said nothing.

Malone stood up to leave, then paused and looked at her with a leer on his face. 'Don't suppose there's any chance of a quick French kiss is there? I mean, it won't do much for you, but I'll have the rest of the night to play it over in my mind, if you know what I mean.'

'Jack, I'm twenty-five years to old for you. So why don't you get yourself one of those teenage magazines to help you through the night.'

He smirked. 'I'll take that as a no then.'

'Prick.'

She stood and walked away from Malone without a backward glance. She had no wish to see the smug look on his face. He knew he held all the cards; aces and everything else in between. This was not good. Plus Dom needed to hear the news about Ian Gilmour and *Fat* Tony.

The officer escorted her through the doors she had entered on her way in. She removed her pass and handed it to the officer on the reception desk. He compared her photo to her face and asked to see her driver's licence once again. Bloody hell, she had been the only visitor in there and doubted she looked anything like Malone. Satisfied, he scanned the barcode on the pass into his computer and released the barrier for her to walk through. If this was the care they took to let visitors leave prison, then what the fuck did they do when inmates left?

Blagging your way out was not an option.

As she walked to the lockers, the front entrance doors slid open and the same man she had seen leave came back in. He glanced at her briefly, then walked up to the side of the reception desk and removed his jacket to be X-Rayed.

Cassie gathered her belongings. There was the same nagging feeling again. Where had she seen this guy before? Why was he memorable?

Someone at the desk must have cracked a joke, because the man and the two other officers burst out laughing. She looked up, and then it hit her, coming together in a white rush of memory. A blurry image of him came sharply into focus, triggered by his high-pitched and squeaky laugh.

She knew where she had seen him.

Smiling, she instantly realised he could literally be their key to unlocking the prison.

FIVE

The heat hit Rossi like a physical barrier as he stepped out of the airport terminal. If he had thought it was warm in Glasgow, then the Costa Del Sol reminded Dom of what a real summer could be like. After he'd left his excuse for a mother and confirmed with Cassie the girls had arrived as scheduled, he had contacted Miguel Orejuela about the Gilmour deal. Orejuela had wanted to meet the next day in person. A bit quick, Dom had thought, but here he was. It would be good to touch base with his Cartel contact again anyway. Marti Galbraith was with him, a Glasgow hard man, sixty-five, the typical strong silent type, still well able to hold his own. His brooding presence had helped keep Dom isolated on the flight and given him some well needed thinking time. Rossi had been happy to get away from Glasgow for a bit. Jack Malone had been uppermost in his thoughts, especially as the prick was looking at serious prison time, but Cassie would deal with Malone in his absence, and although Gilmour's part in his father's death had been pushed to the background, he had not forgotten.

Dom looked at Galbraith standing beside him. 'Marti I need to ask you a few things, so be honest with me.'

Marti nodded.

Dom considered how to broach this, but with Marti the direct approach was normally the best. 'Did Ian Gilmour have my father murdered?'

He saw Marti swallow before answering. 'From what I've heard Dom, yes he did.'

Rossi shook his head. 'Why for fuck's sake? I thought they both worked together?'

Galbraith nodded. 'They did. Your dad sometimes used Ian as his backup man when he was doing some of the more difficult hits.'

'So what happened?'

Marti paused. 'Dom, this was a long time ago. A lot of things were happening then. Your dad was working - a lot. People were disappearing everywhere. You were inside at the time, so well out of it.'

'And?'

'Well, one of the 'disappeared' was a guy called Finbar O'Boyle. He was the son of Eamon O'Boyle.'

'From Manchester?'

Marti nodded. 'He came up here and started acting like a prick. Throwing his weight around, trying to start up on his own. That didn't go down well, so some of the bosses teamed up and decided to have him dealt with.'

'And my father was asked to do it?'

'Yes. Franco told me over a drink one night, he got Gilmour involved. He knew O'Boyle would have security so Ian was to run interference while your dad dealt with Finbar.' Marti paused.

'Go on'

'They did their jobs. Finbar was dealt with and things settled down; for a while anyway.'

'What do you mean, for a while?'

'You know Ian worked for his brother in law, Jamie Phillips?'

Dom nodded.

'Well Phillips wanted to go legitimate. Clean his money completely, start developing properties down here and out in Tuscany. Gilmour didn't like that idea. He enjoyed being a gangster, loved the lifestyle, everything about it.'

'So?'

'So Gilmour had Jamie Phillips taken out?'

'By my father?'

Marti shook his head and paused before answering. 'No, by me.'

'You? Shit.'

Galbraith shrugged. 'It was all just business Dom. He paid me. I didn't really know Phillips. Had never worked with him. So I did the job. End of.' Galbraith turned and looked at Rossi. 'Now only three people know. Me, Gilmour and now you.'

Dom was silent for a while. Marti was right. It was business. The world they occupied was lucrative, but it could also be deadly, especially when you least expected it.

'But what does all this have to do with my Father's death?'

Marti took a breath. 'Not long after he took over, Ian wanted to expand, so he decided to do a deal with an English based gangster who had money and muscle.'

'Who?'

Marti looked at him. 'O'Boyle. But Ian was worried O'Boyle might somehow find out he had been involved in killing his son and the only way to ensure that didn't happen.........?'

'Was to silence the trigger man.'

'Exactly. Once Franco had been dealt with, he knew he was home and dry and he's been working on and off with O'Boyle ever since. But I don't know who pulled the trigger on your father. Believe me if I did I would have taken care of it myself.'

Rossi was angry. He looked at Galbraith but his gaze softened as he realised that Marti had only been doing a job. 'Thanks Marti. At least you were honest with me.'

'Dom I could have told you this year's ago. You're not angry with me?'

'Marti, we all have secrets. No, I'm not angry with you. I'm only angry with Gilmour - and Malone.'

Dom felt Marti looking at him, an emotionless stare on his scarred face. 'What?'

'Now you know, what do intend to do about Gilmour? He might not have pulled the trigger, but he orchestrated the act.'

'To be honest Marti, I haven't given it much thought. I need all the cash for this deal in my accounts before I decide on anything. The last thing Gilmour needs to think is that I'm gunning for him because of my dad. Anyway, solving the problem of Jack Malone is a more pressing need right now.'

Marti simply nodded.

Rossi despaired of Malone. When they'd first met in Barlinnie, Dom hadn't been entirely sure about him. They hadn't shared a cell, but had met at recreation and they found they had a few mutual acquaintances, some of whom Malone had even represented. One thing led to another and Malone eventually offered to put together an appeal against Rossi's three-year sentence for attempting to bribe a cop. Dom realised Jack was only in jail because he was stupid enough to gamble with client's money. But he had a quick legal mind and serious expertise in IT, especially financial control systems. He also knew a lot about the Dark Web, how it was used to maintain anonymity and launder large amounts of cash in relative safety. Malone had grown on Dom. Along with a dark side, he had a sharp wit and a dry sense of humour. Dom did realise he had perhaps let slip too much about his own business when they had worked on the appeal, but Malone never mentioned it or tried to gain any leverage through it.

Rossi's appeal failed on a technicality, but he told Malone he'd keep him in mind when they were both released in case anything came up that suited his talents. So he had employed him, just as the drug importing had taken off and he'd needed to start laundering larger sums of money. But now? Now he had grown soft. He gambled in a manner suggesting he had a private mint in his basement churning out hundred pound notes. And now this. Prison facing at least fourteen years for being a drunken arsehole.

Dom was naturally worried about what his incarceration would do to the financial systems he depended on. Cassie would see Malone today to find out what she could. The girl was good. Competent. Quiet. Effective. She had proven herself capable when dealing with the *Spas.* The latest handover had gone well. No hiccups. All fifty girls had arrived, the money handed over, counted and the Serbians had gone away happy. He needed to trust someone. There was too much for just him and Jack Malone to manage. Malone? Fuck, his entire IT system was Jack Malone's baby. He might be an alcoholic and sleaze after the younger girls working for Dom, but he could play a computer like a piano.

The server tucked in a cupboard in Dom's office in a ventilated, fireproof cabinet held all the information on the Rossi's finances, legal and otherwise. Every Scottish business, every bank account, every holding company, and every overseas tax haven he owned, recorded on there somewhere. It was *air-gapped,* with no internet access. It couldn't be hacked from the outside. A combination of passwords, PIN numbers and Iris Scans protected it. Malone called it a *closed loop system.* All the laptops Dom owned were the same. Only he and Malone could log onto them and then into the server. But only Malone understood the fine detail, how much you could withdraw or deposit into any particular account at any given time, where was the best place to filter larger sums of cash. Plus, he handled the payoffs to corrupt officials working with them. Dom had asked Cassie to shadow Malone, learn how the money was washed and where. The idiot was going to be sent away for years, so perhaps his caution at getting her involved would pay off. He just hoped she had the skills to allow him to dispense with Malone entirely.

A black Range Rover slowed to a halt beside them at the airport pickup point. The passenger window rolled down and a head nodded at them. Both he and Marti stepped around the steel anti ram bollards into the back seat, then the vehicle moved off. The drive to Migeul's Villa in Mijas was uneventful. They pulled up outside a set of tall wrought-iron gates set into a high decorative wall surrounding the estate. A CCTV camera mounted on a pole panned around and tilted to look at the car before the gates opened. He eyed Marti sitting beside him, but he was his usual inscrutable self

'Stick close to me Marti until I'm happy Miguel and I are still on friendly terms,' he whispered. Galbraith nodded but said nothing.

The car stopped at the end of a long, paved driveway. Dom glanced out and saw Miguel standing by the main door of the ultra modern villa, sunglasses on and a glass of something cold in his hand. He took this to be a friendly sign. They exited the car and walked towards Orejuela. Rossi looked about as if taking in the view. He noticed bodyguards around the compound, counting at least nine, much more than he would normally expect to see. Even on a day as warm as this, they were all wearing jackets no doubt concealing their side arms. This security seemed like overkill.

'Ola Miguel. Cómo estás?' he asked, with the little Spanish he knew.

Orejuela grinned. 'I am fine my friend, just fine. I trust your journey was not too uncomfortable?' They shook hands then grinned and embraced in a friendly hug. He looked at Dom's companion.

'It's always good to get away for a bit,' Dom replied. 'This is my colleague, Marti Galbraith. I hope it won't inconvenience you too much to have him here?'

'Not at all. We have plenty of space for the friends of our friend. But come, please. I have refreshments ready for you. Let's relax a little before we discuss business.'

Dom nodded. He turned to Marti and gave him a look which said, everything was fine. 'Marti, organise the luggage to be taken to our rooms? I'll meet you later tonight.'

Marti nodded and walked back to the car. Orejuela barked something in Spanish and one of the nearby bodyguards went with Marti to show him their rooms. Miguel took them along a wide veranda at the side of the villa to a walled garden at the rear. There was a fountain in the middle. Clear water trickled to an ornamental pool over and down stone rocks, only to be pumped back up again in an endless cycle. A trellis gazebo stood in one corner, with shade plants growing through it. A set of four hardwood cushioned chairs sat on riven stone paving below the trellis, surrounding a hardwood table. An unlit stone barbeque lay off to one side. Dom noticed one chair was occupied. This perhaps accounted for the four guards standing at each corner of the garden, plus another one near the trellis. As they walked over, the guard at the trellis stepped forward and held up his hand stopping Dom going any further. Dom looked at Miguel, who simply shrugged. Rossi was to be searched. Turning back to the guard Dom raised his arms wide, his grey tailored jacket opening up like a pair of bat wings. The body search over, the guard nodded at Miguel. Orejuela half smiled and invited Dom to move forward with an outstretched arm.

'Thanks for the show of trust Miguel. Remind me to invite you to Scotland some time then I can get someone to show you what a full body search feels like – including all the cavities.'

Miguel grinned 'Please forgive me my friend, but it was a necessary precaution, believe me. Come I'd like you to meet someone very special. Someone we both owe our livelihood to.' He walked toward the table. Dom followed, his curiosity about the mysterious guest growing.

'Domenico, can I introduce you to Senor Antonio Barrera from Colombia, the brother of Carlos Barrera. Antonio oversees the transportation of all our goods into Europe. Senor Barrera, this is my good Scottish friend and business associate Domenico Rossi from Glasgow.'

Dom stood there for a second. Had he just wandered into a deleted scene from the Godfather? These people were so polite it was scary. They were also incredibly dangerous. He turned to the elder gentleman and gave a slight bow. It seemed appropriate. He was after all sitting there like a King. Barrera was small even seated, no more than five foot five in his socks. He wore a white shirt turned up at the cuffs. He was also out of condition. Not fat but heavy, an obvious lover of rich food. His moustache was so obviously died that Dom almost felt compelled to keep looking at it.

'I'm pleased to meet you Senor. I had no idea anyone from the other side of the Atlantic was coming over to discuss this deal.'

Barrera grunted, merely glancing at Dom quickly before returning his attention to the tablet he was holding. 'Do not flatter yourself. I was already in Spain for a meeting when Orejuela informed me you wanted to discuss a large deal with him. It seemed opportune to sit in and find out how he goes about making these deals.'

Dom looked at Miguel. He simply shrugged. 'Senor Barrera and I work closely together, but seldom in person. You have hinted at buying a large volume of product, so with him being in the country, it seemed too good an opportunity to waste. Don't you agree?'

He didn't, not really. But he nodded.

'Sit down, both of you,' grumbled Barrera.

Rossi and Orejuela sat in seats opposite each other. Barrera was to Dom's right, so he angled himself slightly to give the portly South American the impression he was in charge. Miguel poured them all a drink of iced lemonade from a pitcher on the table.

'Well, what is your proposal Mr Rossi,' Barrera kicked off, placing the tablet on the table. 'I have a flight to Bogota this evening from Madrid which I do not intend to miss.' He paused for a second 'Do you know we also have a Madrid in Bogota?' he asked Dom.

Dom shook his head.

'No, not many people do.' He waved a hand for him to continue.

So much for a quiet refreshment before talking business. Where should he start and how much should he give away? His mouth was surprisingly dry. He took a sip of his drink.

'I have a client in Scotland who has approached me regarding the importation of a large quantity of cocaine.'

Miguel swirled the lemonade in his glass. He looked at Barrera, who stayed silent, then back at Dom. 'Then I am sure Senor Barrera is wondering why we do not simply deal with your client?'

He hadn't expected that. Was Miguel trying to big himself

up in front of the Barrera Cartel second in command?

'Well, you could try that Miguel, but remember, I've spent years building up a wholesale operation insulating all the players from the heat that would come if they were caught importing. And believe me without my input and help, they would be found out.'

'How?' Barrera asked quietly. 'Would you betray them?'

Dom bit back his reply. He shook his head instead. 'They'd betray themselves Senor. Most of the smaller ones are greedy and stupid and don't have the know how. There will be a lot of attrition. My client would require to build a new organisation, and it would be hard to easily compartmentalise. Separating the importation from the distribution and sales side would be virtually impossible. Plus, a lot of the leaders are just thugs. They're not even thugs with brains. They let their emotions rule their heads and worry about consequences later. I don't. I plan. I sweat the details.' He shrugged. 'My reputation is impeccable. I've lost only two shipments since I've begun.'

'But we would still get our money,' Miguel put in. 'What happens to the product when it arrives in Scotland is not our concern. If the authorities take it......?' He left it hanging there.

Dom considered for a second. 'If the authorities take the product, they'll also take the buyers. Pretty soon you'll have no one left to sell to. Plus, I'm reliable, and you can't say that about many people in our business.'

He eyed them both. They seemed to speak to each other silently, in a language made up of their own facial expressions. Well, taking the initiative had always worked for him in the past. He reckoned he had little to lose right now, his life excepted.

'You realise if you deal with anyone else in Scotland, you'll need to get your own people on the ground, find the contacts, bribe or blackmail them yourselves? And if they're taken down it could break your supply chain all the way back to Bogota.'

Both men were silent. What the hell was Miguel playing at? Why the interrogation? They had worked together for years without an issue, so what else was going on here?

Barrera sat forward, inching nearer to Dom. He half expected a knife to be driven through his thigh at any minute - and then one across his throat.

'The man you are dealing with in Glasgow, Gilmour. How well do you know him?'

Rossi was taken by surprise. 'Senor Barrera, how do you know about Ian Gilmour? He's a big fish in a small pond. Not a player I'd expect someone at your level to be interested in.'

Barrera patted Dom on the knee and gave him a cold smile. 'Do not underestimate the value of the Scottish market to the Barrera family. Yes, we make most of our money selling in the States, but in Europe, your Celtic brothers and sisters consume more of our product per head than anywhere else on the Continent. So it pays us to know who we are dealing with. Plus, there are rumours he has also been looking elsewhere for his deliveries.'

'Senor Barrera, no one else in Britain can import in quantity. They don't have the skills. I do. So if Gilmour's talking to anyone then it must be at the source, in Colombia.'

'But our competitors already do business in Europe,' Miguel interjected. 'Perhaps they have contacted Mr Gilmour? Perhaps it would be in our best interests if we also made contact with him, no?'

Dom placed his glass on the table and sat back in his seat. He drummed his fingers in the armrests, looking back and forth between the two men, acutely aware what he said and did next could be the difference between walking out of here or of being carried out.

'Fine Miguel, you do that,' he smiled. 'Speak with Gilmour. But I'm telling you, respectfully, you will lose your shipment. Gilmour cannot do this on his own.' Dom realised this was high risk but he had run out of options. He didn't know if they were testing him or if they were serious about cutting him out of the loop.

Barrera looked at Dom calmly. 'And just how much cocaine

does Mr Gilmour want?'

Rossi paused for a second. 'One metric tonne,' he said, 'delivered in a single shipment within the next six months.'

Orejuela looked straight at Barrera, his surprise clear. 'That is a significant value of product Senor. As I mentioned to you in the past, our relationship and dealings with Mr Rossi have been nothing but fruitful for both of us.'

So Dom thought, Miguel is still batting for me. It's this idiot from Colombia who needs convincing.

'Yes, I am aware of the close relationship you have with him, but my worries still exist. Perhaps it would be more beneficial, and profitable for the Barreras to set up their own distribution network with Senor Gilmour? That way we control the supply and more importantly the price.'

Rossi sat silently, unsure of what to say. He watched as Antonio Barrera took a sip of his drink then pinched the bridge of his nose. The gold rings he wore on all four fingers of his hand were huge, meant for ostentatious show. Plus, they could also be used as a first class knuckle duster in a close up fist fight. How the hell did Barrera know about Ian Gilmour? There were no South Americans in Scotland asking questions or trying to make contact. If there were, Dom would have heard about them. Something else was happening, but what?

Barrera misunderstood his look. 'My sinuses,' he said. They always give me problems when I come down to sea level. I much prefer our higher Colombian altitudes.'

And you're giving me a headache to you bastard, Dom thought grimly.

'Let me take a few days to think about things Senor Rossi, days that will make no difference to our plans should we,..... should I decide to go ahead with Miguel's usual arrangements.'

Rossi looked at Miguel, the disquiet evident on his face, but Miguel's subtle shake of the head told Dom to leave it be. It would be sorted - one way or the other.

'Very well Senor Barrera, I'll wait until I hear from Miguel. All I can say is the work we have done in the past has been good for both our organisations.' Dom stood up and held out his hand to the Colombian.

Barrera nodded and also stood. He took Dom's proffered hand, his fingers barely touching it, as if Dom had some contagion which would pass to him with even fleeting contact. Saying nothing else to Rossi, Barrera turned to Miguel.

'I will leave now for the airport. Walk with me to my car.' Miguel nodded and followed his fellow Colombian back towards the house, signalling to Dom with the flattened palms of his hands behind Barrera's back to stay where he was. The bodyguards stationed around the garden quickly followed both men out, leaving Dom alone.

Rossi fought to keep his anger in check. The risks he had taken for these bastards over the years were innumerable. Who the fuck did this arsehole think he was, coming here unannounced and hinting Dom was potentially of no further use? Everything he had built since his release from prison, and before, was now on the line. His biggest payday was looking as far away as Malaga was from Glasgow. But there was something else, something niggling at him since Barrera had mentioned it. How did he know about Gilmour? Did he have a traitor in his own organisation? Only Billy knew about Gilmour's visit to Dom and he knew nothing of the detail. But someone was stirring the pot as it was obvious Barrera knew more than he should.

After ten minutes, Miguel returned, his arms held out in supplication. 'My friend, I am sorry about what just happened, but as you can see I had no choice. Antonio is my boss and much as I like you, I value the head on my shoulders much more. You understand, don't you?'

'Fuck Miguel, you might have given me some heads up. That prick has just put my entire business at risk. If anyone I deal with finds out about this, they'll write me off quicker than a car in a head on collision.' He turned away and took a deep breath, trying in vain to calm down.

'You know I could not do that. If he even suspected I had

tipped you off it would not have gone well for me.' Miguel seemed genuinely contrite.

'And what *about* you my friend?' Rossi asked with more than a touch of sarcasm. 'Do you feel our relationship has run its course? Should I be looking elsewhere at alternative suppliers?'

The Colombian shrugged. 'I do not think that would be wise Domenico. The tentacles of the Barrera Cartel are long. If you try to compete with them or introduce another player to the market? Well, I will leave you to imagine what the repercussions might be for you and your entire organisation.'

Dom shook his head in clear frustration. 'This is bullshit Miguel and you know it. Your idiot boss does not understand the complications of getting a product into an island as small as ours. I can guarantee his first major shipment will be lost.'

Orejuela walked over to Rossi and placed an arm around his shoulders, propelling him gently back towards the house. 'Please, leave this with me. Things change and there can be many pitfalls to overcome on any path, especially the one Senor Barrera is considering walking. Things will work themselves out, you will see.'

Dom went to answer him when he felt the mobile phone in his jacket pocket vibrate. He took it out and looked at the number. Cassie.

'Fine Miguel, fine. I need to take this call – in private please.'

'Of course. My garden is yours for as long as you need it.'

He pressed accept.

'Hi Cassie. What did Malone want?' No point in small talk. Besides he didn't feel like it.

Dom listened. His jaw clenched, as she detailed the *safety measures* Malone had set up in the system. He swore the bastard would pay, but right now he had to find a way around this, find a way of regaining control of his burgeoning empire. He was being attacked on two fronts; by someone he had thought of as his friend and by the people he needed to keep his small empire standing. Lost in thought for a second, he hadn't realised she was still speaking.

'What? Tell me that again.'

As he listened, a slight glimmer of hope appeared. A dim spark in an otherwise overcast, cloudy and uncertain future belying the weather here in Spain and back home in Scotland.

'Okay,' he said, nodding to himself. 'Send the video to my mobile. Get Billy to run down this guy's life. I want to know where he lives, is he married, does he have kids, what are his shift patterns, what car does he drive, the works, and tell Billy I need it last week. I'll change my flights and be back tomorrow morning. I want you and Billy to pick this guy up and bring him to the Villa tomorrow afternoon. Then we can discuss a plan of action.'

He disconnected the call and stood facing the Iberian sun, head back, eyes closed. Why did shit all have to happen at once he thought? His screw up of a mother had said things usually come in threes, but right now he would settle for the two biggest threats he had faced in ten years being his last.

Then again, she had also said 'whit's fur ye will no go by ye,' and Dom aimed to make sure that particular saying came true.

SIX

Dan Ogilvie stood in shirtsleeves looking at the ruins of Bothwellhaugh Roman baths, marvelling any civilisation seventeen hundred years ago, could build structures such that any part of them lasted, especially against the ravages of Scottish weather. He often came here to Strathclyde Park after a hard day shift had ended at HMP Glasgow. At fifty five, he knew his chance of becoming a Governor was gone, so all he thought about each day was getting in the next five years until his retirement. The brown nosing and funny handshakes among the younger managers did nothing for him. Few had walked a hall. They hadn't had to go into a cell where the floor was slick with the blood of a prisoner who had slashed his wrists during the night. Or held on to the legs of someone who had had hung themselves after a bad visit from his girlfriend while your partner cut them down. Fast track managers someone had called them. Well, by the time he was Fifty he realised he was on the fast track to bumping right into a glass ceiling he hadn't even known was there. He had risen as high as they would let him. The Head of Operations was okay, but it wasn't Governor or even Deputy Governor.

He heard footsteps, and glanced around. A man and a woman walked towards him. The woman was in her mid-thirties, severe tied back hair, black skin, good looking, high cheekbones wearing a thin white blouse, tight blue jeans and some ankle length boots that did not look designed for walking in a park. Not bad at all he thought. A vague memory stirred of a previous encounter, but he couldn't pin it down.

He nodded politely. 'Hi,' he said. 'Grand day for a walk isn't it.'

The man smiled. 'A bit too warm for my liking, I prefer autumn.'

The woman nudged him playfully in the ribs, 'Aw c'mon now grumpy, it's a smashing day. You could just sit in the shade for ages looking at videos on Insta' of cats opening doors, and people falling on their arses.'

'That you could,' he said as they both stepped closer to Ogilvie, 'if I even had a clue what Insta' was that is.' They stopped, one either side, looking at the ruins of the baths.

'I bet you can find lot's of other videos on that Youtubey thing as well,' the man said while looking over the ruins. He nodded toward the baths. 'Is there anything on the internet about this place?' he asked Dan.

Dan shrugged. 'Probably,' he replied. 'I've never looked. I just read what they put on the notice boards.' He pointed to one close to the ruins of the building.

The man nodded.

'There are some weird ones kicking around though,' the girl said. 'Nothing filthy, mind you. But I mean, have a look at this one will you.'

She held her iPhone out, directly in front of Ogilvie's face. Her friend also turned to look. Dan watched it politely, feigning interest. It was a short mix of idiots being, well idiots, each looking for their elusive five minutes of fame.

'I don't tend to watch much of that stuff,' he said with a smile. 'Always seems like a waste of ten minutes of my life every time I do.'

The woman nodded. 'I know. It does become addictive after a while. I mean for this next clip I had to watch over three hours of the most God awful, boring stuff to get it, but when you see it I'm sure you'll agree, it was well worth it.' She grinned.

Dan looked at her a bit quizzically, but she flashed him a bright, flattering smile.

'Go on then,' he smiled back. 'Let's have a peek.'

She swiped her screen to the left, brought up the next video, pressed play and held it up to Ogilvie. 'Now you need to watch it carefully to get the full impact,' she told him.

As it played, all he saw at first was a hallway of what looked like a high end hotel. Striped wallpaper, green patterned carpet. The image quality of the video was good, but there was no sound. As it played, a few people walked across the screen in ones and twos, none of whom he recognised.

'Is something supposed to happen?' he asked with a frown after a few minutes.

'Just keep watching Mr. Ogilvie. You'll see it in a minute.' The woman said.

He nodded, then turned his head to look at her again. 'How, ...how do you know my name.' he asked suspiciously.

'Later,' she said, the humour gone from her voice. 'Watch the video.'

He looked at the older man, who smiled tightly and nodded towards the phone in her hand. Turning his head back to the video, Ogilvie watched as two figures walked along the corridor facing the camera. One of them was a young girl. She had long hair and wore a tight, low cut dress, finishing just above the knee. Walking beside her with an arm around her waist was an older man in his fifties, slightly heavy but with his own greying hair. He was talking and laughing with the girl, but just as they passed the camera, he looked to the front and it was clear who it was. It was also clear to him now where it was.

It was him. In a private brothel, in Perth just after he'd visited the prison there.

'And you know what Dan,' The girl said, edging a bit closer. 'She's only sixteen. I know she looks older, but it's amazing what a push-up bra and a bit of slap can do for a girl, don't you think?'

'What the fuck is this?' he asked angrily. 'Who the hell are you two?'

'We,' said the girl, 'are either your worst nightmare or all of your dreams come true. Which one depends on how you want to play it! After all,' she smiled coldly, 'we can't have this wonderful piece of reportage footage getting into the wrong hands now, can we?'

'This is rubbish. The video show's nothing. You try to blackmail me and I'll have you arrested before you leave the park. Do you know what I do for a living? Do you have any idea how much trouble you'll be in?'

Dan tried to move away, but the man grabbed hold of his arm in a surprisingly strong grip. 'Mr Ogilvie, I suggest you listen to the young ladies proposition.' He smiled at the girl. 'Sorry for using that word pet.'

'She is sixteen Dan,' the girl told him. 'I have the proof. I have her passport and her birth certificate.' She paused. 'And I haven't shown you the quality stuff yet by the way.'

He shrugged himself free of the grip. 'What do you mean the quality stuff?' he asked, half turning towards the girl, his fear increasing.

She smirked. 'Surely you don't think we only have cameras in the corridors Dan? I mean what would that say about us if we didn't look after our girls in their actual places of work?'

'What? Are you fucking kidding me?' He looked frantically between the two of them. CCTV in the bloody rooms. He had seen no cameras. But then again, they were so small now you could fit them anywhere, and he should know.

'Oooh....!' the woman said through puckered lips. 'You do have some kinky little foibles Mr Ogilvie. I mean the thing you do with your tongue when she's on her knees? Well, let's just say it was a new one on me.'

Dan felt his legs weaken. His stomach dropped. He knew if this got out, it would ruin him. Shit, he'd end up spending time among the beasts he helped keep locked up. His gut knotted. This couldn't be happening, it couldn't! But it fucking was.

'Wha,.....what do you want from me?' He looked frantically between the two of them. 'Money? Inside information? Someone dealt with? What?'

'What I want you to do right now Dan is call your wife. Tell her you've been held up at work. Some security incident or other only you can deal with. Then you'll go with this gentleman in your car. He'll drive to where we need to get to. Okay so far?' The woman fixed him with a frosty stare.

He nodded dejectedly.

'Good. I'll follow in my car and then? Well, we'll see.' She saw the look of fear on his face. 'Oh, don't worry it'll be nothing bad, not physically. Now on you go, make the call.'

He looked at them again before walking off slightly, pulling the phone from his back pocket and dialling a saved number. After he had finished his conversation, he turned to look at them, still shocked and worried.

'Okay. Let's go,' the man said.

They reached their cars. The man held out his hands for Ogilvie's keys. He handed them over and got into the passenger seat expectantly.

'Now,' he told him, easing himself into the driver's seat. 'Don't be a dougball and do anything stupid Mr Ogilvie. I may be getting on a wee bit, but believe me, I can still whack your napper off that dashboard if you try anything daft. Got it?'

Dan nodded nervously.

'Good.'

Ogilvie watched as the man adjusted the seat backwards to accommodate his longer legs, tweaked the rear-view mirror and started the engine. 'Off we go then,' he smiled.

An hour later, Dan was in the kitchen of some massive Villa on Glasgow's south side. The windows in the wall to his right and in the sitting area were shaded with Roman blinds.

'Over there and take a seat Danny boy. We'll be getting to the good stuff soon.'

Dan walked across the quarry-tiled floor, chancing a look at his escort before he sat down in one of the two-seater couches in a breakfast area. 'We waiting on someone else?' he ventured nervously.

'Danny, sit there and calm down. I'll get you a wee camomile tea for your nerves, shall I?'

Just then the woman walked in followed by a man he hadn't seen before. He looked to be in his early to mid-forties. Tall, dark, good looking. He glanced at Dan, unsmiling then looked at his escort. 'Any problems?' he asked.

'Not a one boss, not a one.'

Ogilvie swallowed as the middle aged, but fit looking newcomer sat down on the two-seater couch facing Ogilvie. 'Before we start.....' Ogilvie physically flinched at the words. The man smiled. 'As I was saying, before we start I just want you to remember what's at stake here. All the CCTV footage together with evidence about the girl's age will go straight to the press if you refuse to help us. Understand?'

He nodded. 'Hel,.....help you do what?' he stammered.

The woman moved and sat next to his interrogator. The *heavy* leant on the door from the kitchen leading into the main house.

'Simple. 'We need you to get someone out of your prison, not in a year, but now, within the next two weeks. So, how can you help us? What kind of paperwork do you need to create to make that happen?'

Dan eyed them quizzically. 'Are you serious? Get someone out of prison, just like that?' Ogilvie shook his head in bewilderment. 'You people have gone to a whole lot of trouble for not much return.'

'You're the Head of Operations. Surely it's not beyond your no doubt considerable skill set, to create paperwork letting our.......,' he paused before continuing, searching for the right word, 'friend, out of prison?'

Dan was silent for a while before shaking his head. 'It doesn't work like that.'

'No!' he said. 'Then tell us Dan, how does it work?'

Ogilvie was silent, considering his options, which to be honest he knew were limited. So he supposed there was no harm in telling him. 'Like everything else in the world, you can't do a thing without having someone somewhere create an electronic record of it. The second I logon to any SPS system using my ID, it's recorded.'

The man held up his hand. 'How do you create the correct paperwork?'

Dan laughed and shook his head slightly. 'What paperwork? Everything is electronic. You need a PC audit trail to let any move happen.' He gazed at the three of them in turn. 'I can't believe you didn't know that's how things are done. I mean, you simply expect me to create some kind of non-existent form and waltz your friend straight out of prison? Give me a break.' He sighed. 'Look, who are you people anyway?'

The man looked at the other two and shrugged. 'No harm in being on first name terms I suppose. That's Billy, she's Cassie and you can call me Dom.'

Ogilvie watched as Rossi sat back on the couch and folded his arms. 'Okay, that's the introductions out of the way, and the first option.' Ogilvie looked bemused. Dom shrugged. 'I had to ask. It might have been simple, so this way we deal with the obvious first then look at other scenarios.'

'There are no other scenarios,' Ogilvie said quietly. 'You remember what happened a few years back? We *lost* four prisoners during hospital visits, terrorists, when a couple of the private cars we used for external transports were rammed and hijacked. That put an end to it, especially after one of the escort officers ended up losing a leg. Now, every hospital visit has four officers to each prisoner, and everyone is transported in secure vehicles, not bog standard cars.'

Cassie looked at Dom. 'It would be too messy anyway boss. We'd have cops breathing down our necks before we could leave the hospital car park. And ramming anything could cause as much injury to our asset as anyone else.'

He nodded in reply. 'What about breaching the wall with something? Starting a riot as a cover to getting him out? Any chance that would work?'

'Unless you have a spare M1 Abrams sitting around somewhere complete with explosive ammunition, you can forget all about breaching any wall.'

'I thought HMP Glasgow was a local prison, not top security? I can't see the Government spending any more money than they need on a jail to lock up poxy drug dealers and junkies?' Dom stated.

Dan shook his head. 'Folklore and fiction. There is no such thing as high or low security. There is just security, plain and simple. Castle Huntly apart, every other prison in Scotland is designed and built to the same standard.'

'Which is?' Dom queried.

'Let me put it this way. If Scotland had any gold bars of its own, we wouldn't need to build our own Fort Knox. We could just create a concrete bunker in the middle of a prison and keep them there.'

Dom looked at Cassie. 'Any ideas?'

'Getting through a cell wall, or the bars on a cell window,' Cassie said thoughtfully. 'At least you would have time to plan, think of some way of getting over the wall before you start.'

Ogilvie said nothing.

'Answer her,' Dom instructed, angrily.

Ogilvie smirked. 'It isn't a question worth an answer. I mean, how many prison staff do you think haven't seen the Shawshank Redemption? Okay, okay,' he continued quickly as he noticed the menacing look in Billy Jenkins' eyes. 'The walls of each cell are 150mm thick double reinforced concrete. If by some miracle you got through that, you then have a layer of steel mesh embedded in the wall cavity before you even got to the external brickwork.'

'What about the windows?' Dom put in. 'Cassie mentioned them.'

'Forget them. The bars are rectangular, made of carbon steel composite. On the inside of the cell there's a sheet of anti vandal polycarbonate covering the entire window.'

'That cannae be too tough to break,' Billy observed from his position at the door.

Dan shrugged. 'You'd still have the external glass to deal with. A five layer laminate with two, three millimetre layers of vinyl in between.'

'Okay,' Dom put in. He stood up and walked around, thinking.' But it's not impossible?'

'No,' Ogilvie agreed. 'With the right tools, no.'

He stopped just inside the kitchen and turned to face them. 'So we have a starting point then!' He looked at Ogilvie expectantly.

'No you don't'

'Why?' Dom asked, bemused.

'Yes, you might remove or break the glass, and maybe you could do it without being heard if you were clever enough, but no, you still couldn't get out through the window.'

'Again, why?'

'The bars,' Dan said. 'They're 30mm wide. The gap between is only 95mm. You can't squeeze through it.'

'But you could prise them apart,' interjected Cassie, 'make the opening larger. I've heard about it and seen it in films. All you need is a towel and a hefty piece of timber.'

Fuck, if this was happening anywhere else I'd be pissing myself laughing instead of just pissing myself Ogilvie thought. He sat back and looked towards the guy called Dom that seemed to be in charge. 'You people do not understand do you?'

'No, we don't,' hissed Dom. 'So stop with the sarcasm, and just answer the bloody question. Can you do it?'

Ogilvie took a deep breath. 'Okay. I'll cover all this in one go so we can stop dicking around. You can't do what she said, just accept it. You can't hacksaw through the bars because each corner of every bar has an even harder material built in that will ruin any hacksaw blade you can come up with in seconds. The only way you can get through them is with an oxy-acetylene torch. Each cut takes forty minutes, and you have at least two cuts to make for every bar you want removed. You can't break him out, period.'

Ogilvie watched as Dom walked to the large American style double refrigerator and opened the door. The interior light spilled out into the kitchen bringing with it some well needed cooler air.

'What happens when you have a fire? How do you evacuate prisoners? Where do they go?' Dom took out a plastic bottle of fresh orange juice, twisted the cap off and took a drink. He turned to look at Ogilvie again.

'If the fires in a cell, then nothing. It's automatically extinguished by a water mist system built into each one. If the fire is anywhere else, an officer needs to confirm it before they evacuate prisoners down the fire escape stairs.'

Dom walked back to his seat. 'Where do they go once they're in the stairwell?'

'Usually nowhere, but if you need to get them out, then you contact the ECR and ask to have the final fire escape door unlocked. Then you enter a fenced off secure area.'

'ECR,' Dom asked.

'Electronic Control Room,' Dan replied.

'Is there any chance of them getting to the wall from that secure area?'

'Snowball in hell comes to mind,' Ogilvie muttered.

'What?' Dom asked.

Ogilvie looked up at him. 'No, none. The internal fence is at least fifteen metres away from the building. After that, there's an empty seven and a half metre wide strip before you even get to the perimeter wall. The fence and the wall are both five point two metres high, and we top the fence with razor wire. And let's not mention the perimeter intruder detection system built into the fence.' Ogilvie sat back and folded his arms. 'You people need to face it, we've thought of everything. Once you're inside, there's no way out.'

Dom shook his head. 'You're wrong. Nothing is totally secure. There are always gaps, blind spots that people haven't seen. We just need to think laterally, not literally.' Ogilvie watched as Dom eyed him menacingly.

'And you are going nowhere until we figure out where that one gap that single overlooked blind spot is.'

Ogilvie slumped back in his seat and looked dejectedly at the floor.

'What about smuggling him out inside a vehicle,' Cassie looked at Dom, then Ogilvie. 'From what I saw, there are people going in and out all the time. In fact, it's like bloody Sauchiehall Street.'

'What's his name?' Ogilvie asked.

Cassie looked at Dom. He shrugged.

'No harm in telling him I suppose. He's called Jack Malone and we need you to keep a close eye on him.'

'Remand or convicted?'

'Remand,' Cassie told him.

'Then it's not possible. He won't get anywhere near a vehicle. Remand prisoners don't work, they don't have to. They're still officially innocent.'

'Plus?' Dom asked, knowing he was leaving something out.

'Plus,' Ogilvie continued, 'everything moving in and out of the vehicle lock is checked with a heartbeat monitor. The curtain sides are also checked with a carbon dioxide sensor. Anyone in there will be found.'

Dom blew out a long breath. 'Okay let's get back to basics,' he said. 'How do you leave the prison every day? How do people know it's you walking out the door and not someone else that's just stolen your keys?'

Ogilvie looked surprised. 'Are you kidding? People will know it's me by simply looking.'

'But what if someone new starts? It'll take them a while to recognise everyone, even the Management. So run me through it Mr. Ogilvie, what happens when you leave to go home?'

'First off, Malone's in a Houseblock and I don't work there. Believe it or not I usually work in an office. To leave a Houseblock, you need to open three steel doors with electric locks. The first two you can open using a programmed fob, which is just a token that operates in much the same way as your contact less car key works. The door into the corridor is controlled by the ECR.'

'What then?' Dom urged him.

'Then, there are a bunch of other steel doors, all with electrically operated locks, each of them requiring the fob to open.'

'What happens if your fob hasn't been programmed for the door?' Cassie queried. 'How do you get out then?'

'All the doors have a Video Communication unit attached to them. You use that then the ECR opens it – if they recognise you that is.

Dom nodded. 'But you, given your job, your fob will get you all the way out of the prison won't it?'

'No!' Ogilvie replied with a grim smile. 'It won't. Even the Governor isn't trusted enough for that. No one gets through the last three doors using their fob.'

'So the last three doors out of the prison are controlled by this ECR you're talking about!' Dom concluded.

Ogilvie nodded.

Cassie gave a small sarcastic laugh. 'Then maybe we should be blackmailing someone in the ECR just to open the doors when Malone leaves?'

'It still won't do you any good,' Ogilvie said to her with a smirk. 'There are hundreds of CCTV cameras in the prison. Your *'friend'* will be caught long before they are anywhere close to the final door in the Gate Building.'

'Hundreds of fucking cameras,' Billy said in amazement. 'No wonder our taxes are so high.'

Cassie looked at him. 'Billy, you don't pay taxes.'

He smiled.

Ogilvie wondered about their thought process. Did they think it would be easy? They might have a low opinion of Civil Servants, but prison staff had been doing this job for a long time. They were clued up. They thought differently. They *were* lateral thinkers. He had shot down every idea they had put forward.

Dom sighed. 'Shame we can't make him look more like you, Mr Ogilvie?'

Cassie suddenly sat upright. She turned towards him, and snapped her fingers. 'That's it.'

'What's it?' Dom asked her.

'You said it's a shame he couldn't look like him.' She bit her bottom lip for a second. 'I might just have something,' she said half smiling. 'It's a bit of a long shot, but from what he's told us, we aren't going to get Malone out in any conventional way. All we need just now are two things, one of which is for him,' she pointed to Ogilvie, 'to keep his mouth firmly shut. The other? Well, the other needs me to do a bit of apologising and hopefully get back on the good side of someone I know. If it goes smoothly, then we could be in business.'

'How?' Dom asked her.

'Give me a day or two,' Cassie said standing up. 'I need to make a call first and hope she's still speaking to me. Then I need her to tell me she can do what I have in mind, without me giving too much away.'

'Don't tell me it's another wee lassie you've dumped after using and abusing,' Jenkins grinned.

Cassie glared at him. 'You shouldn't be so smug Billy. Your future's as much at stake as mine.' Ogilvie sat silent as she glanced at him then looked at Dom. 'We need to send him home. He needs to keep acting like everything is fine. Go to work. Go home. Shag the wife, whatever it is he normally does he needs to keep doing it. If he doesn't and someone gets suspicious then nothing will work.' She paused and looked directly at Ogilvie. 'Just remember exactly what we have Mr Ogilvie. Do as you're asked, and everything will be fine. Okay?'

He nodded quietly.

'What do you have in mind Cassie?' Dom asked his interest piqued.

She grinned. 'We're going to walk him out.'

SEVEN

It was another glorious day. Shimmering currents of air rose from tarmac roads and pavements making distant streetscapes dance in the heat. It brought a latent promise of lasting forever, and people's lives had slowed to walking pace to deal with it. Cassie parked her car at the Exhibition Centre and strolled along the riverfront past the gleaming, painfully bright steel finish of the Armadillo that reflected the crisp, blue sunlight. She continued on towards the sloping, shaded, glass frontage of the Crowne Plaza, the BBC building across the water mirrored in it's facade. The sun was still high in the north east sky and the structures on the opposite bank of the Clyde basked in its rays, the curves of the Science Centre standing out in knifelike sharpness. The light was almost painful, so she pulled the Ray Bans from the top of her head across her eyes and polarized dimness descending.

She often went running down here, along the banks of the river, her and many others, stepping unknowingly in the footsteps of long dead shipbuilders and Dockers. Now though, she walked slowly, trying to gather wandering thoughts. Pen them in. Make some sense of them. Make sense of the last fifteen years. A black girl, from an old mining village in Lanarkshire that had last seen a real mine over forty years before she had been born. God, how she had struggled. Not so much with people. She was after all tall, strong, athletic, fairly good looking, always had been. There had been fights and name calling, usually 'Paki Bastard,' which always amused her. Her mother was Nigerian and her father had been a mine foreman in Africa, but had come from the village. She had been born in South

Africa, but he had sent them both back as he said they would be safer, bought them a house in the village away from the schemes, in the posh *Main Street.* But safety was all relative. They would always be *incomers*. She realised that from the age of six. But her strength and innate cunning helped her survive. Plus, she could run like a gazelle which helped against the bullies. When he died though, she was ten and the money dried up. The mortgage payments fell behind, then the Council Tax, then; well then everything. Her mother sold the house, and the Bank took the money and the Council gave her a two bed flat in one of the schemes her father had sought to protect them from. And they got on with it.

Little money meant no treats, just the grey blandness of a same day existence. She screamed inside, not knowing who she was or what she wanted. Her mother, dropped into an alien culture she knew little about, unable to guide Cassie through its many pitfalls. She had friends, and she had enemies. Sometimes they swapped. So she fought with them all, and she never lost, ever. But it cost her black eyes, and loose teeth and bruises too many to count. She matured, grew out of it. She found boys, tried them again and again, hated them again and again, convinced the next time would be better. She hated the fumbling in the parks and other quiet places they took her. Hated the roughness of their fingers prodding inside her when she let a few of them get to third base. Hated the way her underwear dug into her thighs and hips as they pushed it aside. They always seemed to enjoy it, always insisted she stroke them off after they had squeezed as many fingers in as they could, and licked and smelled the fluid she involuntarily produced. It did nothing for her. There was never a home run. There were a few bruised testicles on a couple who 'insisted,' but no one ever got her above one on the excitement scale.

No one that is until Sandra.

It was at a party in the nearest town in a large, stone-built house. Bay windows. Too many rooms. She was seventeen and got dragged along by one of the enemies of old, recently turned friend. But the party was nice. Mostly other sixth year pupils like her, from a couple of the local high schools, partying their way through January and February into the exam season beginning in March. There was booze aplenty but Cassie and alcohol had not always gotten on. Hangovers, sore heads and gut wrenching puking had hit her badly, often after just a few drinks, so she had learned to stay well away. Someone had seemingly hit the big time though, as there was a *White Room.* Cassie had never tried coke before, except in a bottle. Egged on by a few others she *did a line,* both nostrils, then she sneezed and sneezed and blew a few hundred quid's worth of the white powder all over the carpet. People were not happy, not amused. Cassie was not happy. But someone behind her was. They were giggling, hand held over her mouth to stop the belly laughs wanting to erupt. Cassie turned and looked at her, anger on her face. But she mellowed and smiled when she looked into the other girl's eyes. No condemnation, no criticism. She just thought it was comedic. That had been it. They said hello, hung out for a while talking, smoked some dope, wandered into a bedroom, found a space and lay down in each other's arms. The kiss happened naturally, no hesitation on either part, and later, much later, when the party was breaking up they made an excuse to stay and put the relative solitude to good use.

First loves seldom last and this was no different. Sandra went to University in England. Leeds, Cassie remembered. Cassie herself wandered into hospitality, running pubs, hotels and nightclubs. It didn't pay especially well, so she took to buying some Class A's from people who did that kind of thing in the nightclubs. and selling them to people she felt she could trust. Which is where she met and got to know Domenico Rossi. His effortless charm was a bit seductive and even when he found out she was gay, he smiled, shrugged and said he didn't have many actual friends so who cared. About five years ago he asked her to run his *Spas*. He was up front about what went on in them but insisted the girls he employed were never forced, never mistreated. When she found out for herself this was true, she went for it. She did not agree with it, but as she became better off than she could ever have imagined, her conscience wandered into a recess in some dark part of her mind and set up camp, enjoying its break.

After yesterday's meeting though, she had found it hard to sleep in her city centre flat, blaming the heat, the humidity, the sounds of the city wafting in through her open window. The truth was though, she loved those sounds. They were her lullaby. She felt uneasy without them. No, she had not slept because of what she was about to do. To apologise for something she had done with the best of intentions. But wasn't that what the road to hell was paved with? After twenty minutes walking, she arrived at Glasgow Harbour Terraces. Scanning the numbers and names, she found the right one, well the number anyway. The name was unfamiliar. She pressed it regardless and listened to the distant buzz reflected in the tinny speaker.

After a few seconds, maybe ten, a voice answered back. 'Hello. Who is it?'

Distorted as it was, the voice was one familiar to her from a nine month relationship she had ended a few short weeks before. She contemplated saying Amazon delivery just to get the door open, but that would be an inauspicious start.

She gulped. 'Hi Claire.' It was almost a quiet rasp. 'It's Cassie. Please, please don't hang up,' she continued quickly. 'I need to talk with you. I know you think I'm a bitch, but I'm honestly not. Please let me in.'

There was silence from the other side. A pause so pregnant with expectation it felt explosive. Eventually, she heard a click. The door unlocked. She entered and climbed the stairs to the top-floor flat facing the river to the south. She saw the door was already unlocked, slightly open. She pushed it gently with her hand, but there was no one behind it. Walking into the hall she made her way past the bedroom and bathroom and stopped just as she entered the living room. Claire Mercier, stood with her back to Cassie, arms folded, staring out of the window. She had just stepped from the shower, her auburn hair slightly damp, uncombed, wearing a knee-length cotton dressing gown. Her feet were bare. The smell of scented soap hung in the air.

Cassie coughed softly. 'Hi again Claire. I'm sorry. I should have called before coming round.'

'You forget a toothbrush or something even less important Cassie?' Claire said angrily, not bothering to look.

Cassie sighed. 'Please, let's not fight. I'm here to apologise and explain. It hasn't been easy for me either, you know.'

Claire laughed. 'Oh my, are the poor me's coming now? Not interested Cassie. Shit, I don't even know why I opened the bloody door for you.'

Except, she did know, because Cassie felt the same way. She swallowed hard. 'I've missed you. How have you been?'

Claire's head bowed slightly, and her shoulders slumped. 'Cassie, I fucking gave you everything. I opened up with you more than I've ever done, even with my mother, and you repay me by walking out one night. Leaving a note for me. Being a coward.'

'You never called,' Cassie mumbled. 'I,...I didn't know what to think. Were you happy it was over? Were you mad at me? Disappointed?'

Claire turned, her lips set in a thin, tight line. 'Did it mean anything to you Cassie? Us? Was it ever more than just physical with you?'

Cassie sat down on the leather sofa, the seat so wide her feet barely touched the rug on the timber floor. Good for curling up in, but not designed for sitting. Her hands lay loosely on her lap.

She looked up at Claire and shook her head sadly. 'I had no choice,' she told her haltingly. 'I was getting so close to you it physically hurt every time we left each other. I just wanted us to be together, but I couldn't drag you into the world I occupied with all its seedy little secrets and undercurrents of violence. That wasn't what I wanted for you.'

Claire marched over and stood in front of Cassie, arms folded like protective armour. 'What are you talking about? You told me you were a nightclub manager. What the hell is so seedy about getting people pissed you thought walking out was a better solution? Did you ever for just one second consider I couldn't give a shit about your work or the people you might know? Why do you think I never asked you about it, or them? All I needed was you.'

Cassie bowed her head and looked at the floor. 'It's not that simple,' she told her quietly.

Claire sat down beside her, the dressing gown sliding open a little, one ivory knee and thigh peeping out. 'Cassie, you might not believe this but I know more about the underbelly of life in this town than you might imagine.' She reached forward to take her hand then quickly withdrew it. 'Fuck, what am I doing? You left me. I was so angry with you. I still am.'

Cassie reached out and held one of Claire's hands lightly in her own. She didn't flinch or pull away. 'I know. I would be too. I was a coward. I didn't want to face you. It's,.......it's not like me, but I just couldn't have handled seeing your face when I told you.'

Claire looked at her hand in Cassie's and pulled it quickly away. 'What do you want Cassie? I don't have time for this. Just tell me what's on your mind and then get out.'

Cassie smiled a little. She could sense the anger in Claire's voice was a little fake. Perhaps there was a chance after all.

'I won't lie to you Claire. I missed you, terribly, but something has come up in my work and I need your help with it.' Pausing, she looked at her hopefully. 'And I thought at the same time, well, maybe I could apologise. Explain in more detail. Ask for forgiveness. Perhaps even start over again.'

Claire laughed. 'You want my help? After you broke my heart, you want my help? Jeez, you have a real brass neck Cassie.'

'Claire,' Cassie replied, 'I *need* your help.'

'Then start by explaining why you had to leave? What big

secret about your life is so bad you couldn't tell me about it? Why are you so special? What abo............'

'I work for a gangster,' Cassie blurted out, stopping Claire in mid flow. 'He's not like Tony Soprano,' she half lied, 'he doesn't whack people or organise hits on them, but he is a criminal.'

Cassie stood up and walked to the window. She gazed at the still waters of the Clyde, sparkling in the sunshine like diamonds. Except being Glasgow it would likely be cubic zirconium. 'I met him years ago, in one of the nightclubs. I did some dealing. Class A's. He bought from me a few times and we got talking, got friendly, then he offered me a deal I couldn't turn down.' She half turned, not knowing what to expect. Claire just sat on the couch staring at her expectantly.

'Do you want to hear more?' she asked tightly. Claire said nothing, but her eyes spoke volumes. 'Okay. He owns a string of high-class brothels.' She walked towards her. 'He needed someone to run them and look after the girls, I mean really look after them, keeping all the street shit away from them. So I took the job, mainly because it was too risky dealing and I hated the hours in the nightclubs.' She stood facing her.

'Doesn't sound to me like he's on anyone's most wanted list, so why couldn't you have told me this before?' Claire asked looking up, seemingly unconcerned her recent lover had a dark, secret life in the shadows.

'Bloody hell Claire, you work in the film industry. How the hell would I know how you'd react to me running hookers?'

She shook her head. 'I told you, I have a few family connections on the wrong side of the law myself. But there's more, isn't there? This man you work for, he does something else, something more dangerous?'

She nodded. 'And I needed to shield you. If he's ever taken down, then I'm going too and everyone I know will be under suspicion.'

'But now you need my help, although I can't imagine why or what I can do for you. I'm a special effects artist for God's sake, not a bank robber.'

Cassie sat down again beside Claire. They both turned slightly to face each other, knees almost touching. Claire's dressing gown fell open a little, exposing her right breast and Cassie felt herself take a light, involuntary gasp.

'It's your skill set I need,' Cassie told her, lifting her eyes to her face. 'I have a problem, and it needs a fairly unique solution?'

'Which is?'

No point being coy about this she thought. 'I need you to help me get someone out of prison.'

Claire said nothing for a while. She just looked at Cassie, her eyes darting over her face. Then she laughed. 'Tell me, when did I let on I'd joined the Magic Circle, because even I know it will take someone bloody talented to pull that off.'

Cassie smiled and nodded. 'I know. That's the reaction I had when I first thought of it. But please, it's not as mad as it sounds. We have someone on the inside we want to make our prisoner look like, and after seeing your workshop a few months back, well, you might just be able to pull it off.'

Claire looked confused. 'What does my workshop have to do with it? I can't invite this prisoner around for a full facial makeover can I?'

'No,' Cassie agreed. 'But you have a state-of-the art 3D printer, and I've seen it in action making some of those prosthetics for the films and TV programmes you're working on. You've put together masks for all kinds of productions. You just need to treat this like one of those.'

'Cassie,' Claire whispered, pulling her dressing gown around her. 'I don't need to do anything, remember. We aren't an item any longer. You closed that door a month ago.'

'I was stupid, I know that.'

'But would you be back here if it wasn't for this other thing?' Claire asked. 'You can't just tune me up and play me like a violin and then lock me back in a case when your poor fingers get sore. I'm not that fucking easy.'

Cassie sat back. She picked at her fingernails and looked

blankly out of the window. 'I would have come back, eventually. But you're right, this is too soon, I still hadn't worked out in my mind how much I wanted to tell you. Now I don't have an option. You needed to hear everything.'

Claire stood up and walked to a sideboard standing against one wall. She removed the stopper from a bottle of Chianti she had started the night previously and poured herself a large glass. After a few second's hesitation, she poured another glass and came back to the sofa handing one to Cassie. She took it with a tight smile.

Claire sat down again and took a sip of her drink. She sighed. 'This doesn't mean I forgive you Cassie, but what do you need me to do?'

The relief Cassie felt was surprisingly immense, not just because Claire seemed willing to help her, but because she also seemed willing to give her another chance, if not now then at some point in the future.

'Thank you Claire. I know this must be hard for you.' She wondered just how much she should give away? She didn't want Dom finding out someone outside the organisation knew they were potentially in serious trouble without their banker. But that wasn't knowledge Claire needed to get this done.

'What do you need to print a full head face mask? One that someone else can wear? Hair, facial complexion, the works? And it has to be accurate.' She waited.

'Preferably a 3D laser scan of both of their heads plus a complete set of high resolution photographs of all four sides of the donor head, for skin tone and hair colour, that kind of thing.' Claire told her.

'Well, you're kind of in luck. I can get the donor to meet with you. To be honest, he won't have much choice. Scanning him won't be an issue. But the guy in prison! Well, that isn't going to happen, at least not the scanning part. So, can you do it from just photographs of him?'

Claire appeared to think for a second or two. 'Yes, I can do it. But I'll need some information on the guy wearing the mask. I can give you a list.'

Cassie considered. 'Okay, I'll get as much as I can for you.'

They both sipped at their wine, silent for a long minute. 'When do you need this Cassie?'

'Is ten days pushing it too much?'

Claire shook her head. 'That'll be fine provided you get the guy in question into my workshop soon.' Claire paused for a second, then glanced at Cassie, a worried look on her face. 'Will I be safe? What you're trying to do is illegal and if the authorities suss out how he did it then.......? Well let's just say there aren't too many visual effects artists in this neck of the woods who can do what we're discussing.'

Cassie smiled bitterly. 'Don't worry about him. He's a nonce and I have him by the bollocks. If he even unzips himself without asking me first, then the papers will get all the nice little home movies I've collected of him and the *underage* girl he's been visiting in the Health Spas.' She noticed the concern on Claire's face. 'It's okay,' she continued quickly. 'She isn't underage, but she looks it.'

'I know I shouldn't ask, but why is this so important?'

She shook her head. 'You're right. Don't ask. The less you know the less comeback there will be if it all goes tits up.' Cassie swirled the wine around in her glass. 'If this works Claire, maybe we can look at getting away from here. Starting over somewhere else. To be honest, being a de facto brothel madam doesn't sit well with me. I know I can score big from what's planned after we get this guy free. We could disappear anywhere we liked.'

'Yeh, right.'

They sat in silence for a while. Cassie felt the earlier tension had eased. They had just seemed to spark off each other when they had first met in that West End bar. Their conversation had been easy, funny and free flowing. It hadn't been difficult to like her, but after a few months she hated not being honest with her, hated knowing she could never be honest with her. That was why she left. But now? Now she still wasn't being totally honest, not about the drugs, and she wasn't sure she could ever bring her in on that.

She looked at her again sitting beside her on the couch. 'You said earlier you had experience of the murky Glasgow underworld. What was it? Dad a petty thief? Mum does a bit of dealing on the side? A brother in prison for stealing bottles of Buckfast from the corner shop?' She smiled at her. 'You don't need to tell me if you don't want to.'

Claire sat back on the sofa, crossing her legs, the dressing gown opening up again, Carries eyes wandering. 'Then I won't. Let's just say growing up in Ferguslie Park meant crossing paths with lot's of low and high level crooks.' She reached forward and placed her glass on the low table in front of them, Reaching over, she took Cassies from her hand and did the same.

'Now,' she said softly, standing up. 'It's been a month.' She undid the belt of her dressing gown and let it slide from her shoulders. She was naked beneath.

Cassie smiled and reached for her.

EIGHT

Ian Gilmour sat at his favourite table in the French Café he owned in Glasgow's West End. It was eight thirty in the morning, and despite his reputation he didn't mind rising early. He spooned one teaspoonful of sugar into his Café au Lait, proper coffee, made with half espresso and half warm milk. It gave the brown liquid a creamy texture, not the harsh bitterness of chain store coffee shops. A warm croissant sat on a side plate with a little tub of strawberry jam. Gilmour knew this wasn't exactly what most people expected bad assed gangsters to eat for breakfast, but he had always liked France, especially Paris and a little town on the south coast called Villefranche. He had spent more than a few long weekends there with various ladies of his acquaintance. A two and half hour car journey from Marseille where he had run drugs from North Africa in the past, it was much quieter, more civilised. He glanced at his wristwatch, then the door. A couple of his soldiers occupied a table near the window, glasses of water in front of them, facing the door. Domenico Rossi was due to arrive soon.

Gilmour knew Rossi was an enigma in the business. In the past, everyone had gotten their gear from a supplier in Manchester, who worked for another mob from *The Smoke.* But when the government down south began to take drugs seriously, importers had been busted, prices rocketed, demand went crazy and supply dried up. Rossi then branched out from the hookers and brothels he operated and started supply runs for anyone who would pay him. Surprisingly, it worked. Rossi had gotten into the game at the right time and although Gilmour hated to admit it, the bastard could be trusted. But Dom

Rossi did not figure in Ian Gilmour's future plans. That was why he had asked *Fat* Tony Smith to find out if Jack Malone could be 'persuaded' to jump ship and join him? With Malone onside, it would have crippled Rossi and forced him to do a deal with Gilmour amounting to a takeover. But the answer had been an emphatic no, so he had fallen back on Plan B. Get rid of Malone, watch Rossi struggle and then swoop in to pick over the bones. Except the two pricks Tony had sent to make that happen had fucked it up. Malone was banged up in Barlinnies replacement, out of reach until Ian could come up with another way of getting rid of him permanently. And seven civilians were dead. Not something Ian was happy about, but as he'd lost his conscience many years ago he didn't dwell on the death of innocents for too long.

Now he had to do it the hard way. He needed Rossi's contacts and expertise one last time, and had to squeeze him for every drop of information he could. Routes, contacts, bribes, landing points. By the time he had sucked him dry, he would have the monopoly on importing everything into the country. And a meeting with a certain Colombian in Amsterdam six months earlier had reinforced his ambitions. But he required someone inside Rossi's organisation. Someone he could trust with no ambition of their own. That was why he was here.

The door opened and a blast of city noise, dust and heat wafted in. Even this early in the morning it was warm. Scotland was having one of those Mediterranean summers everyone loved but everyone complained about. Two women walked in, both in their early thirties. One was around five foot eight with auburn hair cut short, shaved at the sides. The other was smaller by a couple of inches, with longer bleached blonde hair reaching her shoulders. Both wore loose fitting cotton blouses, one white the other a light shade of blue. They had on jeans which suited their full but not heavy figures. Unless you knew, you would never have taken them for twins.

Gilmour looked up and smiled. 'Angela! Gabby!' he said. 'Good of you both to come. What can I get you? Tea? Coffee?

Anything to eat?'

They walked over and kissed him on the cheek in turn, before sitting down.

'Thanks Uncle Ian. Coffee would be good,' Gabby, the auburn haired girl said. Angela nodded, looking glum.

Gilmour got up and walked behind the glass fronted display holding the French pastries he loved. They did mostly have some fruit on them. Mandarin slices, Strawberries, that kind of thing. But the gelatine covered pastry and custard was always what did it for him. He placed their cups half filled with espresso on a tray, sans saucer, then frothed a jug of hot milk in the steamer before bringing it all over to the table where they sat.

'So how's my sister doing then?' he asked, sitting down. 'Still enjoying the Canary Island sunshine?'

'Can't get her off the beach,' Gabby laughed. 'She's slowly roasting herself alive.'

'Tell her to watch it. She'll get all leathery and wrinkled.'

Ian poured the hot milk into their cups. Both girls took a sip.

'Now I suppose you're wondering why I asked you here?'

They both sat quietly and waited.

'Well, I've got a wee job for one of you,' he told them eventually. 'Nothing taxing. I just need someone I can trust to monitor something for me and feed me information.'

Angela shook her head unimpressed. 'What? Become a spy?'

'In a way,' her Uncle replied.

'So who would we be spying on?' Gabby asked. 'And exactly why is it so important?'

Gilmour considered for a moment. He supposed it was only fair they knew some of the details. 'You would be working with a guy called Domenico Rossi. His organisation brings in practically all the drugs sold in the country, and I want to take over that role. There are only two or three principal people that work for him of any importance. Apart from Rossi himself, there's his accountant, Jack Malone and some girl who looks after his other business. He's also got Billy Jenkins and Marti

Galbraith. They're old timers, but more personal bodyguards than anything else. He has a few others, some soldiers and suchlike, but they're just fillers making up the numbers.' Gilmour leaned forward. 'I need to find out as much about their import operations as I can over the next few months. And who better to do that than one of my favourite nieces. Not to mention he will also have a fair whack of my money and I want to know it's safe.'

'Why one of us?' Angela asked.

'Because,' their Uncle said, 'they probably think I'll send some big knuckle dragger like one of those two behind you. They won't be expecting anyone from the fairer sex. And not anyone with brains.'

Gabby looked at her uncle. 'So just who is Domenico Rossi? I've never heard of him.'

'I'm not surprised,' Gilmour retorted. 'His organisation isn't big. They don't supply the street dealers or do any dealing themselves. The Rossi's are purely wholesale. '

Angela sat back, her face in a sulk. 'Sounds boring to me Uncle Ian. You haven't got anything a wee bit more exciting have you?'

He looked seriously at them. 'This is important girls. I wouldn't ask you otherwise.' He turned to Gabby, the question evident on his face.

'I know I've done some work for you in the past Uncle Ian, but what if I get found out, or nabbed by the cops?'

'The cops won't be a problem. You'll be on Rossi's books as a Management Consultant, nothing else. Plus Rossi will know all about you. In about twenty minutes in fact. I've asked him to meet us here so we can go over a few things and I can introduce you to him properly. Make sure he understands what I want him to think your role is.'

'Fine,' she sighed. 'One of the places I work is closing for refurbishment and won't open again for a few months. I have a small private contract to complete, but after that I'm free,' she smiled.

Ian nodded. 'That's my girl.'

They sat for twenty minutes, drinking more coffee, discussing old times. Times when they were kids and Uncle Ian took them to the seaside and the park, in between his time in prison that is. He asked again about his sister. She was in her fifties, slightly younger than Ian and had retired to Spain then the Canary Islands when her husband, Jamie Phillips, had been shot and killed in a shooting years before. Annabelle Phillips had no interest in anything her husband had done apart from handle some of the books. She was happy to live off the profits, but equally happy to ignore how they were generated. But Ian had always been driven, always looking for the big result, the ultimate score. This time he thought, he might just have done it.

Gabby stood up. 'I need to go a place before they get here.'

Ian nodded and pointed to the right of the counter. She got up and left.

A minute later the door of the café opened again. Both of Ian's boys stood up, instantly alert as Domenico Rossi walked in, sunglasses, open necked shirt, designer jeans and well cut jacket. All as Ian had expected. What surprised him was the girl behind him. He hadn't met her before, knew nothing about her, but he guessed she was the one that looked after the brothels and the hookers. Not too shabby looking either. Black. Smartly dressed, like her boss, but her hair was pulled back tight, giving her a strained, menacing look.

'Its okay boys,' Gilmour said. 'I'm sure Mr Rossi will vouch for his friend, who I didn't know was coming.' He nodded at Dom, whose mobile phone suddenly rang. Rossi held up his hand to Gilmour, then answered it, said little but nodded a few times throwing in the odd 'Si' every now and again. After a few minutes he ended the call and put the old Nokia style phone back in his jacket pocket. A burner Gilmour guessed. Rossi walked over to Gilmour not even looking at the two bodyguards. The girl followed silently. They stopped in front of Ian's table, and he took off his sunglasses.

'Well, I could have brought Marti with me Ian, but what kind of impression would he have made?'

Gilmour eyed the woman up. 'Well, be a gentleman Dom, introduce me then.'

'Cassie Hughes, meet Ian Gilmour, soon to be boss of the biggest crime empire in Bonnie Scotland if what he's hinted at comes true. And you Ian, who is this lovely young lady you're with.'

Dom sat down in the chair next to Angela, directly opposite Gilmour. Cassie pulled a chair from another table and sat at right angles to them both, leaning back relaxed but watchful.

'This is one of the terrible twins,' he told Dom. 'Angela Phillips this is Domenico Rossi, the long time associate I've just been telling you about.'

She looked scathingly at Rossi. 'That seat's taken,' she told him.

He looked around in mock confusion. 'Funny, doesn't feel like I'm sitting on anyone's lap.'

'She'll be back in a minute,' she said, glaring at him. 'And she won't be happy.'

'Well, we can't have that then, can we Ian?'

'Angela, leave it out darling, just for a wee while okay?'

He noticed Rossi's eyebrows rise at this, and smiled crookedly. Let him wonder. Then he heard someone come approach from behind and turned his head. 'Gabby, come and meet Mr Rossi and his associate.' He looked back. 'Your sister already has,' he grinned.

As she neared the table Gilmour noticed she slowed down. Her gaze drifted between Rossi and Cassie, lingering slightly longer on her. For a second he thought he saw surprise in her face, but it vanished as quickly as it appeared. Cassie also stared hard. Perhaps she just fancies her, he smiled inwardly. He knew Gabby was gay.

Gabby dragged over a chair from another table and sat facing Cassie. They avoided eye contact. Shit, this could be a problem, Gilmour thought. He needed her to keep close to the centre of things, without falling out with anyone.

'Okay Ian, we're here to iron out some details about our deal, so let's get on with it,' Rossi said impatiently.

Gilmour simply nodded. 'Gabby will be the person looking after my interests. She'll be the one working with you. Any issues with that?'

'None,' Dom replied. 'Happy to have her on board. Maybe I'll send her out to Colombia for a wee field trip during all of this? What about it Gabby, do you have a passport?'

'Rossi, you had better be kidding.' Gilmour leaned forward menacingly, arms on the table, bumping the empty coffee cups. 'These two precious young ladies are my nieces, and apart from my sister, their mother, they are my only living relatives. If anything happens to Gabby, I guarantee I will go all medieval on you, understand?'

'Whoa. Don't worry Ian she won't be going on a holiday anywhere. I'll handle the Colombian side myself. Which brings me to point number one. My fee! That call was my contact letting me know the Colombians are grateful for our offer to purchase such a large quantity of product and will enter detailed negotiations with us, - well, with me. To do that though, I'm going to need the twelve million as working capital within the next few days.'

'Not a problem Dom. I have a warehouse full of the proverbial greenbacks just looking for a new home. I can get my boys to drop a lorry load off anytime and anywhere you want.'

Rossi shook his head. 'Ian, I know you came up through the ranks when things were done differently, but even you know that won't cut it nowadays. It would take me years to launder that much cash. No, here's how it will happen. I'll be issuing you with invoices for work some of my consultancies have done for several of your property development businesses. You know, architects, project managers, engineer's fees, that sort of thing. The full twelve million will be transferred, legally, into said consultancies bank accounts. Once it's there, I'll get the deal moving. You just give me the company names, I'll do the rest.'

Gilmour was silent. He looked at Dom, his jaw clenched. 'That isn't how I work Rossi,' he said through gritted teeth.

Dom shrugged. 'That's the way it has to be Ian. If we don't keep up the pretence of legitimacy, then we're fucked. Plus, I have nowhere to store vast amounts of hard, cash and I don't want to stand guard on it twenty-four seven. I'd rather the banks looked after my money. Oh,' he said as if just remembering something. 'The final amount will be paid anonymously via a Dark Web Cayman Islands account I'll set up.'

'Fine,' Gilmour growled. 'I'll get you the names of the property companies you need to invoice.' He paused for a second, a puzzled look on his face. 'And what the fuck is the Dark Web when it's at home?'

Rossi grinned. 'Don't worry about it Ian. I'll let you know what to do when the time comes.'

The three girls sat silently through all of this. Angela seemed bored, but Cassie and Gabby were avoiding eye contact. Cassie was silent. Gilmour felt she was here to watch and learn. But Gabby was being very quiet. Even Rossi had noticed.

'Your girl isn't saying much Ian. I thought she would be desperate to know what I have in store for her?'

'Aye, but she listens pretty well. She'll find out what's going on fairly soon,' Gilmour said with a menacing smile that never reached his eyes. 'Oh, that reminds me Dom. The grapevine's been humming with all sorts of talk. It seems your Mr Malone has been a bit of an all round dickhead. Gotten himself banged up in jail when he was pissed and drove his car off the M8. How many people died in that crash? Six? Seven?'

Rossi sighed. 'It's an inconvenience Ian, I won't deny it. Malone does a fair bit for me, but until we can get him out on bail, it means Cassie and myself will need to step in and pull double shifts if we have to. It won't affect anything we've been discussing.'

'It had better not,' Gilmour grunted. 'Because once things begin to move, they'll motor along quickly. I can't have you standing there waiting for some judge to decide if your boy is going to get out anytime soon, understood?'

Rossi nodded. Ian though, wondered just what kind of impact having Malone banged up was having on him.

'So what's my role in all this?' Gabby eventually asked. 'Are we expected to swear allegiance to you Mr Rossi, down on bended knee and all that? Sign the official secrets act or something?'

'I'm getting the impression your heart's not in this wee temporary arrangement,' Dom grinned. 'But no. It'll be very simple. You'll be working with Cassie here. You follow her. Do what she asks you. If she's doing nothing, then so are you.' He glanced at Ian. 'Plus there won't be any trips out of the country for you. My suppliers are suspicious of people they haven't vetted first and they hate surprises. I'll be doing that part on my own if needed. Understood?'

Gilmour noticed this Cassie bird did not look over enamoured with Rossi's babysitting arrangements. She either had some kind of problem with Gabby, or just didn't like her looks, but something was going on. Well too bad. That was for Rossi to deal with. But what Rossi had said did not sit well with him.

'If you want twelve million of my hard earned readies Dom, then sorry, that isn't good enough. Gabby will become your new best friend. Where you go, she goes, including meeting your overseas contacts. Understand?'

Rossi stood up, pushing back the chair, sliding it across the Karndean floor. 'Then I might as well just walk out of here right now Ian, because that will not happen.' He looked directly at him and shook his head. 'Do you have any idea what these mad Colombian nutters are capable of? It's taken too long to get them to trust me. The last thing I'm about to do is waltz in to see them with a total stranger walking beside me.' He looked at Gabby and then back at Gilmour. 'I do and you'll never see either of us again. Understand?'

'I don't like being threatened,' Gilmour said menacingly. 'Not by you or anyone else.'

'For fuck's sake Ian, it's not a threat. It's just how things are. These guys stay under the radar by being careful. If they mess up, they'll get their head taken off by a chainsaw; without anaesthesia. If you think we play hardball in this overpopulated little patch we call home, then you are sadly deluded.' He paused. 'Why the lack of trust all of a sudden?' he spread his hands toward Gabby. 'I mean embedding your girl in my organisation! Tracking the money! Double checking everything we do! We've worked well together in the past, so just what the hell is all this? Just who are you running scared of?'

Gilmour stood up quickly. His chair went flying behind him where the back of his thighs caught it, clattering it into the glass fronted counter. The two goons also stood, startled by the noise, waiting for a signal from their boss. 'I'm scared of no bastard,' he snarled. 'And never say that to me again, do you hear? You run a two bit organisation that owns a one trick pony. You're nothing. Like I told you before, I can do this on my own if I have to. Clear.'

Rossi smirked at him.

The three girls just sat there calmly watching.

Then Cassie yawned dramatically 'Well,' she sighed, lifting her eyes toward Gabby. 'Looks like the big macho boys want to have a little fun to themselves.' She leaned forward. 'Why don't we girls bugger off and do some work while they sort it out amongst themselves? Seems like they've forgotten all about us for now.'

'Cassie's right,' Gabby said. 'Let's get out of here until these two sort out who's got the biggest swinging dick between them. Then perhaps we can sit down and discuss the options rationally. What do you say, ladies?'

The other two nodded and stood up, grabbing their handbags and headed towards the door.

'Wait,' Gilmour shouted while still staring at Dom. He looked at Gabby over Dom's shoulder. 'Now is that anyway to talk to your old Uncle Ian.' He flashed his own, cold smile at her. 'Come on. Sit back down.'

Gabby nodded. 'Well, if you two can stop trying to head butt each other and start talking as if we're here, then yes, we'll sit back down. Otherwise you can wipe each other's arses, because we won't be doing it for you.' She eyed Cassie, who nodded in agreement.

Cassie turned and moved back towards the table. 'This will be tough enough without your male egos getting in the way.' She looked at Gilmour. 'Mr Gilmour, you know exactly why Mr Rossi can't accept truck loads of cash. It would be stupid and irresponsible and too damned easy to track.' Her head swivelled, taking everyone in, lingering a little longer on Gabby. 'I know honour among thieves is not supposed to exist, but honestly, if you don't start to trust each other, this will not happen.'

Gilmour looked at Gabby. Her eyes and expression confirmed she agreed; that and an almost imperceptible nod.

'Everyone, sit back down,' Gabby asked. 'Let's start from the beginning again, okay?'

The girls took their seats. Gilmour and Rossi retrieved theirs from where they had tumbled and placed them back at the table then sat. The two heavies followed suit, looking confused.

'Now,' said Cassie, taking charge before either of the two men could say anything, keeping their alpha male egos in check. 'Let's go over the basics from the beginning, and I'll do the honours,' she continued quickly as Gilmour tried to interrupt. 'One, Mr Rossi will generate invoices for the twelve million. Two, Mr Gilmour will pay those invoices.' She glanced at him, almost daring him to speak. 'Three, Gabby will join our organisation temporarily to look after Mr Gilmour's interests. Four, Mr Rossi and I will do all negotiations for the delivery of the product, and only Mr Rossi will travel if he needs to. Clear?'

After a few seconds pause, Rossi smiled and nodded.

Gilmour clapped his hand and rubbed them together. 'I like this girl of yours Dom, I do. She has real balls and talks more sense than most of the twats I have working for me. Fine,' he said before standing up. 'That's sorted. But right now I have places to be, people to shaft.'

Rossi also stood. 'Do we need to shake on this Ian or do we have enough witnesses?'

Gilmour walked over to Rossi and placed an arm around his shoulders. 'Nah, Dom boy. We can trust each other by now. Those girls are pretty good at the old arbitration thing.' He winked at him. 'Let's walk to the cars together and enjoy the morning sunshine before it gets too bloody hot.' He looked around. 'Coming girls?'

'I want to have a talk with Gabby if that's ok.' Cassie answered. 'Get her up to speed on how things will happen from now on.'

'Fine.' He tossed her a set of keys. 'Lock up when you leave. Gabby will get them back to me.'

Angela followed the men out, including the bodyguards. When they had the place to themselves, Cassie turned and looked at Gabby.

'Looks like I wasn't the only one keeping things back, was I - Claire?'

NINE

Dom took the mobile phone from his pocket, the one Miguel had called him on earlier. It *was* a burner. He opened the case, removed the battery then the SIM and broke the card in half. He would incinerate it later, back at the Villa. The handset itself had been located automatically on the network by its fifteen digit International Mobile Equipment Identity number. This differed from the SIM, but in theory could still be traced. It was a small risk, but the handset would also be destroyed by hammering it flat. The SIM number had been sent to Orejuela via Dom's Dark Web email account, so only he would know it. But in this business, there was no such thing as being too careful.

Fucking Colombians, he thought angrily. He had lied to Gilmour. Miguel had called to say Antonia Barerra had made a decision regarding the shipment, and strongly hinted it had not gone in Dom's favour. Barerra wanted to meet again with Dom back in Mijas. He had a good idea why. If the South American intended to run his own shipments into Scotland via Gilmour, then he didn't want any potential competition. And as that competition was Rossi, Dom knew this would be his last run. Gilmour had no idea how to get the product safely into the country, which was why he had foisted his niece on him, to get the detail.

At least Miguel was sympathetic to Dom's situation, no doubt because of all the money he kept for himself from their deals. If South America became directly involved, then cash control would be much tighter and even Orejuela might become surplus to requirements. When Dom got back to his

Villa, he would contact Miguel again via the Dark Web and give him another single use number from the multitude of pre-pay SIM Cards he had. He needed to speak with him, not just use email. The biggest deal of his life looked like it could be his last, and he was not about to let that happen. Dom knew his organisation was small. Important yes, but simply a gear in the cogs running the machine from Colombia all the way to Scotland via Spain. That needed to change. He glanced in his rear view mirror. Cassie was walking back towards the car. She opened the door and climbed into the passenger seat. He let her settle down and clip on her seat belt. Her face was impassive, but there was a tension about the way she held her shoulders that let Dom know something was bothering her.

'Everything okay Cassie?'

'Fine Dom. Thanks?'

He didn't believe her, but started the car which hummed almost silently into life and set off for the Villa. He became aware of Cassie looking at him.

'You never told me much about what happened when you saw your Mum last week. Was everything okay?'

His knuckles tightened on the steering wheel. 'Cassie, my mum and brother are a waste of space. If I had the time and energy, then I might try to do something about them. Get them into rehab or detox somewhere. But they don't want to go. I'll get Marti to sort out some local dealer that's been roughing them up and drop some cash off to them every week, but that's it. In any case, they'll just snort it or shoot it up,' he sighed. 'Enough about them. Bring me up to speed on Malone? You said you needed time to check something out. Have you done that?'

Cassie looked down at her lap.

'Cassie?' he asked again.

'I've found something that might work,' she said hesitantly. 'We'll need Ogilvies help to pull it off, but with luck and some planning, it should be doable.'

'Given what you have on Ogilvie, and more to the point what he thinks you have, I doubt he'll be a problem.'

'Me neither.'

'Okay, don't keep me in suspense. What do you have in mind?'

'Based on what we know about prison security, we aren't going to break him out. We don't have the resources for that. However, Ogilvie and Malone are both roughly the same shape and size. The obvious problem is they don't look like each other, general head shape apart. But something he said at the meeting yesterday sparked an idea.'

'Yes. You mentioned walking him out.'

'And I meant it.'

'Okay. Tell me more.'

She took a deep breath. 'Look, this might sound a bit crazy, but hear me out. I had a relationship with a woman that works in the film industry. She, ... she's a special effects and make-up artist. Her real skill is in creating masks for people to wear when they're on set. You know, if you want an actor to look like the King, that kind of thing. I thought if we could get one of Dan Ogilvie that Malone could wear, we might be able to get him out.' She paused and glanced briefly at Dom.

'Cassie, what are you not telling me? I've known you too long, so don't hold out on me. This is too important to play games.'

She glanced at him and nervously played with a tassel hanging from her handbag. 'It's about Gabby.' She paused. 'Gabby is the friend I was telling you about. She's the special effects artist.'

The car swerved slightly. 'Wait, Ian Gilmour's niece will make a fake Ogilvie mask for Malone, the same Ian Gilmour I'm keeping in the dark about Malone's betrayal. That's what you're telling me?'

She nodded. 'I nearly died when I saw her in the café. She did too. She had no idea what I did for a living and I, ... I thought her name was Claire.'

Fuck. This was just getting better and better. Now the one person he couldn't afford to find out about Malone needed to find out about Malone to get the fucking mask done. Jeez, what an absolute shit week this was turning out to be.

'How well do you get on with her now? Has she agreed to work with you?'

'Well, lets just say we made up yesterday,' she smiled, embarrassed. 'And she said she would do the work.' She turned and looked at him urgently. 'Dom, she won't say anything to her uncle. I can talk to her. Make her see we need to do this so everyone can get a payday. She's a bright girl. She'll play ball.'

'Will she Cassie, will she?' Dom stated, anger in his voice. 'She didn't even tell you her real name for God's sake. How can you trust her?

'Because we both lied for the same reasons. We're both involved in crime, maybe not her as much as me, but she does occasional work for Gilmour and she told me in the café her father was Gilmour's brother-in-law. In fact, he used to be Gilmour's boss until someone took him out. Her mother is Gilmour's sister and he still bankrolls her.'

Dom was silent for a while, thinking. Her father had been murdered and Dom now knew by who. Perhaps there was a way to get Gabby onside after all. 'So what does she need?'

'We need to get Ogilvie to Gabby's workshop,' she continued. 'She needs a scan of his head. Plus, we also need as many photographs of Malone as we can dredge up, front view, side view, anything we can get.'

Dom thought for a moment. 'The only person who can give us the photographs is his wife, and I'm not sure he and Kelly are on speaking terms right now.'

'Not surprising Dom. You do know he's turned into a right sleazeball?'

'I don't care what he's turned into. All I know is he'll lock me out of my money in less than two weeks unless we get him out of jail, and he will not lock me out. That will not happen.'

He paused for a second as they hit some traffic. 'Look Cassie. I'll be up front with you. There's been a few snags in Spain that require my personal attention. I'll be gone for a few days sorting them out. With Malone out of the loop you are the only person I can trust to handle things at this end. That means dealing with Ogilvie, getting him where you want when you want. Convincing him he's integral to our plan and it will also be worth his while.'

She glanced at him, 'What, you mean offer him cash? But we have the blackmail video?'

He nodded. 'I know, but after this he'll be finished so some money in his pocket won't hurt. I'll get the basics in place, set up an offshore account for him.

Cassie said nothing and stared out of the windscreen at the upmarket south side streets they had begun to drive along, streets that hid the city's dark past.

Dom drove on, thinking. 'Cassie, tell me, can it be done? Is it possible?'

'Honestly, I don't know. We need to use Ogilvie for a big part of this. He's the only one that'll be able to smuggle the mask into prison. Plus, we need to think of what Ogilvie does with himself while Malone is escaping. If what he's told us about the number of cameras is true, then we can't have two of them wandering around.'

'Do you think you can convince him to do this? If he's caught, it will mean the end of his career. Jail time. He's got a lot to lose.'

Cassie nodded. 'Even without the in room video, we have enough on him to ruin his life and career. This way, he has a good chance of coming out of it to live another day. I doubt he'll be a problem, especially if we can also offer a financial incentive.'

Dom agreed. Despite racking his brain over the last few days, he had been unable to come up with an alternative. 'Okay, how long will it take to create the mask?'

'About ten days, but Malone needs coaching on what's expected of him. He needs to act like Ogilvie. Carry himself like Ogilvie. Have the same body language as Ogilvie. Someone needs to go see Malone once we've bottomed this out and tell him exactly what to do at each of these final three locked doors. I can't see anyone doing that other than Ogilvie.'

Dom thought for a second. 'Ten days is cutting it fine, but get Ogilvie to Gabby's place tomorrow. I'll come with you. Might be better if I show up anyway, just to reinforce who's in charge and that we're not letting him away with anything. Okay?'

'Dom, I can handle this myself.' Cassie sounded irritated.

'I know you can, but I want to have another look at this girl, try to suss her out a bit more. See what she's made of. Make the arrangements and then let me know when. I'll get Marti to speak with Kelly and dredge up as many photographs of Malone as she can. Plus, I might have a way of making sure Gabby is onside with us.'

Cassie simply nodded. They drove on in silence and when they arrived at the Villa, Dom leaned over and pecked her on the cheek. She smiled weakly, went to her own car, and drove off. Dom walked to the front door and went straight to the living room where he threw the broken SIM card into the log fire. Next he went into the garage. Parked there was a Ferrari he only used on occasional weekends when the weather was good and the cobwebs were many. Well, right now the weather was bloody great, and the cobwebs were being spun at an alarming rate in his head, but he ignored the car, found a velvet drawstring bag in a drawer and placed the battery less mobile phone in it. He pulled the drawstrings tight then placed the bag on the concrete floor. With four hefty whacks of a mallet, he rendered the mobile phone useless and untraceable. Billy would dispose of the shattered remnants later.

Tossing the bag onto a shelf, he walked back into the house and went straight to his office. He was alone. Billy and Marti were out delivering cash generated by the Spa's and smaller drug runs to businesses around Glasgow. They also ensured fake receipts were generated to satisfy any Tax Inspector's prying eyes. The money would eventually make its way into each businesses bank account. Except all those bank accounts belonged to Dom, holding his millions generated over the years, the millions he desperately wanted to hang onto, the millions he wanted to add to. Feeling weary, he sat, ran his fingers through his hair and opened the screen of his laptop.

He booted it from his Flash Drive. Malone had talked him through setting this up years before. There were only three shortcut icons on the screen. One his wi-fi router login, one his Virtual Private Network and the other the TOR browser itself. He logged into the router, ran his VPN software then logged into his internet account. Next, he clicked the onion shaped icon and booted up the TOR browser then waited until the software made a secure, untraceable, encrypted connection to the internet. This software was God-given for criminals like him. Malone had told him the US Navy had developed it for secure, anonymous communications. But it depended on people or organisations running *nodes,* special, untraceable computers, so in two thousand and two they had released into the public domain; the best way to create the network they had surmised. What they forgot to do was build in a back door, so organisations like Dom and the Cartels used it freely to communicate, arrange deals and transfer vast sums of money. And no one could track them. Your ISP might know you were using it, but not the websites you were accessing. And using the VPN got around even that risk.

Dom opened his Dark Web email account. There were no messages. But now the burner SIM had been used, he needed to provide Miguel with a new single use contact number. Walking to the wall safe behind the framed painting, he opened it, removed a bundle of SIM cards, took one at random, and replaced the rest. There were another four Nokia phones there. He took one, closed the safe and walked back to his desk. He looked at the number printed on the cardboard surrounding the SIM. This he typed into a new email in his anonymous account. It read simply 'D to M –' followed by the eleven digits he read off the card. He retrieved Miguel's convoluted email address from a previously sent cryptic message and copied it into the new one before hitting send. The SIM card went into the phone which he put on charge and switched on. Then he sat back, clasping his hands behind his head.

Malone crossing him was bad enough, but this business with the Colombians had kicked him in the guts. It had taken Dom years to build a relationship with Orejuela. The shaky start was now one of mutual and beneficial respect. Their business was good. The Colombians dealt mainly in Cocaine, the white happy powder Europeans just seemed to love and in Scotland, it was the party drug of choice, that and Ecstasy. Dom did not doubt other markets with larger populations were more profitable on a one off basis for the Cartel, but he had become a regular; practically the sole UK importer, and he would fight to stay at the top. Because everything he now had, where he was in life, was so different from where he'd come from.

TEN

Growing up in Milton, Dom realised from an early age he did not have the football skills of its most famous sons, a certain Sir Kenneth Dalglish or Frank McAvennie. This severely limited his life choices. Finding another route out of the schemes was possible, but the rewards for getting a *'job'* were, to him, not that great. At school, he had not been stupid, but he had been lazy, playing on the local's fear of his father to avoid all the usual bullying shit that came with childhood. His dad was feared and admired in equal measure. Quiet, unassuming, he never spoke about his work with his family. When Dom was young, he didn't understand why people were wary if not frightened of his dad. He was never violent towards his family, and Dom's mother doted on her husband. She came from Milton and seemed content to remain there, happily staying at home looking after all three of them. But when his dad went away to *'work'* she fretted endlessly until he returned home.

Dom had no aversion though to playing on a reputation he barely understood, using it to make easy money running drugs for local dealers then eventually dealing himself. But Milton was violent and dealing drugs could bring the two things into sharp focus quickly. So he had joined a martial arts class, preferring his fists and feet to a knife or a gun. Then one night a conversation with a desperate junkie revealed all. The guy was around twenty-seven, ten years older than Dom, strung out, rattling, desperate for his next fix. Except he had no cash and the quickest way to become poor in this game was to give anything to a drug addict on credit. They would never pay. The guy had spotted him behind a set of local shops, where the alcoholics and junkies gathered after their benefits had been paid and they had splashed out on their next fix. Bonfires were lit from broken up wooden pallets, and the occasional black wheelie bin set on fire where the desperate would try to enhance their high by sniffing the toxic fumes. They used this space because it had no CCTV. Neither did the shops, or the street outside.

Around midnight, Dom had a few wraps of heroin left. He walked there on the off chance that even in the middle of the month someone would be desperate enough to want to buy something to take the edge off. He trod carefully, avoiding the used needles and broken glass, not wanting to spoil his Nike AirMax trainers. The place was deserted, but he waited. Ten minutes later, *'it'* appeared, dishevelled, shaking, shivering, hugging himself, barely able to walk, wearing grubby jeans, and a dirty worn parka. His sunken eyes and emaciated frame told Dom he was a mainliner. Dom looked at him, making no attempt to hide his disgust. The guy smelled like he'd been living in a sewer for weeks. Rossi thought he had probably seen him before, but after a while all these idiots began to look the same.

'Got anything man?' he asked Dom, sniffing back the snot threatening to dribble down his face.

'Wow,' Dom told him, holding out his hand, palm out. 'You are boggin.' Don't come any nearer.'

He stopped, shuffling his feet. 'I need a fix man. A'm going' fuckin' nuts here. You got any gear?'

Dom looked at him dispassionately. He could never imagine what drove a person to these depths. To become so self unaware that even when you looked like a skeleton with a skin graft, you kept coming back to the thing that would eventually kill you.

'I've got a couple of wraps,' Dom said coldly. 'Twenty quid each if you want them.'

The junkie sniffed again. 'I haven't got twenty pence man. Nothin'. Fuck all. 'Any chance of getting them on tic?'

Dom would have laughed if he'd even found that statement vaguely funny. 'Piss off mate. You think I'm a charity worker or something? Twenty quid or keep rattlin'.'

The junkie shook his head. He looked from side to side unsure of what to do. 'Look man,' he said, taking a step closer. 'I'm good for it. You know me, well you know my wee brother Tony. He was in the same class as you at school.'

'Tony fucking who?' Dom snapped.

'You know, Tony Reid. Wee guy, red hair, buck teeth. Plays the guitar.'

'So what if I do? It's you that wants the hit no yer wannabe Jimi Hendrix brother. No dosh, no smack, understood.' Dom could see the guy was flipping to the wrong side of desperation.

'Wha ...... What if I gie ye a blow job? I mean I'm good at it. When I can get up the drag, I make a fair few quid from the pervy auld men up there.'

Dom bristled. 'What the fuck do think I am you snottery little bastard. Fuck off before I kick your cunt in.'

He wiped his runny nose with the sleeve of his jacket. 'You better gie me it, cause a know whit yer auld man does. I'm gonnae go tae the polis and tell them everything.'

This was interesting. 'What the fuck do you know?' Dom asked curiously.

'About the fact he's a fuckin' hit man for hire. I know two ae' Tam Gault's guys. They let me suck them aff now and again in a flat they have in Clydebank, when I'm cleaned up like. They talk a lot when they're pished and they think when I'm jagged up I canne hear whit they're sayin'. But I'm a sponge. You know that murder up in Edinburgh last week? Two guys found up at Arthur's seat wi' a bullet in the back of their heids? Well, that wis yer da' He did it. Tam Gault fell oot wi' somebody over there and wanted tae send a message. That's whit yer da' does. He whacks people and if ye don't gie me they drugs, I'll tell everything I know tae the cops.'

Dom stood and looked at him for a minute. He knew his dad

kept funny hours and worked away a lot, but this! Shit, he'd never even been in jail as far as Dom knew. How the hell could he be a mob hitman? This wasn't the fucking Soprano's. Yet for all this half dead junkie's obvious defects, he somehow felt he might be telling the truth. Franco Rossi was a quiet man. Hard but fair. He never raised his hands but he also never showed Luca and Dom much in the way of emotion.

Once, when he was six or seven, his mum had come back from the local shops, agitated. Seemed a couple of young Neds were hassling people, snatching purses, strong arming them for money or drugs. She had seen them have a go at a few of her friends. Not her of course, she was untouchable around here. Franco had patted her on the back, asked if she was all right and where he could find these two. Dom had been in his bedroom with the door open listening. As his father left the house, he quietly followed him, keeping well back as he made his way to the place his mother had mentioned. The Neds were there, laughing and annoying other people. They were about eighteen, fearless, able to do anything so they thought, but when they saw his dad walking towards them, they both looked at each other and stood still. His father stopped in front of them, he leaned in and spoke quietly. Dom was too far away hiding behind a hedge to hear what he said, but he could see both boys looked terrified. They both nodded.

First one then the other held out an arm. Dom watched as his father turned the arm of the first over so the elbow was pointing almost upwards. The boy slipped to his knees, his arm bent behind him, shoulders and head touching the ground. Then his Father stamped on the arm at the elbow. The crack was audible for hundreds of feet, and the scream that followed a lot farther. The second boy stood trembling, a puddle of urine appearing at his feet. When his dad had finished, both of them lay on the ground, holding their arms, screaming. Franco Rossi simply walked away.

Dom looked at the waste of space in front of him. 'Who in their right mind would believe anything your slimy little mouth said? One word from you to anyone, and I'll come after you even if my Dad is locked up. Understood?'

Tony Reid's brother looked crestfallen and turned away, head bowed. Suddenly he spun back around fast, much quicker than Dom expected. His right hand came out from below his jacket and he held a knife, a large one, stolen from someone's butcher's block from what Dom could see in the little light permeating back there.

'Gie me the fuckin' wraps ya bastard. Now, or I'll stick this knife right in yer guts.' He moved slowly towards Dom, determined desperation now on his face, the knife waving in front of him.

Dom said nothing, but watched as Tony Reid's brother walked towards him. He watched his eyes, not the knife. His Sensei had told when someone went to stab you they always looked at where they were going to plant the knife. Watch their eyes and you'll know where they want to open you up. So Dom let him come on, his arms easy at his side.

When he got to within a few feet, Dom stepped back slightly. 'I'm giving you fair warning. Put the knife down, back off and walk away. Do that and I'll forget this ever happened okay?'

The junkie's eyes flicked back and forth across Dom's face and body. Then they stopped, appearing to focus for an instant on Dom's stomach. As he lunged, Dom stepped quickly to the side. His right hand came down at an angle and blocked the knife away from his body. His left hand bunched into a fist and he quickly snapped out a punch hitting the right temple of the junkie. This pushed him back a little, stunning him, but the knife was still in his hand. He swung blindly at Dom, desperately trying to make a connection. Dom was now beside him. He pulled his right arm back across his chest and side stepped into his opponent, hitting him squarely on the cheekbone with his elbow. There was a dull crack. The junkie let out a yell and dropped the knife to the ground, both his hands clutching at his now broken jaw, trying hard not to scream as that was too painful. Considering someone with a knife had never attacked him before, Dom found he was surprisingly calm. He walked to where the knife had fallen, picked it up and moved closer to the junkie. The smell was overpowering, but he grabbed hold of the guy's hair and lifted his head up, staring him straight in the eyes.

'Piece of shit,' he whispered.

Then he plunged the knife hard, straight into Tony Reid's brother's neck, right at the part where you carry out a tracheotomy. He pulled the unfortunate junkie towards him. The ten inch long blade penetrated the soft skin at the front of the neck and went all the way through the trachea. Dom kept pushing until he felt it hit the spinal column at the back of the head. Then he pressed some more. The tension left Tony Reid's brother's body as he died without a sound.

When Dom bent down and withdrew the knife, he was surprised at the relative lack of blood. He had missed the jugular, but he knew he had severed the windpipe and badly damaged the spinal cord. He stood there for a few seconds watching as the junkies last breath gurgled into the night, his body paralysed, foaming blood escaping from his throat through the deep cut. Then he looked around slowly, but no one had witnessed what he had done. It amazed him how easy it had been. He should have felt something, even some feeling of satisfaction. But there was nothing, just cold dispassion. He discovered that night just what he was capable of. Was this how his Father felt every time he carried out a hit? He walked away without a backward glance.

When he got home, he hid the knife under a loose floorboard in his room before breaking it up and disposing of it over the next few days in bins throughout the city centre, carefully wiped clean of his prints just in case. They never caught the junkie's killer. The entire area was a smorgasbord of DNA, and as Dom himself had never been arrested, his wasn't then on file. There was nothing to connect him to the crime. When eventually he was arrested and convicted for attempting to bribe a cop, they got a hit, but it was only another one of well over two dozen and they didn't even interview him about the murder. The death of a junkie from Milton wasn't worth the effort.

As he matured, Dom realised he wanted more, deserved more. So on the back of his father's reputation, he became a major dealer in Milton. He had girls in his life, but no one special, no one he couldn't live without. Relationships, he rationalised, would complicate things, restrict his ability to be where he needed when he needed. Marriage was never even a dream. He earned money fast, learned the ropes, made the contacts he would need later in life. Even crooks need to network. He was also careful, was never caught, but he realised that was only a matter of time. Making the amount of money he wanted to from dealing drugs at street level was too risky, so he ploughed most of his profits back into property, buying derelict old mansions for cash and renovating them before selling them on for a legitimate profit.

His lawyer introduced him one day to someone looking to retire but wanting to sell his business as a going concern, capitalising on the goodwill he'd said. Intrigued, Dom had wondered what this *going concern* was, and started digging around a bit more. He discovered the guy ran a brothel in an isolated old mansion out in the country between Glasgow and Fenwick. Still illegal, thought Dom, but not nearly as dangerous as the drug trade. So he had a look. Tested the goods, liked the potential, did the sums, looked at the figures and went for it. He bought the business.

He ran it as a Country Spa, but like the Edinburgh saunas, most people including the cops knew exactly what went on and were content to turn a blind eye, glad it was controlled, monitored. Occasionally there would be a visit from Immigration checking the girls were legal, not trafficked, not underage. But they were. Dom made sure of it. In twelve years he had added another nine 'Spas' to his portfolio. They were amazingly profitable. He easily grossed fifteen million a year and even after expenses, like buying the girls, paying their cut, his profits were still immense. But his success soon brought him to the attention of some larger families in Scotland who were 'interested' in his business and wanted a cut. Some wanted to cut him out altogether, so he had to pay sizable amounts of protection money to keep operating. It was still worthwhile, but the parasites were getting greedier every year.

Then it all changed. Most of Scotland's drugs came up the M6 from Manchester, or via Cairnryan. But Joe Public was sick of the chaos and carnage caused by County Line dealers and the gangs invading and occupied entire neighbourhoods. Their kids were dying. They were used as cannon fodder by the bosses who didn't give a shit about how they made their money. The vulnerable were being *'Cuckooed,'* their innocent properties taken over and used to grow, deal and store. Then an ostensibly Tory, but hard right wing, overtly nationalist Government was elected on the back of an eradication policy. And eradicate they did. Special SAS trained flying squads of police and volunteer soldiers hammered the gangs. No real due process. Just heavy handed para military style units going in where they *thought* crime gangs operated and blitzing the locale until these cancerous families were essentially wiped out.

The supply of everything from the continent dried up. Cairnryan could not cope with the increase in demand. It wasn't large enough, didn't have the capacity. Plus every container, every vehicle was examined. Seizures were up and Dom saw an opportunity. He had kept an arm's length interest in the dealing business. You had to keep your options open he'd always thought, so he ran a few dealers out of two flats in Glasgow. Nothing big, but enough to maintain a presence. Much of this had happened while he had been banged up in the BarL. His jail time amounted to a three-year sentence. He'd been caught on tape trying to bribe the wrong cop to look the other way while a punishment beating he'd been asked to organise was taking place. While he was inside, Cassie, with Billy and Marti, had kept the Health Spas running, and the two dealers working for him supplied with gear. In prison though, he had kept himself abreast of the developments in the supply side of things.

On his release, he spoke with Ian Gilmour now in charge of Jamie Phillips' crew, and Tam McGraw through in Edinburgh. He knew they were having cash flow problems due to a lack of supply, and offered to get him a new shipment within a set time period or else he didn't need to pay. Plus, he promised it would be a no risk venture for them. He would arrange the import, take any flak that came his way. He would get the product delivered straight to their front doors. Surprisingly, they accepted.

He said he needed a fee, a large one, 25% of the wholesale purchase price, in advance. They accepted.

He said he wouldn't be paying any more protection for his other businesses. They accepted.

They said if he failed to deliver, he would become a permanent underwater feature in a deep part of the river Clyde. Rossi accepted.

Now all he had to do was what he'd promised - deliver.

Marti Galbraith and Billy Jenkins had been *professional* friends of his father. They had all been in the *business* since their early teens. Franco was the trigger man. Marti preferred a knife. Billy stuck to using his fists. They had worked for Dom since he'd bought his first brothel. They were still capable, but were older and wanted a slower pace of life, especially after their friend, his Father, was murdered. Controlling the Spa's helped. They also had contacts with anyone worth speaking to. Dom had Billy set up a meeting with a criminal down south that used to work for a now defunct family. He had eluded the clutches of the Police and had lain low for a while. But he still needed money and when Billy told him Dom was willing to pay for any information he had on his old contacts, he was happy to oblige. A few weeks later, Dom was in a bar on the Costa Del Sol, speaking with Miguel Orejuela, outlining his plans for the future, detailing how they could both profit from him being the sole importer of the cocaine he had to sell, into Scotland. He also guaranteed to pay up front and cover any losses he suffered himself. Miguel liked that part of the deal.

So why the fuck, thought Dom, am I sitting here waiting on the guy I've made millions for, to call and tell me his Colombian prick of a boss wants me out and probably dead? He looked at his Rolex Sub Mariner. The call should come soon. He switched on the new mobile and waited until it had carried out a first time boot sequence. It recognised the SIM card, connected to the prepaid network. Fifteen minutes later, the phone buzzed. Dom looked at it for a second, still wondering exactly how he was going to play this. With a sigh, he picked the handset up from his desk and pressed the green accept button. As with all his mobile conversations, he needed to keep this one as vague as possible. Despite denials, the NSA and GCHQ vacuumed up every voice call and text they could before running it through their algorithms to identify keywords of interest. Terrorism was their main agenda, but references to a full tonne of coke would not go unnoticed.

'Hello Miguel.'

There was a pause from the other end. 'How are you my friend? I trust our last conversation did not prove too awkward for you?'

'No, not at all Miguel. I always enjoy having my feet kicked from under me just as I'm sitting down with a client wanting to spend more money than I've ever seen. It just makes my day.' Rossi was angry, but tried to control it.

'Domenico, I tried all I could. But my immediate superior is determined to start up an import business of his own. I'm sorry.'

Dom felt there was some genuine regret in Orejuela's voice. 'Well, sorry will not be much comfort to me when I go permanently out of business. Entender?'

'Yes, yes, I understand, but right now there is little I can do about that. I cannot speak with my contact for at least three days. That is when he is flying in.'

'You realise Miguel, if this alternative import operation is established you will lose your substantial commission from me on top of what you already earn from elsewhere?'

'That has been uppermost in my mind. The last thing I want is to seem redundant.'

I'll bet you do Miguel, smiled Dom, because in your game the redundancy payout is permanent.

'And is he bringing his entire sales and security team with him again?' Dom asked.

'No, not this time amigo. This time I am being trusted to handle that side of things myself. After all, I have been in business with him for a long time.'

Where was this going Dom wondered? 'Have you made any arrangements yet for his arrival?' he asked the Colombian.

'Not as yet,' Miguel answered.

'When you do, would you be willing to share it with me?'

There was another pause this time longer. 'Yes, yes I would. It should give you enough time to prepare a suitable welcome for our guest.'

Well, well thought Dom. Was Miguel thinking along the same lines he was?

'Okay,' Dom continued. 'Would there be an opportunity perhaps to have an earlier encounter with our mutual friend, before he arrives at your villa?'

He could sense Miguel hesitate. 'It is certainly possible,' Orejuela said, 'but you will require to get the correct people in place and make the appropriate arrangements to allow it to happen yourself.'

Dom smiled. Miguel *was* on board. 'Good. I'll be in your vicinity the day after tomorrow. That gives me just over a day to engineer something. I'll arrange the welcoming committee. Just make sure the meeting is at your Villa. Are you happy with that?'

'Si. I will email you the details as per our normal route.'

'Good,' agreed Dom. 'I *trust* all will be well at your end on completion?'

'Absolutely.'

There was a pause again, and Dom waited, wondering what

Miguel would say next.

'You realise this is a one off opportunity, with much more risk for me than for you? I hope whoever you decide to put on your team is up to the task, as once it is done there will be no going back; even if God forbid it should fail?'

Dom thought about Marti and Billy's skill sets, plus their extensive network of contacts for this type of work. 'The team will be fine,' he told Miguel. 'They have considerable experience in negotiating deals and making tough decisions.'

'Good. They will need it.' Miguel said then hung up.

Dom ended the call at his end. The phone would go through the same process as the previous one, untraceable until the end.

He thought about what Miguel had said. Thought about the danger the Colombian was putting himself in. The trouble was, Dom was in just as much danger if this entire thing became a fiasco. Colombian Cartels were not known for their ability to forgive. More importantly, the germination of the plans seeding his imagination depended on it working.

He pulled out his normal phone and placed two calls in succession, one to Jenkins and one to Galbraith asking them both to meet him tomorrow and to make sure they brought their passports. They were all going on another brief trip abroad.

ELEVEN

The few friends he had, often asked Dan Ogilvie why more people don't escape from prison? He usually just smiled and said little. From the visible five point two metre high concrete wall with its accompanying five point two metre high steel fence, to the fence's movement detectors and motion activated perimeter cameras, monitored twenty four seven by the Electronic Control Room, to the internal cameras and controlled doors, escape was effectively impossible. Everyone and everything entering or leaving a prison was checked, verified, logged and recorded.

As Head of Operations, Dan Ogilvie knew all this, and more. He knew every corner of every houseblock, knew there were no blind spots. He knew this because he'd spent years finding and removing them. He had lied to the man blackmailing him about the cameras. There were exactly one thousand, seven hundred, and twenty-four. His prison was escape proof. He had helped make it that way. Except, now he had to help a bunch of lowlife pond scum he would cheerfully see locked up, find a way of getting one of their own out.

Just how in the fuck had he gotten into this, he wondered? But he knew. His marriage had been less than one of convenience for many years. They moved in different circles, had different friends, different hobbies. She had lost interest in him a long time ago. They had separate rooms. He hadn't seen her naked for over five years, but he had always been a sexually driven person. Affairs were too messy, hence the use of prostitutes. He had graduated from the saunas of Edinburgh to visiting a few of the upmarket brothels that were in every city with a prison. It was a visit to the one in Perth that had led to his current predicament.

He realised he had no real alternative but to go through with what they would eventually ask of him. If that bitch he'd spoken with at Strathclyde Park had the video evidence, then there was no other option. He knew exactly what happened to child molesters in the general population. That was why they were all *on the numbers* in a separate houseblock landing. But getting involved was one thing, getting away with it was different, and he had to get away with it or else he would spend a large part of his remaining years being tucked in each night by old colleagues. So perhaps the best thing was just to get away?

Thirty five years in the Service had let him see, and do, many things those on the outside would need a massive stretch of imagination to even conceive of. He'd tramped the leaking halls and galleries of prisons built when Queen Victoria still reigned gloriously. Job titles had been many, as had promotions. The riots and standoffs with prisoners out to make trouble for no reason other than boredom had not been a problem for him. As a younger man he had been fit, active, ready to rumble at any opportunity. Kitted up in his black riot gear, plexiglass shield and steel toe capped boots, he enjoyed the thrill of rushing a hall still smoking from the fires of burning mattresses and 'persuading' those out of their cells to return to them. Steel toecaps meant you didn't feel much, even while you were breaking the occasional arm or leg. His worst two years were as a new First Line Manager, in charge of the 'Digger,' the place where the bad boys bad boys were sent to give the bad boys some peace. That had been two years of assaults, hunger strikes, food strikes, convicted terrorists and dirty protests. God how he hated those dirty protests. After all that, the sacrificed hours, the double shifts, the loss of sleep to the job, when he retired he would end up just about being able to survive on his pension, roughly half of what he earned. But there would be no luxury travel, no Caribbean cruises. Anyway, who would he go with? His wife? She hated him. She would also make sure she got her cut of his lump sum.

So these lazy, blackmailing bastards sickened him. They were just crooks who hadn't been nailed yet. But they were rich enough to afford somewhere big and isolated to run their sordid empire. The cavern sized kitchen he'd been in told him that. His job was to keep locked up their associates who had been caught. The murderers, rapists, drug dealers. All very admirable, but the profits they continued to make even when they were inside, still went to the creeps on the outside that ran things. What did he get in comparison? A pathetic government salary and an even worse pension. He drummed his fingers nervously on the desk in front of him. He knew the next step he took would be a big one, the most decisive of his life. If he was going to do this, then he had to make sure it wasn't for nothing.

He felt his personal mobile in his pocket vibrate. Cell phones were banned inside a prison; a criminal offence to even try to smuggle in, far less possess. Theoretically, they were even banned in the Gate building. But they allowed Senior Staff some leeway, so Dan always had his with him, only leaving it behind when he went down to the prison proper. He looked at the display. No name came up. He didn't recognise the number. He swiped to accept and held the phone to his ear.

'Hello,' he said.

'Dan, how are you? This is Cassie, your friend from the park the other day. Where are you just now, at work?'

'Yes,' he mumbled.

'Fine, when do you finish?'

'I'm on day shift this week. I'll be leaving here about three o'clock. Why?'

'Well, if you have any plans for this evening, cancel them. We'll be visiting a friend of mine. I'll pick you up at four, outside the Gallery of Modern Art. Don't be late,' she said, before quickly hanging up.

Dan sat for a second, the phone still held to his ear. Shit. These idiots seemed determined to go through with this even after he had told them just how impossible it was. And he hadn't told them everything. It wasn't just a matter of getting through some locked doors and escaping into the wide blue yonder. If they thought that, then obviously none of them knew much about what an officer had to do to get out of a modern jail. Maybe he could use that to his advantage? If they were so desperate to get this one guy out, then there had to be a good reason for it. He needed to make them aware there was another layer in place, a layer that could not be bypassed. They would also need codes, and that would cost them. If he had to disappear then he wanted as much money as he could take with him, because that would be all he had to live on for the rest of his life.

But first, he had to look this Jack Malone prick in the eye and find out what was so special about him. He pulled his keyboard and mouse towards him. Typing in his login ID and password, he accessed SPIN; the Scottish Prison Information Network, and logged on to the Prisoner Records system, known as PR2. His clearance level as the prison's de-facto security manager allowed him unrestricted access to every data system in the establishment, so logging into this would not arouse any suspicion. Eventually he came across Malone's name and clicked on it. Malone's file was sparse. Yes, he'd had a spell in the BarL some time back, but there was nothing more of any interest in there. He had kept his nose clean or at least never been caught since and no one seemed to have a grudge against him. He was just a drunk driver, but one who had killed seven people.

Mind made up, he logged out of the system, closed his PC and went to collect his keys, radio and officer alarm. He nodded to a few people as he made his way down the prison's main spine corridor, a multi coloured enclosed external tunnel of steel cladding and polycarbonate glazing linking all parts of the prison together. Arriving at Mungo House, he had the ECR let him through the corridor access gate and then used his electronic key to open the door into the building itself.

Each four storey accomodation block in the prison had three

wings running at angles to each other. They held approximately six hundred convicted or remand inmates. In total, three houseblocks held eighteen hundred bodies, from short six month terms to forty-year lifers. With doubling up, they could extend this to over two thousand. Each floor was controlled from a central core by only eight officers, so if, as they sometimes did, the one hundred and fifty inmates on that level wanted to express their frustration, they withdrew their co-operation and things went tit's up for a while. Ogilvie knew the public had the impression officers were in charge of every prison and though ostensibly true, operations depended on the willingness of every prisoner to take and comply with instructions. Otherwise, you would need as many officers as prisoners. Luckily today they were compliant.

Remand prisoners were held on the fourth floor. Ogilvie used the lift. This always smelled of stale food delivered to each wing in hot trolleys. He wore a light grey business suit, white shirt, blue tie and black shoes. Managers did not wear uniforms. His name badge and job title hung on a lanyard around his neck. Arriving at the fourth floor he exited the lift and again used his fob to open the last door onto the level. To his left was the control desk, carefully positioned so officers could see down all three wings without having to move. Nodding to the First Line Manager in charge, he walked through the open grille gate onto the wing leading to Malone's cell. He pretended to inspect things as he walked, chatting with prisoners who passed him. Some he recognised as *frequent flyers,* confident enough to engage him in conversation. Others looked scared, nervous, newcomers with no idea what to expect. Bright, contrasting, primary colours with pastel accents had been used on the concrete walls in an attempt to soften the look of the building. But most newcomers simply hurried along, staring at marmoleum covered floors, avoiding eye contact with anyone.

The door to Malone's cell was open. Ogilvie stopped and looked in. He was lying on his bed, seemingly asleep. A plate of half eaten food lay on the Corian worktop next to the bed. As he was on remand, Malone did not have to work or go to any of the classes on offer. He could stay in here all day and watch Homes under the Hammer on the small fourteen inch, LCD television that sat on the same unit beside the kettle and half eaten meal.

'Something wrong with the food?' Ogilvie queried. There was no response. He stepped closer. The blue painted steel door was fully open. 'I said, is there anything wrong with the food Mr Malone? You don't seem to have eaten much. Guilty conscience perhaps?'

This time Malone opened his eyes and wearily propped himself up on the thin, memory foam mattress. He looked Ogilvie up and down. 'Who are you then? The Master Chef food critic or something?' he smirked.

Ogilvie stared straight back at him. 'Just showing some concern for my charges. Is everything okay for you? Everything to your liking? Staff being nice to you are they?'

Malone sat fully up and swung his feet off the bed. He stood, ran his fingers through his messed up hair and smoothed down his ruffled blue shirt and jeans. 'I have no idea who you are pal and I don't know how you even know my name, but I don't intend to be here long enough to become annoyed by all the crappy rules and regulations you have in this place. So why don't you piss off and let me sleep.'

So, Ogilvie thought, he knows his friends are working on a way to get him out, because from what Dan had seen of the charges against him, he was as guilty as fuck and would spend at least the next fourteen years in a cell similar to this one.

'And why would you think you'll be getting out Mr Malone?' Ogilvie asked, stepping into the cell. 'From what I've seen you'll be our guest here for a long time.'

'You think so? Don't you know I have one of the best lawyers in Scotland working for me? I'll be home and tucked up in my own bed by the weekend,' Malone grinned. 'Oh, and now you've asked, I do have some complaints.' He turned and lifted what looked like a blue slab of plastic from the bed. 'Who in their right minds ever decided this was a pillow?' He banged it against his fist to demonstrate just how hard, rigid and inflexible it was. 'I'd be better off balling up my clothes and lying on them.'

'Sorry about that Mr Malone. I'll make sure I inform the housekeeping staff of your concerns and organise our special pillow delivery service for you. Okay with that?'

'Aye, hilarious.'

Dan grinned broadly and walked back out of the cell. Nope, he didn't like this bastard one little bit, and it would grate on him forever that he had to help him escape.

TWELVE

Angela rolled onto her back and stared at the plain white ceiling. She was still glowing, tingling from the sex. A smile played across her lips. She couldn't fathom why Gabby liked women. Men could do things to you that were indescribable, especially if the man was as talented as Charlie Easdon. She turned her head to the side and watched him lying with his naked back towards her. As soon as they had finished, he had pecked her on the cheek and then fallen asleep as he normally did. The first few times it had happened she had been upset, but it was just the way he was and she had come to accept it. She had needed this. After the meeting in the café with her Uncle Ian and Domenico Rossi, she had not been in the best of moods. As usual, all her Uncle had thought to do was to give her the menial, boring tasks. The last thing she wanted was to be baby sat by some brothel Madame just in case she heard a juicy snippet that might be useful to Uncle Ian bloody Gilmour. She intended to get more than that in life. Spying for Uncle Ian was not what she wanted. If Gabby was happy doing it, then let her. She reached across with one hand and dragged her nails lightly down Charlie Easdon's flesh, watching the white tram-lines fade as the blood flowed back into the skin.

'You up for more then Angie?' Charlie Easdon rolled onto his other side and faced her. She watched his face light up with a smile and she leaned in to kiss him, the duvet falling down exposing her naked breasts.

'I'm not sure I could take any more today. It just wouldn't be as good. But I could do you if you like?' she smiled coyly, reaching under the covers and fondling his growing hardness.

'Well now, that would be nice.'

With a wicked grin, her head disappeared under the duvet. Easdon lay back, eyes closed.

When she had finished and cleaned up, they both sat up in bed. Charlie reached into the bedside table drawer and took out a couple of joints he had rolled. He lit them both with the zip lighter sitting on the nightstand and handed one to Angela. They each drew in a long lungful and held it for a few seconds to get the maximum hit, before exhaling in a cloud of smoke.

'Good thing you've disabled the smoke detector,' she giggled.

Easdon looked at her. 'Angela, what do you want from me?'

'What do you mean?' She seemed confused.

'I mean, is this is it? Is this all the time we get to be together because you're the boss's niece and I'm just a guy that works for him?'

'Aw c'mon Charlie. You're more than that. You've got your own wee business going here and you're making good money. Shit, you've got a Porsche outside. Imagine that thirty years ago in Drumchapel.'

He smiled and took another draw on the joint.

'Although,' Angela said, drawing on her own joint. 'It would be nice if you could go a bit more upmarket than this two bedroom flat.'

'And just how am I going to do that,' he complained. 'All my contacts are here, all my street dealers. This is the only place I can keep on top of them.'

Angela pulled the duvet up over her breasts. She looked at Easdon. 'What if you could start up on your own Charlie? What if I knew where you could get as much gear as you need? Enough to buy protection? Enough to become your own man?'

'Angela, it's only your Uncle Ian and Tam McGraw through in the East who provide people like me with gear to sell. I can't see your uncle being too happy if I set up in competition with him.'

'McGraw then, what about him? I'm sure he'd be happy to see someone sticking it to Uncle Ian, especially if you can source your own product at the outset.'

Easdon sat up and turned towards Angela. 'Look, I know I can get some gear from the Rossi outfit, but I don't have enough cash for that, not for the amount I'd need to make it worth their while. And as for going into competition with Gilmour? There's no way he'd allow it. He'd be seen as a soft touch if he did.'

Angela sighed. 'Who said anything about the Rossi's? Look, I know where there's a warehouse full of the stuff. I'm pretty sure they wouldn't miss a couple of pallets if we did it the right way.'

Easdon looked at her in amazement. 'Are you serious?'

'Charlie I want to be with you all the time. Do you think I enjoy doing the odd manicure and living on charity dished out by my uncle? God, I'm in my thirties and I'm still being treated like a teenager. I want things to change. I want to be the partner of someone who's going places, and I want that someone to be you and it can't be if you still work for my uncle.'

Easdon looked at his hands in front of him on the bed. The joint burned away between two fingers. 'This warehouse,' he turned and said to her. 'Your uncle wouldn't own it by any chance would he?'

She nodded. 'That, plus everything in it. Money, drugs, you name it. He even runs a legal storage operation out of there just so he can filter some cash through the accounts.'

'And how do you know about it?'

'I've done some jobs for him there in the past, so I've had plenty of opportunity to eyeball the place.' she told him, the enthusiasm building. 'I can get you a set of keys and the alarm codes. I'll also give you a date when there will be no one there. You'll need to disable the CCTV and remove the hard drive, but I can also tell you where that's kept.'

He eyed her. 'How do you know all this stuff?'

'Because my uncle still treats me like a brainless blonde bimbo whose only just turned twelve. I told you, I've picked up stuff from the warehouse. He just gave me a set of keys, told me what he wanted then let me get on with it.'

'And he doesn't have it guarded twenty four seven?'

Angela shook her head. 'The place is a fortress. He's reinforced the perimeter walls so it would take a tank to get through them. Same with the gates and the roof. They're high security ram proof ones. Plus the alarm goes off in ten seconds if it's not disabled, so that would be your first task.'

'You're talking as if I've agreed to this.'

Angela swivelled her legs out of bed. She reached around on the floor for her underwear and pulled on a pair of lilac knickers. She stood up on the hardwood floor and turned to face him with her hands folded over her bare chest.

'Fuck Charlie. I'm handing you an opportunity on a plate to break out and be your own man. All you need is to convince a few others who want the same thing. Surely you know somebody?'

Easdon stayed silent, thinking. 'Alright. Let me speak to a couple of guys I know through in Edinburgh. I'll need to convince them, so you'll need to get me some proof as to how much gear is in there.' He got out of bed and stood there naked.

She smiled and held up a finger. 'Give me a second.' She padded over to where her jeans lay on the floor and bent down, her breasts hanging pendulously in front of her. Glancing at Charlie, she saw he was getting erect again and grinned inwardly.

She stood and walked over to him while looking at a mobile phone. As she reached him she turned the phone around. A video was playing. Although the inside of the warehouse was dim, Charlie saw row upon row of plastic wrapped bundles containing what looked to be a mix of white cocaine powder and brown heroin. There were also some blocks of skunk stored between them. He had never seen so many illegal drugs in a single place.

'Bloody hell Angela. When was this taken?'

'About three months ago, but the place is always full.'

'Okay. Send this to me. I'll need to show it to the other people I was telling you about. This should convince them.' He smiled at her, then walked forward and wrapped her in a hug. 'If we do this right, then Uncle Ian won't even know we've been in there, will he?' he whispered in her ear.

She broke away from his embrace. 'I need a shower, she said. Coming.'

He grinned. 'I will be soon.'

THIRTEEN

Cassies Fire Red Tesla 5 pulled up outside the Gallery of Modern Art. Ogilvie stood looking around nervously. She gave a short blast on the horn and he walked over, opened the door and climbed into the passenger seat. Dom watched silently from the rear seat. It took Ogilvie a few seconds to realise he was there, and he did not look happy about it.

'Problem?' Rossi asked. Sarcasm dripping.

He looked at him grimly. 'Given you've fucked up my life, I'm not entirely sure who I was expecting. Bible John? Jack the Ripper?'

Dom shook his head. 'You need to de-stress Dan. It'll be the death of you.'

Cassie moved off. They drove silently through George Square, turning right at Queen Street Station past the old North British Hotel now the Malmaison, before heading left up Montrose Street to where the Rotten Row maternity hospital used to be and on to Cathedral Street. From there, she hung a right and travelled on until she came to the left hand split at Stirling Road, onto the M8. They travelled east until they reached Junction 11 of the motorway then took the slip, eventually driving into the old Queenslie Industrial Estate. After a few minutes she stopped outside a small, nondescript unit with a roller shutter door and a pass door to the side inset into a brick wall.

'Okay, we're here. Follow me.'

They got out of the car and walked up to the timber pass door, where she rang the bell screwed to the wall. Some time later it opened and Dom caught a glimpse of a good looking, average sized female with short auburn hair who was ever so slightly overweight. It was Gabby, and from the look on Ogilvies face, he wouldn't have kicked her out of bed. She wore denim dungarees over a white t-shirt and had on blue running shoes. She looked at them both, then at Ogilvie.

'This him then?' she asked Cassie, who nodded and walked through the door held open by her lover. The woman beckoned Ogilvie to follow with a nod of her head.

Inside, the unit was larger than Dom had imagined. Strewn around, lay all kinds of different - what, he wondered? They looked like puppets, or figures waiting to be animated. Along the wall to his right sat a workbench containing a variety of what appeared to be half completed heads. There did not appear to be any office as such, but to the rear of the unit, tucked into one corner, was a computer work station, complete with printers and a few other machines he didn't recognise.

Cassie turned. 'This is Dan,' she said by way of introduction. 'And you've already met my boss. Dan this is Gabby. Do what she tells you.'

They walked to the back of the unit, towards the computers, but Ogilvie didn't move.

'Well?' Dom said. 'What are you waiting for? A gold plated invitation? Get your arse over here.'

Rossi watched as Dan slowly walked towards them. There was a chair. Behind it was a white background. In front was some kind of contraption Dom didn't recognise. There were also two bright LED lights at forty-five degrees to the equipment pointing back at the chair and two similar lights behind the chair pointing in the opposite direction. Even Dom thought this was a hell of a lot of trouble to go to just to get a photograph. He hung back slightly, his eyes wandering around the workshop, taking everything in.

'Sit down here Dan,' Cassie said to him, pointing. 'Gabby is going to explain what will happen once we start, okay?'

Ogilvie said nothing, but he did sit down. The chair was in the middle of a circular track allowing the *camera* move around him. Cassie looked at the other girl and nodded.

'This,' Gabby said pointing to the contraption in front of him, 'is a 3D laser scanner optimised for facial features. In a few minutes it will begin to scan your head, a full three hundred and sixty degrees. Do not move while it is operating, understand?' she said forcefully. Ogilvie nodded agreement. 'Good, that's all you need to know for now.'

Dom watched as Ogilvie rubbed his chin and looked around at Dom then back to Cassie. 'We need to talk,' he said, 'and before this James Bond moment starts.'

Cassie stared at him. 'Ogilvie, you do realise what we have on you hasn't gone away?'

'Perhaps not, but you need me as much as I need you. So if you want to have any chance of getting your Mr Malone out of jail, then there are a few additional things you need to know.'

'Which are?' Dom asked from behind Ogilvie, who turned his head and watched as Rossi walked toward them.

Ogilvie smirked. 'Not so fast. I'll need something from you in return.'

'Mr Ogilvie, don't be under any mis-apprehension. If you piss me about, then I'll have no hesitation in bringing you down and then bulldozing through the front door of that jail of yours to get what I want. Understand?'

'Listen,' Ogilvie swallowed hard. 'If I do whatever you have planned for me, and Malone escapes, then I'm finished in the Prison Service. There will be a massive investigation into his escape. I'll be fired even if they can't prove anything against me. So my life and career will be over.'

Dom shrugged. 'So what, at least you won't be known as a peado.'

He bristled. 'Perhaps not, but I don't want to live the rest of my life on the pittance of a pension I'll receive – unless they also take that away from me too.'

Dom sighed. 'You don't exactly have the upper hand here Dan.'

'Look, without me you have nothing. I don't know why this

Malone guy is so important, but he clearly is, so I need a financial cushion or else the deals off and I'll take my chances.' He smirked. 'And I don't suppose it'll do your rep any good if it gets out you have underage girls working for you, will it?'

Rossi was surprised. Ogilvie had clearly had a chance to think things through over the last few days, and he was right about one thing. It would do Dom no favours if there was even a hint of anyone underage working in his Spa's.

'How much?' Dom asked.

Ogilvie smiled. 'Considering I need to hide away for the next thirty years or more, then I reckon a couple of million should do it,' he answered. 'Tucked away in a nice little Cayman Islands offshore account only I can access.'

Dom shook his head. 'You have been taking the brave pills haven't you? Where do you think I can lay my hands on two million quid just like that? Screw this, I'll just hand the videos over to the newspapers and laugh as your world comes crumbling down.'

Ogilvie shrugged and stood up. 'If that's how you want to play it, fine. But I'm key to this entire thing. Without me, Malone stays banged up, and whatever shit you're in just gets deeper and smellier.'

Dom hated being blackmailed, by anyone, especially by someone he himself was blackmailing. But he knew there was little else he could do. Ogilvie was key to all this.

They all stood in tense silence for a moment. 'All right. I'll transfer the money and send you the details, but you need to sit down and have this scan done. Then you tell me everything else I need to know about getting out of your damned jail. Understood?'

Ogilvie smiled as if he knew he had the upper hand. 'Sure, do the scan. That's not a big deal, but I hold on to the information you need for the last part until I know the money is in place. Oh, and I need a new passport. My face, different name. I assume you can do that?'

He glared at him. 'Sit.'

He sat.

Gabby tapped an icon on a computer console. The contraption before Ogilvie lit up and two green lines, one vertical, the other horizontal began to slowly scan his head.

'How long will this take?' Dom looked at Gabby.

She shrugged. 'About an hour for each scan. We'll need three to be sure.'

Dom saw Ogilvie bristle at this. 'It is what it is, Mr Ogilvie. Just sit there quietly until she's finished.'

'You know,' she told Dom. 'You don't have to be here while this is happening. This is the boring part anyway.'

Dom looked around the workshop. 'Maybe,' he replied. 'But I was hoping you could show me around.' He glanced back at her. 'To be honest, I'm still not sure this will work. It was only because Cassie said you had convinced her I thought it worth a try.'

'Thanks for the vote of confidence,' she smirked. 'Tell you what. Wait here a couple of minutes and I'll show you something. A demonstration if you will. I won't be long.' With that she disappeared to a part of the workshop hidden behind a set of moveable partitions.

Dom looked at Cassie, who just shrugged. 'No idea,' she said.

Ogilvie sat there. Dom could see he was looking confused as to what was going on, but then he didn't need to know the relationship between Dom, Cassie and Gabby. Rossi was more interested in Gabby being Ian Gilmour's niece, the daughter of the man her uncle had murdered so he could move himself forward in the cesspit of a world they all occupied.

'Okay. Are you ready?' Gabby's voice asked from behind the screens.

Dom shrugged. 'Can't wait,' he replied.

The light was slightly dim in the workshop, but as Gabby walked around the partition Dom was taken completely by surprise. For a few seconds he thought Ian Gilmour had wandered into the unit by some back entrance; except he knew Ian Gilmour would not be wearing the clothes Gabby wore. He stole a glance at Cassie, and she stood open-mouthed. Even Ogilvie looked surprised.

Gabby walked slowly forward looking slightly incongruous, her head that of her Uncle, even down to the shading in his hair and the lumps and bumps on his skin.

She stopped in front of Dom. 'Believe me now?'

Dom shook his head and smiled. The full head mask looked near perfect. Even the lips seemed to mould themselves to Gabby's face. The only strange thing was the voice; it was hers and not Gilmour's. That was disorientating.

'When the hell did you create that?' he asked, suitably impressed.

'I did it to play a joke on my Uncle. That scanner there,' she pointed to a machine sitting on the worktop, 'creates a full three dimensional representation of the subject's head. If we don't have the head, I can do the same thing with photographs if we have enough of them and a measurement for a frame of reference. That's what I used for Uncle Ian.'

Dom looked behind him again at the machine scanning Ogilvie. 'Okay, I can see how the digital capture works, but how in God's name do you get from that to,...... this?' he turned and pointed to her face.

'Over here,' Gabby indicated to her left. They walked to a worktop set on the back wall. On top of this sat a plexiglass booth, the same size and shape as a large commercial fish tank. Inside the booth, Dom noticed another piece of kit. This had nozzles, and a wire, head shaped frame.

'This is a 3D thin membrane latex mask printer. It's only been around for a year, but it's revolutionised what we can do with special effects in cinema and TV,' Gabby told him, proud of her equipment. 'In the past we could build a rubber or silicone mask and then hand tint it in an attempt to make it as realistic as possible. It wasn't always a hundred percent,' she shrugged, 'but with this, the accuracy is incredible. It means you don't need to use software in post production to change people's appearances, which in turn saves time and money.

Plus, it can also print the fine strands that go to make up hair. Plus the substrate is incredibly thin; just like another layer of skin. The person who developed this is a bloody genius.'

Dom looked at the equipment and then back at Gabby. He had heard of deep fake videos, but they wouldn't help him get Malone out of jail. He walked around Gabby, taking in what he was seeing, judging its effectiveness from all angles. Stepping back a little, he looked again at her face, this time more critically. Then he saw it. Her head size. It was too small to be Gilmour, yet the mask fitted her perfectly. How?

'Tell me,' he asked her, rubbing his chin. 'How do you get the mask to fit your profile and contours?'

She smiled, reached up behind her neck and pressed something Dom couldn't see. Ian Gilmour's features sagged and went slack. Gabby then grabbed the mask by its hair and pulled it easily from her head. She was also wearing what looked like a thin swimming cap.

'That's clever,' Cassie said. 'Although not very sexy looking.'

Gabby laughed, enjoying showing off her talents. 'Yes it is.' She pulled off the cap and shook her hair loose.

'Okay, how exactly does it work?' Dom asked.

'Well,' Gabby said, holding the mask in front of her. 'The material is specially formulated to conduct a mild electric current. There are incredibly thin wires built in so when a small lithium battery is inserted here,' she pointed to a small holder on the back of the mask, 'and this button pressed, the wires become energised and stiffen into an underlying grid giving the mask its tension.'

Dom looked thoughtful for a few seconds. 'But how does it mould itself to your underlying features, especially your eyes and lips?'

Gabby shrugged. 'Same process,' she said. 'The mask foundation is keyed towards the individual who will be wearing it. Again, it's better if I can do a scan of their face, but photographs will let the software have a pretty good attempt. The only thing they need to do is wear a skullcap or shave their head to allow it to sit flush at the top. Plus,' she continued, holding up the mask, 'it also goes over the neck and onto the upper part of the shoulders. That means it's pretty seamless.'

'So Malone will need to shave his head just before he puts the mask on?'

Gabby nodded. 'Preferably, yes.'

Dom looked at Cassie. 'Malone's photos?' he asked

'I have them in the car. Marti went to see his wife yesterday. He told her we were working on getting him out and the photographs would help.' She shrugged. 'Apparently she wasn't over enamoured about that, but Marti told her to go see him and pass on the news.'

'Good. This is all looking better minute by minute. 'Now Mr Ogilvie,' he turned towards where Dan was sitting, the lines of the scanner still working. 'We will need you to get this mask to Malone, together with the battery. Any problems with that?'

Ogilvie sat stock still. Dom looked at Gabby. She shook in her head in frustration. 'You can talk Mr Ogilvie. Just try not to move too much.'

Ogilvie relaxed. 'Yes, I'll be able to get it in, although I'm not sure what you want me to do with it afterwards.'

'Get it to Malone, what do you think?'

'And then what?'

'And then you need to swap places with him? You need to be in his cell pretending to be him until he's out of the prison. We can't have two of you walking around the jail at the same time can we?'

'Are you nuts,' he smirked. 'I look nothing like Malone, and I'm not wearing a mask of his face. I do that and there will be no doubt about my involvement.'

'Then we need to pretend he's attacked and overpowered you. He can tie you up, gag you and dump you under the blankets on the bed. Just lie there as long as possible to let him get away. Plus, you'll need to swap clothes with him.'

'Bloody hell, this is getting more like a military operation every time I hear about it.'

Dom was becoming irritated. He walked up to Ogilvie and stopped in front of him, careful not to disrupt the scanning beams. 'Listen you perverted prick, I don't care what you think about it. I don't care how complicated you think it's becoming. You do whatever's needed to get Malone out of jail. If he has to whack you over the head and truss you up, then that's what he'll have to do. Understand?'

Ogilvie swallowed hard, not daring to move his head.

Cassie coughed softly behind him. After a few more seconds staring at Ogilvie, Dom turned his head and looked at her. 'What?' has asked, more harshly than he intended.

'His voice?'

Dom looked confused. 'What about his voice?'

'Well, I know both of them have similar build and physique, but their voices are totally different. If anyone talks to Malone on the way out, then it's game over. They sound nothing like each other.'

Dom turned and looked pensively at Gabby. 'I don't suppose you have a voice synthesiser to go with this hi-tech mask do you?'

She shook her head.

It was Ogilvie who came up with the solution. 'Laryngitis,' he mumbled.

They looked at him. 'I could lose my voice completely for a few days before the escape. That way, if anyone speaks to me I just point to my throat, then mouth I've lost my voice.'

'That'll work.' Dom said. 'But won't they tell you to take time off work in case you infect anyone else?'

Ogilvie laughed, then remembered the scan. 'The place is so short staffed that even if you're suffering from Covid 19 they'd still have you working double shifts. Don't worry. It'll work.'

'So', Dom looked around at them all one by one. 'When do we do this?'

Again, Ogilvie provided the information. 'The end of the backshift is best. They leave the jail between nine and nine forty-five in the evening. The prison then goes on lock down and only the ECR can open any doors. Once the staff are in it's normally quieter.'

Dom smirked. 'Looks like you're buying into all of this after all Dan. We'll make a gangster out of you yet.'

He smirked. 'Perhaps, but you still need to show me the money in my bank account. Without that, Malone goes nowhere.'

Dom looked at Gabby. 'Will you be okay alone with him here while Cassie takes me back into town?'

She grinned. 'Oh, I think Dan and I have an understanding, don't we Dan?'

Ogilvie scowled.

'Good, but I need a word with you about something else before we leave. In private.'

She screwed up her face. 'I'm only in this for one thing. Don't get me involved in anything else.'

'It's not anything I want you to do Gabby. Its information you might find – how can I put it - interesting.'

'Fine,' she sighed. She walked towards the partitions where she had just come from. Dom followed her. Behind them stood a small make-up table and chair. Gabby sat down and Dom perched himself on the edge of the table. He folded his arms and looked at her. 'It's about your father,' he began.

'What about him? He's been dead for years.' Gabby sat playing with the mask in her hands.

He nodded. 'I know, but I thought you might be interested in finding out what happened to him. Discovering who killed him?'

Gabby looked at him coldly. 'You know who killed him?'

I've only just found out, and the information I have comes from a source I would trust with my life.'

'Okay. Let's hear it.'

Dom thought for a second about how to approach this. He wanted Gabby to know about her Uncle Ian. What he didn't want was her running off hysterically and then accusing him. That wasn't how revenge was done in this business. It needed to be much more clinical. But he couldn't tell her about Marti Galbraith being the hitman.

'When your dad and Ian were in business together your dad was the majority partner. He was in charge, and made all the decisions. Gilmour was okay with that provided he could do his own thing, but your father began to move in a different direction, become more legitimate. Your Uncle had other ideas. He wanted to negotiate a big deal with a gang down in Manchester run by a guy called Eamon O'Boyle to supply even more drugs, but your dad put the kibosh on that and Ian wasn't too thrilled.' Dom paused looking at her for any reaction.

'And?'

'Well, the only way that deal would happen was if your Uncle Ian took over. And the only way he could do that was if......'

'My dad was out of the picture,' she finished

'Right. But your Uncle Ian had to make it look like he'd been taken out by another player.'

Gabby's head jerked up at that. 'From Edinburgh?'

Rossi looked a bit surprised. 'You know more than me then?'

'Something Uncle Ian told me. They got word a guy called Mickey McGuire from Edinburgh had been involved, but before anyone could question him he fell to his death from the top of the Balmoral hotel. Then Uncle Ian clasped a few hands, greased a few palms and took over the business.'

'You knew this already?' Dom asked, surprised.

She shook her head. 'Not that my Uncle was involved in killing my dad.' She sat back in the chair and crossed her legs. 'Why are you telling me this? He looks after my mum, so taking revenge on him would be counterproductive. Tony Smith would probably get it all.'

'Aren't you angry about what he did?'

'Of course I'm fucking angry, but what can I do about it?'

'On your own, not much, but my father was also working for Gilmour when he was killed?'

'And what does that have to do with anything?'

'It shows how ruthless he can be, that no one is safe. Look my dad was no saint. He was an enforcer, a gun for hire, and the last person who hired him was Ian Gilmour.'

Gabby looked confused. 'And you're saying Uncle Ian had him killed. Why?'

'Because years ago your Uncle and my dad were contracted for a hit on a young up-and-coming nutter from Manchester that was making a nuisance of himself up here. They took him out, but Ian is now trying to set up another even bigger deal down in Manchester. And guess whose son it was they iced a few years before.'

'O'Boyle's,' she whispered, realisation dawning. She looked up at Dom. 'So he had your father killed to cover his tracks just in case he told O'Boyle Uncle Ian had been involved in the death of his son.'

Rossi nodded. 'And now he's trying to expand again. In fact, he's trying to set me up so he can take over my operations with the Colombians. That's why you're here, to get as much info on my operations as you can. I know he's all nice and charming when we meet but he's a scheming, cold, devious bastard.' Dom walked over and stood in front of Gabby. 'If you work with me and Cassie on this, then I promise that Gilmour will pay for what he's done to both you and me. But you need to act normally around him. Wait until the time's right. Can you do that?'

Gabby stood up and looked Dom in the eye. 'Rossi I've just met you. Teaming up to kill my Uncle with someone I don't know isn't what I had in mind when I got involved in this.'

'Gabby I didn't say anything about killing him. I want to take him down, yes, but at this point his murder will just be too messy.'

'So what are your plans?'

Rossi shrugged. 'I'm still thinking them through, but I thought you should know about his part in your father's death.'

Rossi waited. Gabby looked thoughtful for a while, but her

expression was unreadable.

'Okay,' she eventually said. 'I'll keep quiet about it for now. Mainly because it's not something my mum or Angela need to know.'

'Good,' said Rossi. 'You've made the right choice. Now, let's get back to Mr Ogilvie.'

'Wait. I need to give my Uncle something, information he might already know but important enough so it will look good coming from me?'

Dom thought for a few seconds. 'Okay, tell him I'll be in Spain tomorrow to meet with some Colombians in a few days' time.' He thought some more. 'And you can tell him with Malone in jail, I'm running around trying to dig money out of as many accounts as I can. It's not much, but it should do for starters.'

They both walked back. Cassie was waiting on them, a curious expression on her face, but Dom shook his head slightly, a sign for her not to ask.

'Let's go,' he said. Then he stopped. A thought had just occurred to him. He pointed at the mask of Ian Gilmour Gabby still held in her hand. 'Do you mind if I take that with me?'

Gabby raised an eyebrow.

'I just want to scare the shit out of some people,' Dom grinned.

Gabby handed it over.

Yes, Dom said to himself as they walked out of the workshop back to Cassie's car. I want to scare the shit out of someone, but that someone certainly won't be expecting it.

'Come on Cassie, I need to arrange an urgent passport.'

She looked surprised. 'I didn't know there were more girls coming over?'

'There aren't,' he told her.

She knew not to ask too much, especially in front of Gabby and Ogilvie. She shrugged. 'McGovern's then.'

Rossi nodded. 'McGoverns. And get me a passport photograph of Ian Gilmour.'

FOURTEEN

Jack Malone lay on the bed in his cave trying his best not to scream. The year he had spent in Barlinnie had, he thought, been bad. But either he had gotten less able to deal with frustration the older he had become, or this place was infinitely worse. Everything from the hardness of the four inch thick foam mattress sitting on top of the cold, steel mesh bed, to the even harder and thinner 'pillow' he now lay his head on, made him angrier every minute he spent in this god forsaken concrete asylum.

Because that's what it was. A madhouse.

It was never quiet. Every cough, sneeze, move of a plastic chair or kettle boiling seemed to reverberate around the wing regardless of how far away it was from his cell. There was the jarring metallic crash of doors being slammed shut. The shouts of inmates desperate for attention despite only having pressed their cell call buttons seconds before. Then there were the spice zombies. Except they weren't stupefied the way you would expect the living dead to be. They moaned. They sang. They made all sorts of incomprehensible noise at volume mark ten. That usually set up a cacophony of shouts and demands from other inmates to 'shut the fuck up or they would be getting it.'

Officers walked the association space at night, their radios clicking occasionally with one sided conversations. Heavy grille gates slammed closed as they made their never ending rounds, their routes recorded by their officer alarms. The scratching sound of your cell door viewer being lifted then allowed to bang down again, usually just as you had dozed off.

Toilets being flushed. People playing guitars at three o'clock in the morning. Concrete was not renowned for its sound absorption qualities. It was fucking madness.

Daytime, like now, was little better. The boredom was soul destroying. Malone's life on the outside revolved around laundering vast amounts of cash, setting up deals for Rossi, buying over failing businesses, ostensibly turning them around. Then, he enjoyed the fruits of his labours in the nightclubs of Glasgow and especially the *Glasgow Grace*. But life on remand was mind numbing. Daytime TV was mind numbing. Nearly everyone on the remand wing was below the age of thirty and was either a frequent flier in for petty offences, or had lashed out in a drunken blackout and killed or seriously injured someone. Not too dissimilar to his own crime he knew. He had been here over a week, with no sign of a trial date being arranged. It had taken him days to dry out with the help of the diazepam prescribed by the prison doctor. But the urge, the obsession with alcohol was still there. The only positive he could take from all of this, was the realization he was an alcoholic and would need to do something serious about his drinking when – if he ever got out.

With a sigh, he sat up on the bed. When he fully realized what he had done on the motorway, he had panicked. He knew conviction was certain and there was no way he would survive fourteen or more years in this place. The only ace he had up his sleeve was the financial hold he had on Rossi, well that and the fact he knew so much about his organisation that he could bring it down around his ears if he wanted to. Initially, he had thought about making a deal with the Fiscal. Immunity from prosecution for the driving offences for him turning Kings Evidence about the Organised Crime Group Dom ran. But even he realised the best he could hope for was a ten-year sentence instead of a fourteen year one. With seven people dead, three of them children, there was no way in hell this would be forgotten. All he could hope for now was that Rossi would find some way of getting him out, either legally or otherwise. He laughed bitterly to himself. Who was he kidding? He had just asked his boss to do the impossible, to do something that hadn't been achieved in over thirty years. A hospital visit or a funeral used to be the favoured means of escape, but even he knew this had been tightened up after a string of inmates had managed to pull that off.

Standing up he yawned and stretched. The walls of the cell he occupied were peppered with dabs of dried up toothpaste where other inmates had used it as glue substitute to hang their photographs and posters. He had none of these. No one apart for his lawyer and Cassie Hughes had been to visit him. He existed in a seeming vacuum. Even his bitch of a wife seemed to have deserted him. His cell door lay open. This was *association* time where inmates could mingle and talk with each other in the large six-metre wide space outside of the cells. The problem was, he knew no one in here and hadn't felt like introducing himself to any of the other lowlifes, as he saw them.

It was around two thirty in the afternoon. Although half of the inmates were out in the exercise yard, the hall was still echoing with the sound of voices and the clacking of the balls on pool tables. He wandered into the association space and noticed an officer walking towards his general direction, white blouse, black trousers, key chain swinging at her side, easing past the fixed metal tables where they sat and had their meals, if you could call it food.

'You've got a visitor Mr Malone,' she told him, stopping just before she reached the pool tables.

Jack wasn't expecting anyone, although he realised at some point Cassie would need to come back and tell him what they were doing. And she had only a few days left to do so.

'Who is it?' he asked her.

'What am I? Your social secretary or something.? I just know someone's here to see you and if you want to know who, then you'll need to come with me.'

'Okay, okay. I'm coming. Lead the way.'

He had left the houseblock on a couple of occasions, but still found it hard to recognise where he was. He had been marched down from Reception on his first night after being strip searched and showered. The only other time he had been out was to see Cassie. All he could recall was a lengthy walk through a corridor looking like a glorified bus shelter. Plexiglass windows let you see the outside world, well to other parts of the prison, and there were multi coloured wall panels dotted at various intervals to break up the monotony. There were also cameras everywhere, hundreds of them. He followed the Officer up towards the Visits area in silence. She walked behind him, calling out instructions at the direction changes they took. Eventually they arrived in the Visits Holding area after having passed through a metal detection portal. He took a seat but after only a few minutes he was asked to stand, where the same Officer waved an electronic wand over his body. It remained silent.

'Follow me,' she said, bored.

It took him a second to find his visitor in the room. He was surprised to see it was his wife. He had married Kelly twenty-four years ago, and the last twenty had been miserable. She sat there, a hard expressionless look on her face, no smile of recognition. Walking over to the glass topped table she was sitting at, he stood for a second looking at her, slightly confused. They hadn't spoken in weeks. She was too busy socialising, keeping up the pretence of normality, whilst he was too busy feeding Dom's machine with cash and getting pissed on the *Glasgow Grace* most nights. For a fleeting second he thought about leaning in and kissing her, but then realised there would be no point. He instead sat down and stared at her, a brief smile playing across his lips.

'If it's money you're after Kelly, then I'm afraid I can't help just now. For some reason they won't let me anywhere near a computer, if you can believe that.' He grinned.

She just looked at him, arms folded, face like fizz.

He eyed her quizzically. 'All right, just why are you here? I know it's not out of love or compassion.'

'I had a visit from Marti Galbraith.' She replied in clipped tones. 'He advised me it might be a good idea to come here. Gee you up a bit. A wee morale booster.'

'Why the fuck did Marti Galbraith come anywhere near you? He could have asked you to come here with a simple phone call.'

'That's what I was wondering. Seems he wanted me to give him some photographs of you. He didn't say why.'

Photographs, Malone thought. What did photographs have to do with getting him out of here? 'Did he say anything else?'

She shook her head. 'Nothing, He just sat there, impassive as usual, drinking tea, waiting until I'd dug out as much as I could from the attic.' She shook her head. 'He's lucky I hadn't already burned them all, you creep.'

'Somehow I don't believe you Kelly. There's no way you would have come here just to please Marti Galbraith and give me some grief. So what else do you want?'

She crossed her legs and looked at him with pure venom. 'I've to tell you Dom is working on a way to get you out of here, although God knows why after what you've done. When the time arrives, someone will approach you with detailed instructions of what you need to do. You are to follow them to the letter. No deviation, no doing things your own way. Follow the plan and you'll be fine.'

Malone raised an eyebrow. 'And who is this someone? How will I know them? Is it another inmate?'

'I don't know Jack,' she said, clearly exasperated. 'I'm simply passing on a message.'

'Well, you better tell Dom to get his arse in gear and move things along a lot faster. The clock's ticking.'

'I have no idea what that means Jack. It's not as if you can be choosy about the timing is it?'

'Just tell him.' He sneered. 'He'll know exactly what I mean.'

Uncrossing her legs she leaned forward, staring Malone directly in his yellow tinged, bloodshot eyes. 'Do you feel any guilt about killing those people, any?'

He shrugged. 'It was an accident. I didn't mean to do it. Some prick cut me up and caused me to swerve. It's all on the dashcam.'

'You were drunk, you idiot, at least seven times the limit. Do you think that argument will fly with any judge.'

'It doesn't matter. I'll never get to court.'

Kelly looked at him, amazed at his arrogance. 'If Dom's lawyers can't get you out of this place, then where do you think it will end up?'

'You can pass this on to Dom. Tell him if he can't get me out of here, then I will do anything to make sure I don't end up spending the next fourteen years cooped up in this fucking madhouse. Anything.'

She stood up. 'Why the hell did I ever stay married to you? I should have binned you after the first affair.'

'Maybe,' he snorted. 'But then you'd still be that poor little minimum wage care home worker, getting pissed every weekend to get the smell of shitty Alzheimer's patients out of your nostrils and looking forward to a quick shag every couple of weeks or so. No Kelly, you knew exactly what you were doing hanging on in there.'

'Fuck you Jack.' She turned her back and walked away heading for the exit. A Visits Officer followed her.

'Remember Kelly,' he shouted after her. 'Tell Dom. Tick tock!'

FIFTEEN

The Easy Jet flight to Malaga from Glasgow with Billy and Marti was turbulent. That just about mirrored the current situation thought Dom. After he had spoken with Miguel, he had organised seats for the three of them and booked them into a hotel in Benalmadena. He would not be staying with Orejuela this time. The issue with Gilmour was eating at him. The bastard was making all nice, clapping him on the shoulder, getting his niece involved to keep an eye on them, but he knew that soon, Ian Gilmour would be in for one hell of a terminal shock. It had been a risk to tell Gabby what little he knew. She had seemingly gotten on with her uncle, but when he put the facts to her, well as much as he knew, he saw something change in her eyes, a steely determination. For the time being, she had agreed to say nothing to Gilmour or her sister and equally not to her mother. No confrontation, no ultimatums. Dom told her when the time came she would be included in whatever he had planned. After that it was up to her how she wanted to play it.

Years before, Marti Galbraith had spent some *enforced* time on the Costa Del Sol, lying low after a few big bank robberies. He had gotten to know some of the players and they had utilised his special services a few times in his self-imposed exile. Marti told Dom he hadn't missed the bleak, Glasgow weather. There were worse places to seek refuge in. The couple of hundred grand he and Billy had made from the bank robberies was enhanced by the cash he received from carrying out the few hits asked of him. Hits he handled effectively and efficiently. While Marti had been enjoying the sunshine, Billy Jenkins had stayed behind in Scotland, working for a while with Franco

Rossi. He eventually let Marti know the cops had dropped their suspicions about the two of them and he was free to come back. Billy had taken a risk in staying behind, and Dom knew Marti was grateful to him for it. So the two of them had teamed up again when he returned and went back to their old ways of being hired guns, enforcers, working again with Franco, until Franco had become a problem for Ian Gilmour. Dom had wondered if it could have involved either Marti or Billy, but their reaction of bristling indignation when he had put it directly to them gave him peace of mind on that score.

Luckily, Marti still had the right contacts on the Costa. After Dom outlined exactly what he was planning, both Billy and Marti said they were in. The plan was simple. He needed to get rid of Antonio Barrera - permanently. And make it look like the work of some disgruntled faction trying to muscle in on the Barrera's empire. Once they knew exactly when Barrera would arrive, they would plan the hit in as much detail as time allowed. Miguel was to give them information on how it should be *styled* to make it look like the work of a rival gang. That meant anyone travelling with Barrera would also need to die. It also meant both Billy and Marti would need to be part of the team carrying out the killings. They had no idea of the numbers travelling with the Colombian, so Dom figured three of them were a minimum. The risks were high. Any slip-ups meant certain death for them all, either here on the Costa or back home in a more considered fashion. He knew Marti and Billy had killed before, both of them for a living, His one kill had been anger driven, but the coldness he felt afterwards let him know he could do it again if needed. If they were to survive this, they had to work as a team. They only had two days to plan, and it would have to be enough. His other worry was Cassie back in Glasgow. Was Ogilvie still co-operating? Could the mask plan work? He had to resist the temptation to call every hour for an update, realising it would just give the impression he had no confidence in her abilities. She was probably as capable as he was, but Dom had instructed her not to action anything until he returned from Spain. She was just to make sure everything was in place as he still needed to tweak the final details of the plan.

The three of them sat beside each other on the flight, barely speaking. After a few glasses of red wine, Dom felt himself drifting off into a dreamless sleep, interrupted two hours later as the Cabin Crew asked them to prepare for landing. He took a deep breath and fought from scratching at an itch on his face he couldn't quite reach. After the plane landed, they moved through the airport separately. Now he stood with Marti outside in the heat at the airport pickup point. His laptop bag over his shoulder, his overnight case beside him. Sweat dripped down under his collar.

'So,' he said to Marti. 'Any feedback yet from your contacts down here?'

He shook his head. 'Not yet boss. Too early, They said it would be later today when they would get me a list of kit available at short notice.'

Marti stood gazing at nothing in particular. He wore a beige jacket over a cream shirt and light brown trousers and shoes. At sixty five, he was slightly younger than Billy, but he had a hard, careworn look of someone not to be messed with. An old knife scar running from his left ear across his cheek, stopping short of his upper lip only enhanced the impression. Dom had never seen Marti flustered or upset, ever. He had a single setting on the emotion dial, fixed at one but incorrectly wired to ten. When you asked him to do something, especially with a knife, he never failed. His workouts in the gym at the Villa four times a week, stretched even Dom when they exercised together.

'It's likely this will be a close up job, Marti. So something with suppressors would be good. Uzi's preferably.'

Marti grunted. 'Would be boss, would be. But more likely to be twelve gauge double barrelled pieces. Things have been pretty quiet down here for a while. I'm not sure how much heavy kit there is floating about.'

'Well, let's make do and mend then, eh!'

Jenkins arrived at the pick up point with the car. Cases went in the boot and they piled in, Marti up front and Dom in the back.

'Straight to the hotel boss?' Billy asked him.

'Yes, I just need to check my messages on the way.'

Dom took the TOR Tails memory stick from his pocket and slipped it into a USB slot on the side of the laptop and booted up. He configured his mobile phone as a 6G wi-fi hotspot and when the laptop was up and running connected the inbuilt wi-fi to the phone. After his VPN connected, he loaded TOR and logged into his emails. As expected, there was one from Miguel just as he'd promised. He opened it. Barrera would arrive tomorrow, flying in on a connecting flight from Madrid to Malaga. Miguel had provided the flight number. There would be three bodyguards not the veritable army he had brought with him the last time. Either Barrera felt he was under no threat or he did not want to attract attention. He would also hire his own car and drive up to Mijas. Miguel had not been asked to supply any additional security on the way from the airport. Good, thought Dom. That would make things easier. Plus, he would not have to get rid of any of Miguel's people as collateral damage. There was also some information on how to make it look like a rival cartel hit. Dom swallowed hard when he saw this. He replied to the email with a simple acknowledgement, deleted it, then logged off and shut down the laptop.

'Okay, we're on. Once we get to the hotel, we dig out the maps and look for the best place to spring the ambush.'

He looked at Marti in the passenger seat. 'You need to push your contacts down here Marti. We need the weapons as soon as possible.' Galbraith nodded. 'We may also need the help of some local *soldiers* who know the area. We'll need to boost some cars. This is hired, so we can't use it. Make sure the people you get are trustworthy. They need to keep their mouths shut.'

'I know some people who'll fit the bill boss. They aren't young, but if it's just driving, then they'll be fine.'

'Good,' said Dom. 'I'll give you some cash to pay them up front.' Marti nodded again.

When they reached the boutique Hotel Pueblo Por el Mar, they quickly checked in, found their rooms and dropped their luggage. Dom had Billy come to his room, and they waited while Marti spent some time on the phone making calls. When he joined them, Dom fired up his laptop and opened up Google Maps, selecting a satellite view of the road between the airport and Mijas. There were three primary routes Antonio Barreras could take. The quickest and most obvious was along the infamous 'highway of death,' AP-7. This would take them through Torremolinos and close to Benalmadena before swinging to the right up into the hills of Mijas with its randomly dotted Villas. The problem? There was no place to set up an ambush until Barrera had left the main road and began the climb up towards Orejuela's villa. Dom looked at the other routes, but these were longer and there was no guarantee he would take any of them. The only common choke point was in the hills.

The three of them poured over the map for nearly an hour, looking at options, switching between the maps Street View and 3D View. I wasn't as good as the real thing. Dom knew they would still need to visit, but the semblance of a plan formed in his mind. Barrera's car would eventually need to connect with the A-387. From there, it would turn off onto the Camino Fuente de la Seda, then left into the winding Calla Sta. Rosa that began a gentle climb up to Miguel's Villa via the Calle Los Naranjos. There was a hairpin bend along the Calla Sta. Rosa, surrounded by scrubland and trees. It had a parking area to one side of it where cars could sit while their occupants admired the view; or simply waited. The entrances to two villas were slightly downhill from this hairpin, and the right-hand turn into the Calle Los Naranjos was set uphill from it. In between, there was nothing but road, shrubs and trees, a total distance of around 100 metres. The trick, Dom realised, was to make sure Barrera's car was the only one on this stretch of road when they made their move. This would require two roadblocks, one just after the Villa entrances and the other shutting off Calle Los Naranjos and Calla Sta. Rosa further up the hill. They needed to trap the South American's vehicle, get it alone then hit it hard. Setting up fake road works downhill was one option. They could then stop all vehicles after Barrera's. Numbers were also now the problem. Someone had to shadow Barrera and his bodyguard from the airport and pass along details of the car they were in. He would now need at least two other teams, one to block the road at the points needed to trap them and one to operate traffic lights. He put the options to them.

'We'll need at least two vans, and two sets of manually operated traffic lights. That should stop any other cars coming up or going down hill,' Billy told him. 'Then we need to find some way of blocking their car at exactly the point we want them. Plus, it needs to be blocked both ways, up and downhill to stop them trying to escape anywhere.'

'Could we use the vans for that?' Dom asked.

Billy shook his head. 'No. We need something that will straddle most of the road otherwise we'll just leave space for them to get through. I'd recommend those water tankers you see at road works. We can have them set up at an angle so we roll them back onto the road when we need them to.'

Dom thought for a moment. This would need a lot more people than he'd envisaged, not to mention all the equipment. Given what they had discussed, they would need seven bodies, four more than he currently had. Billy would tail Barrera from the airport. Dom and Marti would lie in wait in the shrubbery with weapons ready. The Spanish based hired help would need to steal or borrow the equipment and then drive it into position at the right time and set up the fake road works and traffic lights. Dom sighed heavily. There was too much to go wrong. Too many people were becoming involved. But he had no other options.

'Marti, get back on the blower and have a chat with a few people. Tell them what we need and when, but I'll hang fire on the location until we check it out. And get us half a dozen two-way radios.'

Marti nodded and left the room. Dom went back to staring out the window. Billy wandered over and stood beside him.

'You know boss, Marti and me have danced this tango a few times before. We know all the steps. Follow us and you'll be fine.'

Rossi smiled at the analogy, but Billy was right. He needed to trust these two old hands.

ΔΔΔ

Dom received the last message from Miguel in the early hours of the following day. Barrera and his four bodyguards had boarded Iberia Flight IB 6586 from Eldorado International Airport Bogota to Barajas airport Madrid. The flight time was approximately ten hours. This would see them arrive in Madrid at ten-fifteen in the morning local time. They would then board an Iberia flight operated by Air Nostrum at eleven fifty-five for the one hour fifteen-minute trip to Malaga and exit the terminal just before two in the afternoon local time. Miguel had surprised Dom by telling him Antonio Barrera had managed to keep himself off the authorities radar in Europe. He never handled drugs. Went nowhere they were grown. Never entered the company of those known to be associated with their importation. Instead, he had the carefully cultivated persona of a Colombian coffee importer, meaning he travelled First Class to and from Europe.

Dom had informed Miguel in as cryptic a fashion as he could of what they were planning. He was to make sure none of his people were anywhere near the location when this went down. Miguel had also been asked to somehow get irrefutable video evidence.

Billy had earlier parked up and was waiting in the main arrivals terminal at the airport. He needed to find out what kind of car Barrera hired and its registration number. He would text this with an accompanying photograph to Dom. Once done, he would get back to his own car and follow them if he could. If not, then he would make his way to the ambush site as quickly as possible to act as an emergency backup.

Barrera and his three heavies walked out of the customs area together, carrying their suitcases and hand luggage. One of them headed towards the car hire desks. Billy stood patiently wearing his best blue suit, holding a sign with a name on it, fake as far as he knew, but designed to make it look like he was a limo driver. Barrera's phone rang. After listening briefly he hung up and indicated to the other two to follow him. Billy shadowed the group as they made their way out, throwing the paper sign in a bin. He watched as they went towards a black Range Rover Dynamique EV. Pulling out his mobile, he surreptitiously took a snap of the car and the number plate and sent it in a text to Dom's personal mobile. Then he turned and walked back to his car.

At the Camino Fuente de la Seda junction with the Calla Sta. Rosa, some workmen and their vehicles had pulled up a couple of hours previously. They had driven to the lay-by, parked up and erected two sets of traffic lights, one just after the villas and the other at the junction with Calle Los Naranjos. This was a private road, not public. A few inquisitive Spaniards asked what they were doing, but were happy when Marti's expat friends told them, in fluent Spanish, it was work being funded by a developer. The vans in the lay-by had been moved forward slightly and turned to point downhill. Dom and Marti drove up and swung around to park their own car behind them, also facing downhill. All the vehicles had been *borrowed* to order yesterday. They would be returned intact after the operation was over. The owners had been paid to keep their mouths shut and the authorities in the dark. When Dom had visited the location late yesterday afternoon with Marti and Billy, he was concerned it wasn't isolated enough. The villas close by were surrounded by two- metre high walls, but there was a footpath running through scrubland just downhill of the road and they could do nothing about anyone walking there. They would wear masks so Dom hoped if anyone did appear, they would be surprised and confused by what was happening.

Dom and Marti got out of their car. They both wore thin, running gloves, incongruous for the weather, but they could not afford to leave any fingerprints. They also wore masks. Walking to the car boot, they removed two holdalls and without a word climbed over the low wall on the north side of the road. Dom walked to his left, slightly uphill, while Marti went right into some trees just before the hairpin. To ensure good coverage, they would need to fire from two angles. If anyone escaped from the car, then Marti would have a good view of them clambering down the hill to the right of the road and be able to take them out. Settling down into the cover they had identified yesterday, both opened their holdalls and took out the suppressed Heckler and Koch MP7's Marti's Spanish contact had been able to get for them. These were not the most powerful or accurate weapons available, but outside of special forces equipment, Dom knew they would work. They each come with three, forty round magazines. With a rate of fire of 950 rounds per minute, Dom knew he and Marti had to be quick and precise. The reflex gun sights and red laser dot of the weapons would not be of much use this close up. It was more a case of spray and pray.

Dom switched on his radio. Marti, Billy and the two work gangs also carried them and they were all tuned to the same channel. Then he settled down and waited. Eventually his mobile phone vibrated. He looked at the message from Billy. They were on their way. He pressed the transmit button on his radio and passed the details of the vehicle to everyone else. All the participants were now in play and it was simply a waiting game.

Rossi was aware no plan survives first contact with the enemy. This was one plan which did not even get that far before seemingly falling to pieces. A Civil Guard transport arrived and began to climb the hill up towards the roadblock. Dom saw it soon after it passed the first set of traffic lights. Rossi had no idea where they were headed, as there were only more holiday villas farther up the hill. He hunkered down and hoped Marti was doing the same. The marked four by four, pulled up before the second set of lights. Someone in uniform got out and shouted towards one of the 'workers' in Spanish. Dom had no idea what he was saying, but the two of them engaged in a conversation for a few minutes, before the Guard got back in and continued up the hill.

Dom clicked transmit. 'What the hell was that about?' he asked quietly. 'Have they gone?'

There was a hiss and a click in return. 'Their Colonel owns a Villa further up the hill at the end of this road. He sent them on ahead to check and make sure it's okay before he arrives tomorrow.'

'Does that mean they'll be here for a while?'

There was a pause. 'They say they'll be doing an overnight. Guess they want to get the use of the pool and other facilities.'

Shit, thought Dom. If they're on the ball, they might recognise the suppressed gunfire if they are close enough. Plus, they've spoken to one of Marti's people. If they recognise him or record the registration numbers on the vehicles they could be in big trouble. His radio clicked again.

'Do we scrub boss?' It was Marti, asking the obvious question.

He was about to answer in the negative when he noticed the Civil Guard vehicle had stopped again and someone had clambered out of the passenger seat.

Now what? He wondered.

The guard approached the workers at the first set of lights and began pointing at them and the water tankers parked nearby. He could not hear what was being said, but as it was all in Spanish it made no difference. The man the guard had been speaking to turned and walked down the hill, As he did so he raised his radio and spoke into it. 'Everyone, the Civil Guard has just told us to pack up and move. They don't want any work happening while their Colonel is here. What do we do?'

Fuck, Dom mouthed. This was their only chance to take the bastard out before Barrera got to Miguel's and told him officially Dom was soon to be out of the loop. But short of taking out the Civil Guards in the transport, he couldn't see any way of keeping the traffic lights in play. With a sigh, he hit the transmit button. 'Okay everyone, stand down. Marti and I will wait here until these guys leave and then head off. The rest of you get the cars back to their owners. I'll call Billy and let him know. Pack up, now.'

Dom watched for a while as the 'worker's dismantled the traffic lights and hooked the water tankers back up to their vehicles. The Civil Guard officer stood for a few more minutes watching then satisfied they were going, turned and tramped back up the hill toward his waiting vehicle. Dom took out his mobile and called Billy.

'Yes boss?' came Billy's clipped tones. The sound of a car engine was in the background.

'Billy, we're a bust. The whole thing has gone arse over elbow. The Civil Guard turned up and ordered everything moved.'

'Shit. Where are you boss? Did they spot you and Marti, ... and the tools?'

'No, we're both still fine. We're hiding in the trees waiting until its clear enough for us to get back to the car. Head for the hotel. We'll meet back there and figure something out. Where are you just now?'

'I'm about ten minutes out. I've just passed Barrera's car. I can come and give you a hand if you want?'

'No need,' Dom told him. 'See you later.' He hung up and looked back to the road. The Civil Guard four by four had disappeared up the hill. Dom called Marti on the radio. 'Marti, Barrera and his goons will be here in ten minutes or so. Let's get back to the car.'

Marti answered by standing up so Dom could see him. They each made their way separately to the road, the Heckler and Koch's safely in the holdalls. Dom reached the car first, bag over his right shoulder. He opened the boot then looked around him. Marti's friends were busy putting everything back into the trucks, their yellow vests flapping in the light breeze. Apart from that it was silent. The only other noises he could hear were crickets and the occasional cawing of a bird somewhere high overhead. He found the sun and lifted his head towards it, eyes closed. The heat didn't penetrate, but Dom always preferred the stillness of the countryside when he went to the continent. The tourist trap resorts were too garish and busy for him. Up in the hills like this, life seemed on hold, and a moment could be made to last for an hour.

Footsteps made him look.

'Hope your wearing factor fifty, boss.' Marti smiled at him. They had both kept their masks on.

'I hate getting beaten Marti. If this prick gets past us, then we're finished. We might as well just cash in and retire down here, because Miguel won't risk dealing with us again.'

Marti stopped beside him. He swung his bag into the boot. 'You know Dom, when me and your dad were pulling jobs together, we often used to talk about what it would be like to retire. Get up late, have a swim, spend all day reading a good book or playing golf.' He paused and looked at Dom. 'Then he used to remind me I was shit scared of water over three feet deep, I couldn't hit a football with a tennis racket and he was dyslexic. So fuck off with this retirement talk. You'll end up like Billy and me, tied up and dead in the saddle.'

Dom said nothing.

'Look,' Marti turned to him. 'You'll find another way. These guys always make mistakes. You just need to be there and in place when they do.'

The sound of a truck starting up attracted Dom's attention. Both vehicles had completed loading and were moving off. Dom would make sure Marti spoke with them later. He had to ensure they kept their mouths shut. As the truck disappeared back towards the A-387, complete silence descended on the hillside. No voices, no children playing in pools, no car engines revving, no dogs barking, no one out for a walk. Dom stood quietly for a minute, wondering. Just then, coming up the hill, he heard the sound of an artificially enhanced electric car engine. He looked quickly at Marti.

'We can do this,' he suddenly blurted. 'The roads empty, there's no one here. We know it's a Range Rover. They'll need to slow right down to get around this corner.' He paused. 'Well, how about it Marti? Want to take a gamble?'

Marti smiled, tugged his mask, pulling it even tighter over his head, unzipped his holdall then took out the already loaded machine gun. Dom did the same, leaving the boot lid up to provide him some additional cover. They checked the magazines, cocked them and slipped off the safety catches. Dom checked Marti's disguise, a black ski mask and Marti did the same for him. With a nod, Marti walked around to the offside front of the car, dipping down slightly behind the wheel arch. This gave him cover but also let him see downhill for the approaching Range Rover. Dom held the gun hidden inside the boot in his left hand, ready to use at a seconds' notice. They waited.

'Here they come,' Marti said calmly.

Dom's mouth had gone dry. It surprised him to find he was nervous. He supposed knifing a jagged up junkie was just a bit different from taking out the number two in one of the world's biggest drug cartels.

'Okay, wait until they've gotten parallel with the front of our car. I'll open fire first and try to get the driver, but whatever happens, for fuck's sake keep on firing.'

Dom hesitated for a second, then reached into the bag and pulled out a large hunting knife. He took it from its sheath and stuffed it into the rear waistband of his trousers. The Range Rover climbed the hill and slowed down to take the left-hand hairpin. It came level with Dom's car, but the driver paid it little notice. As the front of the Evoque reached the nose of Dom's car, he swiftly took the machine gun from the boot. His right hand went straight to the trigger and he stepped out from around the car. His first burst was low, but went into the

Range Rovers front right tyre, shredding it. The sound was no more than a loud buzz, the suppressor working well. As the car slewed to the right and headed for the wall, he fired his second burst through the front passenger door, the four bullets destroying the ribcage and lungs of the unfortunate bodyguard. Dom noticed Marti stepping out from behind the rear wheel arch a second after he had fired. He let go a continuous burst into the back window of the SUV, shattering the glass with a bang.

The Evoque driver had recovered a little from the initial shock but instead of throwing the car into reverse, he pulled a handgun from somewhere inside the SUV and turned to lose some shots at Dom through the shattered windscreen. By now, Rossi had moved to the front of the car and ran closer, firing as he went. As the handgun shots whistled past him, Dom traversed slightly to his right and pumped another four round burst into the drivers chest through the broken window. Marti had moved to the passenger side rear door and loosed off some more shots through both the window and the door itself. Dom circled the SUV to the opposite side. He angled a shot through the drivers window into the back, but the bullets thumped into the headrest. Dom hurried past the rear door, weapon held in front of him. He reached forward with one hand and pulled the handle, swinging the door open. Marti did the same on the opposite side. Inching forward, they both carefully looked into the back seat.

Inside, the car was a charnel house, the cream interior forever stained crimson. Marti's shots had taken off the back of the head of the man closest to him. Bits of brain, bone and gore were spread along the rear seat and all over the inside of the roof. The man sitting near Dom breathed heavily, blood bubbling from his mouth. He had been hit, probably somewhere in the back but Dom could not see exactly where. He was alive though, and it was Barrera. He looked at Dom in puzzlement for a few seconds, wondering just who it was that had arrived here to assassinate him. Then he recognised the face and shook his head, bewildered. Dom reached behind his own neck and pressed a button. Then he grabbed the top of the mask and pulled it off, one handed, revealing his true identity. Recognition dawned for Barrera and his face twisted with a mix of pain and anger. His hands reached out to Dom, a desperate attempt to grip his throat, before falling back with the effort.

Dom leaned in towards him. 'That's right you greedy Colombian prick. This is what you get when you act like a smart arse and try and put me out of business. Oh, and Miguel says hello.'

Barrera's face contorted in rage. Rossi replaced the mask, stepped back to avoid the blood splatter and fired another four rounds point blank into Barrera's chest. He slumped down, eyes closed.

'Marti, check the ones in the front. Make sure they're gone as well.'

Placing the gun on top of the car roof, he reached into the waistband of his trousers and took out the hunting knife. This was the part he was not looking forward to. Miguel had told him what to do to make it look like a rival Colombian gang had carried out the hit.

Taking a deep breath, he leaned into the car and took hold of Barreras top lip. With the serrated edge of the hunting knife, he sawed through the soft tissue from left to right. Dropping the lip in Barreras lap he did the same with his bottom one, leaving them both lying there. He looked up to see Marti staring at him silently.

'We need to make it look like a Cartel hit Marti,' Dom told him quickly, as he moved to the front seat passenger to repeat the process. 'Miguel told me this is the signature of one of their rivals.'

Marti shook his head. 'The rest are all dead Dom,' he said. 'We need to be quick.'

Dom moved around the SUV taking the lips from the Colombians and leaving them lying in their laps. He wiped some of the blood from his hands on his trouser legs. Picking up his machine gun, he looked back up the hillside for a few seconds and then hurried to the car. He looked at Marti. His clothes were speckled with blood splashes as Dom knew his would be. Once back at the hotel they would get cleaned up, burn the clothes on a quiet beach somewhere and Marti would get the guns back to their owners.

The entire hit had taken only two minutes from start to finish. No cars had passed. The Civil Guard had stayed up at their villa. The air was still again after the frenzy of the shooting, and the mutilation which had followed. They both put the guns back in their holdalls, which then went in the car boot. They had left their hired car parked up in a Torremolinos side street where they had gotten this stolen one, which would later be found burned out. Dom climbed into the driver's seat and switched on the ignition. He selected drive then stopped as he sensed Marti looking at him.

'What?' he asked softly. 'Have we forgotten something?'

Marti pursed his lips. 'I don't know whether your old man would be proud of you or not,' he answered. 'I watched him carry out a few hits in my time, but even he showed a wee bit of nerves occasionally, and he never had to take out four people at once, especially after his plan had gone tits up.'

'Yeh, well, believe it or not this isn't my first tango either Marti.' He glanced across at him and could see something on his face, a mix of both surprise and admiration. 'I know. I'm full of surprises. Let's get out of here. I need to get back and update our real Colombian friend.'

As Dom drove down the Camino Fuente de la Seda to the A-387, he knew further up the hill, someone was hiding amongst the bushes watching and recording. The Nikon Z11 with its 500mm f4 lens was mounted on a tripod for stability. The pan and tilt head was set to move slightly and keep tracking the point of action. The 4k video taken from the 60 megapixel full frame sensor would allow extensive cropping. This meant it would be simple to identify individual faces. The photographer stopped recording as Dom and Marti drove off and switched the camera from Live View into Review Mode.

She pressed play and quickly reviewed the video from the beginning, nodding with satisfaction as she watched. Good, she thought. Miguel should be happy with this.

Even at its lowest magnification, there was no doubt only two people had carried out the hit - but only one of them was wearing a black ski mask.

There was also no doubt as to the identity of the hitman who had been stupid enough not to wear his.

To those who would later see the video and who knew him, there was no mistaking the face of Ian Gilmour.

SIXTEEN

Dom stood in the ground floor hallway of his Villa at the foot of the Grand Staircase, and looked one last time at his reflection in the gold framed wall mirror. Satisfied, he walked over and opened the front door, then stepped on to the porch, waiting. Since coming back from Spain, he had been on edge. Billy and Marti had taken everything in their stride. They had shown no emotion he could see. In fact, they both nodded off on the flight back from Malaga whilst he had sat there wondering if he had done the right thing. Too late for doubts though. Miguel had contacted him on his return to Glasgow. Everything had gone as planned. His partner Mariana had managed to take the video of Gilmour assassinating Antonio. Carlos Barrera had been contacted and informed of what had gone down and he intended coming to Spain to seek his own retribution. Miguel had spun him a tale of betrayal and of how he was doing everything he could to find the culprit in league with Los Malvados. Dom had asked him to keep the video of Gilmour to himself for the time being. When the time was right, Dom knew he somehow needed to engineer a meeting between Gilmour and Barrera to permanently ensure Ian was not a future problem.

The electric gates at the bottom of the driveway swung slowly open. Marti's Jaguar pulled in and parked up. Billy sat relaxed in the passenger seat. They both got out, nodding to him as they climbed the steps and walked past making their way into the office at the rear of the building. Next to arrive a couple of minutes later were Cassie and Gabby. Cassie's car crunched over the gold coloured gravel, pulling to a stop beside Marti's.

Dom waited until the girls had walked to the front door. They climbed the steps. Gabby had a small, white, cardboard tube in her hand together with her handbag. The mask? Dom wondered.

'Thanks for coming, ladies. No problems I hope?'

Cassie shook her head. 'Are you expecting any?'

Dom shrugged. 'Just nervous I suppose. Things are moving fast.'

'Still a long way to go,' Cassie reminded him. 'And we need to find out from Ogilvie what little secrets he's keeping from us.'

'Indeed.' He turned and looked at Gabby. 'How are you feeling Gabby? Have you spoken to your Uncle since our last talk?' he asked warily, They stepped into the main hallway and he closed the heavy, red, painted timber door.

Gabby gazed around her at the opulence. Polished marble tiled floor. Stucco plaster cornicing and friezes. A chandelier you wouldn't let Del Boy and Rodney anywhere near. 'I'm impressed Dom. You didn't strike me as the type to go for the classic Victoriana look. This is a nice place.'

'Thanks,' he replied quickly. 'But your Uncle? Have you spoken with him?'

She tore her gaze away from a framed original painting of a Highland stag on the wall behind Dom and shook her head. 'No. Last time I did was just to pass on the info you gave me in my workshop. Word has it he's down in Manchester today.'

Manchester? That means O'Boyle, thought Dom. Has to be. 'Okay. Let's get set for Ogilvie arriving. I want him to see the money in his account and then get the last part of the plan put in place.'

They followed Dom into his office. He had moved some chairs in earlier so everyone could be seated, and they spread themselves around. Quickly booting up his laptop, he connected to the internet and loaded up the screen displaying the Cayman Islands account where he had legally deposited the two million he had already laundered. He paid his taxes. He paid his National Insurance. He did everything by the book, apart from the fake receipts Malone generated every week, spread across the hundreds of businesses, owned in some way, by Dom. Malone had once told him he *employed* nearly five hundred people. The honest workers. Those with no idea their labours were used as cover for a massive money laundering operation grossing millions annually.

A soft chime announced Ogilvie had arrived at the gate. Marti had relayed Dom's address to him earlier in the day. Rossi stood and went to let him in. Ogilvie stopped as he crossed the threshold, his eyes roving around the expertly restored Victorian details of the Villa.

'Understated,' he said to Dom, sarcasm in his voice.

Dom ignored him. 'This way.' He led him back down the hallway.

Dom introduced Marti, who grunted at Ogilvie. 'Okay, first things first.' He beckoned Ogilvie to join him on the other side of the desk and pointed at his laptop screen. 'This is your account. As you can see, I've transferred all the money just as you wanted. All I need to do now is give you the final login information, and it's all legally yours. Just make sure the taxman doesn't come asking questions about where it came from.'

'How do I know the account's real?' Ogilvie asked, nodding towards the screen. 'You could have mocked something up for me to look at and this is nothing more than a ruse to get me to hand over the final bit of info Malone will need.'

Dom whistled through his teeth. 'All right. Set up a payee form to your own bank account. Once you're done, transfer some money. You'll see it arrive almost instantly.' He shook his head. 'I won't look.'

Dom walked from behind the desk and stood beside Marti. He watched as Ogilvie moved his fingers across the keyboard, occasionally clicking the mouse on some unseen icon. He pulled his mobile from his pocket, opened a text, then entered some details into a form on the laptop screen. After a minute or so, he stood. 'Okay, seems to have worked,' he said. 'But I've changed the account password so only I can access it.

Not that I don't trust you,' he smirked.

Dom said nothing. 'Let's get down to business.' He walked back to his seat, currently occupied by Ogilvie, who reluctantly moved aside and took the chair next to Marti. 'Gabby can we see the mask?'

Gabby removed the plastic disc at one end and opened the cardboard tube. She held it up and something flesh covered with hair slipped out into her hand, looking like a dead fish. 'This is it,' she said to no one in particular. 'I completed it quicker than I had envisaged, but it looks good and behaves well even if I say so myself. I tried it on a dummy I made of Malone's head to make sure.'

Dom held out his hand. She gave the mask to him. He picked it up, turning it around against the light, noticing the skin tones, the natural blemishes, the open pores. It looked realistic, even with no one wearing it. He looked at Gabby.

'Should we try it on,' he asked.

She looked pensive. 'It's been custom made for Malone, Dom, so I wouldn't advise it, but I've brought a second one along that was part of an initial test run. I thought Ogilvie could see it being put on someone else so I can show him how it's done.'

'Billy you're up.' He turned to Ogilvie. 'You'll need to show Malone what to do when you give him this, okay?'

He nodded. Gabby took the spare mask from her handbag and turned to face Billy.

'Smooth your hair down as much as you can.'

Jenkins ran his hands across his head, flattening his hair as best he could.

'Now take off your jacket and tie and undo the top few buttons of your shirt.'

He grinned. 'I love it when a woman takes control.' With the tie off and the buttons undone, Gabby took the mask and pulled it over Billy's head and the top of his shoulders. Once she was satisfied, Gabby reached behind Billy's head and pressed a small, metal stud that covered the CR2032 battery. Electrical impulses shot through the filaments in the masks sub structure, instantly tightening up facial features and moulding them to Billy's own contours. When she had finished, Dom looked between Billy and the real Ogilvie sitting next to Marti.

'Well fuck me,' Dom whispered. It was perfect. He had never seen anything so surreal. If he had walked past Billy in the street while he wore the mask, he would have sworn it was Ogilvie. Even at the lips and eyes, there were no tell-tale give-aways where a joint between skin and latex would have been most obvious.

Cassie smiled at Gabby. 'Bet you're glad she's on our side Dom. I can only imagine the mayhem that we could cause if we had these masks for certain other people who need taken care of.'

Dom looked her quizzically, then slowly shook his head. 'Isn't science wonderful? So, it looks like it'll work then, at least this part of it. You can take it off now Billy.' Dom turned to look at Ogilvie. 'Now it's your turn. We have a mask that work's, you have your money safely tucked away where nobody can get at it, so let's hear what those final pieces of the puzzle are.'

Ogilvie sat in silence for some seconds, eyes downcast. Dom realised he knew this was the penultimate point at which he could turn back. The last one would be handing the mask to Malone and watching as he took his keys and made his way out of the prison. He saw him take a deep breath.

'I start backshift as Duty Governor in three days, so it can't happen before then.'

'Shit,' said Cassie. 'That's cutting it fine Dom.'

'I know. But as long as we get him out and back here before midnight then we'll be okay.' He turned to Malone. 'So what does he need to know?'

'Before he leaves his cell wearing the mask, he has to change into my clothes including the shoes. He also needs to take the set of keys I carry with me.'

'Why can't he just take the fob he needs to open those doors you have control over?'

'The fob is attached to the key bunch. You can't take it off.

Plus, before I leave the prison each night, I need to put my keys, my radio and my officer alarm back in their various locations in the Key Vending room.'

'What happens there?' Dom asked.

'All the key bunches for every officer and manager in the prison are kept in there. They're electronically locked into a wall rack. But to access the rack, you need to key in a PIN and then put the keys into the correct slot. A light will flash red to let you know which recess to use and then turn green when your keys are inserted. And it has to be the correct rack. They are all programmed to only accept specific key sets. Then the radios and the officer alarms need to be placed into their respective charging racks for use the next day. Plus, you need to use your token to access the Key Vending room itself.'

'Fuck,' Billy laughed. 'You'd need a Ph.D. in the Krypton Factor for all that shit.'

Rossi ignored him. 'So,' Dom said. 'You need to tell Malone what your PIN number is and also tell him which rack to use? Correct?'

Ogilvie nodded.

'What if he gets it wrong,' Cassie put in. 'What happens then? Does an alarm go off or something?'

Ogilvie shook his head. 'There are ten racks and only two of them accept my keys, so he can't get it wrong. There's no warning in the vending room either. It's the return of the key bunch that's critical. The radios and officer alarms don't need to be seated as accurately. If they don't charge up overnight, then it won't make any difference to Malone getting out.'

'What's stopping him from just walking out of the jail with the keys tucked into his pocket?' Billy piped up. 'Seems a lot less trouble to me.'

They all looked at Ogilvie again. 'You know,' he said sarcastically, 'we've been running prisons in Scotland for a wee while now. Maybe we've thought of something like that.'

'Enough with the attitude,' Dom barked, his frustration getting the better of him.

Ogilvie sighed. 'He can't take the keys out of the prison with him. There's an alarm at the main entrance that will activate if someone tries to take them out. It's triggered by a microchip hidden in the key ring, and even I don't have access to that.' He looked at each of them. 'Malone will just need to follow my instructions, step by step. It shouldn't be too difficult.'

Dom gazed at each of them individually. 'If there's anything else you want to say, now's the time?'

'How does he get away from the prison?' Marti asked. 'It's not as if one of us can just turn up and bundle him into a car.'

Dom nodded. 'You'll need to give him your car keys,' he said to Dan. 'And then tell him exactly where your car is parked. I want him away from there ASAP. Got it?'

'I'm not supposed to take my personal keys into the heart of the prison,' he replied.

'Will anyone stop you if they do? Will they even know? You are the Head of Operations after all.'

Ogilvie shook his head and said nothing.

'Okay, then. In three days' time Jack Malone will walk out of HMP Glasgow ostensibly a free man, and you Mr Ogilvie, will need to accept a few bruises for your troubles.'

Ogilvie looked at him wondering what he was talking about.

'If Jack doesn't make it look like he's clobbered you over the head, then it won't take the plods long to piece together most of what's happened, will it? He'll be gentle. I promise.'

Dan scowled.

'What else can you do to avoid suspicion?' Cassie asked him.

'Well, I've already worked at losing my voice, so on the day I'll be hoarse. I'll make a point of visiting as many inmates as I can before then, pretending I'm getting feedback from them, listening to their complaints, that sort of thing. It's not something I'd normally do, but it isn't unheard of.'

Gabby shook her head at him. 'And just how are you going to achieve that if you've been struck dumb then?'

'I'll think of something,' he replied. 'Anyway, I'm the Head of Operations, so no one will stop me.'

'Anything else?' Dom looked around one last time. Everyone was quiet. 'Okay, once Malone gets out he drives to the waste ground behind the retail park at Springburn. When he gets there, Billy will be waiting to pick him up in another car.' He leaned forward and gazed directly at Ogilvie. 'Malone needs to know everything he has to do, step by step, from the second he leaves his cell till the minute he arrives at the pick up point. We're depending on you.' He lifted the tube with the real mask in it. 'I'll leave it up to you how you'll get this into the jail, okay?' He handed it to Ogilvie, who looked at it like it was a snake then handled it like a burning fire stick.

'Now, disappear. I don't want any of you around here for the next couple of days.' They all stood up and went to leave, including Ogilvie.

'Oh, just one more thing Dan. It's not that I don't trust you or anything, but now you have access to all that cash in your offshore account, I want to be sure you'll stay on board with us and see this thing through.' He smiled wryly. 'After all it wouldn't take much for you to vanish somewhere.'

'I'm not going anywhere. I have too much to lose if you ever release those videos.'

'Still,' Dom said to him. 'I'll feel much better if you can put up your new best friend for the next few nights.' He pointed to Marti.

'You've got to be kidding.'

Dom shook his head. 'Not about this, Dan. Not about this.'

SEVENTEEN

Fucking Marti Galbraith! Dour bastard. He had been with him for two days now. Day one he had escaped by being at the prison on his last day shift, but yesterday and today Galbraith had been babysitting him before he went on backshift. Marti had followed Dan to HMP Glasgow, to ensure his safe arrival he had told him. On the second and third long, boring, monotonous days, Marti never left the house. Dan avoided answering the phone in case it was someone from work and he gave away his intentions. His wife had decided to go and stay with her sister when he had brought Galbraith home. He didn't think his excuse that Marti was a colleague between house moves sat well with her. Or perhaps she just needed a reason to piss off and leave him. Well soon, she would get her wish of being alone, except he would be the one doing the pissing off.

Those two obvious dyke birds Cassie and Gabby had turned up last night to double check the mask they had handed him at Rossi's Villa. They had stayed for a while, talking with Marti more than him, and then buggered off to do whatever lesbians do when they're getting it on. That kind of sex had never interested him. Dominating young birds was more his style, and look where that had fucking gotten him? Galbraith had not allowed him near a computer. In fact, he had disconnected the internet, just in case Dan had any thoughts about accessing his Cayman Islands account and doing a runner. He sat in his kitchen at a little fold-up breakfast table nursing a mug of coffee, liberally dozed with Jack Daniels. It was only eleven o'clock in the morning, but his nerves were twitching and he needed something to steady himself. Pity he couldn't take this into work with him. His shift started at one thirty, an hour before the day shift ended to allow for any handovers needing to be done and to make sure the prison had coverage twenty four seven. The door from the dining room into the kitchen opened, and he turned to see Marti Galbraith standing there. The girls had brought him a change of clothes, blue shirt, blue jeans, black shoes. He looked like a retired rodeo rider and came across as tough as nails, not to be messed with.

'Dan I can smell the booze all the way to the front door. Pour it down the sink and just breathe, okay. It'll help you relax. I know, I've tried the whisky route. It nearly drove me mad. It was much easier just to live with my demons.'

Ogilvie sighed, took another long swallow of his coffee and went to pour away what little was left. He rinsed and washed the mug and placed it on the draining board to dry. 'Tell me Marti. How do you guys live with yourselves?'

'What do you mean?' Galbraith asked, sounding puzzled.

'I mean all the violence you've dished out over the years, all the people you've beaten up?' He looked straight at him. 'All the people you've killed? How do you deal with your conscience?'

Marti looked at him, a smirk on his lips. 'Maybe I don't have a conscience anymore? Maybe my conscience got left behind when that first prick of a school teacher took me aside and told me I would be his favourite. Or perhaps it vanished when I watched my father beaten up and left brain damaged by some low level nineteen seventies street gang. Or maybe none of those happened. Maybe I just don't give a shit. I do as I'm told, I get paid, I go home. End of story.'

Ogilvie shook his head and smiled back at him. 'You know I've met more than my share of murdering, vicious psychos banged up for life.' He walked over and dried his hands on a towel from a wall rack. 'For the first few years they were like you, all bravado and jail time is nothing and I'm still King of the Hill. And then slowly, gradually, as other slightly less evil men were released, it dawned on them; this was it. The best years of their lives were to be spent living in an echoing concrete chamber. They would be old, broken, bitter men when they were released, if they ever were. And everyone they ever knew would have forgotten them or would be dead.'

'Well, good thing for me I'm not banged up any more. I never liked prison food.'

'Who the fuck does,' Ogilvie laughed. 'Where did you do your time?' he asked him.

Marti thought for a second, then shrugged. 'No harm in telling you I suppose. E Hall, Barlinnie. I did a five-year stretch for assault with intent.'

'And did you?'

'Did I what?'

'Have any intent?'

Marti tilted his head. 'Let's put it this way, the guy fucked off to Spain when he heard I was getting out, but I still tracked him down. Now he's a permanent resident of a flyover column somewhere on a Spanish motorway.'

Ogilvie walked back and sat down at the table. 'So they never caught you for anything else? Your entire criminal career and you only have one conviction?'

Marti nodded and walked over to the table, pulling out another chair, scraping it across the quarry tiled floor before sitting down. Dan noticed the edge of a tattoo peeking out from beneath his shirt cuff. Galbraith was looking at him closely and Dan became uncomfortable.

'What?' he asked him, his body shifting slightly backward in his chair, putting a few more millimetres between him and Rossi's paid henchman. If they had been having this conversation in prison with Galbraith locked up, then Dan would have felt a lot more at ease. He'd had meetings with some of Scotland's most notorious killers, questioned them even, together with a psychologist. Peter Tobin, Luke Mitchell, Angus Sinclair - on the inside he had always felt a sense of superiority. In his opinion their crimes had been their own choice. No one forced them to do any of it. They had brought it all on themselves. They were psychopaths or sociopaths. But now here he was, sitting talking with an ex con in his own kitchen, one he knew should have been tried for numerous murders, but who had somehow escaped that official label. And he had no choice. No say in what was about to play out to its conclusion, good or bad.

'I always wondered?' Marti asked softly, the scar on his face twisting it slightly into a lopsided expression. 'What makes someone like you become a screw? You obviously have a modicum of intelligence, so why do you want to spend your working life around scumbags like me? Oh! Don't worry,' he laughed eerily, as he noticed Dan flinch at his self deprecating barb. 'I know what you people think of us, but remember, if we weren't here, you'd be out of a job. You'd probably be working as a shelf stacker somewhere.'

'Maybe gangsters like you fascinate me?' He relaxed into the chair, the Jack Daniels in the coffee kicking in. 'Anyway, I *was* a shelf stacker for a while. I worked as a Saturday boy in Woolies for years until I was seventeen. Then I got a job as a trainee Architect's Technician with the local council. Took me another few years before I moved into the Estates Department of the Prison Service then five years later I went Operational.'

'So you go from building things to what? Trying to rehabilitate thicko's like me that come from crappy rundown council housing estates where if you didn't steal or sell drugs you just became everybody's whipping boy?' Marti shook his head. 'Doesn't seem a logical route to me.'

'You might be a lot of things Marti, but thick isn't one of them. You're smart. You understand exactly what's going on here. I'd be surprised if you weren't working an angle yourself. That's what fascinated me most about working the Halls, walking the levels. I used to think clever prisoners like you and few others I could name were just lazy. You had all become crooks because it was an easy option. But I was wrong. You became crooks because you loved the buzz. Crime was your alcohol, pure and simple. You needed it to feel alive. You still do. Yes, there were the psychos like Tobin and Sinclair, but they were the exception.'

'I doubt you'd understand what drives me Dan, no matter how many cons you've talked to or analyzed in your own way. How can you, coming from this?' He swept his arm around the room followed by his gaze.

Dan laughed. 'You seem to think I'm hiding a silver spoon up my arse. I was dragged up on the same streets as you Marti. A council estate in a wee Ayrshire mining village that didn't have too many opportunities if like me, you were crap at football and liked to sit and read books. I only survived because I gave as good as I got with my fists and feet and got the fuck out of the place first chance I could.' Maybe it was the whiskey, or perhaps he was now just at the stage where he didn't give a damn anymore. Dan felt something build and push him close to breaking point. 'You know what annoyed me the most though? What always stuck in my craw? Even though you were in the nick, you probably still had more money and a better lifestyle waiting on the outside than I would ever have. I hated you all for that. I didn't pity you. I didn't envy you, I hated you.'

Marti stared at him unblinkingly, then touched his hand to his chest in a mock gesture of supplication. 'I'm hurt Dan, I truly am. And there was me thinking you did it from a sense of duty. You've disappointed me, you have.' He smirked. 'Now, let's go over everything one more time, okay?'

'I don't need another repeat. I know what I'm doing and if anything goes haywire, I'll deal with it.'

Marti was about to argue when his mobile rang. He took the call. 'Billy,' was all he said. 'Fine, I'll see you in half an hour.'

'Where do you have the mask?' Marti asked Dan.

'It's in my briefcase. That goes through the baggage x-ray, but I can't think of any other way of getting it into the prison.'

'What about the battery? Won't that trigger an alarm?'

'It's just a bog standard CR2032. We have plenty of them in the office, so I'll get the mask in without one installed and then fit it later.'

Marti nodded. 'What about leaving the jail? Don't you need

to pass through an x-ray machine?'

'Now what would be the point in that,' Dan said with exasperation. 'We're trying to stop stuff getting in, not out.'

'Okay, tell me again about Malone? Does he know what to do?'

The after effects of the Irish coffee were wearing off. Ogilvie was tired of the incessant questioning Galbraith had been putting him under.

'Look, I spoke to Malone the day before yesterday. He knows about the mask and how to fit and activate it. I've told him he needs to shave his head so it will fit. I've also told him exactly what he needs to do to make his way out of the prison and gone over it with him at least a dozen times. There is only one direction he can go that won't take him back into the jail. My voice has also 'gone.' I was rasping yesterday and nearly got sent home, but convinced them I'd be okay as Duty Manager today. If anyone asks where he's going, he's to make a steering wheel signal with both of his hands to show that he's going out to the car. He'll have my key vend password and I've told him which cabinet to put the keys in. The only thing I can't do is escort him out of the building, so let's give it a rest with the questions and I'll go and get ready!'

'All right,' Marti smiled. 'Don't want you getting too upset. You put your best suit on and I'll wait here for you until Billy arrives.'

Exactly thirty minutes later, Billy Jenkins pulled up in his silver Mercedes. He tooted the horn twice. A minute later, Marti and Dan walked out of the front door. Dan turned and locked it, then followed Marti to Billy's car.

'Right Dan,' Marti said. 'Same drill as before. We'll follow you at a safe distance and wait until you're in the prison. After that, it's up to you. Make sure Malone knows we'll meet him at the waste ground at the retail park just to the north of the prison. He can't miss it. He's to drive your car straight there. We'll park up somewhere outside the prison and wait for him...., you, to leave, and then follow. Oh, and Dan. We're patient, but I don't want to be sitting there all night. Get in and get him out by nine thirty. You said yourself that's when the jail goes into lockdown, so don't leave it too long to visit him. Okay?'

Ogilvie scowled and walked to his own Audi. As he sat in the driver's seat, a weariness overwhelmed him for some seconds. He could not help feeling this was all going to come down around his ears. They would catch Malone disguised as him, and realise he had to have been in on it. He felt like running, but with Marti and Billy trailing him, that wasn't possible. He started the car and moved off.

ΔΔΔ

Jack Malone paced edgily in the seven-point one square metre single cell he had been living in for over two weeks. When Dan Ogilvie had approached Jack and explained exactly what was being arranged, he had laughed in his face. He had heard nothing so Mission Impossible in his life. It was a fantasy. But then Ogilvie detailed the route he should take to walk to the Gate Building. He explained about the last three doors being remotely controlled and interlocked. Had explained the Key Vending room, where and how to replace the keys and what to do with the radio and officer alarm. He had given him his PIN number for the Key Cabinet and told him which two of the ten he could use. He would deliver the mask the day of the escape. Malone was to shave his head to get the best fit. He also mentioned the laryngitis, meaning Malone would have an excellent excuse not to speak when disguised as Ogilvie. His keys had to be returned to the cabinet. He could not take them out of the prison with him. They would trigger an alarm if he tried. He also needed the car park fob attached to Ogilvies car key's to get out through the final turnstiles and passed the main reception desk. And before he could do that, the prison keys had to be back in their safe.

Malone had sat there in his cell slack jawed, listening, as Ogilvie went through everything with him at least a dozen times. When he said Jack would need to hit him, take his clothes then truss him up in his bed to make it look like a real escape, he'd smiled. He didn't like the condescending prick, even if he was helping get him out, so that part would be a pleasure. Such was his vanity though he had not looked forward to shaving his head. This morning he had almost decided against it. But now, as he ran a hand over his shiny pate, he knew it would grow back so he would just need to keep on dyeing it as it did. Picking up the baseball cap lying on his worktop, he pulled it on.

He walked to his cell window. The clock on his TV read 20:30. The TV sat beside the small white kettle on the single worktop in his cell. The volume was down. Eastenders was about to start. It was the middle of summer, so there was still plenty of light. He saw a group of remand prisoners on one of the Five-a-side pitches, kicking a ball around. There weren't too many people left in the hall, most of them taking the chance of some late evening sunshine. But Ogilvie had warned Dan to stay put even if he was gasping for fresh air. Fifteen minutes later, Jack heard footsteps echoing along the association space. Someone at the Officers station cracked a joke. He heard distant laughter. His cell was at the far end of the level, near the large, grilled window with its panes of opaque, obscured glass. His cell door was open, and he turned, expecting Ogilvie. Instead, it was the figure of another inmate, one he didn't know. The man stood there in his grey jogging suit, arms by his side, hands in pockets, looking intently at Malone. He was younger than Jack by ten years at least, and fit. The scars on his face gave truth to the fact he was no stranger to violence.

Malone stared back, tilting his head slightly. 'Anything I can do for you pal?' he asked in as neutral a tone of voice as he could muster.

'You're Jack Malone, right? One of Domenico Rossi's boys?' It was a statement more than a question.

Malone tensed. What was this about, he wondered. 'You got me at a disadvantage pal, because I have no fucking idea who you are – or what you want.' Jack watched as the man standing in the doorway bristled. Perhaps he should have spoken a bit more gently. 'Sorry,' he said. 'Didn't mean to offend you, but I wasn't aware I knew anyone else in here. In fact, I don't think I've seen you before.'

'Oh, you don't know me Jack. We haven't met. I only arrived a couple of days ago. But I work for Ian Gilmour, well I do when I'm not stuck in places like this for knifing a scumbag dealer who couldn't pay his debts.' He grinned evilly. 'Still, at least I'm out of harm's way, eh!'

'You and me both.' Malone said, relaxing a little. 'I know Big Ian, and *Fat* Tony. He and my boss have done some business in the past. In fact, I was supposed to meet him the same morning I got banged up. What's your name?'

'It's Billy, Billy Nichol.'

'Well Billy, what can I do for you?' Malone looked at the watch on his wrist.

'Are you in a hurry to be somewhere else?' Nichol asked him, taking a step over the threshold into Malone's cell.

He eyed Nichol warily, and shook his head. 'Someone promised they'd pay me a visit. Just hoping they make it on time, that's all.'

'Hmm!' Nichol took another step into the cell.

'You know if the screws catch you in another cons cell, they'll strip any privileges you have. I wouldn't risk it if you will be here for a while.'

Malone watched as Nichol grinned again. 'That's okay Jack. I will be in here for a long time once they get me into a courtroom. Can't argue with the CCTV now, can I? Anyway, I'm just here to deliver a message from Big Ian.' His right hand started coming out of the pocket of his jogging bottoms, but before he got the knuckles past the open top, he was prodded hard in the back and took another step into the cell. Nichol swivelled around, about to lash out at whomever was behind him, but stopped quickly when he saw it was someone wearing a suit, a white shirt, and a tie.

'What the fuck are you doing in someone else's cell?' Dan Ogilvie glared at him, almost daring him to have a go. 'Get the fuck out of here and back to your own cave or I'll have you down the digger for the next two weeks.' Ogilvie went toe to toe with Nichol. 'And I'll make sure you're next to the dirty protest going on.' Dan stepped back and turned sideways in the doorway. Not much, but enough to let Nichol squeeze past him.

'Sorry boss,' he muttered, before glancing at Malone and moving back towards his own cell.

Ogilvie turned and watched him go. Then he directed his attention back at Malone. 'What was that about?'

Malone shrugged. 'Haven't a clue. First time I've seen him. And I thought you had lost your voice?'

Ogilvie appeared unconvinced, but walked into the cell and swung the door closed behind him. 'This'll need to be quick.' Ogilvie was carrying an orange internal mail envelope in his hand. He placed this on the bed. 'The mask is in there. My car keys are in my jacket pocket.'

Malone nodded. Both men undressed. They quickly swapped everything down to their underwear, including, watch, socks and shoes. Ogilvie had to help Malone with his belt and the pouch for his keys and keychain. Malone opened the envelope and took out the facemask. His shirt was undone down to the third button. He looked at the mask, uncertainty evident on his face.

'Don't worry,' Ogilvie tried to reassure him. 'I've seen one of these in action. It will work.'

Malone was unsure, but he realised he had little to lose. He pulled Ogilvies latex face over his head and down over his shoulders. Reaching behind him, he found the plastic stud and pressed. Immediately the mask tightened, small pulses of electricity running through its pseudo peripheral nervous system. He walked into the small toilet cum shower room and viewed the results in the shatter proof plastic mirror. His image was distorted, but it looked good to him. He was Dan Ogilvie. Doing up his shirt, he put on the tie, slipped on the shoes and then the jacket. Ogilvies name badge was on a lanyard and Jack slipped this over his head onto his neck. Ogilvie himself had already finished and was now wearing Malone's shirt, jeans and training shoes. Jack picked up the baseball cap that had fallen on the bed and handed it to Ogilvie, who looked at it disdainfully, then stuck it on his head. They eyed each other. Ogilvie nodded. He handed Malone the envelope.

'Just in case someone saw me carry it in here,' he replied to Malone's quizzical look. 'Now for the last bit,' he finished

Ogilvie sat on the edge of the bed, disorientated a little by his own face looking back at him. He was about to say 'take it easy,' but never got the chance. The punch to the primary pressure point of his left temple was much harder than Ogilvie expected but not as hard as Malone wanted. Ogilvie simply looked dazed, not unconscious. So Malone punched him again. He fell, face down onto the bed. If the second punch hadn't knocked him out, he would have been in agony from the hairline fracture he had suffered.

It surprised Malone just how calm he was. He had earlier pulled his quilt to the foot of the bed, and now lifted Ogilvies legs fully onto the mattress. Drawing the quilt up, he made sure Ogilvies left arm was bent at the elbow, positioned over the left side of his face. Satisfied anyone looking in from the door or through the spyhole would assume this was Malone, he stopped and adjusted his clothes. He tugged down his jacket, smoothed out the creases in his trousers and straightened his tie. Malone took a deep breath and walked out of the cell into the association space. He closed the door, but didn't lock it. He wasn't sure which key to use. Turning left, he moved tentatively towards the Officer's desk. This sat beyond the grille gates separating the Houseblock Core from the Cell Wings housing the inmates.

ΔΔΔ

Two cells along, Billy Nichol sat on the edge of his bed. Turning his head at the sound of footsteps, he watched as the screw who ordered him from Malone's cell passed his own open door. Nichol's wife had visited yesterday. Ian Gilmour had been to see her. He told her if Billy took a message and passed it on to some guy called Jack Malone who was also on remand, then she and their kids would be looked after while Billy was inside, which she knew would be a long time. Nichol recalled how she had twisted her wedding ring and glanced nervously around her, before leaning in over the clear glass table and whispering something to him. He had nodded grimly, but said little. As she stood to leave she turned and gave him the biggest, hardest hug he had ever had from her. Nichol smiled and told her she'd be all right. The loud crash of a door slamming into its metal frame broke into his thoughts. That would be the Manager leaving the level. Billy could now make his way back to Malone's cell and pass on Gilmour's regards. He stood, stretched, took a calming breath then walked out.

Turning right, he made his way along the wide corridor with its multiple shades of pastel colours, until he reached the emerald green door to Malone's cell. Shit, he thought. It was closed. If it were locked then he'd need to find another opportunity later. Glancing up and down the corridor, he saw the CCTV cameras in their metal encasements dotted around. He knew they covered everywhere and missed nothing, and he realised he would be recorded entering and leaving the cell. There was nothing he could do about that. All he could hope for was that no one was monitoring live images. Not that they could do much anyway. Everyone was too far away. Two of the seven officers on duty were at the main desk in the Core, both of them working at separate computers. The other five were outside with the remaining prisoners on exercise.

Nichol tried the handle of the cell door. It turned. With a gentle push, it opened on its pivot hinges then swung quietly into the cell. Malone lay face down on the bed, quilt cover up high, both arms outside of it, one down by his side, the other stretched over his head. He still wore his baseball cap. Nichol was surprised. A few moments before Malone had been wide awake and talking with Ogilvie. Maybe the screw had slipped him something he mused. Whatever, it would make this next part even easier. Nichol walked into the cell, closed the door as far as he could without engaging the lock, then walked to the foot of the bed. His right hand went to a pocket in his jogging bottoms and his fingers wrapped around the plastic toothbrush handles. As he took these out, a long piece of string like white material followed. The string was made from the stripped down fabric of a cotton shirt, wound and twisted together for strength, then tied to the toothbrush handles to form a crude but effective garrotte. The single use garrotte had been a long night in the making. He moved quickly to the top of the bed. With his left leg on the floor, he pressed his right knee into Malone's back between his shoulder blades, pinning him there. Malone remained still and quiet.

Grasping the handles of the garrotte in each hand, he crossed his arms left to right. In one smooth, fluid motion, the garrotte was pulled down across the front of Malone's face to his neck, and then pulled tight. Nichols knee pushed even harder into Malone's back and the effort of strangling him caused the unfortunate man's head to lift from the pillow. Billy kept pulling as hard as he could, staring at the back of his victims head. There was some thrashing, and death throe drumming of his feet, but no clawing at his neck. Jack Malone died quietly and with little fuss. After a few minutes, the drumming stopped. Nichol relaxed his grip and lifted his knee from his victims back. Malone's head fell face down onto the pillow, the brim of the baseball cap squashed against the hard latex of the pillow. Nichol looked around. The door was still shut. No one had seen anything. He pulled the quilt back up as far as he could to cover Malone's body, wrapped up the garrotte and placed it back in his pocket. That, thought Billy, was the easiest hit he had ever done, and inside a bloody prison.

As he left Malone's cell, he closed the door and went back to his own. Nothing else had changed. No one had been alerted.

Entering his own cell, he went into the en-suite toilet, took out the garrotte, placed each plastic handle against a corner edge of the toilet wall at the door frame, and snapped them into four smaller pieces. Placing them in the toilet bowl together with the string, he pressed the flush button. He was allowed four flushes every hour, but after the third, all evidence of the garrotte had vanished. Smiling to himself, he walked over to his bed and lay back, hands behind his head. He knew they would figure it out eventually, but he was going down for life anyway, so at least this way Gilmour would look after his family.

Job well done, he thought.

In his haste, he hadn't noticed the body on the bed had a full head of hair beneath the baseball cap, unlike the bald head of Jack Malone.

EIGHTEEN

Malone walked through the open metal gates, locked back one hundred and eighty degrees, flush with the fixed section of the grille. Moving slowly but steadily, he passed the control desk in the *core*, nodding to the one officer who looked up. She nodded back then returned to her computer. He stopped and placed the envelope he had been carrying on the Corian counter. The female officer looked up again. For a few seconds he felt the first signs of panic, but she smiled and took the envelope, placing it on the desk behind the counter. Malone nodded then walked off.

He walked calmly towards the exit door, fingering the bunch of keys in the pouch attached to his belt, his hand clamped around the token he would need to open the next two doors. On reaching the first he stopped. There was a flat, smooth plate attached to the lock with the symbol of a key printed on it. Malone took the key bunch from the pouch and held it to this symbol. Nothing happened. Then he noticed the token hanging down towards the bottom of the bunch. He adjusted his grip, bringing it closer to the symbol. There was a soft click. A small LED on the panel changed from red to green. Grasping the handle, he turned it anti-clockwise. It released from the keeper, and he gently pulled the metal security door open. His stomach flipped. Shit, this could work. The key bunch and attached chain he placed back in the leather pouch as Malone had instructed.

Once through the first door, he stood in the main stairwell, painted a utilitarian magnolia unlike the brighter colours on the wings. The lift was to his left and the stairs slightly beyond.

He decided on the stairs. His breathing quickened and his heart thumped, but the trudge down the four flights was uneventful. He passed no one until he reached the ground floor, Level One. As he stepped off the last stair tread, the door from the level opened and two officers walked out. The jolt of adrenaline caused Malone's heart rate to spike, but he realised it would have been impossible to leave without meeting someone. All he needed to remember was he had lost his voice. Both white shirted officers reached the door into the link corridor ahead of Malone. One looked older, more comfortable, more experienced. The other, had barely begun to shave. They turned and looked at him.

'Evening boss,' the older man said as he presented his token to the lock reader. 'Are you starting or finishing?'

Malone's eyes widened a little, but he kept his composure. Pointing to his throat he mouthed he had lost his voice then shrugged his shoulders.

'Dan, you need tucked up under a quilt nursing a hot toddy. What are you doing at work? Looks like you've put a wee bit of weight too,' he observed. He laughed and Malone smiled with him.

The mask had passed its first test. Someone who knew Ogilvie had seen it up close and made no comment about him looking strange. The officer opened the door. All three of them walked into the small, ten metre long stub corridor that butted onto the main spine corridor which ran nearly the length of the prison. When they reached the next door, the older officer stopped in front of the Videocom unit and pressed a button. Malone heard a soft ringing sound from the speaker as they waited on the officer in the Electronic Control Room answering.

'ECR. Please identify yourself?'

Formal, thought Malone.

'Hi there. It's Harry Gallagher with John Devine from Mungo Hall, and the Head of Ops, Mr Ogilvie.' Gallagher turned and looked at him.

There was no answer, but seconds later the lock on the door clicked quietly and Gallagher opened it into the main corridor. If he could follow these two all the way out of the prison, then his lost voice would make no difference.

'See you later boss. We're heading down to the digger.' He motioned towards the young officer. 'Mr Devine here has yet to encounter his first dirty protest, so I thought I'd do the honours.'

Gallagher turned left followed by Devine, who grimaced slightly, as they walked away. Damn, Jack thought. There goes my escort. He turned to his right and began the walk along the two hundred and fifty meter length of the main spine corridor. It was empty, but he knew the cameras dotted along its length would record every step he took.

ΔΔΔ

In the ECR, the electronic heart of the prison, three officers sat in comfortable and expensive chairs. They were nearing the end of their shift and if they were honest it had been a boring day. No officer alarms, no fights, no fire alarms, no false alarms, just vehicle after vehicle coming through the large, cavernous gates that could fit a full sized artic and trailer with two metres spare all around, enabling it to be searched. That, and opening and closing pedestrian and vehicle gates between zones had been the sum of their day. At least it was cool. The heat generated by the monitors and PC's meant it was one of the few places with its own air conditioning, something frowned upon everywhere else because of its environmental impact.

A bank of eight, sixty inch monitors were fixed to the wall in front of the control desk. From there, the Officers viewed everything in, out and around the prison. Each monitor was subdivided into twelve smaller virtual screens, displaying CCTV images from a variety of locations around the jail. The SCADA interface allowed either of the two operators to select and zoom in on any of the one thousand seven hundred odd cameras monitoring the lives of the establishment's population. At that minute, one sub monitor showed Malone, disguised as Ogilvie, walking up the main corridor towards the Facilities building.

'Hey Malky,' One of the Operators nudged his fellow officer in the arm. He nodded toward the screen. 'I've heard that bastard Ogilvie's supposed to have lost his voice. That true?'

'Seems so,' Malky replied. 'At least when I buzzed him through the doors on his way down, he just pointed to his throat and shook his head.'

'Well now, you know that's against our standard procedures, don't you Malky.'

'Douglas, just what the fuck are you planning?'

Douglas Renton smiled and rubbed his hands together. 'That arrogant bastard marked me down in my annual review at the end of March. Guess what for? Yep, not following procedures. Bumped me back six months on the pay scale meaning I get fuck all of an increment until September.' He looked over at Malky. 'So now I intend to follow all procedures to the letter.'

'Are you serious? He'll have your arse for this.'

'Tough. Unless he tailgates through with someone else, I'll have him standing there all night.' Renton reached forward to a control panel fixed to the desk. He knew exactly which door Ogilvie would need to get to before he had to use the Videocom. He brought up the image from the camera in the corridor overlooking the first of the final three doors out of the establishment and sent it to his desk monitor. Now, all he had to do was wait until Ogilvie got there, and hope, for a while at least, no one else wanted to use it. Given its location though, it was a busy door, so he guessed he would not have much time, but what the hell, anything to break the monotony.

ΔΔΔ

Malone kept walking. He went through another door in the spine corridor into the Facilities building. As he did so, a young officer passed him, followed by a group of others. Malone looked at them and resisted the urge to run back to his cell. Instead, he stood aside and politely allowed them all to pass him. When those at the rear noticed him, their pace increased, not wanting to hold him back. Malone was beginning to realise the amount of authority that came with being the Head of Operations in a prison.

'Thanks Sir,' a female officer about five-foot two high said as she wandered past him. He smiled back nervously, wondering how in the hell she managed to handle some of the apes he'd seen banged up? Once they had all moved on, he exhaled the breath he hadn't realised he had been holding. As the door closed behind him he walked further into the building across the linoleum covered concrete floor. The building was on two levels, the upper one accessed by two sets of stairs onto a balcony to his right. Malone had already passed the first set when he remembered the exit to the Gate building was via a bridge from next level up. Feeling foolish and nervous, he walked a little more urgently to the second set of stairs. He climbed these, turning back the way he had come until he reached the balcony then turned again to make his way towards the bridge. That door was some ten metres away and desperate as he was to get to it, he knew he dare not run. On reaching it, he opened it with the fob. Ogilvie had told him this was the last door where that would work. The next three would need calls to the ECR.

He walked across the bridge. The first of the three doors controlled by the ECR seemed to recede away from him. His mouth became dry. Time appeared to slow down. Each step felt like it took an eternity. He prayed no one would appear from the other side before he was through. His disguise had stood him well so far, but each time someone spoke with him, he expected them to reach out and rip the mask from his head. Even though the sun was setting, it was still warm, especially on the bridge above the sterile zone, which had glass on each side and no ventilation, and he now began to sweat beneath the latex. His skin itched, but he resisted the urge to scratch, instead using it as a spur to make him move faster.

ΔΔΔ

In the ECR, Douglas Renton watched the view from the cameras displayed on the large wall monitor tracking Ogilvie's movements across the bridge. That was strange, he thought.

'Malky, have a look at this. Do you think Ogilvie's walking a bit funny today?'

The other officer leaned over and watched the screen for a few seconds. 'He seems to have lost the slight limp he normally has from the old rugby injury.' He turned to Renton and shrugged. 'Maybe he's just having a good day.'

'But he's had that limp for as long as I can remember. I mean it's not too obvious, but if you watch him for a while you can usually pick it up.'

'Well, what do you want to do Douglas? Ask the guy who looks like the Head of Operations if he is the Head of Operations?'

Renton said nothing, but continued to watch the screen.

A few seconds later he transferred his attention to the smaller display on his desk. This was the door locking system monitor.

'Nearly there,' you bastard, he grinned to himself.

He saw Ogilvie reach the door, and watched him press the Videocom button. Instantly an alert came from the system and Ogilvie's image was displayed on the LCD screen.

Renton pushed a button on a desktop microphone. 'ECR. Please identify yourself?' he asked, trying his best to conceal his amusement.

The image of Ogilvie on the screen shook its head, pointed to its throat and mouthed something that looked like 'lost voice.' Renton grinned to himself, waited a few more seconds then pressed the microphone talk button again.

'Sorry, I didn't catch that. Can you please identify yourself?' He released the button.

'You're playing with fire Douglas,' Malky told him.

'It's alright. I'll let him through in a few minutes. Just want to see him get mad for a bit.'

Ogilvie gestured wildly at his throat and then towards the door. Renton was enjoying this, but on another monitor he noticed a figure walking towards the same door from the opposite side.

'Bollocks,' he said. 'It's the bloody Governor.' With a sigh, he pressed an icon on his touch screen and released the lock on the door.

ΔΔΔ

Malone heard a click. The butterflies in his stomach settled down a little. He had thought the prick in the ECR wasn't going to let him through. As he reached for the door handle though, it turned, and the door swung open toward Jack. He stepped back to avoid it hitting him. An Asian woman of medium height wearing a grey business trouser suit walked through and noticed him. The unbidden feeling of panic welled up again in his stomach. She looked at him. He nodded back. They stood for a few seconds staring at each other before she finally spoke.

'You not going the wrong way Dan?' she asked

Jack's eyes widened in surprise. He pointed to his throat and mouthed for what he imagined was the hundredth time that he had lost his voice. It was then his eyes noticed the name badge around her neck. This also displayed her title. The Governor.

'Oh, that's right. I forgot you said you were coming down with something. Have you seen a Doctor about that laryngitis?'

He shook his head and gave a little shrug as if to say; you try getting an emergency appointment with a doctor.

'Well,' she laughed. 'You'll not be much use doing a final evening walk round with me before I leave then, will you?'

Malone smiled.

'Best get back up to the office and grab yourself a lemsip or something.'

They both heard the soft sound of an alarm buzzing. 'Oops, looks like we've kept this door open too long. You better get out of here.'

Jack nodded and turned to walk away. Just then, one of the items of kit Ogilvie had given him clipped to his belt began to buzz and vibrate. The one the Governor carried did the same. It was the Officer Alarm. She looked down at hers. Jack quickly mimicked her actions.

'Shit,' she said. 'Looks like it's kicking off in the Mungo House exercise yard. Look, I'll get down there and see what's going on.' She looked up again at Jack.

Thinking on his feet, Jack pointed to himself and then back across the bridge in the general direction of the House blocks.

'No, that's okay. It'll probably be under control by the time I get there anyway. You head off and get yourself sorted.'

The open door alarm was still buzzing, so Jack moved off quickly and closed it behind him before the Governor could say anything else. Breathing a sigh of relief, he leaned against the door. He closed his eyes and tried to recall what Ogilvie had told him to do next. The Key Vending room, that was it. Return the alarm, radio and his key bunch. That should not be too difficult.

He was in a wide vestibule. There was a door to his left that led into the Visits area. He remembered this from his two trips there. Further along this small corridor there were five other doors. One led upstairs to the main office suite where Ogilvie worked, one allowed him to enter the Key Vend room and the other exit it, and one took him into the ECR. There was a fifth door that faced him. This was the way out. The route to freedom. He needed to be quick and look assured. Both this vestibule and the Key Vend room had CCTV coverage. He was so close now he could almost smell the fresh, outside air.

ΔΔΔ

In the ECR, Renton continued to watch Ogilvie as he stood in the vestibule. The guy just looks strange, he thought. There was something off about him. The lack of a slight limp yes, but he also seemed to carry himself differently today. Renton had spent the last three years working in the ECR. He knew everyone by sight. He knew their voices, was aware of their habits and could identify them by their walk alone. The problem was, he did look like Ogilvie. Based on the face alone, he was Ogilvie, so what the fuck, Douglas wondered, was niggling at him.

'Douglas, would get your head back in the game. There's a fucking riot going on down at Mungo Hall.'

Renton pulled himself away from watching Ogilvie and directed other officers from elsewhere in the prison towards the trouble.

ΔΔΔ

In the vestibule, Malone swiped his token against the Key Vend room reader and opened the door. Once inside, he paused to get his bearings. Ten lock cabinets were ranged around the two long walls. Another wall held charging racks for the Officer Alarm mobiles and the Radio batteries. Only two cabinets could receive Ogilvie's keys, numbers three and five. Each cabinet was identified by signage fixed to the wall above it. Malone walked over to them. There was a keypad attached to each cabinet. Number three looked to be full. There may have been the odd space, but it looked crammed with key bunches. He moved onto number five. This was more promising. Malone closed his eyes and tried to recall the code Ogilvie had given him. Six, one, four, nine. He keyed the sequence into the keypad. An LED on the panel flashed green and an alarm buzzer sounded. Ogilvie swiped his fob against the reader on the cabinet. He opened the door and looked for a flashing green light. Shit, he couldn't see one. His eyes moved quickly over the banks of keys already there. 'Come on,' he whispered. 'Come on.'

Just as he spotted it towards the bottom, the LED on the keypad turned red. Fuck. He closed the cabinet door, then keyed in the code again. Same procedure, but this time he had a better idea of where to look and found the flashing green light without too much trouble. Then he remembered. He had forgotten to unclip the key bunch from the chain on his belt. By the time he had done this, the green light had turned to red, again.

He puffed his cheeks and blew out a sigh. He tried again, and this time he inserted the two-inch long key bunch *bullet* into the correct slot in the cabinet. Straightening up, he turned and went to move toward the exit door when he remembered the radio and officer alarm mobiles. Looking at the racks, he walked over, took the alarm mobile and inserted it into a spare charging slot without any difficulty. The radio proved a little more awkward. He needed to remove the battery and place this in its charger then hang the handset on a wall rack. He fiddled with the back of the handset and eventually found the two buttons that would release the battery. This done, he put them in their racks and again moved towards the exit door.

ΔΔΔ

In the ECR, Renton watched Ogilvie on a monitor. He switched cameras to show the view inside the Key Vend room. This room was not normally under observation, but as he waited he saw Ogilvie acting like a probationer. There was no way it should have taken someone with his experience three attempts to insert their keys into the cabinet. Something was wrong, but he just couldn't put his finger on it. Renton had a strange feeling in his gut. Ogilvie just wasn't acting like Ogilvie.

'Malky, I'm going to pop out to the Key Vend for a minute, okay?'

'Douglas, if Ogilvie's there he'll have your balls on a sandwich for leaving the ECR.'

'Let me worry about Ogilvie. I won't be long.'

'You'd better not be. I'm still monitoring what's going on down at Mungo Hall and I can't do that and open doors at the same time.'

As Renton got up and moved to the exit from the ECR, a door open request came through from the Visit's side of the establishment. This was also covered by the three door rule. Renton's monitor had been set to view the Key Vend room but automatically switched to the Visit's door. Malky looked at Renton and shook his head. He leaned over the desk, looked at whose image was displayed on the monitor and hit the door unlock icon without asking for confirmation. Renton shook his own head and waited for Malky to unlock the ECR door for him.

'Don't be long,' Malky said as he pressed the door unlock icon.

Renton walked into the vestibule and across its width to the Key Vend. Using his fob, he swiped and unlocked the door. Ogilvie was standing at the exit door gripping the handle, but he looked around quickly, seemingly surprised by Renton's sudden appearance. The officer stared at Malone disguised as Ogilvie, his eyes moving up and down, taking in everything about him.

'Mr Ogilvie,' Renton said. 'Seems you were having a wee bit of trouble with cabinets. Anything wrong?' He indicated to the cabinet with his head.

He watched calmly as Ogilvie looked at him, appearing uncertain for a few seconds, before he shook his head.

'Hmm! I was also wondering what had happened to that limp of yours. I mean, it's hard to see sometimes, unless you know what you're looking for. Have you been having some physio or something?'

He waited, but Ogilvie simply pointed to his throat instead.

'Oh, that's right. I heard you had a sore throat. Convenient eh?' He walked slowly towards him watching as Ogilvies eyes flicked around, like a man seeking an escape route he thought. As Renton continued to look at him, he saw little details that did not look right. His suit trousers were a bit too tight on his waist. They also seemed a tad too short, not much, but Ogilvie usually had his covering the tops of his shoes. These sat just above. And he looked as if he had gained some weight, just a few pounds, the jacket tighter than he had expected. But the face? It was Ogilvie, of that there was no doubt. So why did he feel something was amiss, just slightly? Shit. Perhaps he *was* simply imagining things, because neither he nor Ogilvie particularly liked each other. Bugger it he thought.

'No problem Sir. I was just concerned you were having some issues with the cabinets, that's all. I'll get back to work now.'

Renton walked over to Ogilvie. He had to pass him to get to the exit. As he reached him, Ogilvie stretched to hit the green 'Request to Exit' button. As he did so, his jacket and shirt sleeves rode up slightly. It was then Renton noticed the tattoo. It began at the wrist and disappeared inside the shirt sleeve. When did Ogilvie get a tattoo he wondered? He looked up at his boss. Then he saw it. His eyes. They were the wrong colour. They should be blue, but instead he was staring at a pair of bright green pupils. The surprise appeared undisguised on his face.

'What......,' was all he could mouth, before a fist struck him hard in the solar plexus, knocking the wind from him. He doubled over and took a step backwards, clutching his midriff. As he did so, he caught a glimpse of a knee rising to meet his chin, which it did with a crack. Falling back, he slammed his head against the worktop holding the battery charging racks, knocking a few of them to the floor. That was the last thing he remembered until he came to in hospital the next day.

ΔΔΔ

Malone breathed heavily. This was not going well. This little prick had somehow become suspicious of him. He had to get out of here quickly, before someone came in and found the officer lying unconscious. The exit door had auto locked after a few seconds. He hit the RTE again and pulled the door open, just enough to allow himself through, making sure he shut it tightly behind him. The vestibule was clear.

Moving to the next door, the second of the three final ones, he tried to compose himself before pressing the Videocom button. He expected a voice to ask him for his name and prepared to give the 'can't speak' gesture, but a soft click told him the door had unlocked. He opened it and walked through, then stopped. Shit, the entire space he stepped into was filled with officers. What the fuck were they doing here? It was a few seconds before he realised this had to be part of the shift change. The few he had seen in the Facilities building corridor had arrived early. As he stood there, people closest to the door turned to look at him but none of them attempted to go through the door he had just used. Seems they weren't that keen to get to their work. He smiled benignly and mouthed again about his voice, all the while pointing to his throat. There were a few return nods, mainly from younger members of staff, who moved aside for him. The old hands simply looked at him then resumed their conversations, otherwise ignoring him. He threaded his way through the throng and reached his destination; the last door. After that, he would be free.

He was about to push the call button, when that door opened and more officers entered the *crush hall,* waiting to begin their shift. Malone grabbed the door as it closed, and made his way through into the main public reception area of the building. So much for no tail gating, he thought. His mind was racing and his heart hammered out the staccato of a woodpecker. He knew once the first of this group reached the Key Vend to collect their keys, they would discover the unconscious officer. Then he guessed the prison would go on lockdown.

In front of him was a waist high, tripod style turnstile. He moved up against it but it refused to budge, despite his pushing. An officer on duty at the reception desk looked his way with a frown. Malone's anxiety was growing. Then he remembered the other token, the car park fob. He quickly reached into the leather pouch and pulled out the key chain, but there was no fob, nothing to open the turnstile with. He again panicked and patted the jacket pockets. He felt the rattle of the car keys. Taking them out he was relieved to find there was a token attached to them. Malone held this against the reader on the turnstile. The lights on the centre housing blinked green. He gently pushed his way through, then turned and gave the desk officer a smile and a shake of his head to show how stupid he was. The officer nodded, but Malone noticed him watching him closely as he made his way through the sliding front doors of the prison.

He concentrated hard on slowing himself down. Walk, don't run, he repeated. He had made it. He had fucking made it. Dom's crazy plan had worked. Now all he had to do was find Ogilvie's car and head straight to the pickup point. He held the car keys in his hand and walked in the twilight to the general area where Ogilvie had told him his car was parked. He kept pressing the open button. Eventually he saw some lights flash on an Audi A4 at the end of the row. Walking quickly to the car, he got in, started the engine and began to drive. To get to the exit, he had to pass close to the main entrance again. As he drove he noticed some kind of commotion. White shirted officers streamed out of the building. They began gesturing looking around the car park. He drove past them slowly, not daring to catch anyone's eye. Looking in his rear-view mirror, he saw one of them shout something and point to the car he was driving. Then he started running after him, but Malone sped up and exited the car park, only slowing down for the barrier to rise.

He turned left, as Ogilvie had instructed him to, not right which would have taken him to the M8, the most obvious escape route. This would take him to Springburn. He had been instructed to pull into some waste ground about two miles along this route and wait. He was on a high now, giddy with adrenaline. He failed to notice the other car pull out from where it was parked and start to follow. Behind him he heard and saw – nothing. It would take time for the prison to alert the police and brief them, so Malone knew he was home and dry. He found the waste ground and parked up, switching off his lights but keeping the engine running so the a/c would work to combat the humidity in the air. A few moments later another car joined him.

Billy Jenkins climbed out of the passenger seat and walked over to Malone. He opened the driver's door, then stepped back for a second, surprise on his face. Malone wondered what the problem was, then he remembered he was still wearing the mask. He had become so damned used to it he had forgotten. Reaching behind his neck he found and depressed the button. Immediately, the mask lost its shape. Jack reached up, grabbed the hair and pulled it off. He looked up at Billy and smiled.

Jenkins glared back at him. 'Make sure you get a hair transplant when you're older Jack. You look fucking stupid as a baldy.'

'Aye, and I love you to, ya prick.' He got out of the car and stood for a few seconds, breathing in the warm night air. He turned and looked behind him. A helicopter now hovered over the prison, its searchlights panning back and forth even though it was still light, no doubt its infrared capabilities turned up to maximum. 'Let's get out of here,' he said to Billy. Malone smiled at nothing in particular. This was the best day of his life. He had put one over on the establishment and after he sorted Dom's accounts out, he would disappear to some millionaire's playground on the other side of the world.

He fingered the mask. He might even keep this Dan Ogilvie persona alive.

Yes, that would be fun.

NINETEEN

Dom sat in the living room of his Villa cradling a glass of Glenmorangie over ice. Whisky purists would have decried the sacrilege. Water should be the only accompaniment. At twenty four degrees though, it was too warm for just water. Apart from a ceiling fan and a Dyson free-standing unit, there was nothing to temper the air in the room. He wore a pair of light grey chinos and a cheap t-shirt someone had once bought him as a Christmas present. On his feet, he had a pair of dark blue, leather slippers. Shit he thought, get me a pipe and I'll become my grandfather. It had just gone one in the morning. Malone had arrived earlier with Marti and Billy. He was smiling, talking away like a demented budgie. Marti looked as though he wanted to deck Malone just to get him to shut up. When Jack had noticed Dom standing in the hallway he smiled and walked over to him, clasping him in a bear hug, thanking him profusely. Dom did not return the hug. Malone stepped back and nodded knowingly. He looked behind Dom and noticed Cassie standing there. He even smiled at her and mouthed thank you. Billy and Marti squeezed passed with a glance at Dom and went into the kitchen to get themselves something to drink.

Fifteen minutes was all it took. Fifteen minutes for Malone to log into the system and change the master password to one Dom gave him. When it came to the part where the software asked him to scan his iris, he slowly turned, pushed his chair back a little from the screen and held out his hand inviting Dom to step forward. As Cassie watched, Rossi placed his right eye in front of the scanner and waited whilst the low-powered laser digitally scanned his unique eye pattern. The software asked him to do this twice more as verification, and after a few minutes, control of the system was his alone. Finished, he asked Malone to go sit with Billy and Marti then logged back into the system with Cassie standing behind him. He realised he would need someone as a backup for emergencies, and he knew it would likely be her. It was time for her to move up.

Navigating to the bank accounts of the three legitimate property consultancy companies he had set up, he confirmed Gilmour had delivered. The full twelve million was there. 'So, he wants me to think this is still on track,' he said to Cassie, some relief evident in his voice.

'Looks like it,' she replied.

He had looked at his watch. Eleven fifty five. Five minutes to spare before the system would have been locked. After midnight, new deposits would have been impossible. After midnight payments would have been impossible. Five minutes! That was how close he had come to losing all he had. All because he had stupidly trusted the one person he thought he knew.

'Cassie, I want you to do something.'

'Name it.'

'I want you to trawl through as much of the system as you can tonight. I need to know the how, why, when and where of every transaction we carry out on a regular basis. Which accounts we pay money into, how much and how often, who we bribe, who we blackmail. When do we pay them off, that type of thing.'

Cassie looked at Dom. 'Are you trying to set me up as your banker or something?'

'Cassie, I need someone I can trust to run all this for me.' He waved his arm at the computers, as though he could visualise the money they represented. 'I trusted Malone once and look where that got me. But you've proven yourself to me repeatedly and asked for nothing in return. Find out as much as you can before tomorrow and then we'll talk about a more permanent arrangement. It's time you moved up from running brothels. In fact it's time we both moved on from that.'

'You're thinking of selling up?'

'Yes. I have been for a while now.'

She nodded. 'Okay then. I'll see what I can figure out.'

Dom logged out of the system then watched as she accessed it with her own credentials, much more restrictive than his own.

Now, as he sat in the darkness of his living room, he swore he would only ever fully trust himself again. But Cassie was the next thing to family for him and he couldn't run things on his own. He had to let go a little, he realised. But Malone had let him down badly. Antonio Barrera had tried to destroy his business and Ian Gilmour? Well, Gilmour betrayal's was the worst of all. He had betrayed Dom's father and had him killed. He had betrayed Eamon O'Boyle by killing his son then doing business with him as if nothing had happened. But worst of all, he had betrayed Dom by trying to do a deal with Barrera to make sure Rossi was taken out of the equation for future imports, something that would have killed his business as much as Malone's betrayal.

Dom swirled the amber liquid and the quickly melting ice, around in his glass. Marti and Billy had finished their drinks and left soon after with a drunken Malone in tow, the best part of Dom's drinks cabinet inside him. Marti had been told to get him to one of the safe houses and make sure he stayed there until Rossi decided what to do with him. He served no useful purpose anymore. In fact, he was a liability and would need 'taken care of.' He knew too much about Rossi's business to fall into the hands of the police again. Dom would have only a day at most, before the cops knocked on his door asking all sorts of questions about the last time he had seen Malone and if he knew where he was. Sammy McGovern, one of the best hi-tech forgers in the country had already created a fake passport in another name for him, but Dom was in two minds about using it. It had just gone three thirty in the morning though, and there was little else he could do right now. Cassie had finished her trawl through the system, She needed time to compile the results, and was in her office catching up on that and what had happened at the brothels. But not before she had rung Gabby and informed her their plan had been successful. Dom would make sure a sizable sum of money found its way to the girl soon.

He took another sip of his whisky; his third of the night. He didn't drink much and its effects were beginning to tell. A feeling of calm contentment drifted over him. Home poured measures were always larger than those in pubs. Bringing down Ian Gilmour was his next task. And that needed some subtle handling. He somehow had to deliver Gilmour to Carlos Barrera for suitable punishment. Dom knew Gilmour's demise would not be swift, but both he and Gabby had a stake in extracting some kind of revenge from him for the deaths of both their fathers. He wanted to be there to confront him. He was sure Gabby did too, but he couldn't risk that. There was also O'Boyle to consider. Dom was certain O'Boyle was putting up a large part of the funding for this shipment.

He wondered why he had not come directly to Dom, instead of letting Gilmour run with it? It was probably Tony Smith's idea, and given what he knew about Ian's operations, there was no way in hell he could come up with another twenty two million as his part of the payment. No, O'Boyle had to be the major partner in this. He needed to get O'Boyle fully on his side. To do that he would need concrete evidence of Gilmour's involvement and he would also need to 'give up' his father as being one of the two hit men who had taken out O'Boyle's son. With his father already dead, O'Boyle could do nothing against him, but Dom had some worries he might be the eye for an eye sort and reciprocate by taking Dom out. Although with Gilmour involved and still alive, it was more than likely he would go after him, - he hoped. The best means of exposing Gilmour was Poirot style, with everyone in the same room at the same time. Gabby already knew about Gilmour's part in her father's death, which just left Eamon for his son and Carlos for his brother. Dom knew getting Carlos to fly the Atlantic had not been difficult after Miguel convinced him he would deliver his brother's killer into his hands.

Dom sighed and drained his glass, placing the empty tumbler on the table beside his chair. By nature he wasn't a born manipulator. He had read Machiavelli once, well a few chapters, but wheeling and dealing and double crossing had all seemed just too much hard work. He had built his reputation on straight talking. Tell me what you want, I'll tell you what it will cost and we'll go from there. That had been his resendetre for years. Now, he was having to plot and scheme; something new to him. But if he was going to survive and come out the other side, he had no option. He needed to become good at it, quickly.

A gentle rap on the living room door brought Dom from his reverie. For a second he wondered who it was, before remembering Cassie was still in the Villa.

'Come in Cassie its open.'

The door edged open a little and Cassie's head appeared around it.

'Dom, sorry to interrupt but I've just seen something on the news you need to hear.' There was an edge to her voice, an urgency Dom rarely heard.

'Which channel?' he asked as he walked across to a table on the opposite side of the room. He picked a remote control, turned towards the original fireplace and aimed it at the sixty inch Panasonic LCD hung on the wall above it.

'Any UK news channel,' she said walking further into the room. 'They're all carrying it.'

Dom looked at her. 'It's on every channel?'

She nodded and chewed her bottom lip.

Rossi quickly scrolled to the news channels and went to the BBC. He listened with Cassie for the next few minutes while the newsreader and the reporter standing outside HMP Glasgow detailed what they had been told of the night's happenings.

'Shit.' He shook his head. Just what the fuck was going on? He threw the remote control back on to the table. 'Cassie, phone Marti. Find out which flat he's in.'

She nodded.

Ten minutes later they were in Dom's BMW travelling fast into the city centre. After his three large double whiskies, Cassie was driving. Malone was in a building close to the Broomielaw and the Riverboat Casino, where all of these problems had started nearly three weeks before. Arriving, he buzzed the flat number. Marti let Cassie and himself in. They climbed the stairs and when they reached the front door it was already open. Billy stood there in the hall, drying his hands on a towel, waiting expectantly. Dom raised an eyebrow.

'Marti called and asked if I would come over.' Billy said. He paused for a second. 'In case you have something in mind for Malone.'

Dom said nothing and looked at Marti who stood further along the hallway, just outside a closed door. He indicated to it with a nod of his head and Dom walked over. Opening the door without knocking he went in and switched on the lights. Malone laid spread eagled; face down across the bed, fully clothed in Ogilvie's suit. He would still be drunk, but Dom needed answers. The mask was on a nightstand beside the bed. Dom walked over, grabbed Malone by the shoulders and shook him hard, his head bouncing and flopping with no resistance.

'Jack, wake the fuck up.'

Malone grunted and after a few seconds came to. Dom let go and Malone rolled over in bed onto his back. 'Wha........, what the hell?' he slurred.

'Get up Jack, now. Get out of bed. We need to talk.'

Malone propped himself up on his elbows and looked at Dom, drunken confusion in his bloodshot eyes, trying to register where he was.

'Jack.....?' Dom said.

It was more a threat than a question. Malone gave his head a shake and brought Dom's face into focus. 'Is it morning already?' he asked, still unsure as to why he was being woken.

'No it isn't. Now get up and get some coffee. You have a hell of a lot of explaining to do.' He stormed from the bedroom and walked through into the tastefully furnished living room. Cassie was already there, standing expectantly by the fireplace. Marti still stood in the hallway, and looked at Dom as he walked past.

Do we have a problem boss?' he asked, coming to join him.

Dom glared at him, his face set in a grim mask. 'Get some coffee ready to pour into that arsehole, Marti. If he doesn't give me the right answers then you'll be taking him for a swim in Loch Lomond.'

Marti nodded, knowing better than to ask anything else.

A few minutes later Rossi grimaced as he heard the sound of retching coming from the bathroom. Malone eventually stumbled into the living room, wiping his mouth on the back of his hand, his hair tousled and clothes rumpled. He stopped just as he came over the threshold, his eyes moving between Dom and Cassie. He looked around and saw Billy standing there, leaning against the fireplace.

Dom stared at him for a second. 'Sit,' he instructed.

Malone went to the couch and sat on the edge of the seat, his hands clasped tightly in front of him. He looked again at Dom. 'What's all this about? You've got control of your accounts, so what's the problem.'

Marti appeared with a steaming mug of black coffee and handed it to Malone who sipped on it tentatively.

Rossi said nothing. Instead, he picked up a TV remote from the mantelpiece and switched on the television sitting in one corner of the room. 'Watch and listen,' he hissed.

Dom eyed Malone. The reporter he had seen earlier re-appeared. He was on a loop, which meant there was nothing new to report. Malone began shaking his head.

'I.........I don't understand. He's saying a Prison Governor is dead. What's that got to do with me.'

Dom shook his head. 'Jack are you trying to tell me on the

night you pull off the great fucking escape, it's a co-incidence the Prison Governor is found dead in their jail?'

Jack was confused. 'But I only met the Governor for a few seconds waiting to go out one of the doors. When I left her she was on her way to deal with a riot.' He looked at Dom, realization dawning. 'Wait a minute,' he said standing up. 'You think I had something to do with her death. That's crazy.'

'Jack, did anybody suspect you on the way out.'

Malone nodded. 'There was one guy, an officer in the Control Room. He came into the Key room just as I was leaving, but I decked him and left him unconscious. He certainly wasn't the Governor.'

Cassie was still standing at the fireplace and was scrolling through her mobile. 'Dom, it wasn't the Governor who died.' She looked up. 'They're all called Governor's above a certain level.'

'Then who was it Cassie?'

She glanced at Malone and then walked over to Dom. She held out her phone and he took it, scrolling through the information on the screen. The printed media were ahead of the TV for once.

'Fuck.' He looked at Malone. 'It wasn't the officer you decked who died.'

'No,' Malone replied, seemingly relieved. 'Or the Governor?'

Dom shook his head. 'It was the Duty Governor.' He walked towards Malone.

Malone shrugged. 'So who the hell is the Duty Governor?'

'Who the fuck do you think he is Jack? Who set all this up on the inside so you could escape?'

He shook his head, eyes wide. 'Ogilvie! But it can't be. Ogilvie was alive in my cell when I left. He was unconscious, but he was breathing. He was lying face down on the bed. I made sure of it.'

'You made sure of something, that's for sure.' Dom snarled

'Dom, I swear to God he was alive when I left.' Malone looked around frantically. 'How did he die?'

Dom glanced back at the phone. 'Sources say he was strangled. Garrotted in fact.'

'Why? And where would I get a garrotte? This doesn't make any sense, none of it.'

Dom looked at Cassie who shrugged. 'He's right Dom. Why would he strangle Ogilvie? We had enough on him to ruin his life anyway. There would be no point in Malone attracting that kind of attention.'

'And yet they're saying this is all to do with an elaborate escape plan, so the authorities seem to be reaching the same conclusion.'

Cassie shook her head. 'I don't buy it. All Ogilvie had to do was lie there with a few cuts and bruises and pretend he had been overpowered. I know there wouldn't be any way he could explain away the mask, but he didn't need to. He had been told to say nothing about it.'

Dom closed his eyes and breathed deeply. When he opened them he again looked at Malone who had sat back down, still on the edge of the couch. 'Alright Jack. Tell me everything that happened from before Ogilvie arrived at your cell until you left it.'

Malone looked over at the TV. Dom turned the volume down as Jack composed himself, then listened as he described Ogilvies arrival, the swapping of the clothes the wearing of the mask, hitting Ogilvie, everything.

'Wait a minute,' he said. 'Who's this guy Nichol?' Dom looked at Marti and then Billy, who now stood in the doorway from the hall into the living room.

'Nichol,' Marti said. 'I know that name.' He looked at Billy. 'Isn't there a Nichol that works for Gilmour as an enforcer? He used to be part of the Clydeside gang before they were all sent down. Bit of a brainless thug. He got arrested a few months ago for knifing a dealer over in Paisley and left his prints and DNA all over the shop.'

Billy shrugged. 'I've lost track of who works for who these days.' He looked at Dom and smiled grimly. 'That's what happens when you have a quiet life.'

'What exactly did he say to you?' Dom again asked Malone.'

Malone thought for a second or two. 'It was something along the lines of Gilmour sending his regards. Come to think of it, it did seem a bit strange. He had this weird expression on his face.'

'But he left when Ogilvie arrived?'

Malone nodded. Dom and Cassie looked at each other.

'So,' Cassie said to Malone. 'When you left the cell disguised as Ogilvie, this guy Nichol had no idea you had swapped places.'

Malone shook his head. 'No he didn't. He couldn't have. The cell door was closed when we did the switch.'

'And did you pass his cell when you walked out?'

Malone shrugged. 'Probably. Mine was the last one on the wing, so yes, I must have.'

'Okay,' Dom said. 'But if Nichol saw you leave, he would have thought it was Ogilvie and that you were still your cell.'

Malone screwed up his face. 'What are you saying? Nichol went back into my cell and killed Ogilvie?'

'Yes, but he thought he was strangling you.'

'Me! Now who the fuck would want to strangle me?'

'You mean apart from any one of us? I'll tell you who. Gilmour.' He could see they were looking at him, unconvinced. 'Think about it. He's already tried to kill you once, or have you forgotten that's why you were there in the first place.'

Malone stared at the floor. 'Dom's right.' He looked at Cassie. 'That night in the casino. Tony Smith was there. I'd avoided him all night, but he eventually cornered me.' He turned to look at Dom, but quickly lowered his gaze again. 'He offered me a deal. He said if I came over to Gilmour he would make it worthwhile.' He shook his head frantically. 'I turned him down Dom, honest.'

Rossi said nothing.

'So what do we do now,' Cassie asked. 'If Jack's murder has gone tit's up, then the cops will be rounding up every known gangster in Scotland. They aren't going to let this go. Fuck, it might have been better if it had been Jack,' she said glaring at him.

Malone scowled but said nothing.

Dom slowly shook his head. 'This is a right fucking mess.'

Cassie yawned, reminding Dom how hard he had been driving her.

'Billy, Cassie. I want a word with you two in private.' They walked into the hallway and Dom closed the door.

'Cassie, you're tired. Billy will drop you off at your flat. No arguments.' She nodded too weary to resist. Dom turned to Billy. 'I need you to get some other things.' Then he outlined them in detail.

Once they had left, Dom came back into the living room. Malone sat shaking, holding his bald head in his hands. He looked up at Rossi. 'Dom, I'm sorry about all this. I didn't mean any of it.'

Dom crouched and patted him on the knee. 'Don't worry Jack. We'll take care of you, Marti and me.' He looked up at Galbraith who stood in the doorway. 'Maybe there is a way Marti,' he said, as if something had just occurred to him. 'You know that estate we invested in up north? The one with the big house, out in the middle of nowhere?'

Marti eyed Dom steadily. 'Yes boss. The one we get away to three or four times every year.' he replied.

He turned to Malone. 'You know the one Jack? Up near Torridon.'

Malone nodded. 'Yeh, I know it. Fucking sheep and heather and bugger all else.'

'But it's ideal Jack. Stuck up in the arse end of beyond. The lodge is empty right now. Nobody knows you up there and I doubt they've even heard about the jailbreak, and if they have they won't be bothered either way.'

Malone looked unconvinced. His gaze switched between Dom and Marti. 'Will I be up there on my own?' He shook his head. 'I'm not sure I could stand that. Too much isolation.'

Dom grinned at him. 'I know what you mean. Tell you what, I could arrange to have a few of the girls sent up to keep you company and attend to your 'needs'.'

'Really?'

'Really Jack. They'll be on my payroll so nothing to worry about in that respect.'

Malone still looked unconvinced. 'Can I think about it?' he asked hopefully.

Dom shook his head. 'Sorry Jack, we need to do this tonight. Billy's going to be back soon. Him and Marti will both drive you up there. It'll take me a couple of days to get you some girls, I mean I know you like the younger ones.' He smiled at Malone and raised his eyebrows. 'But at least you'll have the place to yourself for a while, and you can go outside in the grounds. Nice countryside up there. Good for walking off some of that weight you've put on.'

Malone grunted. 'Oh yeah, you can just see me as part of the huntin' shootin', fishin' set can't you?' He sighed heavily. 'Anyway, you seem to have made up your mind.'

'Good man Jack. It's better this way.'

Dom stood and waited until Malone extricated himself from the chair. He swayed a little, still intoxicated from what he had consumed. Rossi held out his hand towards him. Malone looked at it, confusion on his face, but then reached out and clasped it. Dom gripped him hard.

'There is something that's been bothering me Jack. Why? Why set it up so if you dropped dead then everything I'd ever worked for would have been lost?' Dom watched as Malone looked down at his hand and tried to pull it away, but he held it tightly.

Malone gulped. 'I,...... I don't know. I suppose I'm just a greedy, suspicious bastard and I was worried one day you'd decide to get rid of me.'

'And why would I do that Jack?' Dom shook his head slightly. 'Have you ever given me any reason to?'

'No,' Jack replied, his voice a whisper. 'But I was worried

you'd find out about all the money I was siphoning off into my own accounts. Not much from each transaction, but it all began to add up and over the years it must have come to a couple of million.'

Dom looked puzzled. 'Didn't I pay you enough? Even with your lifestyle and your gambling debts, you got enough from me for two lifetimes.'

Malone shrugged. 'I'm greedy.'

'Jack, I knew you were skimming. I'd have expected nothing less of you.'

Malone said nothing, he simply stood there shuffling uncomfortably on his feet and trying to ignore the pressure from Dom's hand shake.

Dom looked at him unblinking for a minute, then let go of Malone's hand. He stepped back slightly. 'Get anything from the bedroom that's yours Jack, including the mask and then wait for Marti. When Billy arrives you go straight to the car and do what the guys tell you. Goodbye Jack' He indicated with a nod of his head for Malone to move off.

Malone squeezed past Marti and went into the bedroom. Dom walked over to the fireplace and turned to beckon Marti over. He came and stood beside him.

'Billy will bring everything you need with him. Make sure it happens somewhere quiet. I want him to stay hidden forever.'

Marti nodded. 'Consider it done Dom.'

TWENTY

Every crook, from Cain onwards, had their safe haven, the one place they called home, where they held court surrounded by their lieutenants. A place where they meted out punishment. Ian Gilmour's was a farm on the north side of Glasgow near Killearn, halfway to the Trossachs. And today was punishment day, except he had no one to physically hurt. The news had trickled down about the botched hit on Jack Malone, Rossi's bagman. Not that he had any qualms or conscience about one less screw in the world, but Ogilvie had not been the intended target. Billy Nichol had messed up big time. When the bizzies figured out Billy had killed Ogilvie, there was no way he was getting out anytime in the next forty years. And there was equally no way Ian could physically get to him. There were no bones he could break. He had promised Nichol's wife she'd be looked after, but that was off the table. And to cap it all, that fucker Malone had somehow escaped from prison.

His trip to see Eamon O'Boyle had gone well. The Mancunian was still on board, but then word from Spain had reached him. Antonio Barrera was dead! His sleep had been fitful, disturbed by nightmares of the entire fucking Universe conspiring against him. When he had first spoken with Antonio in Amsterdam and put his proposal to him, the drugs kingpin hadn't taken long to see the obvious economic advantage of cutting out an expensive middleman in Domenico Rossi. Getting hold of Rossi's route into the country would give them a monopoly on supply. His problem was, he needed Rossi's contacts, his routes, the how and why of his success. Getting that was a priority before he made Rossi an offer he couldn't refuse, or simply *disappeared* him. But he had to weaken Rossi. Malone was the keystone in their organisation. Take him out and the arch would come tumbling down.

Dom's management team was too tight, too controlled, too dependent on each other. That was Rossi's problem. Dom and this Cassie bird earned the cash and Malone filtered it through the businesses they owned. If Dom needed to spend time doing the filtering himself, it meant he had less time to run other aspects of his organisation. So Ian was setting it up in a way that would let him pounce when the time was right. But with Malone's apparent escape from prison, the confusion he sought was not going to be so easy to accomplish.

He had also talked O'Boyle into the scheme. Eamon would be the English side of the business. He would have sole distribution rights south of the border. But with Ian importing for both of them, he would not have to pay Rossi's exorbitant arrangement fees, meaning they could make more profit all round. The plan had been,...... the plan still was, to get Rossi to organise this last run. With Gabby on the inside, she would feed him the information on contacts, shipment routes, deals and the backhanders Dom made, so when the time was right, he could start operating and dealing directly with the Barrera cartel himself. So far, she had proven her worth, with details about Dom's trip to Spain. Except now with Antonio's untimely murder, he needed to re-evaluate his entire plan.

He had been contacted earlier by Miguel Orejuela. Ian had never heard of him. Antonio had not mentioned his name, but he said he knew Antonio and better still his brother Carlos and had been asked to contact Gilmour and reassure him their agreement was still alive – even if Antonio wasn't. Ian had been wary, but he had to get this deal done. He had already invested twelve million of his hard earned pounds in it and was on the hook for a hell of a lot more with O'Boyle. He had originally given Rossi a target of six months to get the shipment organised, but that was on the basis of being able to take over Rossi's business intact and getting the Barrera's to work exclusively with him. With Malone free and Antonio dead, he had to think about how he could take this forward. It was beginning to give him a headache.

He sat in the living room of the old farmhouse. There was a stone floor with an inglenook fireplace set into the main wall. A leather three piece burnt red Chesterfield and mahogany coffee table were the main furniture in the room. An untouched mug of coffee and his mobile phone sat on the table. Seasoned logs lay in the hearth, unlit now because of the summer heat. Some of his associates found this side of his life a bit strange, if not sad. But Ian had grown up on the far edges of Castlemilk, almost in the country. He had spent hours as a kid wandering the hills between Castlemilk and East Kilbride, talking to the occasional farmer he met, getting rides on some of the old farm horses, the Clydesdales. He sometimes snuck off school at calving time and helped out where he could, fascinated by this life so different from everything his family knew in the city. That had all changed when puberty hit with a vengeance and girls had become more attractive than herds of cattle. Plus, the excitement of becoming a small time and then a bigger time crook had kept him away from the life. But he had never forgotten it. So when he had become rich enough, he set himself up as a fake country squire. Well, he'd argued when anyone asked, everyone needed a hobby. He looked up as Andy Taggart, one of his lieutenants walked in. Andy handled security. He dished out beatings when needed, and worse if necessary. Small, squat and scarred, he looked every inch an enforcer.

'Boss, I've got some news you might be interested in.' Taggart stopped and waited patiently.

Gilmour indicated for him to sit in the chair opposite. 'Alright, let's have it,' he said glumly, expecting more bad news.

'One of our contacts out in the Paisley area says he's spotted two of Tam McGraw's guys drinking in one of the pubs down that way.'

Gilmour screwed up his eyes in confusion. 'Why would two

of McGraw's soldiers risk getting a beating by coming on to our patch?'

Taggart shook his head. 'Don't know for sure Ian, but they've also been seen sniffing around the Hillington Estate.'

This perked Gilmour's interest. 'Hillington! How would they know about Hillington?'

Taggart shrugged. 'I can only think of one way. Someone on the inside has passed on the info.'

Gilmour thought for a few minutes, staring into space. Eventually he looked at Taggart. 'Have them followed. I want to know who they meet and when. Stick a tracker on their vehicle. Find out exactly where they go. But I don't want to let it go too long. Once we have an idea who they're working with, we'll deal with them. Okay?'

'Got it boss.' Taggart stood up and went to walk away.

'Andy,' Gilmour said after him. 'I want to do this personally. I have a few frustrations needing venting, and I can't think of anything better than dealing with a traitor.'

Taggart said nothing and walked off.

Who would have the balls to set up without his permission? Because that's the only reason McGraw's boys would be here. Was McGraw trying to muscle in? Not only that, they looked as if they were trying to find out where he kept his supplies. Was the stupid bastard trying to start a war? He sighed. That was tomorrow's problem. Time to see about Rossi. Reaching forward he picked up his phone. Scrolling through the address book, he stopped at Domenico Rossi's number. He dialled and waited, listening to the ring tones.

'Hello Ian. Must be my lucky day.' Dom said dryly when he answered.

'It certainly is, Domenico. Your Uncle Ian might have a wee present for you.'

'Now why do I feel my life is just about to get more complicated.'

'I thought you liked problems Rossi? That's your job isn't it, sorting them out?'

'What do you want Ian?' Dom asked. Gilmour thought he sounded as weary as he felt.

'Not over the phone. We need to meet. It's time to move things up a gear.'

'In relation to what?' Rossi asked him.

'In relation to what the fuck do you think?'

'Correct me if I misunderstood Ian, but you said six months.'

'I did, but as you are no doubt well aware, certain events have happened in Spain meaning that has to change.'

There was a silence for a few seconds. 'Okay Ian. Where and when?'

'Same place as last time. The café. Seven, tonight, alone. Nice atmosphere there don't you think?'

'Fine. I'll be there.'

Gilmour hung up. As he put down the phone, Tony Smith appeared from the kitchen door. He was chewing on a bite from a large meat sandwich he had made himself. The remainder lay on the plate he carried. Walking over he sat in a chair opposite Ian.

Gilmour grunted at him. 'Nothing seems to put you off your grub, does it.'

'What, this?' he smirked, holding the sandwich up to inspect it. 'A mere snack to keep me going.' He took a paper napkin from the plate and wiped his mouth, then replaced this and the sandwich on the plate. 'We have bigger problems to worry about than my waist line boss.'

Gilmour looked at him quizzically.

'I just had a call from one of O'Boyle's guys. Seems they're not too happy you organised a hit on Malone without their say so. They're even less happy it didn't work.'

'Well fuck them,' growled Gilmour. 'They're not the ones risking everything to pull this deal off. I couldn't have that arsehole Malone getting out of prison. Don't these pricks realise if he's out of the picture then Rossi's organisation will collapse after five minutes – well after this deal gets done anyway.'

Smith coughed. 'But he did get out of prison Ian. I mean, I

know he can't do much when he's on the run, but shit, all you need is an internet connection and a laptop and you could run the world from a hotel bedroom. If he's allowed back in play it becomes more difficult to take over the Rossi's.'

'Don't you think I fucking know that,' Gilmour shouted, standing up and walking to the inglenook fireplace. He put his hands on the mantelpiece, arms outstretched, and looked down at the unlit fire. 'We were always going to have to get rid of Malone in any case to fuck up Dom's organisation. It would have been better if your casino plan had worked, but him being in the nick with Nichol was just too good a chance to pass up.'

Smith nodded, then sat silently for a few seconds, his sandwich sitting ignored on the plate on his lap.

'Something else on your mind Tony?' Gilmour asked him.

Tony took a deep breath and looked up at him. 'O'Boyle's also been talking about the payment and how it's to be made.' Smith paused, and seemed to squirm in his seat.

'Go on,' Ian said ominously.

'He doesn't like the idea of losing track of the cash before the gear leaves Colombia.'

Gilmour screwed up his face in frustration. 'I don't like it either, but these Colombians aren't going to let a tonne of coke wander over here without being paid for it up front. Surely to fuck he knows that?'

'He does. But he wants to speak with your Colombian contact so he can put his mind at ease.'

Gilmour turned and scowled at Smith.

'Hey boss, I'm just the messenger,' Tony replied holding up his hands in surrender.

'And what did you tell him?'

'That I'd need to bounce it off you.'

'Did he give any hint he knew Barrera was dead?'

Smith shook his head. 'I don't think he knows where the gear is coming from apart from that fact Rossi is the main conduit to the South Americans.'

Ian walked to the living room window overlooking the main

yard. He folded his arms and stared. He only stabled a couple of horses there himself. The other ten stalls were rented to a bunch of rich locals who kept their own mounts here and popped over every other weekend for a quick canter around the farm. Ian had nothing to do with any of them and he doubted they knew just what his main line of work was. At least it kept up the appearance of respectability and made the place look lived in and valued.

Getting rid of Rossi was proving more complicated than he had thought. There was too much he didn't know about dealing with the Colombians. Contacting Antonio Barrera and getting him onside had been the first piece of the puzzle he had managed to drop into place. The Colombian side was to have been handled by him. Now, his point of contact with the organisation was this unknown Miguel guy, who for all Ian knew, was also working with Rossi. He needed to convince O'Boyle that Rossi could be trusted, and the Colombians would also play the game. There was no mileage in it for the South Americans to rip any of them off as they needed local distributors to buy their gear, and in this case that was himself and O'Boyle. So he had to convince Eamon paying up front and in good faith was the only way this would work. Yes it was a hell of a lot of cash, but what option did they have? What he needed was something he could promise O'Boyle that would make it worthwhile. Something extra to give him a reason to keep working with Gilmour to see this deal over the line.

Gilmour heard a gentle cough behind him. 'What are you thinking about boss?'

'What I'm thinking Tony,' he said as he slowly turned around. 'Is that I need to seriously up the ante with Mr Rossi.'

Tony sat there looking confused, not entirely sure what his boss was proposing.

Smiling he walked back to the coffee table, picked up his phone and placed a call to O'Boyle. 'Eamon, I need to change the time table, move it up a bit.'

Smith watched as Gilmour nodded his head at the answers

only he could hear. 'I appreciate that, but I promise, it will be to your advantage.' He smiled.. 'I've been doing a bit of digging up here into the death of your son. What if I tell you that once this deal gets put to bed and the gear has arrived, I can deliver the son of the man that took out your boy?'

Gilmour listened intently then smiled grimly. 'No, the gunman's dead, but you get the next best thing Eamon. An eye for an eye.'

TWENTY ONE

Dom parked his car a hundred yards or so from the Café on the opposite side of the street. He looked at Billy in the passenger seat. 'Ready?' he asked.

Billy nodded. He opened his jacket and took the Smith and Wesson M&P9 Shield from the shoulder holster. Dropping the clip, he checked it, replaced it with a slap on the underside of the handle before cocking the gun, leaving the safety on then returned the pistol to its holster. He nodded at Dom. 'I am now.'

They both exited the car. Dom locked it and they walked slowly along the pavement in the general direction of the café, carefully scanning their surroundings for anything out of place, their eyes hidden behind sunglasses. Dom had no reason to suspect Ian Gilmour was going to take him out, especially as he already had his twelve million in the bank, but he had seen people do stupid things before. Dom had on trousers, a short sleeved shirt and a light summer jacket. Billy was wearing his standard suit, although he had forsaken the tie. He still looked a bit incongruous. The street was busy with early evening shoppers and those out simply enjoying the late sunshine. It had threatened to break today - again. To be honest, it was needed to clear the air. It was too humid, too muggy. It made people irascible, prone to errors of judgement. And that was the last thing Dom needed right now. He had been wondering all day why Gilmour wanted to move up the timetable. But as there was only one way to find out, he kept on walking with Billy at his shoulder.

They came level with the café, but on the opposite side of the street. Dom saw it was full of ordinary Joe public punters out for their wee bit of French Mediterranean caffeine fix and sugary sweet pastries. Interesting. A public meeting this time. No closed Café. Maybe Gilmour doesn't trust him either. Dom looked at his watch. He was fifteen minutes early, so he nodded to Billy to follow him. They walked on a few steps and stared into the display window of a second hand mobile phone shop. Dom could see a clear reflection of the café in the glass. Waiters running around, clearing up, ushering folk out. Within five minutes the café was empty. A minute later three people left, one man and two women. They closed the door behind them but did not lock it. Dom glanced at Billy and then turned around to stare at the café. Through the plate glass window, he saw someone moving around behind the counter, a tall figure, wearing a suit not an apron. Gilmour. The café appeared empty otherwise.

'Wait here Billy. Looks like Ian wants to have a nice wee cuppa with me.'

Billy was not happy. 'Dom, there could be someone else in the back. In the toilets, Hiding behind the counter.'

Rossi shook his head. 'Nah! I'm holding too much of his money. This is going to be pretty straightforward.' He turned to look at Billy again and gave him a wry grin. 'But keep an eye out just in case. Okay?'

Jenkins nodded. Dom crossed the road, heading straight for the café. As he approached, all he could see along the street was the normal activity of a summer evening. No one skulked. No one hid. He carried on and reached the door. Stopping, he peered in, looking left and right. It was empty. Just then Gilmour turned around, a red metal beaker of steaming milk in his hands. He noticed Dom and waved with it for him to come in.

Dom pushed the café door open and stepped inside. It was much cooler. The hot air curtain blew cold air and the ceiling cassettes kept the room in the low twenties. He removed his sunglasses, placing them carefully in the breast pocket of his shirt, the right lens uppermost, sitting proud of the pocket lip.

Gilmour carried on working behind the counter but eventually turned and gave Dom one of his big, inane, but dangerous smiles which never reached his eyes.

'Dom boy. Glad you could make it. Grab yourself a seat. I'll be with you in a second.' He turned back to the array of machinery and began filling a clear glass jug with black coffee from a percolator to complement the red metal jug that held foamed milk.

Dom surveyed the café and decided to sit at the table closest to the door, back to the window, just in case an early escape was necessary. Slipping off his jacket, he draped it over the back of his chair then sat down. Gilmour re-appeared carrying a tray with two cups and a jug each of espresso and milk. He placed it on the table and proceeded to fill both cups; half coffee, half white aerated liquid. Dom said nothing. He preferred espresso, but he wasn't here to rate Ian's qualities as a Barista. Gilmour lifted the cups, saucers and jugs from the tray and placed them on the table. He looked up at Dom. There was a hardness in his expression Dom could not remember seeing before. Gilmour took the tray back behind the counter then returned and sat opposite Dom, leaning back in his chair, looking at him intently. Dom sipped from his own coffee and waited.

Gilmour held out his hand. 'Your phone. Hand it over.'

Dom looked at him. 'If you think I'm giving you my mobile then you do have dementia kicking in.'

'Switch it off then, and let me see you do it. I don't want any of this recorded.'

Rossi sat for a moment as if considering, then reached into his pocket, took out his phone and switched it off. He held it out to Gilmour. 'Happy now?'

Gilmour reached out and pressed the screen of Dom's mobile a few times. 'Aye, okay.'

'What's this about Ian? Why the secrecy?'

'Well Domenico. Looks like some wee issues have crept in that might throw the proverbial spanner in the works of our deal.'

Dom inclined his head. 'And what might they be Ian? Everything is in motion at my end. My Colombian contacts seem pretty excited about the deal – and the money.' He smiled confidently.

Gilmour sat forward, elbows on the table, chin resting on his steepled fingers. 'Dom, I'm sure as fuck not stupid. Somehow you've managed to walk Jack Malone out of jail right under the snotty noses of the Prison Service – congratulations on that by the way. But in the process you managed to get a Prison Governor killed.' He shook his head slowly and tutted. 'That wasn't too smart now was it? You'll have every copper able to tie his own shoe laces running around trying to find him. He won't be much use to you hiding under a bush, will he?'

'Let me worry about Malone,' Dom replied. 'He's got nothing to do with our deal.'

Gilmour shrugged. 'Perhaps not directly, but my partners are beginning to wonder if they can trust you to pull this off if your bagman is in the wind with all their secrets.'

Dom sat forward. 'Ian, I don't need Malone. He doesn't run things, I do, and he knows nothing about our agreement. That was put together after he was arrested. Anyway, who are these 'partners you're talking about? I thought this was between you and me?'

Gilmour laughed. 'Now I know you're at the wind up. Where do you think I can find over fifty six million in cash, eh?'

Dom rubbed his chin. 'You know, I don't normally care or worry about where my money comes from, but in this case I'll make an exception. So let me hazard a guess. Eamon O'Boyle? Right? He runs half of England anyway from his base in Manchester.'

'Aye, okay. I don't suppose that took too much guesswork. It is Eamon. We're in business together.'

Dom found it difficult to suppress a laugh. The sheer gall of Gilmour was astounding. He was admitting to working with the father of the man he had killed. At least it wouldn't take O'Boyle too long to track Gilmour down when the time came for retribution, assuming the South Americans let him escape their righteous anger. What Dom needed though was hard evidence, something he could give O'Boyle other than Marti's word Gilmour had been in on the hit with Rossi senior.

'So why this meeting? What's so urgent?'

'I'll tell you what's urgent Dom. The world is a small place. Word gets around. Word like the second in command of the Barrera cartel being taken out while visiting his operation in Spain. Plus, you also disappear for a few days at the same time together with Billy and Marti. Suspicious that?'

'Ian, are you accusing me of something? Because if you are, why not just come out with it?'

Gilmour sat in silence saying nothing.

Dom leaned forward. 'I'll say this once, so listen well. I was not in Spain when Barrera was killed and neither were Marti or Billy. Okay?'

Ian sighed. 'Alright. Play it your way. Eamon is putting a lot on the line over this deal. He wants a meeting around the table with you, me and the Barrera's to sign off on it and get some assurances before he slaps any of his money on the table.'

'And what if I say no? What if they say no. What if it's not even the Barrera's I'm dealing with?'

'Then the deal's off.'

It turned into a staring contest. Dom won. Gilmour blinked. Dom spoke.

'I want to work with you and Eamon again in the future Ian, so yes I will get in touch with the Barrera's and see what I can set up. But first, I select the where and the when. Agreed?'

Gilmour said nothing but nodded slightly.

'Second, I decide who comes to the meeting. Anyone not on the list appears, and the whole thing gets called off.'

Again, Gilmour nodded in the affirmative.

'And third. 'Dom leaned in. 'I want to know why it was my dad who took the heat for the death of Eamon O'Boyle's son when you were both involved in it.'

'What?' Gilmour said, his eyes narrowing with suspicion.

'Come on Ian, do you think I wouldn't find out something like that? Somebody, probably O'Boyle, had him killed and I want to know who the trigger man was? Oh, I don't blame O'Boyle. I would have done the same thing in his shoes, but my father paid for it with his life while you walked away. And you were just as involved, just as guilty. You were the one contracted for the hit on O'Boyle's son, so, I'd like to know why my dad ended up the fall guy?' Dom knew part of that was a lie, but he couldn't allow Gilmour to think he already knew everything. Dom's gaze held steady. Inside he was churning, realising this was perhaps pushing Gilmour a little too far. Ian looked as if he wanted to reach across the table and rip his throat out.

'Aye, it was my hit, but your dad was killed because he couldn't keep his mouth shut,' Gilmour lied. 'He was good at what he did, but he tended to boast a bit too much about his successes. That's fine when it's only low level punks we're talking about, but hitting O'Boyle's son was something else, something in a different league. When we carried out that hit, I knew we had to keep it quiet. But your dad......?' Dom watched as Gilmour's gaze seemed to glaze over, as if he were back somewhere else. 'O'Boyle found out he was the trigger man, and well, that was it. It was a long time ago Dom. Over eight years. It's ancient history.'

Dom held his temper. He knew Gilmour was lying.

'Perhaps Ian, but it destroyed my mother. It turned her into a shell of the woman she used to be. And I can't believe no one else knew about your part in what happened to O'Boyle's son.'

Gilmour shrugged. 'A few did, but they weren't the sort to run off and tell anyone about it. They were old timers. Loyalty meant something to them. Still does.'

Dom nodded again. 'You still haven't told me who killed my father?'

'I don't know who did it Rossi. You'll need to ask O'Boyle. It was his hit after all.'

Yeah, right thought Dom. 'You know Ian, the path you've

taken in the last few years seems to be paved with the bodies of the dead. Finbar O'Boyle, my Dad, Jamie Phillips.' He watched and waited to see Gilmour's reaction.

'Are you implying something Dom boy? Because if you are, be careful about what you say next.'

Rossi smirked. He held out his hands. 'Ian, there's only you and me here, drinking coffee, having a talk about old times. If we're going to work together, we need total honesty.' He took another sip. 'I know you took out Jamie Phillips. Oh you didn't pull the trigger, but I know who did, and I know you know he works for me.'

Gilmour glared at him. 'If Marti Galbraith ever wants to retire, then he better stop spreading nasty fucking rumours about me.'

'Rumours?' Dom laughed. 'If he's nothing else Ian, Marti's truthful. He has nothing to gain by lying to me. He knows I'll find out if he does - eventually. So I'm curious Ian. Jamie was on his way to taking the organisation legit. You would all have made more money than you could spend in a lifetime. So why take him out? It was a bad business decision.'

'It was my business decision Rossi, mine. He was robbing me of my fucking future. Yeh I've got a few legit developments going on, but I'm not some middle class property developer. Jamie may have enjoyed the mind numbing meetings with dozy council officials, but that wasn't for me, or the boys. The business was heading in the wrong direction. All I did was grab the steering wheel and get us back on the right side of the road.'

Dom fought hard to hold in a smile. Gilmour was so easy to provoke.

'Fair enough Ian. Not my business. But Marti is untouchable, okay?'

Gilmour did not reply. He reached for his cup and drained it. The coffee was getting cold. He re-filled his own with a top up from the once hot milk and the jug of black coffee. He held the jugs up to Dom, but he shook his head.

'So, about this meeting?' he asked Dom. 'When?'

Dom considered. 'I'll need a few days to convince Antonio Barrera's brother Carlos the meeting should go ahead. He'll be wary after Antonio's death, but given the amount of money involved, I don't think it'll be a problem.'

'Just do whatever you need to Dom. But make it quick. O'Boyle's not known for his infinite patience.'

Dom grunted assent. 'Now, I have somewhere else to be – unless of course you want me to wash up?'

Gilmour grunted. 'Aye, very funny.'

Rossi stood, put on his jacket, buttoned the middle button and turned to walk out of the door. He paused though and looked back at Gilmour, holding out his hand for him to shake. Gilmour looked surprised, but stood up, pushing his chair back.

'It's just business Ian, remember that. None of this is personal. Not for me.'

Dom waited, his hand outstretched. Gilmour reached silently forward and grasped it firmly. 'Aye, just business,' he said.

Dom turned again and walked out of the café. He stopped just outside the door, took his sunglasses from the breast pocket of his shirt and put them back on. Across the street, Jenkins acknowledged this with a nod, and they both turned in the same direction back towards Dom's car. When they reached it Billy turned and looked at Dom, the question clear in his face. Dom nodded.

When they arrived at the Villa, Dom would download the video files from the micro camera built into the sunglasses. It had captured his entire conversation with Gilmour. At the appropriate time, just when Gilmour thought he had reached the pinnacle of his success, Dom would make sure the video was played in full to him and Eamon O'Boyle.

He smiled grimly to himself. It was a bad day when you had three people gunning to kill you, but Dom knew handing Ian to Carlos Barrera would bring closure to both himself and he hoped O'Boyle.

And that closure would be delivered Colombian style, in a way Gilmour would find especially unpleasant.

TWENTY TWO

Miguel Orejuela sat in the garden of his villa in Mijas beneath the same Pergola where he had recently met with Domenico Rossi and Antonio Barrera. He drummed his manicured fingers on the arm of his chair. Now, Antonio was dead, Dom had been betrayed by the man who had asked him to import the largest shipment of cocaine Miguel had ever handled into the UK, and Carlos Barerra was coming to Spain seeking revenge for his brother's death. But this would be a cartel style investigation, where the merest hint of suspicion could result in your life being forfeit before you even realised it.

Every fibre of Miguel's being screamed that Carlos was looking for a scapegoat. He needed someone to pay for Antonio's death. He could not stop him though. After he had called again last night, Miguel knew Antonio's assassination had been the only thing on his mind. Carlos wanted retribution – swift and terrible. But Carlos himself was a wanted man. His International Arrest Warrant was over five years old, raised initially by the Americans, but signed up to by every European country where the Barrera's were known to have a presence. Antonio had miraculously escaped that trap with a mixture of bribes, payoffs, flying under everyone's radar and getting people like Miguel to do the hard work. But Carlos was the opposite. Loud, brash, given to fits of temper, with no seeming wish to ever leave the safety of Colombia. Getting out of South America and travelling to Spain should be a near impossibility for him, but his worth and value to the economy of Colombia was immeasurable. That and the enormous payoffs he made to high ranking Government and Military officials would however help. He had told Miguel the General in charge of the Colombian Air Force would fly him directly to the Rota Military base just west of Cadiz under the guise of an exchange Colonel of the Fuerza Aérea Colombiana. From there, he would be spirited directly to Miguel's secluded villa in Mijas. Miguel knew he would stay for as long as it took.

Suddenly, the burner mobile he had carried in his pocket for two days vibrated. Miguel fumbled for it, nearly managing to reject the call in his efforts.

'Domenico?'

'Hello Miguel. How are you?'

'I am well. And you?'

He heard Rossi laugh bitterly. 'Run ragged is the best I can describe it. I'm beginning to wish I'd opted for a normal job, like a bag packer in a wee supermercado somewhere in the back of beyond.'

Miguel smiled to himself. He stood, picked up a pair of sunglasses from a table in front of him and strolled from underneath the pergola into the sunshine. He put the sunglasses on and began to walk around his garden.

'Do you have any news for me Domenico? What is happening with our Mr Gilmour?'

'Have you spoken to him Miguel?'

'Yes I have, just as Carlos asked me to. Why?'

'Well, he's reached out to me again. He doesn't have all the money for this deal himself, which is what I suspected. He's working with a fairly high level crime syndicate down in Manchester run by someone called O'Boyle. But it seems Mr O'Boyle is getting nervous about the deal. He wants a meeting with everyone involved before he parts with any of his hard earned pennies.'

'Well, I have good news for you then. Carlos is due to arrive tomorrow. He wants to handle the investigation into Antonio's death personally. That means bad things are going to happen to someone.'

Miguel waited, sensing Dom digesting the news.

'I won't ask exactly how he's getting into Spain, but with him being here we might be able to bring this all to a head.'

'Well, we need to do something my friend. What do you have in mind?'

'You need to convince Carlos to sit in on a meeting with all of us? Me, you, Gilmour and O'Boyle?'

Miguel stopped walking. 'I am not sure Domenico. He may not take too kindly to being distracted from trying to find his brother's killer.'

'Well tell him the man who murdered his brother will be in the room with us.'

Miguel hesitated. 'If I tell him that he will have everyone entering the room taken out and beaten half to death until they confess. Why don't I just send him the video evidence before he leaves Colombia?'

'Because Miguel, I have another reason to make sure Gilmour is in the room with O'Boyle and Carlos.' Miguel waited, hearing the hesitation in Dom's voice. There was a sigh from the other end of the phone. 'I respect you Miguel, so I'm telling you this in confidence. Many years ago, my father and Ian Gilmour carried out a contract hit on a young hoodlum named Finbar O'Boyle. Finbar is,.....was, Eamon O'Boyle's only son and O'Boyle has been looking for his killers ever since.'

'So you want to expose Gilmour to O'Boyle at the same time as we let Carlos know he killed Antonio.'

'Yes,' he heard Dom say.

'But Domenico, won't that also expose your father? Do you want O'Boyle to go after him.'

'My father is dead Miguel. When Gilmour began sounding out O'Boyle about going into partnership with him, he became paranoid my father would blackmail him over the fact he was involved in Finbar's murder. So, Gilmour had him killed few years ago.'

Miguel was surprised. A life of crime in Colombia could be tough, but it seemed even in what he thought of as the backwater of Scotland, intrigue, mayhem and murder happened regularly.

'But don't you want to exact your own revenge on Gilmour? Where's the satisfaction in handing him over to Carlos?' Even as he said it, Miguel realised what Carlos and his Colombian torturers would put Gilmour through was infinitely worse than anything Domenico or O'Boyle could come up with even in their most fevered and delusional moments.

'Miguel, you know where that satisfaction lies. Plus, if I get some brownie points with O'Boyle, that might lead to bigger things in the future. '

Miguel thought for a few seconds. 'Alright my friend, I will have a monitor in the room where we meet setup to show the video of Antonio being killed and of Gilmour's part in it.'

'And make sure you also have the footage of him walking through Malaga airport and a copy of his entry visa. Don't worry, it will match his passport details exactly including all the biometric information.'

'And your evidence for O'Boyle?'

'That's in hand. I'll be bringing it with me.'

ΔΔΔ

Dom sat back in the armchair in his living room and looked around at the four other people in the room. Given the last few days, he had felt a council of war was needed, especially after his meeting with Gilmour and his phone call with Miguel. The local CID had paid him a visit earlier in the morning. A contact had given him a heads up so his solicitor was already in attendance and lacking a search warrant, made sure the police behaved themselves. Then the questions began. Yes he did know Jack Malone. Yes, Malone did sometimes work for him as a freelance accountant. No he had not seen him recently. Yes he would be sure to let the police know if he did. No they couldn't have copies of his security CCTV. Goodbye and thanks officer. And that had been it. Short, sharp, sweet. No doubt they'd return at some point, armed with a warrant perhaps. But there was nothing here. The CCTV had 'malfunctioned.'

Now it was three thirty in the afternoon. He had asked Cassie, Billy, Marti and Gabby to join him, and the living room was more comfortable. Dom and Billy sat in single chairs whilst Cassie and Gabby were cosied up on the two seater. Marti was in the kitchen making them drinks. He had debated inviting Gabby, but felt happier having her on the inside than second guessing from somewhere remote. Cassie had also brought him up to speed on what she had found with the accounts. It was good news. Apart from cash bribes to cops and officials in bed with them, most of what happened was automated, the biggest manual task involved filtering the money from their drug dealing through the various businesses, but she had found a spreadsheet telling her how much and when.

One of his main worries had been the *Wallets* where he stored the Bitcoins he had bought. Jack Malone had some access to these. He had been charged with buying and transferring them, but only under Dom's specific orders. This was not exactly Dark Web currency, but once purchased, it was virtually untraceable and despite its fluctuating value, was one of the main currencies Dom and the Colombians traded in. But he had checked these himself with Cassie sitting next to him, and they all seemed in order. Now he just needed Gilmour, or O'Boyle, he didn't care which, to transfer the balance of the purchase price to him in the same Bitcoins. From there it would go into a Bitcoin wallet, which he would send to the Barrera's as soon as the cocaine was ready to leave the South American coast. Marti arrived with the refreshments and they all grabbed a cup of coffee.

'I had a meeting with Gilmour last night,' Rossi told them.

'Really?' Gabby asked, surprised.

'Yes, He said he wanted to move up the timetable.' He looked across at Gabby. 'And despite having you working here on the inside, your Uncle Ian also seems to have lost a bit of faith in me.'

'How so,' Gabby queried.

'He's asked me to arrange a meeting with my suppliers. He

wants his backers in on it.'

'His backers?' Gabby looked confused. 'I thought my Uncle was funding this himself?'

Dom shook his head. 'He doesn't have that amount of spare capital lying around. He's in business with someone else, Eamon O'Boyle from Manchester.'

'He told you that,' Gabby said surprised. Dom nodded again. 'Shit, he's sailing close to the wind. My mother mentioned he might have been involved with the murder of O'Boyle's son.'

Now it was Dom's turn to be surprised. 'How does your mother know that? I thought she had nothing to do with running the organisation?'

Gabby smiled. 'Dom, gangsters see women as just accessories. They forget we're in the room half the time. The wives and girlfriends hear things, but they know better than to open their mouths to anyone about the snippets they pick up.'

'Except your mum mentioned Gilmour's part in murdering O'Boyle's son?'

'Yes. Once in passing and only to me, but I thought nothing of it until just now. Anyway, what do you intend to do with it?'

Dom sat back in his seat and stared thoughtfully into the fireplace. Billy and Marti were impassive, hands on their laps, listening to all that was being said, but waiting until Dom brought them into the conversation. Cassie lay back on the settee, her left shoulder close to Gabby's, her denim clad leg brushing gently against hers. Gabby was snuggled into the corner of the two seater, her legs drawn up underneath her, her right hand lying lazily across Cassie's leg. They both looked content, still in the early throes of a rekindled love affair. Dom could not help feeling a little jealous. His relationships had all been brief throughout his life. He had not yet met the one person that gut punched him the second he saw her, and if he were honest, he had given up looking years ago.

And then there was the absence of Jack Malone. Dom knew if Malone had been here, the smell of whisky or brandy would have wafted around the room as he gently got himself drunk and ready for his nights sleep. He now realised Jack Malone had grown into a dangerous liability without Dom even realising. His knowledge of Rossi's operations had been extensive. If he had allowed him to *'retire'* there was no way of knowing if he would have kept his own counsel. Jack Malone had turned into a puzzle with only one solution.

'Okay,' Dom eventually said. 'I'm going to bring you all up to speed on what I know and what I.....,' he hesitated. 'What *we* intend to do about it.' He paused and looked at Gabby. 'Gabby, I'm trusting you. Don't let me down.'

She bristled a little. 'Ian had my father killed to get where he is today,' she spat and looked over towards Marti. He visibly squirmed in his seat. 'I owe him nothing. Don't worry about me. I'm with you in this until its conclusion, good or bad.'

'That's good Gabby, because it was your Uncle Ian and my father who murdered O'Boyle's son and then when Gilmour and O'Boyle began to do business together, he became worried my father would blackmail him – or worse. So he had him killed, just like he did with your father.'

Gabby's jaw clenched. 'That bastard has a lot of blood on his hands.'

Dom nodded, knowing he was no innocent himself. 'Yes he does Gabby, but then again so did my father. It was the World they lived in. To them it was just another way of doing business.' He paused for a second. 'Tell me, the people who used to work for your father and now work for Gilmour. How well do you know them?'

'I still keep in touch with a couple of the old timers. Andy Taggart and Cammy Maxwell worked with my dad. They're enforcers and run most of the street dealers and the bookies. They treat Angela and me like their own daughters. Very protective they are.'

'And how do you think they get on with your Uncle Ian? I assume some of them suspect he might have had something to do with the death of your dad?'

'He put their noses out of joint when he brought in Tony

Smith to be his second in command. But to be honest, Tony has a pretty good business head on him. I wouldn't be surprised if he's the one initiating this deal with O'Boyle.'

'Okay,' he replied with a quick nod. 'So if there was a change in leadership within the Gilmour clan, you think the old timers and maybe even Tony would go along with it?'

Gabby looked at Cassie, slight confusion on her face.

'What Dom means Gabby, is that if your Uncle Ian was removed permanently, there would be an opportunity for another side of the family to step in there and run the show.'

'What, you mean me becoming a crime boss? Fuck Cassie, that's never been on my radar.'

Dom smiled. 'Not you Gabby. If things go according to plan, it might be a smoother transition if someone they all knew was able to take over. Someone a wee bit older than you.'

'Who? 'My sister is the same age as me.' Gabby didn't look any the wiser.

'There's your mother,' Dom said with a half smile and a raised eyebrow.

And then he outlined what he had in mind.

TWENTY THREE

Dom slowly drove his BMW into the car park of Gleddoch House. This country hotel was set on a hillside above Langbank, on the banks of the Clyde. It was only a forty minute drive from the city centre, and Dom often used it to meet people from those legitimate businesses he owned. Quiet, secluded, its buildings with their white facades were understated but still spoke of money. He drove the Beamer into an empty space, switched off the batteries and sat waiting. He was early. That was on purpose. He wanted to see who would arrive, find out if they were as interested or as curious as he hoped they would be. Gabby would be here soon, and hopefully not alone. Her mother was crucial to this. He had emphasised that to her a couple of days before. She was someone the others arriving could trust, whereas Dom was an unknown quantity.

He sat back and closed his eyes. The last few nights had been troubled. Sleep had eluded him. Thoughts of Malone kept him awake. Had he done the right thing? Could he have gotten him out of the country and away somewhere safe? But was anywhere safe in this interconnected, selfie driven, social media world? He knew deep down at some point, Malone would either have been discovered or would do something stupid. No, a permanent solution had been his only option. The call had come from Marti at six in the morning on the day he'd said his goodbyes to Malone. It was done and it was quick. He had asked him nothing further. He had no wish to know the details. As far as the cops knew, Jack Malone was still on the run still lying low somewhere and they would get him eventually.

The quiet whine of an electric motor and the sound of

wheels on tarmac caused him to open his eyes. A Range Rover Evoque pulled into a space closer to the hotel entrance. It stopped. Two people got out, both men. They looked to be in their mid fifties. One of them was lean, fit looking, five ten or eleven, wearing a grey suit, no tie, black shoes. His head was shaven close to hide his thinning hair. He gazed around the car park with an ease borne of supreme confidence. No one would take him by surprise. The other man was smaller, around five and half feet tall. He wore a darker suit with a blue shirt and tie and a pair of wine coloured shoes. His gut hung over the waistband of his trousers, but he had the broad shouldered build of someone who had lifted weights for a large part of his life. A full head of nearly white hair was combed back in a style not fashionable for over twenty years. He exuded a bullishness that said don't mess with me. They both walked towards the hotel entrance and stopped outside. The small, heavier set one reached into his jacket pocket and took out a pack of cigarettes. He lit one from a zip disposable then drew in a long lungful.

So this was Maxwell and Taggart. They had been with Jamie Phillips and Ian Gilmour for a long time, over twenty five years Gabby had told him. They had come up the ranks together with Phillips, and when he had set himself up, they had joined him in keeping things running. Maxwell was the brains behind a lot of their early business deals, guiding Jamie through the inevitable quagmires they encountered on their journey up the Glasgow underworld. Taggart was the enforcer, the General that kept all the troops in check and ran a bunch of other thugs whose main remit in life was to dish out as much pain and misery as they were told to.

It was a relief to see them. He had been unsure if Gabby would be able to convince them to meet. He wasn't exactly the enemy and he was certain they knew who he was and what he did, but it was still a dangerous gamble. The least they could do now though was listen. But that depended on Gabby getting her mother here. Her text last night had been good news. Annabelle Phillips had agreed to come from the Canaries and meet with them. Well, she had agreed to come over and visit her two daughters. Gabby, he hoped, was in the process of explaining the real reason she had been asked to come. If she had gotten straight back on a flight to Tenerife, Dom realised this would get awkward. But he fervently hoped Gabby had convinced her to at least listen to what he had to say. He glanced at the clock on the dash. Five minutes until he was supposed to be sitting down outlining the details of how Maxwell and Taggart were ostensibly about to climb the ranks of power once more. Unusually for him he felt tense. His heart rate was up. The last few weeks had been one of turmoil. Things had happened quickly, always dangerous in this business. But if everything worked out, it would change the balance of criminal power in the West of Scotland for the next generation, though it did depend on Gabby getting her mother here.

He looked again at the two men standing at the hotel entrance. The fat one had thrown his cigarette butt on the ground and was stamping it out. The taller, thinner one said something to him and the smoker scowled then bent down, picked up the butt and placed it in a bin next to him. Dom smiled. It was nice to see an environmentally friendly crook. The smoker looked at his watch and gestured around the car park while saying something to his friend, who just shrugged. Dom became worried they would leave. People in his business were not known for their patience. He opened his car door and stepped out. He closed and locked it then turned and began walking slowly towards the two men. They stared back at him. A sound behind him made him stop and turn around. A blue Ford was pulling into the car park and took the space next to Dom's BMW. Gabby?

The car stopped and she got out. Cassie Hughes stepped from the passenger seat. She smiled at him, then opened the rear passenger door. Another woman stepped out and Dom was taken aback by what he saw. His *business* over the last ten years had consumed him. Female company had not been on his radar much and although Annabelle Phillips was in her mid fifties, Dom would have put her closer to forty, if that. She was nearly six feet tall, and with her high heels she towered above Cassie and Gabby. The carved model looks and high cheekbones other women would have paid millions for, looked natural, not plastic or botoxed. He had no idea if the boobs were fake, but they were certainly striking. Her legs were encased in the tightest pair of jeans Dom had seen in a long time; Cassie included. She held a pair of sunglasses in her hand and popped them on to shade her eyes from the afternoon glare, pushing her jet black, shoulder length hair back from her tanned face.

Dom noticed Cassie smiling at him and he felt himself almost blush, caught like a schoolboy lusting after a desirable, untouchable teacher. He waited as the three women walked towards him. Annabelle Phillips looked past him towards the hotel. She stopped, as the other two girls walked on and a smile broke out on her face as she began to follow again. As the three of them reached Dom they all stopped. This time Gabby smiled at him.

'Mum,' she said. 'This is Domenico Rossi. Dom, my Mum, Annabelle.'

Annabelle looked at him and Dom returned her gaze. There was just a hint of a smile around her eyes, Dom thought, as if she approved of what she saw. She held out her hand and Dom's lips creased a little. He didn't know whether to shake it or kiss it.

'Mrs Phillips. Thanks for coming.'

Her expression hardened a little. 'You call me 'Mrs' anything again and I'm going straight back to the airport.' She smiled. 'It's Annabelle, please.'

Dom smiled back. Despite his earlier doubts he thought he was going to get on well with Annabelle Phillips.

'Annabelle it is then.' He turned to Gabby. 'You should have warned me your mother was only sixteen when she gave birth to you.'

'Yeah, right,' Gabby replied with raised eyebrows.

Cassie smiled. Dom wanted to hide – kind of. He was about

to suggest they move into the hotel when Annabelle walked off towards Taggart and Maxwell.

'Well if you two reprobates aren't a sight for sore bloody eyes. Still alive then I see?' She held her arms wide as both men came towards her, hugging one, then the other.

They both grinned at her then the taller, thinner one stood back a little and looked her over. He shook his head. 'You look as if you've gotten twenty years younger instead of ten years older. You got a picture or something in the attic back in the Canaries?'

'Put your eyes back in their sockets Cammy. It's bad for your blood pressure.' She linked arms with the two of them and all three walked ahead of Dom into the hotel, talking amiably.

Now that was interesting Dom thought. He would have given odds Maxwell would have been the smaller, heavier man. Taggart looked too out of shape to be much of a threat to anyone.

'Shall we girls?' He ushered Gabby and Cassie towards the hotel and they fell into step behind the other three.

When Annabelle and the two men reached the steps they stopped and waited on Dom and the girls. Dom nodded to them.

'Let's leave the introductions until we're inside. I've booked us a corner table in the Vista Restaurant. I hope you're all hungry.'

A few moments later they were seated around a large circular table covered with crisp, white linen and set for a meal. They introduced themselves to each other. Dom was flanked by Cassie and Gabby, with Gabby's mum beside her. The two other men sat beside each other. Dom noticed Taggart eyed him with what was almost an assassin's stare. In contrast Maxwell looked relaxed and gazed out over the eighteenth hole of the golf course towards the Renfrewshire countryside in the distance.

'Nice place this. I haven't been here before. Need to keep it in mind for the future.' He turned his gaze back to Dom. After a pause he reached over with an outstretched hand. 'Nice to meet you at last Mr Rossi. Seems like you've become a bit of a one man industry over the last wee while.'

Dom allowed a little smile to play on his lips and shook hands with him firmly. 'I do my best Cammy.' He released his grip and held out his hand towards Taggart, who looked at it for a few long seconds before gripping it in his own. 'And you Mr Taggart. Both of your reputations precede you thanks to Gabby singing your praises.' Dom relaxed, elbows on the table, chin resting on his hands.

'Just how do you know Gabby?' Taggart asked him suspiciously, in a gruff, smokers voice.

Dom looked at Gabby and smiled. 'That is a long story Andy, one best told by Gabby when she feels ready.'

Gabby smiled sweetly. 'Andy, it's okay, believe me. I've only known Dom for a few weeks, but I trust him. Everything he'll tell you here is the truth.'

Taggart looked unconvinced but said nothing.

Dom clapped his hands together. 'Right. I'm famished so let's get some grub in.'

After they ordered, Maxwell broke the brief silence. 'Exactly why are we here Dom? I can call you Dom, can't I?' he asked with a smirk.

Rossi shrugged. 'You can call me anything you like. All I ask is that you give me a fair hearing.' Dom steepled his fingers in front of his face. 'From what Gabby has told me, you two,' he pointed at Maxwell and Taggart, 'were equal number three's in Jamie Phillips's set up before Gilmour took over and made you his number two's. Since then, you've been slowly slipping down the pecking order while newcomers like Tony have been getting closer to the seat of power.'

Dom could see the mere suggestion of their fall from grace had made Andy Taggart angrier than he had seemed a few minutes previously. Anger though was probably a natural state for him, unfortunate for his blood pressure given how unfit he was. Maxwell on the other hand stayed silent, calm.

'A long time ago Ian Gilmour and my father, Franco Rossi, occasionally worked together as a team.'

Maxwell looked surprised. 'I knew your father. He was an enforcer, a gun for hire. Independent, just like you. He worked for the highest bidder. I didn't know Ian and he were involved in anything?'

'It was a sideline for Gilmour. Whenever a job needed more than one person, my dad often called on Ian. They knew a lot of each other's secrets.'

'I'll bet,' Taggart piped up. He nodded his head. 'So your Franco Rossi's boy! I knew your dad a bit. Never worked with him, but Ian introduced us way back.' He paused. 'I liked him. Shame about the way he got it.'

'Yes, it was a shame,' Dom agreed. 'It was also a betrayal.' Dom looked across at Annabelle. 'I'll be up front with you. I have my own personal reasons for wanting Ian put out of business. Because of his paranoia, he had my father killed, not because he did or said anything, but simply because Gilmour was worried he *might* do something.'

Maxwell and Annabelle glanced at each other. 'It doesn't surprise me,' Annabelle said. 'He always had a suspicious nature. Even as kids he would constantly accuse me of running to mum or dad and telling on him for something or other. What exactly was he worried about?' Annabelle asked.

'He's in partnership with a gangland boss down in Manchester called Eamon O'Boyle?'

'Offshoot of the Irish mafia,' Cammy said. 'O'Boyle runs all the drug gangs from Birmingham to the borders. But the problem he has is the same as everyone else - supply. You've worked for him as well then?'

Dom shrugged. 'Just some small jobs. I mainly stick to Caledonia, but I know he buys gear from Tam McGraw, who I also import for. Pretty expensive with their added mark-up, but given how tight everything is coming across the Channel and the North Sea, he doesn't have much option.'

'Okay,' Maxwell said. 'So what does this have to do with your dad and Gilmour's supposed involvement in his death?'

Rossi told them about Finbar

'And my brother and your father handled the hit!' Annabelle said with a slight catch in her voice. She realised where Dom was going with this.

'That's right, and everyone was happy, well apart from Finbar and his father.'

Maxwell also seemed to understand. 'So, when Ian approached O'Boyle about doing business, he became worried Franco would do what? Tell O'Boyle? Doesn't seem likely given his part in the killing.'

'Maybe, or perhaps that my dad would blackmail him, hold the fact of the killing over his head and gain some advantage. Either way he decided a permanent solution was the best option.'

'And we have the evidence to back it up.' Cassie had been silent until now. Maxwell and Taggart turned to look at her.

Dom nodded at her to continue.

'Gilmour gave us the evidence himself.' She looked around the dining room. Dom had asked they be seated in this corner and the tables closest to them kept empty. The few hundred pounds of a tip had ensured no arguments. Gabby took a mobile phone from her pocket and placed it on the table. She pressed the screen a few times and a couple of seconds later Dom's voice could be heard followed by Ian Gilmour's. The accompanying video was not the best quality, but it was good enough so they could see Ian Gilmour. It was also clear enough they could hear him admit to the killing of Finbar O'Boyle. Gabby passed the phone around to each of them in turn as they watched the recording and listened to the audio.

Maxwell and Taggart eyed each other for a few seconds and then Taggart nodded. Maxwell turned and looked at Dom.

'Andy and myself have been thinking about what Ian's been up to for a long time now. He always talked about wanting to become the biggest organisation in the country and take over the mob from Edinburgh, but right now he's on some kind of ego driven power trip to control the Coke market. Tony Smith has a lot to do with what he's up to. To be honest it looks like Smith is setting it up so when Ian pegs it, naturally or otherwise, then Eamon O'Boyle will waltz in and take over; not a prospect that fills me with any joy.'

'Could be. He's asked me to handle a large shipment for him. Given what I've found out so far, he's also trying to take over my operation and I'm pretty sure Eamon O'Boyle's bankrolling him.'

Maxwell shrugged. 'So what do we do about him?' Annabelle started at this. Her face hardened and she looked at Maxwell, concerned. 'I'm sorry Annabelle. I realise he's your brother, but we need to face facts.'

Dom's face took on a distant look, thinking about what else he should say. 'I'm afraid Ian has gone too far now to be able to pull back. He's also about to become wanted by someone else, someone who will take great delight in taking him off our hands.'

'What do you mean?' Annabelle asked.

Dom turned towards her. 'Part of what I mean Annabelle is that not only did Ian Gilmour kill my father, he also had your husband killed.'

'No,' she gasped, spinning around to look at Gabby.

Gabby nodded. 'It's true mum. It all makes sense. We always wondered about Ian taking over and running things instead of you. He stepped in fast, while you were still grieving.'

'I didn't want to run anything,' Annabelle told her daughter. 'Without your dad it wouldn't have been the same.

'But Gabby's right,' Dom said. 'Gilmour wanted to run things his way and Jamie was stopping him from doing that. So he organised to have him taken out.'

'How do you know this?' she whispered.

'Because I know the man that did it. He works for me.'

'What?' she was incredulous. 'He told you?'

Dom nodded. 'Yes. And so did Gilmour.'

She looked shocked. 'Why the hell would Ian admit to something like that?'

Dom shrugged. 'Because he's an arrogant bastard with a short temper. All it takes is a little goading'

Dom nodded again to Cassie. She scrolled through the mobile and found another video clip. Pressing play, she gave the handset to Annabelle. Gilmour's sister watched it in silence. When it finished, she put the phone on the table and slumped back in her seat.

Dom reached over and placed a hand on her arm. 'It was just business Annabelle. Your brother saw a way to get what he wanted and went for it.. Don't think your husband was any saint either. He dished out a few contracts in his day. It's the world we live in. It happens.' He looked across at Andy Taggart and then back to Annabelle, hoping she had not missed the significance. She hadn't. 'I'm sorry Annabelle,' Dom tried to placate her. 'Ian's problems are much bigger than either myself or O'Boyle.'

'What?'

'He tried to deal directly with the Colombian cartel I'm working with. He wanted to cut me out and set up his own operation.'

'I know, you've said that.'

'What you don't know is that for some reason he fell out with the South Americans,' Dom lied. 'I have no idea why, but it must have been bad. He went over to Spain himself and,......well, perhaps it would be better if you just see it.'

'Fuck,' she said. 'This is turning into a right horror show.'

He nodded to Gabby and she lifted the phone from the table. She scrolled through, found the file she was after and opened it. This video was much clearer than the last one, but there was no audio. She handed the mobile to Annabelle first then sat back while it looped. Annabelle watched silently, not understanding at first, but knowing it was violent and realistically deadly. Towards the end of the clip, Dom saw her eyes widen. As the figure on the video turned away from the dead body in the back seat of the car, Annabelle gasped. There was no mistaking the face of Ian Gilmour. Cammy Maxwell reached over and took the phones from her hands. He huddled around with Taggart and they watched it replay again.

'This was taken well over a week ago in Spain,' Dom told them. 'The body you can see lying in the back of the car belongs to Antonio Barrera, the number two in the Barrera cartel. This clip will soon be seen by his brother Carlos, the number one in the cartel, and Carlos is coming to Spain personally to attend a meeting Ian himself has asked for on behalf of O'Boyle.' Dom paused and swallowed a little. 'I doubt Ian will be leaving that meeting Annabelle.'

He could see her nervously chewing on the inside of her lip. Strange, thought Dom. He hadn't marked her as the emotional type. He thought she would have been more pragmatic. He waited while Maxwell and Taggart re-ran the video. Eventually Maxwell looked up.

'Where is this?' he asked Dom suspiciously.

'Mijas, Spain,' Dom replied. 'It's from a public webcam down near the spot where it happened,' he lied. 'Why?'

'Ian didn't mention going to Spain with anyone. He might have said something to me or Andy.' He indicated towards Taggart.

'You think he tells you everything?' Dom stated. 'For instance, do you know just how much cocaine he's buying from me and why he needs O'Boyle?' Dom waited, hoping he had asked the right question.

Both Maxwell and Taggart looked at him blankly.

'See, I told you he was starting to cut you out of all the big decisions. So why would he tell you he's flying over to Spain to carry out a hit on a Cartel boss? If it were me, that's something I'd definitely want to keep to myself.'

Cassie and Gabby looked straight at Gilmour and Maxwell, giving no hint to the truth or otherwise of Dom's statement, their faces expressionless. It was now or never thought Dom. He eyed Maxwell and Taggart carefully.

'If I can get Ian back over to Spain for this meeting without him suspecting he's been fingered for Carlos's murder, then that's the last you'll ever see of him, I can guarantee it. Everyone gets satisfaction. Me for my dad, Gabby and Annabelle for their father and husband, O'Boyle for his son and the Barrera's for the death of one of theirs. But then we have the problem of who can fill the void he's leaving? His organisation's big, but if there's a vacuum, there will be lot's of infighting. You might lose a lot before it's over.'

'Who do you suggest then?' Maxwell asked quietly. Dom thought he detected a faint hope in his voice. Well, sorry to disappoint you pal.

'Annabelle,' he said, noting the surprise on their faces. 'Hear me out. Everyone of note in the organisation knows her. Plus, she used to deal with a lot of the books when Jamie was still alive.' He looked to her for confirmation and she nodded. 'So, until she can put the management on a more permanent footing, Annabelle would be best placed to run things, advised by you two of course. She'll not be seen as a threat by anyone else, and as for Tony? Well, that would be up to you, but I suppose he'll work for whoever's paying him, and from what I've heard, he does have a semblance of a brain in his head.'

Annabelle sat open-mouthed. 'I can't do it,' she gasped. 'I don't want to do it. I'm happy sitting on a beach back in Tenerife and drinking cocktails with my pals. Becoming the boss of a crime gang was never one of my career ambitions.'

'It's not just any gang, Annabelle. It's the biggest in Scotland, which is why the troops on the ground will be looking for some continuity. Your Gilmour's sister and Jamie's wife. You'll be a steady hand until you can make arrangements to hand over to anyone else you might want to.'

Dom waited, hoping she had taken it all in. Ian Gilmour was going down, that was a certainty. He was living his last few days on God's green earth, but the last thing Dom and his operation could afford was a civil war within Gilmour's organisation. That might still happen, but by putting Annabelle in charge she could be seen as a continuation of the previous regime, not someone to stir the pot too much.

Gabby reached over and placed a hand on her mother's arm. 'Mum, it's the best solution, plus I'll help you - well me and Cassie, and these two,' she pointed towards Cammy and Andy. 'Cassie knows a bit more about this sort of thing than I do. If you don't step up, then everything dad built will disappear in a mad feeding frenzy of small time hoods.'

'But he's my brother,' Annabelle said to Gabby. 'And you all want me to sign up for having him killed? How in God's name can I do that with a clear conscience?'

'Annabelle, even if you tip him off and he doesn't go to Spain and decides to head somewhere else, he's a dead man walking,' Dom told her. He placed a hand on her arm. 'The Colombians won't rest until he's caught and they get their revenge. Your best option right now is to stick with us. We'll see you through this.'

'I don't understand.' Annabelle looked at Gabby. 'You always said you wanted nothing to do with this side of your dad's work. Why the change of heart?'

'Well let's just say I've gained a new perspective over the last few weeks. Anyway, it's not about me, it's about you.'

Annabelle Phillips slumped in her seat. Dom could see she realised Ian Gilmour's time in charge was about to end. He gazed around the table at them, one by one.

'Does anyone have a problem with Annabelle running things?'

Taggart glowered at Dom. 'I trust Annabelle implicitly. I've known her for over twenty five years. It's you I have a problem with Rossi. I don't know you, I've never worked with you the truth is I don't even know why you're involved in any of this. So tell me Domenico, what do *you* get out of it?'

'Andy it's fine. I understand where you're coming from, I do. But Gilmour is trying to put me out of business too. Plus, I now know he had my father killed. If those aren't two good reasons for revenge then I don't know what is. But I also need to give the Colombians something. They have to save face, and the only way they can do that is to deal with the man who murdered one of their own. So my view is simple. The Barrera's dish out punishment for all of us. And the show has to go on, so it's better they have a ringmaster Ian's troops can relate to rather than someone new that comes in and starts cracking a big whip. That way lies chaos, which is bad for business.'

Cammy Maxwell turned to Taggart. 'He's right Andy. From what we've heard, Ian's coat's on a shaky nail. If Annabelle can be seen to keep things steady then it will prove beneficial all around.'

'And you two will still be back where you belong,' Dom interjected. 'You'll be able to help Annabelle get things sorted and calm everyone down.' Rossi hoped the flattery would work.

Taggart glared at Maxwell for a few seconds, then sat back and took a long drink from the glass of white wine on the table before him. 'Fine,' he said resignation in his voice. 'It looks like this is going to happen anyway, with or without me.' He looked at Annabelle. 'I'll help you get through this as best I can, but I was thinking of retiring somewhere warm, where my bones wouldn't ache every time I crawled out of my pit in the morning. So I'll give you a year, then you need to promise to buy me out, okay?'

'Andy, I don't know if it's okay or not? If you want to leave you can. I won't stop you.'

They sat silently for a few minutes, each dwelling on what they had heard, wondering just what the future held for them. Annabelle took out her mobile and began texting. Dom wondered for a second if she was warning her brother? Giving him the opportunity to get away while he still could? If she was, there was little he could do about it. Dom signalled the waiters and they began to bring their lunch to them. He hoped Gabby had primed her mother well on the way in from the airport. If what Gabby had told Dom was true, then Annabelle had absolutely no interest in running her brother's organisation. Her life, her friends, everything she had was back in Tenerife. Apart from Gabby and her sister Angela, Annabelle had nothing left in Scotland. Dom hoped all she had just learned about her brother had managed to sway her to his side, his way of thinking.

He knew the agreement they had tacitly reached would change their lives in ways they could never have imagined even a few weeks ago. Plus, he had managed to hide his plans from Maxwell and Taggart until it was too late for them to back out. Annabelle though, was a smart cookie. If Gabby could do the groundwork, he hoped she realised exactly what he was after without him having to embark on the next phase of the charm offensive. His own mobile suddenly buzzed with a new text alert. He reached into his jacket pocket and looked at the message. It was from Annabelle. Gabby had given her his number and asked her to use it when she felt ready, which surprisingly was now. It took everything he had not to reach over and hug her.

It simply said, 'We need to talk.'

In that instant Dom Rossi knew his stock in the Scottish underworld was about to go higher than he had ever previously expected or indeed wanted.

Now it was all about timing.

TWENTY FOUR

Next morning at seven, Dom sat alone in his kitchen having breakfast. Cereal, coffee and toast. All ordinary and boring. His mobile, on the table beside his cup, began to vibrate, buzzing loudly, moving around as if possessed. He picked it up and looked at the number. He didn't recognise it. There was no name. Could be Miguel on a burner, but he would not call this number. Curious, he swallowed the mouthful of toasted brown bread he'd been chewing on and accepted the call with a swipe on the screen. Then he put it on speakerphone.

'Morning,' he said politely. 'Domenico Rossi speaking.' Well, he half smiled to himself, what else could he say? Politeness cost bugger all.

'How doin' Mr Rossi,' a Yorkshire accent replied. 'We haven't met, but we've heard a lot about each other.'

Well, well thought Dom. Eamon O'Boyle! Now why was he reaching out to him this early in the morning?

'Eamon, I presume. Nice of you to call me, if a bit of a surprise. I thought you were asking Ian Gilmour to handle all the negotiations about your shipment.'

'Well, you know how it is Dom, sometimes the organ grinder just has to put the monkey back in its box and do a bit of dancing themselves.'

Dom laughed to himself at the analogy. Images of Gilmour swinging through the trees came unbidden to mind. 'Sounds intriguing Eamon, but everything's in hand at this end. There's not much to discuss.'

'Now c'mon Mr Rossi. I don't live in splendid isolation down here. The grapevine has it you're having some problems with the Barrera's.'

'Well Ian's obviously passed on that my suppliers are the Barrera's, but I'm not sure what grapevine you've become tangled up in Eamon, but everything is going according to plan.' Just maybe not your plan, Dom thought.

'When people at the top of their organisation are dying, you expect me to believe that?'

'Nothing to do with me Eamon,' Dom lied. 'The Barrera contact I deal with is very much alive and well.'

There was a pause before O'Boyle spoke again. 'I need to know my money is safe before I hand it over Mr. Rossi.'

'I understand that Eamon, but you've got to speculate to accumulate, don't you. Plus that's a lot of gear that will be heading down your way. Best part of a half tonne of the stuff if I know Gilmour! It'll be snowing for years in Manchester if you're not careful.'

'What I do with it lad is my business. Can you arrange the meeting or not?'

'I'm already on it Eamon. Ian left me in no doubt it had to go ahead. Give me a couple of hours and I'll get back to you and Gilmour with the where and when.'

'Fine. I'll be waiting.'

Dom hung up. It was now obvious that Ian Gilmour, whether he knew it or not, was just a bit part player in what was becoming a game of brinkmanship. He knew he needed to convince O'Boyle at the meeting, that he should leave any revenge against Gilmour to the South Americans. At least he had managed to talk Annabelle into giving up her own opportunity for revenge. He was still worried O'Boyle might decide it was worth taking out his frustrations on Dom as the son of one of the men involved in Finbar's murder. It was a risk he had to take though. The stakes were too high. Only with Gilmour out of the picture could Annabelle step in and keep the lid on the inevitable fallout and violent jostling for position the rival factions in Gilmour's organisation would try to embark on. Then, with that done, he could work with Annabelle to implement the next part of the plan.

Now though, he had to find out for definite when Carlos was due to arrive in Mijas, then organise Gilmour and O'Boyle to be there along with himself. Annabelle would be in Glasgow with Gabby and Angela. Billy and Marti would stay in Scotland minding the shop. Cassie he would take to Spain. Once Carlos Barrera had taken Gilmour off his hands, Maxwell and Taggart would make sure Annabelle was placed in de-facto charge of her brother's organisation. He finished his breakfast, cleared up and went into his office. Another burner phone sat on his desk already programmed with the number Miguel had given him. He dialled and waited, standing looking out of the large window into the garden.

'Good morning Domenico. I wondered when you would be calling.'

Miguel sounded on edge, Dom thought. Hardly surprising given his part in Antonio's death.

'Ola Miguel. How are things at your end?'

'They are moving along as well as can be expected my friend. Carlos will be arriving tomorrow and I have no idea what mood he will be in. He will still be determined to find his brother's killer.'

Good thought Dom. 'He will find him, Miguel, he will. We'll be serving him up on a platter, remember.'

'I do not think you understand his mentality. He will not rest until everyone involved in Antonio's death faces his justice. That includes finding out who told Gilmour the details about Antonio's visit.'

Dom nodded to himself. 'I've been thinking about that,' he told Miguel. 'Perhaps we can spin it that Antonio himself let on to Gilmour when he would be in Spain again? After all, they were working together to eventually get rid of me. It would make sense if they were keeping each other appraised of where they were going and what they were doing.'

'Si, that might be possible.'

'Good,' said Dom. 'I'd like to get everyone over to Spain the day after tomorrow. This needs to be finished. It's gone on far too long.'

'I agree,' Miguel replied. 'Who will you be bringing?'

'Gilmour and O'Boyle. No one else will be allowed. They both know that. I'll work on the basis we have the meeting on the evening we all arrive. You need to convince Carlos he'll be in the room with the man who killed his brother.'

Miguel sighed. 'Si. I will do that.'

Dom felt concern for his friend. 'I'm sorry you have to bear the brunt of this over there Miguel, but O'Boyle is also going to want to know his shipment of coke will be ready to go when he asks for it.'

'Then he'll just have to take my word for it as well as Carlos's.'

'Forty five million is a lot to pay up front.'

'Domenico, unless he wants to go over to Colombia himself and watch the shipment being loaded, then that is the best he will get.'

Dom heard the frustration creeping into Miguel's voice. 'Okay Miguel, I'll make the arrangements. I want the video of Gilmour killing Antonio ready to play when I say so, plus I'll be bringing another couple I'll need played first.'

'Fine, my friend. I'll see you in a few days.'

Dom hung up and sat the phone back down on his desk, making a mental note to destroy it as usual. He would get back to Eamon O'Boyle later, but right now Gilmour was his main concern. He had thought about asking Annabelle to stay hidden, under cover from her brother until it was time for her to step up. But all it would take was one sighting and one comment to alert Gilmour to her presence. It was better if she made contact. Go and see him, tell him she missed the old country. Keep it simple. He sighed wearily. His trust in people had been dented by Malone and he was having to trust in a lot of people right now. He pulled out his mobile and dialled O'Boyle's number. Time to give him the good news.

ΔΔΔ

Drumchapel! Gilmour looked out the car's tinted windows. This place was now as different from the nineteen sixties as you could possibly imagine. Gone were the four storey high, depressing breeze block tenements. Money had been thrown at this sink estate in recent years. It was now all designer terraced housing with three storey high flats and townhouses. Fuck, he thought, there was even a Porsche outside a shop along the road. Changed days. Gilmour sat in the back of Cammy Maxwell's Mercedes, parked up in the street where Charlie 'Easy' Easdon lived. The tracker had done its work. Tam McGraw's two henchmen had led them straight to 'Easy's' front door. Now all they had to do was wait.

Just then Gilmour's mobile rang. Reaching into his jacket pocket he pulled out the phone and answered the call.

'Hello,' was all he said.

After that he just listened, nodding every so often at whatever was being said on the other end of the phone.

'Fine. See you there.' Then he hung up and held the mobile in his hands.

Taggart looked at Maxwell then turned to Gilmour. 'Anything important boss?'

Ian glared at him. 'Aye, I'm heading for a wee holiday in the sun. Now keep fucking watching.'

They sat for another twenty minutes, by which time Gilmour was getting edgy. He hated thumb twiddling.

'Boss,' Maxwell said, pointing out of the car window. 'There's Easdon. He's with the two boys from the east. Looks like they're getting into the car with the tracker.'

'Right. Let's follow them. I want to see what this bastard is up to.'

Thirty minutes later, the Black Ford Focus GTi pulled into Hillington Industrial Estate. Gilmour told Maxwell to park up in a side street. He knew where Easdon was going.

'It's about time for the cavalry, Andy, don't you think?' Gilmour said

Taggart nodded grimly, switched to his address book and phoned one of the numbers. 'Archie,' he said after it was answered. 'I need you and three of the boys tooled up with sawn offs and a load of clean up gear to meet us at,' he reeled off an address. There was a long pause. 'I don't give a shit what Mikey is up to, or even who he's up, I need you all there in twenty minutes tops. Understand?' Taggart's voice left the guy on the other end in no doubt he meant business. 'Good.' He hung up. 'When the fuck did foot soldiers start to talk back?'

Maxwell climbed out of the car and went to the boot. He came back minutes later with three handguns and dropped them on the seat next to Gilmour. Ian picked up the first weapon, dropped the ammunition clip, checked it and then rammed it back home again before cocking the weapon. He left the safety catch on. The process was repeated with the other two handguns and these were handed to Maxwell and Taggart. Then they waited. Twenty minutes later, a car pulled up beside them and a tall, thin, sickly looking man got out. This was Archie Todd, and Gilmour knew he took great delight in dealing with more recalcitrant people who just hated to give up information. He wore a loose hanging, grey suit that seemed to drown him. He stopped at the drivers side of the car and Maxwell lowered the window. Todd looked around, spotted Gilmour in the back, but said nothing.

'What do we have?' he asked Maxwell.

'Three guys in the warehouse, Two we don't know anything about, but the third one is Charlie Easdon.'

'Easy?' Todd's eyebrows lifted. 'What's he doing out here? I didn't think he knew where the warehouse was?'

'Well he does now,' growled Gilmour. 'Plan is simple. You follow us round and we park up just out of view. I want two of your guys around the back at the fire escape. You,' he pointed at Archie, 'and your other partner will go in first through the front door. We'll follow. And remember, I want them alive. I've more than a few questions that need answering.'

Todd nodded. 'They tooled up?'

Maxwell shrugged. 'No idea. Let's assume they are.'

They moved off and stopped just before their destination. These were old buildings, built just after the war. Refurbished yes, but some still had their original asbestos cement roofs. Most had a roller shutter door in front with a small pedestrian door to the side built into the brick facade. Around the rear was a fire escape. Two of Archie Todd's guys moved off in that direction, their shotguns held low at their side. One of them carried a crowbar. Gilmour nodded to Todd and he walked with his other soldier towards the front door. Gilmour and the other two followed along behind. Their guns were still in the waist-band of their trousers. He watched as Archie Todd and the other man edged closer to the door. They looked at each other. Todd nodded and tried the handle. It opened. 'Easy' was not expecting company. Gilmour and his colleagues hurried and caught up with Todd.

'Okay,' Todd told them. 'Follow me in and stay low. I have no idea where they'll be.' He turned to the other gunman. 'Jimmy, get in touch with the other two. Tell them to make entry in thirty seconds.' The guy nodded and pulled out his phone before passing on the message.

Todd looked around him. Gilmour, Taggart and Maxwell each took out their weapons and released the safeties. With a three, two, one countdown using his fingers, Todd opened the door and he and Jimmy rushed in, followed by Maxwell and Taggart. The door opened straight into the warehouse. Todd went left, keeping low. Jimmy angled to the right. The entire unit was stacked high with packages on racks, not all drugs, as Gilmour did run a legitimate storage business from here. Long aisles radiated from a two metre wide main corridor that ran left and right of where they stood. It was also dim. The lighting from the high level lamps was obscured by the racking and the roof lights had a covering of moss nearly an inch thick rendering them useless, that and the stainless steel mesh that covered them internally. From the rear of the unit, they heard a crash. The other two had just gotten through the fire escape door. Maxwell and Taggart gingerly walked forward, their hand guns held out in front of them. Gilmour followed, refusing to bend down, but holding the pistol by his side, safety off. They suddenly heard a shout from the far side of the warehouse followed by the bang of a shotgun. They all ducked. Todd waved to Jimmy and they moved off carefully down one of the aisles. Taggart and Maxwell went to join them.

'Wait,' Gilmour said with authority. 'No point in employing dogs and chasing rabbits yourself is there? We'll stay here and cut off anyone that gets past them.' A few minutes later they heard four more shots, muffled by the goods stacked on the shelves. And then it was over.

'It's me boss, Archie. Coming out.'

Todd appeared from one of the aisles holding his left hand to his right arm. Blood seeped through his fingers.

'Are you okay,' Taggart asked him. 'Yeh, I know, stupid question. Here let me.' He pulled a handkerchief from his pocket and proceeded to wrap Todd's wound.

'What happened,' Gilmour asked, sure this was not the first time Todd had taken a bullet. He didn't care anyway.

'We had to take one of them out,' he said through gritted teeth. 'The others are alive, but 'Easy' has some pellets in his leg.'

'He'll have more than bloody pellets in him when I'm done. Get them out here.'

'The guys are bringing them.'

Gilmour heard the sounds of someone moaning coming from another aisle. He slipped his gun back into the waistband of his trousers, walked across and saw two of Todd's men hauling Easdon along the floor by his armpits. Blood trailed from a damaged left leg, leaving a long red line on the floor. As he was brought closer, Gilmour saw Easdon's calf muscle had been shredded. His head was bowed and he mumbled something incomprehensible. Behind them, Jimmy roughly pushed a man in front of him who had his hands tied behind his back. He was not coming easily and the muzzle of the shotgun was prodded into his back every few steps.

'Bring them over here where we have a bit more space,' Gilmour instructed, his eyes never leaving Easdon.

Easdon was dragged towards Gilmour and held up just in front of him. Ian looked into his eyes, but all he saw was fear. Easdon was fairly young, about thirty five, and was also a handsome bastard who thought he was god's gift. He wouldn't be so full of himself after this, thought Gilmour.

Taggart went over and grabbed hold of the man with his arms tied behind his back and threw him towards Gilmour. He stumbled and fell to his knees. Ian walked over and stood in front of him. He roughly grabbed hold of his hair and jerked his head up.

'You're a wee bit away from the capital son, aren't you? I thought you east coasters didn't come past Bathgate?' The man looked at Gilmour with contempt in his eyes. He was around thirty, with short, cropped brown hair. There was a scar on his cheek marking him as someone who didn't mind getting into a scrap. A soldier on the make thought Ian.

'Want to tell me how you got in contact with my wee pal over there?' He nodded towards Easdon. The man said nothing. Gilmour let his hair go and crouched down to his level, staring him in the eye. 'Son, the only way you're getting out of this is if you tell me everything. Like, did Tam McGraw put you up to this? Or are you trying to go all independent with that dick over there?'

The man smirked at him. 'I'm getting out of this am I, just like my pal back there did then?'

Gilmour grinned back at him and gently slapped him on the face. He stood and walked over to Easdon where he was being held up, still moaning. Reaching forward he lifted Easdon's head by his chin until he was staring at him. The man chewed on his lower lip, trying to deal with the pain.

'Easy, Easy, look what you've gone and done to yourself. C'mon laddie, tell me, did McGraw approach you or did you go to him? And how did you find out about this place?' he swept his right arm around pointing at the racks.

Easdon coughed. 'I,….. I,' he stammered. 'I'm in fucking pain boss. Get me something for the leg and I'll tell you everything you want to know.'

Gilmour shook his head. 'Doesn't work like that son. You tell me what I need to know first and then I'll get you sorted.'

Despite the pain, Easdon smirked. 'Or what? You'll off me? Nah, then you'll never find out who gave it away. You'll never find out how close to you they are, or how much they hate your guts.'

'Is that a fact?'

Gilmour stepped back. In one swift motion he took out the gun, cocked the hammer then held it to Easdon's head. He watched as Easdon flinched. The smell of hot, fresh urine assailed Ian's nostrils.

In a flash he turned to his right, pointed the gun at the head of McGraw's soldier and pulled the trigger. The noise in the immediate area was deafening. They all watched as the man fell heavily forward onto the floor. Blood, brain and bone splattered from the exit wound. The bullet from Gilmour's gun had burst the temporal artery and blood pressure in the man's body caused a fountain of red to erupt in a wide arc, like crimson liquid coming from a hosepipe. The man behind him jumped clear as it sprayed close to him. Everyone stood still for a few seconds. Easdon had slumped forward, the two men holding him under his armpits struggling to keep him upright. He was retching, the sour smell of vomit overpowering the stench of urine. Gilmour turned back to him and cocked the gun again, but held it down by his side.

'Now, Charlie you can see just how pissed off I am about this whole thing. So why don't you be a good laddie and just give me a name? Look, I understand you want to strike out on your own. Hell, I even admire your initiative, in fact I might just set you up somewhere myself when this is all over. But you do need to tell me what I want to know?'

Charlie Easdon mumbled something.

'Ah cannae hear you son. Try again.' Despite the stench, Gilmour leaned in closer.

'It,..... it was your niece, Ian, your own niece.'

Gilmour straightened up slowly and looked at Easdon. Andy and Cammy could see the anger welling up in his features.

'Hold him up,' he told the two men gripping the trembling man. They hauled on his armpits, lifting him higher. Gilmour took the pistol across his body then swung it in a wide arc. It connected with Charlie Easdon's face, cracking several of his teeth and leaving a long gash on his cheek flowing with blood. He pissed himself again. Gilmour was breathing heavily, not through exertion though, but with anger. His eyes blazed, but his voice was low as he leaned back in slightly towards Easdon.

'Now, tell me that again Charlie and think very carefully before you speak.'

'I'm telling you the truth,' he spat, blood and a loose tooth spraying from his mouth. 'I've been going out with Angela for a while now. She told me about this place.' Spittle and blood dripped from his mouth down his chin before landing on the floor. 'She also got me the keys and the code to the alarm.'

Gilmour closed his eyes and tilted his head back. He had asked Angela to come and pick up some packages for him occasionally. That had been money, not drugs, and he had only done it after she kept pressing him to get more involved with the family business. What had the stupid wee lassie done? Gilmour turned and walked away towards Todd. He handed him the gun. Todd looked at it, a question in his eyes.

'Take care of this?' he nodded back towards Easdon. 'Make sure he disappears permanently, and I want those Edinburgh twats found on their own patch. McGraw needs to know he can't fuck with me. And clean this place up. I want no evidence left behind. Call me when it's done.'

'We found these on him too, boss.' Todd's sidekick handed Gilmour a set of keys. The keys to the warehouse. And they could only have come from one place.

With that, he signalled to Taggart and Maxwell. 'C'mon, we're leaving. I've too much to do to be bothered with this shit any more.'

They walked back to the car silently. As he threw himself into the backseat, he let out a scream. Both Maxwell and Taggart jumped.

'Drive,' he simply told them.

Angela, he thought. What the hell was he going to do about her? His life was just getting more complicated every day. And he still had Annabelle to meet later.

TWENTY FIVE

Cammy drove into the courtyard of Gilmour's farm and parked up close to the front door. Gilmour was angrier than Maxwell or Taggart had ever seen him. Despite having delivered a few 'hits' over the years, they were both still shocked about the casual way Ian had put a bullet into the head of Tam McGraws soldier, except it now looked as if he hadn't been working for McGraw, but for Charlie Easdon. But what had tipped Gilmour over a precipice, was the involvement of his own niece in the betrayal. Gilmour would need to do something, but he had his sister to consider, so the 'usual' punishment might be off the table. This was uncharted territory. Cammy turned to Gilmour in the back seat.

'Anything else you want us to do boss?'

Gilmour didn't answer for a few seconds, his eyes seemingly focussed on something unseen. Eventually his gaze turned to Maxwell. 'I want you to get over to Easdon's and sort out his affairs. Everyone pays what they owe, got it?' His voice was flat and calm, but his eyes were narrow, boring into Cammy's with the intensity of an industrial laser. Maxwell nodded, but there was still the look of an unasked question on his face. Both he and Taggart knew what was in store for Gilmour in the next few days, and the last thing they wanted was to have to deal with Angela before Ian left for Spain.

'What for fuck's sake?' Gilmour snarled.

'What do you want us to do about Angela? Do you want us to find her? Keep her here until you get back? Might be better. Give you a chance to think of something appropriate for her.'

Gilmour glared at him. 'There's only one thing appropriate

for that ungrateful traitorous little bitch.'

'Boss, you do that you'll lose your sister,' Taggart replied.

'Don't tell me what I'll lose,' Gilmour thundered. It was then he noticed Gabby's Ford sitting parked in the courtyard. 'So, they're all here already, are they, good,' he smiled grimly, 'I'll deal with Angela and her mother, and then you two can take it from there. Understood?'

They nodded faces solemn.

'Cammy, you get to Easdon's and deal with his shit. Andy you're with me. Let's get inside.' With that, he opened the door and got out, closing it behind him.

Andy Taggart turned to face Cammy, a worried look on his face. 'I'll need to find some way of getting him to put off any punishment until he gets back from Spain.'

Cammy frowned. 'Andy, he's not coming back from Spain, or haven't you been listening? Look if he wants you to off her just say you'll do it, but you'll need to take her somewhere quiet, out of the way. Tell him he doesn't want another mess like the fucking warehouse to clear up.'

Taggart looked worried. 'Aye, I'll think of something. I better get going or he'll be after my balls too. He's losing it Cammy. The sooner Annabelle takes over the better.'

He opened the passenger door and got out, following Gilmour into the farmhouse. As he entered, he heard voices coming from the living room. Gilmour was smiling and talking animatedly. He noticed Taggart. 'Andy, come and meet my sister and my two gorgeous nieces. I know you haven't seen them for a while.'

'What, so I'm not gorgeous anymore,' Annabelle snapped back at him.

'Now you know you're my sister Annabelle, I can't be saying that about you.' He grinned at them, hiding his true feelings well.

Taggart also smiled, keeping up the pretence of not having met Annabelle yesterday, and walked over towards them. 'Hello ladies. Nice to see you all, especially you Mrs Phillips, haven't seen you since your husband died. You're looking good.'

'Thanks Andy. The warmer weather's been kind to me.'

The girls and their mother were sitting on the leather, Chesterfield facing the fireplace, close to each other. Annabelle and Gabby looked calm, but Angela seemed a little tense, as if this meeting was keeping her from something important. Ian sat in the chair furthest away from the door so Andy took the other one. He looked at Annabelle.

'So Annabelle, what brings you back to bonnie Scotland? I was going to say it cannae be the weather, but we're doin' no too bad this year aren't we?'

She smiled back at him. 'Just thought I'd come and pay my girls a visit. It's been six months since I last saw them and I'd heard the weather was good so, voila, here I am.' She looked across at her brother, the smile fading. 'Gabrielle here tells me she's doing some work for you, spying on some high end drug dealer called Rossi. Is that true?'

'I wouldn't call it spying Annabelle. She's just helping look after a wee investment I've made that's all. No big deal.'

'Just make sure she's kept safe Ian. I don't want anything to happen to her, understand?'

Gilmour glared at his sister, but did not reply. Instead he looked over at Angela. She nervously twisted a ring on her finger, trying hard not to look him in the eye.

'On the other hand,' he said, coldly, 'I don't know what my other wee niece has been up to lately. She hasn't been around much asking for advice – or money.'

Angela lifted her head and started back at her Uncle. 'What do you mean? I saw you not long ago in the café with the guy Gabby's working for. I didn't ask you for anything then, did I?' She sounded insulted he had suggested this.

'No you didn't,' Gilmour replied holding his voice even. 'But a wee birdies told me you've been a busy girl elsewhere.'

She sat up. 'What? Are you having me followed?'

He grinned evilly. 'Now why would I do that?'

'Look Ian, what the fuck is going on. Why are you being like this with Angela?' Annabelle was not pleased and didn't care if her brother knew it.

'Well I found out today our Angela's crossed a wee line, gotten herself involved with someone she shouldn't have.' He fixed her with a hard stare.

Angela looked around at her mother and sister, alarmed. 'I haven't done anything,' she told them. She looked at Gilmour. 'Well? What am I supposed to have done?'

Gilmour sat back in his chair and crossed his legs. He began drumming his fingers on the leather arm of the chair, setting up a rhythm with a cadence aiming for a crescendo. 'Maybe I should just ask 'Easy' Easdon in here and he can explain it all himself. Will I do that Angela, will I?'

She looked scared. There was panic in her eyes.

'Angela, what the hell have you been up to?' her mother asked.

'Nothing, I promise. Nothing!'

'C'mon Angela. It's not the worst crime in the world, going out with one of my minions. I mean it's not something I'd ordinarily approve of, but heh, you're still young and 'Easy' is a good looking guy so I can see the attraction.'

They all watched as she sat silently for a few seconds, obviously considering what to say.

'Alright,' she said through gritted teeth. 'I have been seeing him. It started six months ago, but it's no big deal. I know he works for you, but where's the harm?'

'Just seeing him, absolutely no harm whatsoever Angela.' Gilmour stood up and reached into his jacket pocket. Something jangled as he brought it out. He threw it onto the coffee table in front of them. There was dried blood on the key ring and on the two keys. 'But helping him and Tam McGraw to rob me! Know that's just not on, even if you are my niece.'

Angela looked at the keys in horror. She began to quietly sob.

'Angela whose are these?' her mother asked her as she reached across and placed a hand on her shoulder.

'Tell her Angela? Tell her who's keys they are?' Angela kept crying. 'No. Okay, then I will. They're my keys Annabelle. They open a warehouse I have. A warehouse where I store a lot of my gear and my cash.' He walked around the coffee table and crouched down in front of her, patting her knees. 'Come on, you give them to Charlie Easdon, didn't you? Just nod.'

Angela looked frantically about her, but she had nowhere to go. Her mother still held her arm. Uncle Ian had his hands on her knees. She looked up at him.

'I just want to know for certain,' he smiled. 'I know Easdon's a charming bastard and probably put you up to this, but you'll feel better if you get it off your chest.'

She nodded her head wildly and said something unintelligible.

'What? I didn't catch you Angela.'

'I said yes, I gave them to Charlie, but we only wanted a wee bit of stuff, just enough to get started somewhere else. We didn't mean any harm Uncle Ian, honest? We'd have paid you back.' she sniffed back her tears.

'I know you would have, I know,' he said to her, standing up. He looked at her coldly. 'Andy, take her to one of the spare rooms. Make sure the windows are secured and then lock her in there. Only food and drink till I get back'

Annabelle stood up and faced her brother, her face set hard. 'Don't you dare Ian, don't you fucking dare?'

Gilmour reached over and grabbed his sister by the throat with one hand. Gabby and Angela let out a gasp. Annabelle struggled to breath. 'Don't ever tell me what to do in my own house, and don't ever tell me how to run my business, understand little sister?'

Annabelle could hardly breathe now. Taggart became worried Ian was going too far. 'Ian,' he said quickly. 'Ian, for fucks sake you're going to strangle her. Let her go.' He walked over and placed his hand on Gilmour's outstretched arm gripping her throat.

The fury never faded from Gilmour's eyes, but he slowly

released his grip. Annabelle gasped and coughed, clutching her throat. Gabby and Angela rushed towards her, but Gilmour grabbed Angela by the arm and swung her round to face him. 'Not you. You're going with Andy,......now!'

She began to protest again, terror in her eyes, but Taggart told her to be quiet and then led her off to one of the bedrooms.

'Oh, by the way Angela, 'Gilmour called after. 'Don't bank on seeing charming Charlie anytime soon. He's taking a wee trip to the country with some of my other boys and he'll be gone for a long, long time.'

Gilmour watched as realisation dawned. She screamed abuse at him, struggling and kicking to escape Taggart's grasp.

Gilmour watched impassively and said nothing. As he turned around, he felt a painful slap across the face. Gabby stood there, anger seething out of her pores.

'You're a fucking animal Ian. A psychopath,' she screamed in his face. 'That's your niece you're keeping prisoner, and you almost killed your sister. What kind of deranged fucking lunatic are you?'

He rubbed his cheek with his right hand. 'The kind that runs a successful business by not being soft, that's what. Now you and your mother get out of here before I get really angry. I have things to do before tomorrow. Go. Now!' he screamed at them, bringing his hand from his cheek as if to strike her.

Gabby went to hit him again, but her mother used one hand to hold her back, still clutching the other to her bruising throat. 'Leave it Gabby,' she rasped. 'Let's go. Now.'

'But mum,' she protested.

'Now!' She left no room for refusal.

As they turned to walk from the living room into the hallway, they could hear screams and bangs against a bedroom door as Taggart came back from locking Angela in.

'Make sure they leave,' Gilmour snarled at him.

Taggart ushered the two women to the front door. Once safely outside he turned to them. 'She'll be okay Annabelle. She's scared as fuck, but I won't let anything happen to her.

Don't worry?'

Annabelle nodded, a small sob escaping from her lips. 'Just make sure that bastard gets to Spain tomorrow.'

'What the fuck happened in the warehouse Andy? Was Angela involved?' Gabby asked him. She was shaking with anger.

Taggart glanced behind him to make sure the door was firmly closed then turned and nodded. 'She gave the keys to Charlie Easdon and he hooked up with two of Tam McGraw's guys. Looks like they were going to raid the place for some stuff and set themselves up.' He paused for a second. 'Both of McGraw's men are dead. Ian shot one of them in the head himself at point blank range. Charlie's either dead or about to be. He's with Archie Todd. Ian's lost it.'

'I don't give a shit about any of them just make sure nothing happens to Angela?' It was a plea from Annabelle.

'Annabelle, don't worry. I'll look after her. I'll calm her down when Ian leaves and bring her up to speed on what's going on. Now get out of here before he wonders where the fuck I've gotten to.'

Annabelle reached out and touched his arm then the two women turned and left to get into Gabby's Ford.

Andy Taggart stood where he was for a minute watching as they both left. He had dished out his share of punishment beatings over the years. Broken bones, kneecappings, slashed faces, even five murders. He'd organised even more, but the one thing he always did was maintain a sense of emotional distance. His violence was the dispassionate kind of a sociopath. There was never anything personal about what he did. It was all just business. But Ian had crossed the line. He was allowing his anger to blind him to the realities of what they were. His treatment of the three women was clear evidence he was beginning to unravel.

Andy and Cammy had worked for Jamie Phillips before he had been killed. Phillips had been as tough as Gilmour, but he had a better sense of people and had been easier to work for. Gilmour was temperamental, more prone to anger and allowing it to easily surface. Andy's only hope now was that Rossi could deliver over in Spain, and that Ian Gilmour would be handed to the Colombians. He just hoped when they got him, they gave Ian the chance to go to confession, because he was certain the South Americans had ways of slowly killing you that could make your last hours seem like an eternity.

TWENTY SIX

Carlos Barrera was tired, bored and beaten by the constant vibration from the four Rolls Royce AE 2100 D3 turboprop engines of the C130 Hercules Transport. There was no cargo on board, so they were able to fly approximately 8,000 kilometres before needing to re-fuel. This would just have been enough to fly from Bogota to the Costa del Sol, but the engines would be sucking fumes at the end, so they would re-fuel in the Azores. The entire flight would take just over 15 hours, and Antonio was not known for being naturally patient. It was taking all he had to keep his anger and frustration in check. His seat was utilitarian as opposed to luxurious. There was no tray, no in flight video. The meals he ate were re-heated military rations. He wore the ill fitting fatigues of a Colombian Air Force Colonel and they scratched and itched. His four companions, his 'Soldados', sat some way off from him, dressed similarly but with lower ranks on their shoulders. They had been playing an almost constant game of cards since they had lifted off from the military air force facility at El Dorado airfield in Bogota, giving Carlos his space and privacy. At least now it would only be another few hours until they landed in the south of Spain.

He undid the safety belt he had loosely kept around his waist and stood up, stretching to ease his aching muscles. At fifty one, he was past his prime, but he kept in reasonable shape. Unlike Antonio had with his love of rich food and expensive wines. His dark hair had little streaks of grey in it, but his moustache was black, helped a little by the subtle dye he used. He stepped into the aisle and did some bending and flexing. His movement caught the eye of someone further up the plane, also wearing combat fatigues but with the insignia of a General on his epaulettes.

'Well Carlos,' he said as they approached him. 'Nearly there. I hope the journey hasn't been too boring for you?

Carlos smiled a little. 'Not at all General. It has given me time for reflection, time I rarely get when I am back home running my business.'

General Jorge Sanchez nodded. He knew exactly the kind of business Carlos ran. In fact he had been a significant beneficiary of that business. The bribes Carlos paid ensured the Colombian Air Force stayed well away from those areas where the Barrera's grew and processed their rich crop of cocoa leaves. He had been surprised though when Carlos had requested his help in organising this flight. Leaving Colombia was incredibly dangerous. He was wanted by police forces worldwide, so the reason he was going to Spain had to be important. Sanchez had gotten him the persona of a Colonel in the Air Force, with various ranks for his four companions. This would ensure he arrived safely in Madrid, and whatever happened then? Well, Jorge could only do as he was instructed.

Carlos looked back at his four companions. 'Do you have the weapons and the transport ready for us when we land, Jorge?'

'Si Senor. It is all in hand. The vehicle will be waiting for you on the tarmac when you arrive.'

Barrera nodded. 'Good. Now, I need a piss. See you when we land.'

Some hours later, just after the Hercules had touched down, Carlos and his four Soldados had driven off in a nondescript black SUV towards Miguel's Villa in the hills above Mijas. Standing watching the vehicle drive across the tarmac to a rarely used perimeter gate, General Jorge Sanchez reached into his fatigues and took out his mobile phone. He looked up a number from his contacts list and dialled.

'Si?' the voice on the other end simply asked.

'He has arrived and is on his way with four bodyguards.' General Jorge Sanchez disconnected the call and replaced his phone. He had no option but to make it. A year previously, the Major Crimes Unit of the Policia Nacional de Colombia, had discovered he was being bribed by the Barrera's to ignore their operations in the Colombian countryside. Their ultimatum was simple. If he did not work to bring Barrera to justice, then he would find himself in the nightmare that was the La Modelo prison in Bogota, meat for the grinder of its eleven thousand inhabitants. The authorities also wanted to roll up the network if they could. So Jorge had informed them of this Spanish trip and they had bitten. Also safer for him if Carlos was captured in Spain. Less chance of retribution against himself.

His jaw tightened as the SUV disappeared from view, complete with its satellite tracker. The call he had placed was to the Spanish El Cuerpo Nacional de Policía. He would text the tracker frequency to them and after that, it was up to them to capture Barrera. If he escaped the raid, then Jorge knew Carlos would come after him as no one else knew who the Colonel on board was. Sanchez turned away and began his long, lonely walk to the terminal to await the news – good or bad.

ΔΔΔ

The light was fading by the time Barrera arrived at the Villa, but the building was well lit. He could see Miguel's bodyguards standing outside the wall of the small compound waiting on his car, their weapons hidden, but still there. As they ground to a halt on the driveway, Carlos saw Miguel and Mariana, his lover, standing on the front porch waiting expectantly. He was still undecided about Miguel. After all, his own brother had been killed whilst effectively in his care, or at the least on Miguel's patch. Miguel had been a good servant, but the problem with servants was that over time they could become just a little bit above their station and begin to develop delusions of grandeur. Was that what had happened with Miguel? Had he become tired of taking orders from Antonio, watching him take all the credit for the work Miguel himself was doing? He sighed. Perhaps taking the middle ground was the option best suited just now. Do not be too friendly, but do not make it seem he had already made up his mind. Ask for the facts first and then make a decision. Either Miguel was now to become his main organiser in Europe, or he would become food for the sharks.

The SUV rolled to a stop. Carlos waited until his bodyguards had exited, handguns at the ready. Only when they were happy did he climb from the car, limbs stiff from the long flight. They all still wore their Air Force fatigues, and he stood there in the courtyard, surrounded by his men, feeling incongruous dressed as he was. Their luggage was in the boot of the car, including the made to measure clothes he was accustomed to wearing. He ran his hands through his thick hair, then scratched the stubble on his chin. Looking around, he saw no one else apart from Miguel and Mariana. Miguel's bodyguards kept a discrete distance. Carlos walked towards Miguel, his own bodyguards flanking him, moving in unison. He stopped a few feet before he reached him, then held out his arms wide.

'Miguel,' he said. 'It has been a long time since we last met.'

Miguel walked forward himself, his own arms open, more to demonstrate he was unarmed than through any obvious sign of affection. He embraced Carlos nonetheless. Carlos returned the gesture, but his touch was light.

'I wish it had been under different circumstances Senor Barrera, I truly do. That you came here is not unappreciated, but the reason.........!' Miguel left that part unsaid.

'Thank you Miguel.' Carlos wrapped an arm around Orejuela's shoulders and propelled him back towards the Villa. 'Let me have a shower and a change of clothes, then you can bring me up to speed on where you are with the investigations. Ah, Mariana, it is also good to see you again. I had almost forgotten how beautiful you are. I still think I need to steal you away from Miguel.' He smiled warmly at her as they reached the front porch.

'Carlos, I am so sorry about Antonio. I know who much you depended on him. He was a great man and will be sorely missed by us all,' she lied, leaning over and kissing him on the cheek.

'Thank you, thank you,' he replied solemnly.

'Come, I have your room ready and someone will bring your luggage in. I will prepare you some refreshments and when you are ready you and Miguel can meet in the secure room Miguel has built into the house.'

A short twenty minutes later, as Miguel sat nervously in a dining room chair, Carlos Barrera walked in, almost unrecognisable from the man who had stepped from the SUV. He had changed into a soft, light green cotton shirt and pale blue trousers and looked every one of his five foot eleven inches. His hair had been washed and combed and he had shaved the dark bristle away. Even his Zapata moustache had been carefully trimmed. Miguel stood. Barrera waved at him to stay seated then looked at the spread on the table, mainly fresh fruit and some bowls of salad. There were also two bottles of red wine and two crystal glasses.

'It is good to see Mariana remembered I am a vegetarian, but one that likes to drink,' he smiled. 'Now, sit. Let us eat something and you can tell me what you know.'

Both men sat and took platefuls of fruit and salad. Miguel poured them both a glass of wine. They toasted one another. Carlos looked around the room. It was minimalist in design, The steel and glass table and the chromed high backed chairs were not traditional Spanish style. The room itself was painted in a subtle green. Original prints from many famous photographers adorned the walls, Annie Leibovitz, David Bailey, Andy Warhol. Miguel liked his photography and had sought out some of the best.

'I hope you do not think it is too ostentatious, Senor?' Miguel asked as he cut an apple into quarters for himself.

Barrera shook his head. 'On the contrary. You have good taste. This,' he swung an arm out encompassing the room, 'is understated.' He took a sip of his wine and nodded in appreciation. 'Now. Tell me what you know? And please, call me

Carlos'

He watched as Miguel drew in a long breath.

'Antonio had been approached in Amsterdam by Ian Gilmour with an offer he hoped would be beneficial for both of them. Apparently, he was becoming tired of paying a large fee to Domenico Rossi every time he wanted to import drugs into Scotland.'

Carlos held up a hand. 'I already know that, but perhaps you can explain to me why Rossi seems to be the only person who can smuggle our produce into their country? We used to be able to handle that side of things fine by ourselves in the past. What has changed over the years?'

'The Government and the public's attitude to illegal drugs are what has changed. Around eight years ago, the authorities in England began a massive crackdown that centred around all of the usual routes, mainly the ports in the south and north east of the country. They were successful and for a time we were losing nearly all of our shipments, not to mention couriers.'

Barrera nodded. 'Yes, I seem to recall Antonio telling me something along those lines. So what changed?'

'Our profits were being hit hard and the price of what did get through was incredibly expensive on the streets. I was then introduced to Domenico Rossi by a dealer from England, who used to also import directly from us, but via the continent, mainly Rotterdam. He too was losing a lot of product and a lot money and had all but stopped. Rossi said if we could transport our product to him directly from South America, he would arrange to have it covertly delivered to isolated bays and beaches on the West coast of Scotland. He knew where these were, he had information on the tides and he was able to pay off or blackmail the appropriate officials to look the other way.'

'So,' Barrera said. 'Rossi became an important figure in all of this.'

'Si Carlos. He was key. Until he set up his organisation, our income stream from Britain had fallen to practically nothing.'

Miguel looked at Carlos, a confused look on his face. 'Forgive me, but I thought you already knew all of this?'

'I'll let you into a secret Miguel, Antonio was the brains behind our business dealings. I left all of this to him. I was happier running security and organising the deliveries, so no, I did not already know all of this.'

Miguel nodded. 'Well a few weeks ago, Ian Gilmour approached Domenico Rossi with a request for one metric tonne of cocaine.'

Carlos nodded. He swallowed some salad he had been chewing. 'Now this I did know. When you informed Antonio of the request, he contacted me. He also wanted to discuss an alternative offer that had been made by this Gilmour.'

'Yes. He asked me to invite Rossi over to meet with myself, but he would also be there. His intention was to put him off balance, give him the impression we would be dealing directly with Gilmour instead of him.'

'And was that Antonio's intention? To cut the Reas out?'

Miguel nodded. 'Eventually yes. But Gilmour needed to know just how Rossi was able to get his drugs into the country without being caught, as did your brother. So, at Rossi's first meeting with Antonio, he was given the impression the deal he was looking for would not be going ahead. There was more profit in it all round if Gilmour did not have to pay Rossi and some of that payment found its way to Antonio instead. Rossi was left with the impression his time was almost up. Antonio flew back to Bogota but when he returned that last time, and despite me advising him not to, it was to tell Rossi this next run would be his last.'

Carlos's face hardened. 'So Rossi killed my brother?'

Miguel shook his head. 'Initially that's what I thought, Senor, but I have evidence that it was someone else.'

'Evidence? What evidence?' Carlos sat forward. 'And why are Los Malvados involved?'

Miguel paused for a second or so then looked Carlos straight in the eye. 'Because they have been trying to muscle in on our

European markets for a long time now. We have a virtual monopoly on cocaine coming into the continent. Los Malvados sell mainly in Mexico, America and Canada, but they need to expand to grow. Gilmour was reputed to be unhappy about the cost of importing from us, even after we had cut Rossi out of the equation. I suspect he sought out a Los Malvados contact in Amsterdam and did a better deal with them, well better for him.'

Carlos looked unsure. 'Can you prove this Miguel?'

Miguel reached into his back pocket and took out his mobile phone. He pressed a screen icon then handed the phone to Carlos. He said nothing and waited. 'Perhaps it is better if you simply see it?'

As he watched, Miguel saw Carlos's face change. He had never before seen anyone go purple with rage. He could only imagine what Barrera's blood pressure was spiking at.

'Where did you get this?' he asked tersely.

Miguel told him about the supposed webcam footage they had discovered. He next showed him the CCTV video of Gilmour walking through Malaga airport the day before the assassination and similar footage of him boarding a flight back to Scotland the day after.

'He is coming here tomorrow?' Carlos asked through his anger.

'Si.' Miguel confirmed. 'Together with Senor Rossi and a Senor Eamon O'Boyle who is bankrolling Gilmour.'

'Then I want him dead the second he steps into your courtyard. Understand?'

'Carlos......'

'Understand?' he thundered.

Miguel swallowed hard. 'Senor, that would be too easy after what he has done to you and your family.' He leant forward a little. 'Why not take him back to Colombia and punish him properly? You have access to a military aircraft. No one will question one other person on board.'

'Why should I do that?'

'Rossi told me he needs Gilmour alive to ensure O'Boyle will still be on board after Gilmour is no longer part of the equation. After that, he is all yours.'

'I do not like being told how to run my affairs,' Carlos seethed.

'No Senor, I accept that. Eamon O'Boyle knows nothing of this. He is simply supplying the funds, in fact he asked for this meeting so he can make sure his cash is safe. But Rossi needs to convince him the deal is still alive.'

Carlos Barrera's eyes darkened. 'Is that a threat?'

Orejuela's expression remained neutral. 'It is just,........ an observation.'

Miguel sat quietly. He knew he was taking a major risk in asking, ... telling Carlos what was required. Even if he agreed just now, once he saw Gilmour, that might all change as his temper over rode the more logical part of his brain. Carlos and Antonio had suffered much adversity hauling their way out of the Soacha Comunas of Colombia, and Miguel knew he had no intention of allowing anyone or anything to drag his family back there. Eventually he nodded almost imperceptibly.

'Very well, Orejuela. I will give Rossi some time to deal with Gilmour and any issues he has, but tell him not to try my patience for too long. If he does I will have everyone I think is involved machine gunned to death, including you, and record it for my own entertainment.' Barrera stood up. 'Until tomorrow then.' He walked off without shaking hands.

TWENTY SEVEN

Reas's last conversation with O'Boyle had been brief. Yes, he could meet with Carlos. No, he could not have any bodyguards with him. Yes, O'Boyle could ask Gilmour to come along, in fact Dom insisted on it. Now here he was, two days later, walking out of Malaga airport for the third time in as many weeks, and trying to quell the uneasy feeling in his stomach this was all going to go tits up. He worried he might bump into O'Boyle and Gilmour, but there had been no sign of them. Miguel had sent him a brief text saying Carlos had arrived and they were all expected today. He had not said whether Carlos knew the 'truth' about Ian Gilmour, but as the meeting was still a go, he assumed he did. At seven o'clock tonight, he would find out for certain.

'The car's here Dom.'

He turned at the sound of Cassie's voice and saw the white Audi A6e pull up at the kerb. They both climbed into the back as the driver placed their luggage in the boot. Cassie went to say something but Dom held a finger to his lips telling her to be quiet. He was concerned the cab had CCTV, in which case he wanted nothing recorded. Cassie nodded and they stayed silent on the drive into Benalmadena, both of them admiring the scenery as best they could. They checked into the small boutique hotel Dom had used previously and made their way to their adjoining rooms. Dom asked Cassie to meet him in half an hour in the bar. She nodded and went to her room. As he opened the door, his mobile rang. Dropping his bag at the foot of the bed, he looked at the screen and was surprised to see it was Annabelle. After Gleddoch House, he had not anticipated hearing from her so soon.

'Hi Annabelle,' he said, 'How are you?'

'Angry,' she answered tersely. 'My fucking brother is keeping my daughter prisoner at his bloody farm.'

'Wow, back up. Is it Gabby?' Dom asked, alarm clear in his voice. What the hell had Gilmour discovered?

'No, my other daughter, Angela.'

'Angela! Annabelle, I'm confused. Why would Gilmour want to kidnap her? And what does it have to do with this meeting?'

Dom heard her let out a huge sigh.

'Nothing. I'm sorry Dom. I shouldn't be burdening you with this. It's just, well I needed someone I could talk to who would understand, that's all.'

Dom smiled lightly to himself. Well, well. Annabelle Phillips. Confiding in him. What next? 'Is Angela okay?' he asked.

'Yes, I think so. No, I know she is. Andy Taggart is guarding her'

'So, she's safe then, assuming Taggart is still with us?'

'Yes, for the time being.'

'I don't get this,' Dom said. 'What exactly could his niece do that would make Gilmour want to,......' Dom paused, not sure he wanted to say to Annabelle what he was thinking.

'Want to kill her,' Annabelle finished for him. 'I'll tell you what.' So she did.

'Shit,' Dom said softly. 'What was Angela's involvement?'

'She supplied the keys to the unit and the code for the alarm system.'

There was a long pause, neither of them said anything. Eventually Dom heard Annabelle draw in a long breath.

'I'm sorry Rossi. I shouldn't have called you about this. I know Angela's safe as long as Ian stays in Spain, but he's losing it. Cammy and Andy both say he's been getting more erratic lately. Flying off the handle at the least thing. He's dangerous and, well, I'm worried you might get yourself hurt.'

'Thanks for your concern, Annabelle, and I know he's coming off the rails,' Dom told her. He sat down on the edge of the bed. 'Look, don't worry. If he does anything stupid over here he'll be dead regardless, and once Carlos Barrera gets hold of him, he's going nowhere.'

'I know, but I can't help worrying.' She sighed. 'I better let you go and get ready for this meeting. I'm sorry again for calling.'

'Annabelle, you call me anytime, you hear, even if it is just to vent a little. I don't mind. I'm a big boy.' He smiled despite himself.

'Yeh, right,' she laughed lightly then hung up.

Dom stood and threw his phone on the dressing table. He shook his head. Now where the hell had this come from? Annabelle Phillips? She was years older than him, ostensibly past her prime, but for some unknown reason they had appeared to click. Over the last couple of days he had found his thoughts occasionally turning to her and wondering, what? In his line of business, personal relationships were best kept brief and fleeting. In any case, she would be off back to Tenerife when all this was done. He shook his head.

Today had been a morning flight. Six thirty. Dom hated them. But it had been necessary to ensure his backup plan was in place. There was no need to unpack. A single night stay was all he had ever intended. He picked up his mobile, left the room and headed for the lounge. Cassie was already there at the bar. She was drinking mineral water, he hoped, as it wasn't yet even midday. He sat on the barstool next to her and ordered a Coke. She wore her normal attire. Tight jeans white blouse and high heels. Hopefully she had brought a change.

'So,' he said to her. 'Are you ready?'

She took a sip and looked at him. 'Three weeks ago, I was running your brothels. Now you've got me covering your back in case anything goes wrong in a meeting you're having with a Colombian drug baron.'

'What? You want a pay rise?' he smiled at her.

'I want to know why all of a sudden you're putting so much trust in me? Look what happened the last time you did that with someone.'

Dom picked up his glass and swirled the dark liquid around, ice cubes clinking. He *had* trusted Malone. He thought he knew him, but now realised he had just been lazy. Malone had offered him solutions to problems, some of which he didn't know he even had. And Dom had willingly taken them. He wasn't an accountant or a banker, so had left Malone to organise that side of his business. It was a mistake he would never make again.

'Cassie, Jack Malone is out of the picture. Permanently.' He looked her square in the eye and saw she knew what he meant. 'No one will ever get to run that side of my business again. You'll help, but I'll be in control. No, what I'm trusting you with tonight is more important. It's potentially my life, and I have no problem with that.'

'Shut the fuck up,' she said, going slightly red with embarrassment.

Dom smiled at how uncomfortable she was with the compliment. 'Right, you know where you're going and what to do when you get there?'

'Yep. Any trouble, you send me a text and I come racing up crashing the gates if I have to.' She looked at him. 'It isn't exactly rocket science.'

'Good. I just hope Barrera is as true to his word as Miguel says he'll be. The only one that should have a problem leaving there at the end of the night is Gilmour. When do you pick up the car?'

'Marti said his contact will get in touch with me this afternoon and drop it off a couple of hours before your meeting, at around five.'

'Great. Until then, the rest of the day is yours to do as you want. I have some unfinished business I need to deal with upstairs. If I don't see you tonight, then don't take it the wrong way.' Dom drained his glass of Coke in one gulp then let out a belch. 'Sorry,' he said, glancing at her.

She smiled. 'All men are pigs.'

ΔΔΔ

The taxi arrived for Dom at six-fifteen. Thirty minutes later it dropped him off on the main road outside Miguel's Villa. He stood there for a few seconds, in his dark blue linen jacket and Armani jeans. The ornate wrought iron gates were closed and locked. Dom noticed Miguel had fitted solid panels to obstruct vision, spoiling their look. There were two guards standing outside the gates. Heavy set, wearing suits. Too warm for suits Dom thought, so obviously concealing guns. As he got closer, both guards held their left hand out for him to stop. Their right hands disappeared inside their jackets.

'Tell Senor Orejuela that Senor Rossi is here to meet with him and Senor Barrera.'

He was searched, thoroughly. Patted down expertly, not roughly. The soles of his shoes were examined, his collar felt. The guard indicated to Dom to run his fingers through his own hair. He did. Nothing. With a nod, the guard held out a hand inviting him to go through the gate which he opened for him, and up the steps towards the main door. As he approached, it opened and Mariana stepped out.

'Ola Domenico, I missed you last time.' She said to him.

He stepped forward and embraced her, kissing her on both cheeks. 'Thank you Mariana. My last stay was too short, as will this one be. Invite me back later.'

She smiled and hooked her arm through his as they walked indoors. More guards stood in the large entrance hall.

Dom looked slowly around. 'Did Carlos bring an army with him?'

'Most of these are Miguel's men. He needs this to go smoothly.' She sounded worried despite her smiles.

'I'll bet. So when do I get to meet Carlos?'

'Right away.' She led him through the Villa, eventually reaching a heavy door, metal with timber veneer disguising it as a normal pass door leading into a five metre long corridor with a matte grey steel door at the opposite end. This had to be the rear of the house Dom guessed. Good security. The corridor was a bottleneck. Solid doors. Solid walls. A killing zone. Or a trap for those inside?

Mariana opened the next door and ushered Dom through. He went to thank her, but she had already left. He turned back around. They were all here. He was the last to arrive. They were either keen or he was cutting it fine. This was Miguel's secure room that doubled up as a conference and dining room when needed. The dining table was made of polished marble, including the base and rested on a light coloured limestone floor. There were twelve chairs around the table, high backed, covered in dyed grey aniline leather with mahogany wood legs. The far wall held a large monitor mounted centrally. There were also two doors set into this wall, one at each side. Cupboards, Dom guessed. On the table sat five glasses and a pitcher of water. No alcohol. Miguel stood close to the monitor. Dom noticed there was a laptop on the desk. The others were seated and they all looked at him.

'Ah, Domenico,' Miguel flashed a smile and walked over, hand extended. 'You are the last to arrive.' They shook hands. Rossi slipped him a memory stick.

'Sorry I held you all up, and me the one that likes to be early!' Rossi looked at Gilmour sitting on the left side of the table and acknowledged his presence with a nod. He then walked around to his right where the others sat, bypassing O'Boyle, and going straight to Carlos. 'Senor Barrera,' he held out his own hand. 'It is a pleasure to meet you at last, although I wish it were under different circumstances.' Dom stood there, arm outstretched, waiting.

Barrera looked at the proffered hand as if it were a viper about to sink its fangs into his skin. 'If it were under any other circumstances, then I would not be here,' he spat at Dom, the disdain he evidently felt obvious in his tone. 'As I told this 'chocha' here,' he nodded towards O'Boyle, 'I do not take kindly to being interrogated. If I was not here to find the person who murdered my brother, none of you would have ever met me.

My business is in Colombia, not here. Do you understand that?'

Dom pulled his hand back slightly and tilted his head, looking at his palm. 'Seems to me Carlos that without people like myself and Mr O'Boyle here, you wouldn't have a business in the first place.' He was fucked if this arsehole was going to insult him, no matter how many hired guns he had outside.

Dom watched as Barrera bristled. His eyes narrowed. The veins in his neck began to pop. He looked like an aortic explosion waiting to happen.

'On the other hand,' Dom continued, as if nothing had happened, 'we do need you as much as you need us, So, I agree with you, Mr O'Boyle should not have asked you to prove yourself. In fact, Mr O'Boyle should have been dealing with me alone. So please accept my apologies on his behalf.'

Barrera seemed to calm down at this. What the fuck is it with these pricks and their ego's that need constant stroking, Dom wondered? Business was best done dispassionately, just like revenge. Serve it up cold. There was movement behind him and Dom turned to find O'Boyle standing looking at him, slight amusement in his eyes.

'Ow, do lad?' he asked him rhetorically. 'Nice to finally meet you in person. We tain't ever met before and here you are already apologising for me.'

Dom shrugged. 'Nothing personal Eamon. It just helps to clear the air. He held out the same hand to O'Boyle he had offered to Carlos. O'Boyle grasped it firmly. 'Finally nice to meet the real money behind Ian's grand plans,' Dom told him.

He glanced across at Gilmour who had a grim smile on his face. 'Watch your mouth Dom boy, unless you want to find yourself knocked into next week.'

Dom smiled back. 'Look, let's all be friends. In fact I'll even come and sit next to you Ian.'

Rossi walked around the table and sat in the chair to Gilmour's right. 'Now, that's better. Much more civilised.'

O'Boyle sat down. Miguel was next to Carlos, close to the monitor. Dom noticed he held a small remote control in his hand. Good, Dom thought, time to get this charade over with.

'Before we start on the main business Eamon - and Ian, there's a couple of things I want to discuss first. A couple of videos I'd like you all to see if that's okay?'

'What the fuck is this?' Gilmour asked, looking at him, confusion in his eyes. 'He,' and he pointed towards Carlos, 'is supposed to be telling Eamon how the money transfer is going to be guaranteed until the drugs are in the country. We don't need to see any bloody videos just now.'

Dom watched Carlos become angry again, rising from his seat slightly. Miguel placed a calming hand on his arm and whispered something in his ear. Barrera sat down, but his anger was simmering.

'Ian, humour me. You'll enjoy these,' Dom said. Yeah, you'll enjoy them alright.

Rossi signalled to Miguel who pressed a hidden button beneath the table. A few seconds later one of Orejuela's bodyguards entered the room, then stood just inside the door, hands clasped in front of his groin like a footballer protecting his future family from a free kick about to be thumped at him. Dom signalled to Miguel again. He inserted the flash drive into a USB slot on the laptop then pressed a sequence of buttons on the keyboard. The monitor sprang to life and after a few seconds, a slightly fuzzy, grainy video appeared. It showed the inside of the French Café Gilmour owned in the Merchant City. Gilmour could be seen behind the counter of the Café, moving around, working the machines. He then came over to the table and sat down. Dom could see Gilmour's face as he looked past him to the screen.

'What the bloody hell is this?' Gilmour shouted.

Gilmour had turned to face him, his jaw set hard. Miguel paused the video, which Dom knew had barely started, as did Gilmour.

'Ian, just watch the video, okay?'

'The hell I will,' he said, standing up sending the chair flying.

The guard at the door moved forward, his arms at the ready

as Ian Gilmour went towards it. Dom turned and watched Gilmour frantically searching for some way out, some way to escape what he knew was coming. When he realised he was trapped, he turned on Dom, hands grasping for his neck. The bodyguard lunged forward and grabbed Gilmour in a bear hug, trapping his arms by his side. Dom calmly looked at him, unmoving.

'Ian, don't be a prick. Sit down. Like I told you in the Café, it's just business.'

Gilmour struggled with the mountain of a man holding him tight. 'Let me the fuck go, ya bastard,' he screamed. The guard simply squeezed tighter.

'Alright, alright,' he slumped, the fight seemingly crushed out of him. 'I'll sit.' Dom stood and picked up the chair, placing it back where it belonged. Gilmour sat. The guard stood behind him, his shovel like hands firmly on Gilmour's shoulders. Dom nodded to Miguel and the video re-started this time playing through without interruption. O'Boyle sat impassively throughout, his eyes never leaving the screen. The image quality wasn't great but Dom had enhanced the sound to sharpen it, and together they left O'Boyle in no doubt.

'How did you get this lad?' he asked Dom without emotion as the short clip ended.

Dom reached into the inside pocket of his jacket and pulled out a pair of sunglasses, but ones with slightly thicker frames than normal. 'Built in camera,' he simply said, glancing at Gilmour. 'Isn't technology wonderful.'

'You realise he was going to hand you over to me when all this was over, because your da' killed my son.' O'Boyle said to Dom while looking at Gilmour

'Poetic justice eh! I didn't think you had any soul in you Ian. Not going to deny it then?' Gilmour said nothing. He simply looked at Dom, his eyes blazing with fury.

Rossi turned to O'Boyle. 'The sins of the father don't always need to be visited on the son, do they Eamon?'

O'Boyle sat stoney faced. 'So what's this other piece of footage you have Domenico? One that trumps my claim on this miserable twats life?' he asked him.

Dom watched as Miguel squirmed uncomfortably in his seat. He knew what was about to happen and he was worried about Carlos's reaction, even though he knew Miguel had already shown it to him. 'Okay Miguel, play it now. Senor Barrera, I know you have seen this, but Senor Gilmour has not, so I apologise for putting you through it again.'

Barrera's face was like stone. He stared at him as though blaming Dom for his brother's death. If only he knew the truth, Dom thought. On screen the new video started. There was no audio. It was like watching a macabre silent movie. A snuff film for the deaf. Barrera refused to look at the monitor. Instead his gaze held steady on Gilmour, penetrating him, scooping out his thoughts and trampling them. Gilmour sat and watched grim faced as images of him coming into Malaga airport flicked across the screen. They weren't from yesterday; the date on the timestamp was different. His clothes were different. He knew it wasn't himself in the video.

'This is wrong,' he whispered. 'It's wrong! That isnae me,' he pleaded.

The next clip began automatically. It showed a view down the hillside from somewhere close to Miguel's Villa. There was a car parked in a lay-by. Two men stood beside it. A black Range Rover Evoque appeared on screen, slowing down to take the hairpin bend. As it did, one of the figures beside the car stepped out and pointed something at the SUV. It was a gun. The car slowed and swerved to the right, towards the figure, who stepped out of the way. At the same time someone at the rear of the SUV appeared and began firing.

'What the fuck is going on here Rossi? What have you done?' Gilmour was struggling against the hands of the guard firmly holding him in the chair, desperate to get at Dom.

'Me Ian? Not me. Just watch.'

The video had moved on. It was short in any case. Gilmour looked back at the screen. He could make out bodies lying in the front seats of the car. Someone reached out and opened the rear door, then stepped back. They could all make out the features of Antonio Barrera lying wounded on the back seat, his face screwed up in pain. The image flickered slightly, right at the point Dom knew, where he had removed the mask of Gilmour to confront Antonio before replacing it. Then the gunman simply shot the man sitting in the back seat. The figure that pulled the trigger turned and looked almost directly at the camera. The video zoomed in and froze, Ian Gilmour's face emblazoned across the screen.

'No, that isn't right. That's not me.' Gilmour looked across to Carlos Barrera, fear in his eyes. 'That isn't fucking me. I did not kill your brother. This is all fake.'

Barrera said nothing.

'Senor Gilmour,' Miguel said quietly. 'I have a video of you coming into Malaga and leaving via the airport next day. I also have copies of immigration logs for those two days. It was your passport that was scanned. The only thing I did was edit the part where you took Antonio's lips to spare his brother any more pain.'

'That isn't possible. I never left the fucking country. My passport was in a safe back in my farmhouse.' He banged the table in frustration. 'Someone is setting me up.'

'I do not have the technology or the know-how to create a deep fake video, Senor.' Miguel told Gilmour. 'On the contrary. It took me many days to find all of this evidence and collate it for Senor Barrera.' He paused. 'There is no mistake. You murdered Antonio.'

Dom watched as Gilmour sat back in the chair, looking around at the faces of the three men sitting across the table from him.

'Why?' Gilmour asked. 'What reason would I have for killing Antonio?' He gestured towards Dom. 'Once Rossi here had done this run, I would have known all his secrets. Who to bribe. Where to offload the product. How to transport it. Where to store it. Everything. That's one of the reasons the shipment was so large. After that, I would know how to do it myself. Antonio and I were going to work together and cut out all this middleman crap. It would be a damned site cheaper without bankrolling this leech.'

Miguel shrugged. 'You were approached by the Los Malvados Cartel and offered better prices than Antonio was willing to give you. That's why you had to kill him.'

'Now if that's true, then why the fuck would I carry out the hit myself? I have people for that kind of shit. And how the hell do you know it was these Malvados bastards, whoever the fuck they are?'

'Security,' Miguel shrugged. 'You could not risk anyone outside your organisation knowing about this and we know Los Malvados are desperate to gain a foothold in Europe. They are a rival Cartel to ourselves,' Miguel told him. 'And we know it was them because of the way you disfigured the bodies.'

Gilmour shook his head. Dom saw he was beginning to realise no matter what he said or did, Barrera had already made up his mind. This was just window dressing. Dom had never understood why you had to explain to the person you were about to kill the reasons why they were to die. It wasn't as if they would remember.

'Okay, tell me what I'm supposed to have done to the bodies?' There was resignation in his voice.

'You cut off their lips you bastardo, their fucking lips. I cannot even give my brother an open casket when I get him home.' Carlos Barrera had spoken for the first time since the videos had been shown. 'You will pay for this in ways you cannot even begin to imagine. And then at the end, I will cut off your head with the dullest, bluntest knife I can find.' It was said with a venom that made it clear he meant every word.

'Aye, right,' Gilmour smiled wryly. He turned and looked calmly at Dom. 'Congratulations Rossi. I don't know how you did it but you managed to shaft me good and proper.'

Dom stared back at him for a while. No one else in the room said anything. Even the bodyguard had relaxed his grip slightly as he felt the tension leave Gilmour's shoulders.

'Ian, like I told you before, it's just business. It's the same kind of business you did with Eamon's son. It's the same kind you did with Jamie Philips so you could take over his organisation. It's the same kind you did with my father when you had him killed to protect your little secret.'

Gilmour shook his head, the wry smile still on his face.

'By the way,' Dom smiled. 'Annabelle says hello. She knows you took out Jamie, so to say she's a wee bit unsympathetic to your current predicament is putting it mildly.'

'Well my dear sister is in for a wee shock then.'

'Ah, you mean Angela.' Dom watched as Gilmour's smile faded. He shook his head. 'I'm afraid not Ian. You see Cammy and Andy were also getting worried about you. Have been for some time in fact. So I had a wee talk with them and, well, let's just say Angela is safe in the arms of her beloved mother right now.'

Gilmour's jaw clenched. Dom knew the anger was bubbling up again. Ian hated not being in control. But he hated being conned even more. All of his plans had vanished in the few minutes it had taken while he had sat there and watched the 'irrefutable' evidence against him.

'So, my wee sister wants to take over my business does she? Well, tell her good luck with that. Maxwell and Todd were on the way out anyway. None of the boys will work for her. There'll be a fucking civil war.'

'Oh, they won't be working for Annabelle, Ian. She has no interest in anything but family and soaking up the African sunshine in Tenerife.'

Gilmour looked confused for a few seconds. 'Then who..........!' His face clouded even more as seeming realization dawned. He looked across at O'Boyle, who had sat there quietly throughout, observing, saying nothing. 'You,' he exclaimed. 'You traitorous bastard. I brought you into this, it was all my idea. Then you go and shaft me too.' Gilmour tried to stand up, but the bodyguard clamped down firmly on his shoulders, gluing him to the seat.

'Me lad?' Eamon O'Boyle shook his head. 'Now why would I want anything to do with Jockland? No offence Mr Rossi,' he nodded an apology to Dom. 'You killed my boy Gilmour, and aye, it would be poetic justice, me takin' over your patch,' he intoned in his Yorkshire accent, 'but Finbar's death was a long time ago and he was annoying a lot of people. If it hadn't been you it would have been someone else,' he sighed. 'But I would take great delight in making you pay for that, just so his mother gets some satisfaction.' He glanced at Carlos then back to Gilmour. 'I'm sure Mr Barrera here will come up wi' sumit' suitable to make you regret a few of your earlier life decisions. But running your operation across the border? Not for me, thanks. I'm expanding south, where the real money is.'

'This will also hit your business Rossi. If I'm out and no ones in charge, then who's got the cash to pay for your fucking exorbitantly priced services?'

Rossi smiled and leaned towards Gilmour, patting him on the arm. The guard tightened his grip.

'Now why would I need to pay myself Ian? Not much sense in that. Is there?'

Then he sat back and watched the penny drop. Even with the bodyguard holding him, Gilmour was still able to make a lunge for Dom. Rossi never flinched. The Colombian guard grabbed hold of Gilmour's jacket and dragged him back down into his seat.

Then it all went to hell.

TWENTY EIGHT

There was a noise at the metal door, someone hammering, a muted voice from outside. Miguel hurried over. He looked through the door viewer, then urgently keyed a combination into the keypad and pulled the door open. Mariana tumbled through and into his arms. Behind her was the sound of gunfire from pistols and automatic rifles accompanied by shouting and some screams. Dom glanced over. The door behind her into the main building lay open.

Miguel's partner was out of breath. 'The Police,' she gasped. 'They are breaking into the Villa. They are looking for Carlos.' She looked behind her fearfully.

Dom stood up and edged forward to peer through the open doorway. He saw something being thrown into the hallway and jumped back, slamming the inner door closed. The slam shut lock held it in position. There was a muffled explosion, and seconds later puffs of white vapour began to seep under the door threshold.

'Tear gas,' he spluttered. 'They're firing tear gas. They must want him alive.'

Miguel left Mariana and ran to one of the cupboards on the back wall. He opened the door then knelt on the floor. Reaching forward, he grabbed hold of a small square of carpet and threw into the room. Beneath it was a metal trapdoor with a single bolt securing it. Slipping the bolt to one side, he raised the cover using a recessed handle, dropping it back against the rear wall of the cupboard.

'All of you, down here quick.'

No one moved. Then Carlos ran over, the first to understand

what was going on.

'It's a way out,' Miguel shouted at them as he moved aside to allow Carlos to clamber through. 'If you want to escape, get down here now.' He beckoned to Mariana who quickly followed Carlos down the ladder, her long dress getting in the way.

Dom's eyes were clearing. The tear gas had not gotten far into the room. He grabbed O'Boyle by the shoulders and ushered him towards the cupboard. When he looked back he could see the bodyguard standing there, his hands still on Gilmour's shoulders. The sound of banging on the door grew louder as the police tried to break through the solid metal. Dom had no idea how long it would hold, but he wasn't about to wait around to find out.

'Bring him over here,' he shouted at the guard while pointing to Gilmour.

The bodyguard looked confused for a second. He did not speak English, but then realised what Dom intended and grabbed Gilmour by his jacket collar, dragging him to his feet. Gilmour shrugged off the guards grip and ran over, before he too disappeared through the hatch. Dom nodded to the guard and he followed Gilmour.

Grabbing the loose piece of carpet thrown aside by Orejuela, Dom went into the cupboard. He threw the carpet down the hatch, closed the cupboard door then slipped a bolt on the inside into its keeper. This door was also metal, although not as robust as the door into the corridor, but it would help slow the pursuit and allow them extra time to get – where, Dom wondered? He looked through the hatch and saw metal rungs fixed into the sidewall of what appeared to be a series of pre-cast concrete manhole rings set on top of each other. Dom climbed down part way, then reached up and pulled the hatch cover closed behind him. There was a locking wheel on the inside of the hatch. When Dom turned this, two bolts, one on each side, went into deep keepers built into the sidewall. Miguel had not made it easy for anyone to follow him. The tunnel was lit with emergency lighting dull, but good enough to see by once your eyes grew accustomed.

Rossi climbed the rungs down to the bottom and dropped the last few feet onto the ground. He looked around. There was only one way to go, to his right. He could just make out the back of Miguel's bodyguard as he moved slowly following Gilmour, crouching down to make his way through the five foot high, round, corrugated metal tunnel with its floor set at a gentle slope. In the last two years Rossi had invested in some office properties around Glasgow. He realised quickly what he was in; an attenuation sewer. Designed to hold back water from flash flooding into and overwhelming the public drainage system. The problem was, the only thing at the other end of this should be a one-way valve, far too small for them to get through. However, he had no doubt when Miguel had built this he had also created a way out.

Rossi crouched to follow then realised crawling was a better option given his height. Behind him, he could hear - nothing. A good sign, but it wouldn't last forever. Dom could sense the tunnel gradually sloping down. If it were long enough, it might take them far enough away from the Police cordon he knew had to be in place. Shit, he thought, what the hell must Cassie be thinking right now? He had almost forgotten she was waiting downhill for him. He stopped and lay on his back, not caring what the dust and rubble on the base of the steel tunnel was doing to his jacket. He pulled out his phone then dialled her number.

'Dom,' she cried, answering after the second ring. 'What the hell is happening? It sounds like a bloody war zone up there.' She sounded frantic with worry.

'Yeh, I can imagine,' he replied. 'Where are you? Are you still parked up?'

'Yes,' she answered, 'but I don't think I can get to you. The cops have set up a road block further up the hill.'

'That's okay,' Dom responded. 'I'm coming to you – I hope!'

'How? The place is mad with police.'

'I'll explain later,' he told her. 'Just be ready. There will be a few extra bodies coming too.'

'What?'

Dom had no time to explain. He ended the call then hurried to catch up with the rest, especially Gilmour. Just what the hell was going to happen to Ian now? He should have been trussed up and halfway to a torture cell in Colombia by now. Gilmour must have thought his guardian angel did watch over and protect him. Ahead, he heard the sound of feet and hands on metal sheeting as they echoed around the steel tunnel. It was beginning to get uncomfortably warm and stuffy. He eventually caught up with the bodyguard. Miguel was in front of Gilmour, with Mariana, O'Boyle and Barrera ahead of him. After a while, they came to a stop. Dom glanced behind him again. Still no sign of pursuit. He heard Miguel say something in Spanish, and Dom could just see Mariana pull herself to one side as Miguel squeezed past her. Orejuela then called something out to Barrera who was at the front of the group.

Dom heard some cursing, again in Spanish, before he heard a banging noise and felt a wave of warm evening air waft into the tunnel from up ahead. It seemed Carlos had managed to open another hatch at the top of a manhole mirroring the one they had entered. The group began to move forward again, inch by inch, until eventually Dom was the last one left. He climbed out of the manhole, slammed the hatch closed behind him and secured it with another two bolts hidden on the outside. Then he glanced around to get his bearings. It was around eight thirty in the evening, still light enough to be seen by if they were not careful. He noticed they were in a gulley that was no more than a three foot deep ditch at the side of the road. It was surrounded by dense shrubbery which helped conceal them. The tunnel had led them downhill about five hundred metres, close to the spot where Dom and Marti had ambushed Antonio. Miguel had everyone crouching down afraid any passing Police vehicle would spot them. Rossi clambered all the way out and crawled over towards him.

'What now Miguel?' Dom noticed Carlos also looking towards Miguel, signs of panic on his face.

'I'm sorry Dom, I do not know. I never expected to have to use the escape tunnel.'

The shooting had stopped from the hill above them. They all heard a dull rumble as the Police finally used explosives to get through the first door. There was still time, Dom thought.

Carlos reached out and grabbed Miguel tightly by the arm. 'I cannot be caught, Orejuela, do you hear me? I cannot. Look what happened to El Chapo. Fifty years!' He vigorously shook his head. 'You cannot let them do that, understand?'

Shit, Dom wondered. Where the fuck did this arrogant self importance come from? Did he think he was untouchable or something? Getting caught was an occupational hazard. Accept that or get another line of work.

Eamon O'Boyle crouched beside Dom. 'Any ideas lad?' he asked him.

'Me?' Dom grinned. 'I'm full of ideas.' He crept up to the lip of the gulley and cautiously peered over. Then he took out his phone again and called Cassie.

'Hi. Can you get the SUV up to the lay-by we were talking about earlier? It's on your right as you come up the hill, just past a hairpin bend.' He waited. 'Good, see you in a few minutes.'

Dom signalled to Miguel to join him. 'You see the lay-by,' he pointed it out. 'In a few minutes an SUV will park up there. We can make our way down and squeeze into the car.' He could see Miguel look at him doubtfully. 'Miguel, like you I always have a backup plan. The car will be driven by one of my people. Let your boss know, okay?'

Miguel nodded and crept back down from the lip of the ditch.

Dom stayed where he was, keeping an eye out for Cassie, worried the police would be on them before she arrived. He glanced behind him, looking for Gilmour and his bodyguard. He saw the bodyguard, lying prone on the scrubby grass, face down unmoving. The back of his head was a bloody mess where he had been hit hard with something. Of Ian Gilmour though, there was no sign. None of them had heard a thing. They had been concentrating on finding a way off the hill. It seemed Gilmour had decided to go it alone. Time to worry about him later thought Dom. He turned once more to look back down the hill.

'C'mon Cassie,' he whispered quietly.

A few seconds later a Mercedes Four by Four pulled up the hill and onto the hairpin. It slowed down and swung in a wide circle before coming to rest in the lay-by.

Dom twisted around 'Okay everyone, follow me.' At this stage Dom didn't care if they followed him or not. He saw Miguel turn and hold out a hand. Not to Carlos, but to Mariana. Carlos cast him a look, but said nothing. Dom scrambled over the edge of the gulley. The road was nearly ten metres in front of them. A low, stone wall ran along the edge of the road until it reached the lay-bay, which was downhill, about thirty metres away. He headed for this, keeping close to the ground in a crouching run. He didn't look back. If the others followed fine, if not, that was their problem. Keeping low, he scrambled and slid down the hillside through the scrub and loose stones. As he neared the lay-by, he could make out Cassie sitting in the left hand drivers seat, anxiously looking out the rear window. Dom drew level with the car. He eased himself up and looked over the wall. The road was quiet. There was no traffic. He stood up and swung his legs over then sprinted for the passenger door. Cassie spotted him and slipped the car into drive. Dom climbed in, but placed a hand on her arm.

'Wait,' he told her.

She looked surprised. 'Dom we need to go, now.'

'Cassie, the rest are behind me,' he looked over his shoulder and saw Miguel with Mariana. Then he noticed O'Boyle behind them, helping Carlos who was limping. Shit, he thought, all we need is a sprained ankle. He breathed a sigh. 'Give me a minute.'

Jumping out of the car, he ran back past Miguel and Mariana towards O'Boyle and Barrera, who were still on the opposite side of the wall.

'Come on,' he shouted. Further up the hill he heard the sound of a Police Helicopter. 'We need to speed up.' Grabbing Carlos under one arm, he helped O'Boyle drag him down the hill, ignoring the Colombians' cries of pain. He pushed Carlos unceremoniously over the wall. He landed heavily on the other side and let out another cry as his ankle hit the ground. O'Boyle was fitter than he looked. He jumped the wall and grabbed Carlos under the armpits again. Dom followed suit and they hurriedly ran to the car, throwing Barrera onto the backseat through the door held open by Miguel. O'Boyle clambered in, and lay in the foot well. When Dom had gotten back into the passenger seat, Carrie hit the accelerator and sped off down the hill.

'Slow down,' Dom told her breathlessly as he clipped on his seat belt. 'We don't want stopped for speeding. Just get to the A-368 and then head back to Benalmadena.'

'And then?' Carrie asked, doing as he instructed, but gripping the steering wheel hard.

'Let me think,' said Dom.

He looked back up the hill. The Police had still not fully realised what had happened. The helicopter hovered above Miguel's Villa. No doubt some of his men were dead and some were in custody, but at least *they* had all escaped.

'Is everyone okay?' he asked, turning around in his seat.

There were nods all round, except from Barrera, who was clutching his ankle and mouthing something in Spanish.

'Miguel, do you have anywhere you can take Carlos and Mariana?'

'Si, but I am worried it will have been compromised. If they knew about Carlos coming to the Villa, then what else do they know?'

'Understandable. How did they know about Carlos anyway?' Dom asked curiously. 'If he was brought in on a military flight, then no one should have been aware he was here.'

'It must have been Sanchez,' Carlos growled through the

pain of his throbbing ankle. 'He was the only other person on the flight who knew my identity.'

'And who the hell is Sanchez?' Dom asked.

Barrera shook his head. 'It does not matter. I will deal with him if - when I return. Right now, I need to find someplace to lie low and come up with another plan to get out of the country.'

Dom turned back around in his seat and pulled out his phone. He dialled a number and waited.

'Marti,' he said when the call connected. 'It's Dom. I need a favour from you. Things have gone tits up over here. The cops raided Miguel's Villa looking for Carlos. We've managed to escape with him, but I need somewhere safe where he can go until Miguel can figure out how to get him out of the Country.'

He paused and listened. 'Yes, your old contacts down here? They were what I was thinking about. They must still have some safe houses dotted around where we could stash three people for a while?' Another pause while he waited.

'Fine, get back to me as soon as you can. We'll drive around until I hear from you.'

'Who was that?' Barrera asked him, still in pain.

'One of my people. I'm trying to get somewhere safe for you to hole up in until your people can organise your extraction.'

Dom felt a hand on his shoulder. He looked around. It was Barrera.

'Thank you amigo,' he said through tight lips. 'I will not forget this.'

Dom grunted acknowledgement. 'It's purely selfish Carlos. I don't want to be banged up anymore than you do. Plus without you I have no product to import, and without that I make no money.' He glanced at the floor. 'How are you doing down there Eamon?'

'Don't ask lad, don't ask. Drop me off at my hotel when you get a chance would you?'

'I will, but Carlos is the primary concern, so hang in there. Why don't you squeeze onto the backseat with the rest of them?' Five minutes later he felt his phone buzz, announcing the arrival of a text. It was from Marti and had an address and a name. Dom keyed the address into the car's Satnav. 'That's where we head first,' he indicated to Cassie.

Cassie nodded. The instructions were in Spanish, but she was able to get the gist of it and mainly followed the arrows. It was an address in Malaga. That would take them past Benalmadena. Traffic had built up as they drove along the A-368 looking for the junction to the AP-7 highway. Police cars with flashing lights and sirens sped towards them from the opposite direction. Dom tensed up, waiting to see if they would be pulled over. But the Police drove past, heading no doubt to Mijas to join the Manhunt for Carlos Barrera, one of the World's most wanted criminals. And here he was thought Dom, sitting in car with a ned from the Milton and his lesbian, gangster moll driver. Bonnie and Clyde it wasn't. An hour later they pulled up at the address Marti had given them. It was in a block of modern flats built on the outskirts of the city close to the airport. Cassie switched off the engine. Dom twisted in his seat.

'Okay, it's apartment 4/2. They're expecting you.' He got out and held out a hand to Carlos who took it, then gingerly swung his legs from the car landing on his good foot. Dom held onto his arm. Miguel and Mariana got out of the other side then came around to help. Dom let Barrera's arm go and Miguel and Mariana took over.

'Right,' he told them. 'Better get inside and stay there until you can get in touch with your people over in Colombia.'

As they began to help Carlos hobble to the front door of the apartment complex, Barrera turned his head towards Rossi. 'I will be in your debt forever Senor Rossi. Nothing you ask will be too much trouble.'

'That's good to hear Carlos,' Dom acknowledged, 'but you also better thank Miguel. He was the one with the foresight to have an escape tunnel built. Without him we'd all be in handcuffs by now.'

Carlos grunted a grudging acknowledgement. The three of them turned and walked to the apartment. Dom got back into the car. He glanced at the clock on the dash. Nearly ten o'clock. How time flies when you're having fun. O'Boyle was still in the back seat. 'Where are you staying Eamon?'

O'Boyle gave them the address of a hotel in Malaga. They dropped him off and he said he would be in touch. After he had left, Dom sat back. He pinched the bridge of his nose between two fingers, a building headache threatening to descend. His clothes and footwear were ruined, torn, muddy and scuffed. He would need to run though the hotel otherwise they would throw him out. He looked across at Cassie.

'Are you alright?' he asked her. 'Want me to drive?'

Cassie sat gripping the steering wheel, staring straight ahead as though in a trance. She was quiet. The car also sat quietly, its batteries patiently waiting for their power to be unleashed.

'You don't pay me enough for this shit Rossi, you really don't.' She was half serious.

Dom playfully punched her in the arm. 'You love it, don't you.'

'Jesus Dom, we were this close to spending the rest of our lives in some crummy Spanish jail, this close.' She held up her right hand to him, the thumb and index finger only millimetres apart.

'I know, I know,' he apologised. 'I had no idea things would get so hairy.'

'And what *about* Gilmour,' she asked him. 'Where the fuck is he?'

Dom closed his eyes and lent back against the car headrest. 'I wish I knew. The slippery bastard has more than nine lives.'

'What if he manages to get back to Glasgow? After what you just told him, he'll want to go Hannibal Lecter on everyone.'

'Then we should also get back there Cassie, and organise a welcoming committee for when he does pop his head above the parapet and start shooting at us all.'

'But who will he use? Not Cammy and Andy after they double crossed him.'

'No,' Dom agreed. 'Not them, but he has other soldiers he can call on if he needs to.'

'So what do we do?'

Dom looked thoughtful for a while. He drummed his fingers on the dashboard. 'I think,' he eventually said, 'that we need to get Gilmour to come to where we want him. Somewhere quiet, safe and out of the way.'

'Where?' she asked. 'The Villa? The farm?'

Dom shook his head. 'No. I was thinking of a place much more remote than that. And then, when we're ready, we'll drop a few hints Gilmour can't miss and deal with him on our terms.' He smiled across at her. 'Ever been to the Scottish Highlands?'

TWENTY NINE

The small estate sat off the road between Inveralligin and the Alligan Shuas. It wasn't as remote as you could get, but it was pretty close. There was one road in and the same one out. It ended not far past the entrance to the estate, and was the last paved highway on the north side of Loch Torridon. Dom had bought the Victorian mansion years before, intending at one time to turn it into a 'Spa.' But it had proven too remote. The roads in this part of the Highlands were not the best. It could take you four and half hours to get there from Glasgow on a good day, and nearer five and a half when the roads were blocked. So he had turned it into his private retreat, one he used a few times a year when he could. The rest of the time it was looked after by a well paid factor or rented out for corporate events, some of them *'ghosted'* to allow for some cash laundering. On arriving back from Spain, he had gathered everyone together at the Villa in Pollokshields, including Angela. He explained the fiasco that was the meeting at Miguel's to them. He told them Gilmour had escaped, and was no doubt gunning for them all. When he informed them about Alligin House and what he planned, none of them had raised any concerns. Gabby had brought Angela up to speed on their Uncle Ian and what Dom had done to him, or tried to do. So, they had packed up in three hired diesel Four by Fours and driven here. They had taken supplies for all of them, including Marti and Billy. Dom emptied the safe of handguns and Marti had managed to get them a couple of semi automatics. Coupled with the few shotguns kept at the House, it would have to do. They had arrived two days ago. The factor had been told to take a holiday. Dom had set up a solar powered motion activated camera covering the road into the estate. It was linked by it's on board wi-fi to the main CCTV and was watched by one of them twenty four seven. Gilmour, if he had managed to make it out of Spain, would no doubt find them, in fact Dom was banking on it. The only question was who would he bring with him?

Cammy Maxwell and Andy Taggart had decided to hunker down in their own safe houses in Glasgow. They had reasoned Gilmour would come after Dom before anyone else, and if Dom did not get the better of him, then a quick escape from Glasgow airport to somewhere nice and warm would be easier to make from down there.

Alligan Estate was set in a broad windswept expanse of moorland and hillside. What few natural trees there were, had been stunted by the Atlantic winds that often swept in across Loch Torridon. The lack of cover meant Gilmour and whoever he brought with him would find it difficult to surprise Rossi. Dom though had built a granite wall around the gardens of the house. It was only one and a half metres high, but he had planted rows of mature Scots pine in front of the wall, intended as screening as he liked his privacy. But the closer anyone got the more cover they would find, which wasn't ideal.

There were a couple of farms along the road near the Estate, but they had been doing badly for years and Dom had bought them out, further enhancing his isolation. Then he had simply allowed them to fall into disrepair over the years. The main Estate building was accessed by a mile long paved, single track driveway. This led to a set of high, wrought iron, decorative gates set into strong, grey granite pillars attached to the wall and topped with a stone arched lintel. Two pedestrian gates were set in the wall allowing access to the land beyond. The one directly at the rear butted an old drovers road that could itself be accessed from further along a single track road leading to - well, nowhere. The other was to the left of the house also at the rear, allowing people to access the loch via a path Dom had built some time before.

The village of Diabaig, reached along the east shore of Loch a'Mhullaich, was nothing but a small collection of farms and one bed and breakfast. If you didn't live there then you didn't go there. If you weren't local then you wouldn't know about the old drover's path. So Gilmour's point of access would be straight and direct. The gates at the front of the House had been padlocked and barricaded using old machinery from one of the two storage sheds that lay within the boundary. Dom hoped it would be enough but knew it wouldn't. They would just hop the wall.

He sat in an upstairs bedroom converted into an office. A table and a chair were set into the alcove of a large bay window, where he worked in peace when he needed to. It also allowed him to look out over the loch towards the sandstone monolith of Sgorr Rhuadh. He had climbed the peak a few times, leaving from the Beinn Eighe car park near Torridon. Today would have been good for that. The heat-wave affecting the entire country had only tickled the edges of the Highlands. The weather was clear but not as warm as further south a relief given everyone had been suffering for the last six weeks or so. It was on visits here and further north and west years before, where he had identified secluded coves and inlets, ideal for the semi-submersibles and yachts crossing the Atlantic from Colombia. Right now though, he simply sat in the chair and contemplated what might happen next. A gentle knock on the door drew his attention.

'Yes,' he said, swivelling around in his seat.

Annabelle Phillips entered the room. 'I hope I'm not disturbing you?' She smiled pleasantly at him.

He returned the gesture. 'No, come in. Please, sit.' Dom stood up and stepped further into the window recess.

'No, I'm fine thanks. I'll stand.' She walked over and stopped beside him, folding her arms, their shoulders almost touching.

'Glorious, isn't it? 'Dom said to her.

She looked at him, smiled and nodded. 'It is, but a bit too out of the way for me. I like my social life within easy reach.'

'You should see it in the winter Annabelle. The hills covered in a thick blanket of snow and the mist rising off the loch early in the morning. That's when it's at its most beautiful.'

She laughed. 'Sorry Rossi, I'm a sun worshipper. I like to get as far away from the cold as I can.'

'Well, there's always a roaring log fire and bottle of wine to come back to. Kind of makes it worthwhile. 'He turned to look at her. 'Perhaps I'll show it to you one year?'

Her face took on a mischievous look. 'Are you propositioning an old bird like me Dom?'

Dom looked quickly away. He could feel the blush starting under his collar. What the hell was it about Annabelle? But deep down, he already knew. She had presence, she had courage and, most of all she had balls. When he had detailed her brother's betrayals, she hadn't balked at agreeing to do what was needed.

'Hey,' she said apologetically, placing a hand on his shoulder. 'I didn't mean to embarrass you. I'm only joking.'

'Well I'm not,' Dom replied.

Turning, he took hold of her face between his hands and quickly moved in and kissed her. It started off slow and soft, but as he felt her respond, it became more intense. She grabbed the back of Dom's own head with her hands and pulled him in closer. Her lips parted and her tongue snaked out, pressing against his teeth, which opened with no resistance. Eventually they pulled apart and stood looking at each other.

'Wow,' was all she could muster. 'Where the hell did that come from?'

'I don't know. Well I do know. Ever since we met I've wanted to do that.'

'Dom, I'm in my mid fifties. What in God's name could I offer you?'

He smiled at her, and kissed her again gently on the lips. 'I know men my age aren't meant to say this, but every time I see you my stomach does a little flip.'

She stepped back and held him at arm's length, 'Domenico,

you've only met me three times.'

He shrugged. 'Hey, you asked how I felt.'

Before she had time to answer, there was another knock on the door.

'Yes,' Dom said, stepping back from Annabelle.

Marti walked into the room. He looked at the two of them with a raised eyebrow, but said nothing. 'Boss, we just got word from one of our contacts down south. Looks like Maxwell and Taggart were wrong. Gilmour wasn't coming after you first. He took both of them out yesterday. He's on his way up here now.'

'So he got to Cammy and Andy did he? Any idea who's with him?'

'There's talk about Archie Todd and some of his boys. No real heavy hitters, but Todd can be a vicious wee bastard if he gets you alone in a room when you're tied to a chair.'

'Hmm, well let's make sure that doesn't happen to anyone then. Any idea when they'll be here?'

Billy shook his head. 'Maxwell and Taggart were dealt with yesterday, so it could be tonight or tomorrow.'

'Not that it matters, but do we know how Gilmour got out of Spain?' Dom asked.

Marti shook his head.

'Okay. Thanks Marti,' Dom motioned him to leave. 'Oh, and tell Billy to get the hardware sorted and primed while he's monitoring the CCTV. I want to be ready to rumble as soon as Ian gets here.'

Marti nodded and left the room.

Annabelle walked over to Dom and put an arm around him. 'I guess that'll be a rain check on anything else then?' She reached up and pecked him on the cheek, before turning and walking away.

Dom called after her, 'Annabelle, you and the girls get into the basement. There's an old wine cellar down there with a metal door on it. You should be safe until all this is over. And make sure Cassie goes with you, okay?'

She nodded. 'Hope you left some wine down there,' she

winked as she walked from the room.

Dom turned and looked out the window again. He was developing real feelings for Annabelle. That kiss had been coming from the first day they had met, and he was eternally glad he had not embarrassed himself. Could there be something in this? Yes she was ten years older than him, but he had never wanted children so that wasn't a problem. Anyway, with modern technology, they could have kids if either of them were desperate. He caught himself. Bloody hell. Kids!

He was also concerned about Gabby. She had helped immensely these past few weeks, but he wondered what her long term future would be after this was over. Would she go back to her day job? Or would she join Cassie in his Organisation? Until he dealt with Gilmour though, all of that was moot. It was time to get ready, to brief the troops, well Billy and Marti that is. Fuck, it was more like Dads Army. At forty-five, he was the youngest. Billy and Marti were in their late sixties. At least that's what the two of them were admitting to. If Dom's father had still been alive he would have been seventy-two himself. His mother and father had been married for a long time before he had been born and then Luca a couple of years later. Work had gotten in the way he supposed. Now though, it was time to put all of these feelings aside. He had to get ready for Gilmour.

It took until midnight before anything happened. Dom's two way radio crackled. 'Boss,' Billy said. 'We're on. It looks like they've manned up from somewhere. I counted three cars in total, so that could be around fifteen or more.' He paused for a second. 'Where the hell did he get all the soldiers from? His organisation isn't that big.'

'I don't know Billy. He probably paid some low life street thugs with promises of a place in his setup when all this is finished. For now though you stay there and monitor the CCTV. See if you can pick them up as they get close to the house?'

Dom was still standing in his top floor office, lights out, looking through the bay window. He was dressed in outdoor gear, dark waterproof trousers and jacket. His footwear consisted of strong walking boots as he knew this fight would end up outside at some point and he did not want to slip and slide all over the place wearing shoes.

'Dom, I'll be more useful tackling these bastards head on than stuck in here looking at the telly.' Billy wasn't happy.

Dom was about to reply, when a voice from behind him said. 'He's right you know. I can watch the monitors for you.' He turned to see Annabelle standing there together with Cassie and Gabby. He had been so engrossed in trying to see Gilmour out of the window he had not heard them come in.

'Shouldn't you all be down in the wine cellar by now?'

Cassie walked forward. 'Dom, if you think we're going to leave the three of you up here to deal with this on your own then you don't know us, do you?'

Dom smiled. 'I suppose you got a taste for this kind of stuff over in Spain eh?'

'If Gilmour does manage to win this and take the three of you out, I doubt us girls will have much longer to enjoy life. Ian's on a mission to eradicate all of us, so we may as well help as much as we can, while we can.'

Gabby stood beside her mother, hands on her hips, with Cassie on the opposite side, leaning on the door frame. They all wore dark clothing. Black fleeces over black jeans and dark blue sweaters. Cassie's dark skin blended in well with her outfit.

'A Monstrous Regiment of Woman,' Dom sighed. The two younger girls looked at him, puzzled, but Annabelle laughed softly.

'Less of the monstrous thanks.' She looked at the girls, then back at Rossi. 'I see our education system is still as good as ever then.' She shook her head.

Dom looked behind them 'Where's Angela?' he asked.

Cassie hesitated. 'She *is* in the basement, Dom. Charlie's death and what Ian was intending to do to her are still preying on her mind.'

'Okay. Annabelle, you get to the caretakers office and relieve Billy. He'll leave a two-way radio with you. You need to keep us up to date on anything you see. Cassie, Gabby, you pair get on to the roof. There's a wide parapet gutter behind a waist high wall running around the perimeter of the house. I'll have Marti bring you a couple of shotguns with some shells and a radio. Keep low, but keep patrolling. The second you see something, let me know. Got it?'

They all nodded. Dom contacted Marti, told him what to do and then to join him in his office when he had finished. As the girls left, Dom couldn't help feel a sense of pride in them. He knew he was a crook. He knew he dealt in chemical death and prostitution. But these people were his friends, and right now the situation they faced had nothing to do with business. It was all personal, because Ian Gilmour had made it that way. He placed the radio on the desk and pulled the mobile phone from his inside jacket pocket and dialled a number. It was answered after the second ring.

'It's going down,' was all he said by way of introduction. 'Remember to use the old cattle trail at the back of the estate. I'll let everyone know not to fire on anyone coming from that direction.' He nodded at the reply then hung up.

Dom took out the Smith and Wesson 686 Plus revolver from his waistband and checked the safety was off. This gun was a seven shot model, not the standard six, and was chambered with 0.357 Magnum cartridges. It was a single action. It was loud, had a hell of a kick and when one of these shells hit you anywhere on the body, you stayed down. Dom had never fired a gun in anger before, until he had taken out Antonio Barrera that is. His practice had come from gun ranges he had visited on the continent and a few in America before his conviction, but with his life on the line, he was sure of one thing, if Ian Gilmour appeared in his sights he would take him down and worry about repercussions later. As he replaced the gun, he heard the extra shells jingle reassuringly in his pocket. Marti walked into the room carrying one of the Purdey's usually kept locked in their cabinets.

'Shouldn't that be broken?' Dom asked him, a grin on his

lips. 'Don't want you peppering me by mistake.'

Marti grunted then simply placed the barrel of the gun on his right shoulder.

Picking up the radio, Dom keyed the transmit button. 'Check in everyone.' They all responded in turn. 'Listen up. I have some cavalry arriving to help us out. They should be here in about twenty minutes. They'll be coming in from an old road at the back of the house, so keep an eye out for them. Anyone comes from the front or sides, let them have it.'

Dom opened a pocket in the front of his jacket and put the radio in there. He could sense Marti staring at him. 'What?' he asked, looking up.

'Cavalry? We got John Wayne and the 7th riding to our rescue then have we?' Marti looked confused.

'If memory serves, the 7th all died,' Dom answered him. 'Anyway, the Spanish are much better shots.'

'The Spanish?' Marti seemed confused then he nodded and smiled.

They made their way down the winding staircase and then to the rear of the house into the old caretakers office. Billy stood beside Annabelle, the two of them still watching the screens. There was no movement. They could not see where Gilmour and his crew had parked up. The camera coverage only went as far as the rows of trees encircling the house.

'Billy, I want you to go to the back of the house and find some cover outside. I have help coming in from that direction. Once they arrive, if we're not already in a fire-fight, move them around to the front of the villa. You stay at the back and keep two of them with you.'

Billy nodded. 'And if we are in a fire fight when they get here?'

'Then make it up as you go along. Remember, the best laid plans only survive until first contact with the enemy.' He heard Annabelle snigger. 'What?'

'You been watching Band of Brothers or something?' Billy smiled at him wryly.

Dom shook his head in despair. What is it with Scot's and dark humour under adversity.

'Marti, you're with me.'

They both moved to the front of the house. There were two rooms facing the garden, one a drawing room and the other a large dining room. The furniture was still covered with dust sheets. There was a set of French doors in the dining room and two large full height Bay windows in the carpeted drawing room.

'Marti, you take the dining room and I'll head for the other one. If the girls on the roof see any movement, they'll give us as much notice as they can.' Dom looked at him. 'Do you have your pistol as well as that blunderbuss?'

Marti patted the pocket of the lightweight, summer jacket he was wearing.

'Good. Let's hope Gilmour waits until our backup arrives. Go.'

They both moved into their respective rooms, keeping low, crouching behind the furniture to get better cover. The lights were off. Dom eased up to one of the bay windows and sneaked a peak above the window ledge. It was dark as Hades outside and all he could see were shadows and trees moving in what little starlight there was. Perhaps it was time to do something about that. He took out the radio again. 'Annabelle, do you copy?'

A few seconds later he heard a click. 'Eh, copy Dom.'

He smiled. 'Annabelle on the wall to your right, about half-way up, there's a lighting control panel. Can you see it? Over.'

'Yes, I have it. Over.'

'Good. Now find the switch for the external lights. It might say floodlights or garden lights or something. I don't know. I never use them. Over.'

'Got them,' Annabelle replied after a minute or so. 'Do you want me to switch them on? Over.' The humour had gone from her voice.

'Yes,' Dom told her. 'If you can, leave the rear garden lights off, but switch on everything else. Over.'

There was a pause. 'Okay. Here goes.'

The LED lights fitted to the front of the house at high level, instantly flashed on, bathing the garden in a flood of daylight balanced light. Dom again peeked over the window sill. This time the garden came into full view. Nothing was hidden. But there was still no one there. Where the hell had they gone, Dom wondered? It had been twenty minutes since Billy had seen the vehicles arrive, yet Gilmour and his hired hands had made no move. What were they waiting for? Then Rossi felt the mobile phone in his pocket vibrate. He took it out and looked at the name on the caller display. A wry smile spread across his lips.

'Hello Ian,' he said as he took the call. 'Here was me thinking you'd be safely tucked up a nice warm Spanish jail by now.'

'And why would the Spanish want me Dom boy? I wasn't their public enemy number one was I? No, that title fell to your pal Mr. Barrera.'

'Well if it hadn't been for their interference, you'd be a guest of Carlos right now enjoying all of his not inconsiderable hospitality. In fact, I bet he has people looking for you as we speak.'

He heard Gilmour laugh. 'I don't give a flying fuck about him Dom. The only reason he was after me was because you set me up somehow. I still can't figure out how you did it, but I know it was you. If it was about your da' you should have come and talked to me, man to man.'

'Ian you're a coward. You act like a hard man, but you'd rather ambush people and take them out when they least suspect it. My father would never have told O'Boyle about what the two of you had done to his son. Even O'Boyle knew his son was a prick.'

'You don't get it Dom. It wasn't about your da' telling O'Boyle! He couldn't have done that anyway without getting himself in the shit. No, it was about someone having something on me they could hold over my head in the future. I didn't like that. It was an unknown. So at the end, taking out your father was just business, nothing else.'

Dom was tired of listening. 'Gilmour, you're full of shit. Either put up or shut up, okay?' He ended the call and put the phone back in his pocket. Gilmour's answer was quick in coming.

Thirty seconds later a fusillade of gunfire erupted from the tree line where Gilmour's men had been hiding. Bullets of all calibres thumped into the granite stonework of the buildings façade. Windows along the front elevation shattered. Glass rained down into the garden. Rossi ducked behind the raised wall of the bay window, confident the stonework would protect him from anything but an RPG. Wood and glass splinters crashed to the floor. The barrage went on for a couple of minutes. The damage being done to the elegant Victorian structure was immense. Dom doubted any of the sash and case windows would survive this intact. The shrouded furniture inside fared no better as everything in the ground floor rooms was riddled with bullets. All the floodlights to the front of the house were taken out one by one. It ended as suddenly as it had begun. The last of the glass from the upper floor crashed down and fell onto the footpath running around the perimeter.

Then he heard two shotgun blasts. He thought it had started up again before realising it was the girls on the roof making their presence known. He smiled. Big balls those two. Taking out the pistol, he risked kneeling up and aiming through the broken window. He began losing off shots wildly, randomly targeting figures he couldn't see hidden in the lower foliage of the trees. Marti opened up from the room next to him with his Purdey. After he had loosed off seven shots, Dom stopped and re-loaded, dropping the empty shell casings onto the rug he knelt on. Compared to what Gilmour had inflicted on them though, this was peashooter stuff. Good he thought, let the bastard think this was all they had. The firing had stopped. Everyone was taking a breath, realising that randomly taking pot shots would achieve nothing. The radio crackled.

'Dom,' it was Cassie. 'You okay?'

'Fine Cassie,' he replied. 'Just contemplating what our next move should be.'

'Well you'd better contemplate fast. I can see some movement out front just past the gate. They're trying to flank us.' Cassie paused. 'Dom, there are too many of them for us. Where's this backup you were telling us about, because if it doesn't arrive soon this lot will overwhelm us.'

They had both forgotten the niceties of two-way radio use.

'Cassie, everyone else, we don't need to take them all out. The only one we need to deal with is Gilmour. Once he's down the rest of them will melt away.'

'And just how do we get to Uncle Ian?' It was Gabby. 'We're high up here and even we can't pick out any real targets, especially now we have no lights.'

Dom sat with his back against the wall thinking. Finding Gilmour in the dark without having one of his goons shoot them, would be difficult if he didn't keep them occupied. All he could do was hold them off until the people he was waiting on showed up. There was also the problem that this level of gunfire at this time of night was pretty unusual up here. Scaring crows was a daytime activity, as was clay pigeon shooting. It wasn't beyond reason to think some curious local driving past might decide to investigate or have the Police do it for them. He needed help now. He pressed the radio transmit button.

'Billy, any sign of anyone? Over.'

There was no reply. 'Billy?' Dom said urgently. 'Is everything okay?' Still silence. Just as Dom was about to try a third time, he heard the hiss of static indicating a transmission in progress.

'Boss, it's me. You'll never believe who just turned up?'

'Billy, I don't care if he has horns and cloven hooves, just get him and his men inside the house. No point in sending them around the front just now, they'll only be shot to pieces. I'm coming to you.'

Dom crawled across the floor of the drawing room pistol in hand, knees crunching on broken glass and bits of wooden furniture. It was only when he reached the door into the hallway he risked standing up before running to the rear of the house. As he reached the Caretakers office, the corridor in front of it was crowded with around ten men, all armed with the type of weapons Dom never suspected could be obtained in this country. As he pushed past the bodies lining the hall, he saw a familiar face at the rear ushering the last of his men inside.

'Hola Miguel, you took your time!' He walked over and embraced the Colombian.

Miguel returned the welcome. 'Your roads are dark at night amigo,' he flashed Dom a grin, something he was not known to do often. 'So, where do you want my men?'

'Gilmour has us pinned down in here. He has about fifteen gunmen hidden in the trees at the front and sides of the house, so he has us in a bit of a cross fire. He's trying to get men around the back as well. You were lucky to make it.'

Miguel nodded, understanding the situation. 'I will have some of my men work their way down one side further out and try to get behind them. If we can take them from there we will have a better chance.'

'Okay, if you think that'll work. It's not as if I do this sort of thing every day. Just one thing though. If we can take Gilmour out then this will all end. He's the key. So why don't you and I concentrate on finding him? Leave a couple of your guys here to guard the rear of the house, just in case some of them do make it around. If the rest of your people can make enough of a nuisance of themselves, you and I can slip out and around the other side. I'd rather Gilmour was the only one who dies tonight if I can help it.'

'Si.' Miguel pointed to two men standing close to him and said something to them in Spanish. They disappeared back out the door into the garden at the rear of the house.

'Billy, take a couple of these guys up to the roof and get them to help Cassie and Gabby. Just keep firing to get them to keep their heads down, and let me know if you see any movement?'

Billy nodded and signalled for two of Miguel's men to follow him. They looked uncertain, but Miguel said something sharply to them in Spanish and they quickly obeyed. Dom turned and looked into the caretaker's office. Annabelle was still there, peering at the screens. They were all dark, filled with static, no movement in them. Luckily the cameras had been too small to be seen as targets and had survived intact.

'See anything?' he quietly asked her.

She shook her head. 'Too dark. I can't even make out shadows.'

'Nothing we can do about that now,' Dom said, walking in and standing behind her. He glanced at the monitors. She was right. It was coal mine dark. Dom placed a hand on her shoulder and she looked up at him. 'If this goes badly, get the girls and run into the hills behind the house until morning. Your brother doesn't want you, he wants me.'

'But......' she began.

'Promise me?' Dom cut her off.

She nodded and smiled tightly. Dom bent down and gave her a kiss on the cheek.

He stood up. 'Get the rest of your men moving, Miguel.' He pressed the transmit button on the radio. 'Billy, Marti, in a few minutes I want you to open up with everything you have. Miguel's guys have got some machine guns with them which should scare the crap out of Gilmour. Once you start we'll make our move from here. Over,' but not he hoped out.

'Which way do you want my men to go?' Miguel asked him.

'Send them through the back gate and then get them to go right. Gilmour's cars passed on the other side to the left. If you and I can find them, then we can start looking for him from there, and Miguel........!'

The Colombian looked at him expectantly.

'Tell your men to take it easy. I don't want a blood bath if I can avoid it – too hard to cover up in this country. Just do enough to scare the shit out of Gilmour's men. They're probably junkies who had no idea what they were getting themselves into. Understood?'

Miguel nodded then hoisted the machine pistol he was carrying further up on his right shoulder and gave his men the necessary instructions.

The end game had begun in earnest.

THIRTY

'Now us amigo.' Dom nodded and they ran out the back door, immediately turning left, staying low hugging the stone wall of the building. None of the bullets from the fusillade at the front had penetrated this far, so there was no broken glass to give away their movement. The house was in darkness. It was a cloudless, moonless night. The only illumination was the faint background glow of the Milky Way. Their progress was slow, but eventually Miguel held up a hand. He had reached the end of the building. Tentatively he peered around the corner. There was no gunfire in reply. He turned to Dom.

'I do not think they can see us.'

Dom agreed. He pointed to the far corner of the garden. 'There's a gate in the wall just back there. If we can reach it we can use the trees as cover to get closer.' He looked at his watch, but the face and hands were not illuminated and it was too dark to see the time. 'Billy and the girls should be opening fire anytime now.'

They crouched, waiting. Suddenly, there was an explosion of gun-fire. As soon as it began, Dom tapped Miguel on the shoulder and led them off across the garden at the side of the house towards the trees. It took only seconds that seemed like minutes to get there. Dom scrambled around feeling with his hands, frantically searching for the gap in the wall hidden in the trees. Eventually he came across the wrought iron gatepost. He felt along a little further and found the round, ring handle of the gate lock. Twisting it, he pulled the gate towards himself. It opened with a squeal of unused hinges and he hurried through with Miguel hard on his heels. As expected there was no one on the other side. The gunfire had increased in intensity as Gilmour's side had overcome their surprise and were now firing back.

'Which way?' Miguel whispered.

'Down to our left.' Dom replied.

The two men crept down the length of the wall towards the front of the property, making their way past trees that had grown to over seven metres tall. As they reached the point where the wall turned left, they paused.

'Gilmour must have parked his cars out of sight further along the road to our right.' Dom pointed across the open field that would eventually take them to the road and the shore of the loch. He turned to Miguel. 'The main road is about a mile away from here, over some rough and broken ground. It'll take us a while to get there.'

'Then we had better make a start,' Miguel replied, rising to his feet and stepping forward. He had only taken a few steps when there was a shout, and a shot rang out in their direction. Dom ducked then looked to his left, his eyes following the wall along the front of the house. There were two of Gilmour's men crouched behind trees about thirty metres away, close to the main gate. He could just make out their shapes in what little light was available. He lifted his pistol and fired off two shots at each target, knowing he would be lucky to hit anything but hoping it would force them to keep their heads down.

'We'll need to make a run for it Miguel.' Dom looked, but Orejuela was not there. Then he heard a groan from a couple of feet in front of him. Miguel lay face down on the heather, his arms outstretched the machine gun lying beside him on the ground. Shit, Dom thought.

'Miguel? Miguel? How badly have you been hit?' has asked him urgently. There was another groan followed by more shots from the two hiding in the trees. Damn. He needed to get Miguel back under some cover, but these two were making that pretty difficult. He loosed off another two shots then stuck the pistol back in his waistband, before crawling towards the

Spaniard. As he reached him, he leant past and reached for the gun instead. It was the same Heckler and Koch model Dom had used to kill Antonio Barrera. Lying flat on his back, he checked the magazine, cocked the gun and ensured the safety was off. In his head he counted down from three to one, doing his best to ignore Orejuela's groans. On the count of one, he rolled clear of Miguel, towards the wall. He quickly knelt up and at the same time let off two short bursts from the machine gun, sweeping the ground in front of him from left to right. Splinters of wood and bark spun in all directions as most of the bullets hit the trees, but all he was trying to do was keep their heads down until he could pull Miguel back under cover. He threw the gun over to his left. Swiftly turning, he moved forward and grabbed hold of Miguel's ankles, then crouching, pulled him back towards some cover. Miguel groaned in pain, but Gilmour's goons stayed silent. There was no return fire. Once back in the trees out of the line of fire, he rolled Miguel onto his back and looked to see where he had been hit. It was his shoulder.

'How are you doing Miguel?' Orejuela's eyes were closed and his breathing was shallow. The wound did not look too serious. There was little blood, but Miguel was going into shock. Regardless of what the movies portrayed, Dom knew having a hole punched in any part of your body was bloody sore and your mind reacted in the way it was designed to do by going into survival mode.

Dom slapped Miguel gently a few times on the cheek. His eyes opened and he smiled weakly. 'Sorry my friend. Looks like you are on your own.'

'Can you move?' Dom asked him.

Miguel nodded and using his other arm tried pushing himself up onto his elbow, but fell back with the effort.

'Look, you're in the trees. You should be safe here until this is finished.' Rossi pulled Miguel's jacket aside and ripped a length of material from the mans shirt. He wadded it up and placed it in Orejuela's other hand, then pressed the makeshift dressing hard against the wound. 'Hold it here Miguel. It will help the bleeding.' Dom looked at him, resignation in his eyes. 'I have to leave you here, but I'll be back, okay?'

Miguel smiled wanly and nodded. He pointed to his jacket pocket with another nod of his chin. Dom reached in. His hand went around the cold metal of another ammunition clip. He took this and stuck it into a pocket in his own jacket. With a nod, he crept back to the edge of the wall and looked around it carefully. There was still gunfire towards the House, but it now seemed more sporadic in nature. No one had called him on the radio. Even with the volume turned down as it was, he knew he would have heard something. His mobile, also on silent, hadn't vibrated either. Dom hoped Miguel's men had pushed Gilmour's back a little or had at least stopped them moving forward. There was no sign of the two gunmen who had fired at them and wounded Miguel.

Dom took a breath and moved off, gaining the cover of one of the trees in front of him. He realised trying to reach Gilmour's cars across the field was pointless in the dark, so he intended to move along the wall, rolling up the flank of anyone Gilmour had put on this side. If he could make it to the main gate, then he might be able to get onto the road and back down towards the loch. He crabbed down the length of the wall, moving from trunk to trunk, getting closer to the gate. It looked like most of Gilmour's forces were concentrated on the far side of the road. Pausing, he sat, back against a tree. As he did so, he heard the jangle of something in his jacket pocket. The bullets for the pistol, Shit, he had forgotten he had fired five shots earlier. He now replaced them. But he only had four shells. He also put the fresh clip into the machine gun. Time to up the ante again, he mused.

He took out his mobile and dialled a number. It was answered quickly. He hadn't heard a ring tone anywhere in the darkness, so Gilmour was not close to the fighting.

'Well Dom boy. Looks like we're having our own wee Battle of the Alamo here doesn't it?'

'Ian, the way I figure it, you're in way over your head. Why don't you just call your dogs off, pack up and toddle off back to Glasgow, eh? We'll let bygones be bygones and start afresh next week. How about it?'

'You really are a piece of work Rossi,' Gilmour laughed. 'I'll give you credit for getting some hired guns from somewhere, but there's still that wee matter of Senor Barrera thinking I took out his wee brother. And not only that, ya jumped up wee prick, you hand me over to him like we don't have any history together, and then turn my own fucking family against me!'

Dom sniggered into the phone, taunting Gilmour. 'Oh, it's much worse than you think Ian. You see, not only did Angela try and do you over, which by the way had fuck all to do with me. No, Gabby was the genius who created a more than lifelike mask of your ugly head. Lifelike enough to fool everyone including airport security.'

'What?

'Yes, after I told her you had Marti kill her father, it wasn't too hard convincing her to put her skills to good use taking you down.'

'Fucking bastard,' Gilmour voice roared in his ear. Then the line went dead.

Dom noticed the incoming gunfire had stopped. Strange he thought. What was Gilmour up to? There was a rustling noise nearby, something scrabbling through the undergrowth. Dom, looked but could see nothing. Probably just some smart local wildlife getting the hell away while things had calmed down a little. Dom put the phone back in his pocket. Kneeling up, he peered around the tree trunk again. There was still no one to be seen, but suddenly, he heard a sound from close to the boundary wall. It seemed to be coming from no more than five metres away.

'Psst! Psst! Dinnae shoot. I want tae talk.'

Dom spun to his left, his handgun pointing in front of him. The Heckler was on the grass beside him. 'Who the fuck are you?' he hissed.

'It disnae matter.' There was a pause. 'Look, promise ye wullnae shoot if a come out. I just want tae talk. Awright?'

Going by the nasal tones, it sounded like one of Ian's street dealers he'd press-ganged into coming up here. What was this about, Dom wondered?

'Okay, slowly. Crawl over here, but throw your weapons out first; all of your weapons.' Dom held his aim steady as a shotgun and large kukri style knife landed a few feet in front of him. He had no idea if this was all the gunman had, but he would simply have to hope it was. 'Good. Now crawl over towards me and stop when I tell you.'

Dom reached forward and pulled the weapons towards him. Out of the gloom he saw a figure appear on all fours, scrawny individual, young, dressed in black jeans and a dirty, pale blue t-shirt with a faded logo on the front and a denim jacket. He was wearing a pair of bog standard trainers on his feet and no socks. Not exactly special forces attire. But he also held something in his left hand. Dom tensed up until he realised it was a two-way radio.

'That's far enough,' Dom told him. 'Now speak. What do you want, and make it quick?'

The man sat back on his haunches. 'What me and the rest of the lads want is tae get the fuck out of here,' the man - boy really, told him. He could have been no older than twenty three or four and looked scared shitless. 'That mad bastard Gilmour said we'd be doing a wee quick job. In and out, no problems. He didnae say anything about starting a fucking war.'

Dom eyed him curiously. He could see the guy was a junkie. He was scratching his arm, starting to rattle. 'Then why the firepower? Why did you all come tooled up for a fight?'

He shrugged. 'He telt us it wis just in case man, know whit a mean?'

Dom shook his head. 'No. I don't know what you mean and right now I don't care. You said you wanted to talk, so talk before I put a bullet in your jagged up little face.'

The guy held up his hands in surrender. 'Aye, awright man,

nae need to come over awe aggressive, ye know.'

Dom shook his head. God preserve us, he thought. 'Just tell me what you want for fucks sake?'

The firing had died down completely by now. None of Gilmour's men seemed to have any interest in attempting to rush the house and Miguel's soldiers were keeping themselves under cover, just as Dom had asked.

'Big Ian gied two of us a radio. The guy wi' the other wan is wi' everybody else over there.' He indicated with a nod of his head. 'Am gonnae call him and tell them aw tae get tae fuck back tae the cars. He's no paying' us enough for this shit. Just you tell yer guys no to shoot, okay.'

Dom eyed him carefully for a few seconds, wondering if this was some kind of trap. But going by the way he looked he doubted the addict would have the gumption to come up with anything too clever. 'Fine,' Dom eventually said. 'I'll tell my guys no firing for the next five minutes until you lot scarper back down the road, but you'll need to watch out for Gilmour and Archie Todd. They won't be too happy.'

The other man nodded. Dom took out the radio and passed his instructions to everyone. The junkie did the same and seconds later Dom heard the sound of feet from the other side running along the single track road back in the direction of the loch. He quickly glanced to make sure they were all retreating and by the time he turned back around, the junkie had also vanished, presumably following his pals. Now all Dom had to do was wait and see what kind of reaction this 'retreat' would get from Gilmour. It came within seconds. There were loud shouts from the direction the group of men had all run. A couple of shots rang out, then more shouting, then silence.

Dom waited, wondering what was coming next. Picking up the Heckler and Koch, He crept from his hiding place and edged closer to the road. Eventually he gained the cover of the last few trees before reaching the road itself. He knelt down beside a trunk, the machine gun held in his hands, pointing towards where he expected trouble to come. The closed and barricaded wrought iron gates to the house were to his left. In the distance, he heard the sound of car engines starting. Diesel or petrol, not electric. At first they faded off, heading back towards the village. Dom hoped they had all given up, perhaps even convincing Gilmour. Then one of the engines grew louder, revving hard. Dom held the gun up to his eye, sighting along the barrel, straining to see what was coming.

About two hundred metres from the gates, just around a slight bend, there was a dip in the road. As Dom watched, a pair of lights disappeared into the depression, before launching themselves into the air as they sailed out the other side. The four by four they were attached to crashed back down onto the tarmac with a suspension breaking thud, swerving a couple of times. Dom thought it was about to roll, the high centre of gravity fighting to win the battle against the three tonne weight of the Land Rover. It stayed upright however, the driver gunning the engine, speeding up, heading directly towards the gates. Dom knew it had to be Gilmour. This was his one last desperate attempt. Without thinking, Dom aimed low. He fired a long burst from his machine gun towards the Land Rover's tyres. Some of the bullets hit the grass. Some the road. A few went into the upper body. But enough hit the tyres causing both front and rear to blow out. The vehicle wobbled again and swerved from side to side, the driver fighting desperately to maintain control. The Land Rover did not stop accelerating, but it had become hard to steer.

It had been aiming for the gates, intending to burst through them. Instead, it rammed into the left hand gatepost attached to the granite wall. The wall gave slightly, but held. The gatepost though was torn from its resin anchor fixings. One of the gates popped open at the side, leaving a gap into the grounds, its hinges burst from the impact. The stone arch swayed, and then toppled, hitting the ruined bonnet of the vehicle. The front of the four by four had collapsed in on itself. Steam erupted from the radiator. Brake and engine fluid poured from beneath it onto the road surface. For a few, long seconds there was silence. Nothing moved. Then, there was a noise of someone kicking. The passenger door was stuck, the frame bent by the impact. There was a crash, and the passenger side window broke. White powder from exploded airbags drifted into the night, quickly followed by the head and arms of a figure struggling to exit the vehicle. Dom was too far away to see who it was, but he lifted the machine gun and pulled the trigger. There was only the click of an empty chamber. Shit, he thought.

He reached for the extra clip on the inside pocket of his jacket, but all he found were threads. It had fallen out somewhere. Throwing the useless gun aside, he took the pistol from his waistband and ran forward, leaving the cover of the trees behind, half expecting to be fired on any second. But he wasn't. As he closed the gap to the Land Rover, he could see the person scrambling from the broken window had fallen head first onto the ground. They were now trying to pull themselves up. As Dom got closer, he stepped on a dry twig that snapped. The passenger from the vehicle looked around and Dom saw it wasn't Gilmour. He didn't recognise him, but it had to be Archie Todd. Todd appeared to notice the gun in Dom's hands and looked frantically for something he had dropped. His left arm hung uselessly beside him. Kneeling, he picked up his weapon from the grass where it had landed. Todd then let off a series of three wild shots, none of which came anywhere close to Rossi.

Dom didn't hesitate. He slowed, knelt on the grass with one knee, gripped the pistol two handed, and aimed. This was the only way to be sure. Waving his gun around and trying to shoot while running would result in nothing but wasted shots. He took a shallow breath, and aimed at Todd. Gilmour's hired thug half stood up and started moving in a panicked run towards the rear of the Land Rover, losing off two more shots in Dom's direction. Dom tracked him and fired. He heard the screech of metal as the bullet thumped into the side of the car. He fired again, trying to lead Todd. More screeching of metal. Steadying himself, he squeezed the trigger one more time and watched as Todd stumbled, dropping his own weapon and reaching down to hold his leg. He turned to look at Dom, terror in his eyes, obvious even in the dim light. Rossi did not hesitate. He fired again, hitting him square in the chest and Archie Todd instantly fell hard onto the road at the side of the car.

But Todd hadn't been driving.

Dom edged back towards the wall, near the trees. Using it as cover he crept along slowly, heading towards the Land Rover. As he did so, a figure appeared from behind it and fired off a series of shots aimed towards where Dom had been kneeling seconds before. Without thinking, Dom loosed off two shots in quick succession towards the figure, knowing it could only be Gilmour. Then Rossi suddenly felt the cold metal of what he took to be a pistol pressing against his neck. He froze. A thin arm snaked around him and pulled him back. The muzzle was then pressed into his temple, hard.

'Ah've got him Mr Gilmour. He's goin' nae where.'

Dom grimaced. It was the little jagged up thug with the radio, the one he thought had run with the rest of them. Seemed he had a plan after all.

'Drap the gun, ya bastard.'

Rossi did as instructed.

Dom heard a voice from behind the Land Rover. 'Good lad Sandy. Looks like you'll be taking over Easy's patch after all.' He stepped out from behind the car, his gun held out in front of him. Despite the situation, Dom fought hard to suppress a laugh as Gilmour walked towards him. He was wearing a suit! Shirt, tie, jacket, trousers, the whole shebang. Ian always liked to look sharp. 'Well Dom boy,' he continued, 'Things haven't worked out well or either of us, have they?'

As he walked forward, Gilmour shouted loudly, making sure everyone heard him. 'Tell your wee army no heroics Dom or their general takes one in the guts and cops it for a long slow death. Do it, or so help me I'll get Sandy to put one in you right now.'

Dom looked at him for a few seconds. He knew all it would

take was a single well placed shot and Ian would drop like a stone and he wanted so badly to deliver the shot himself. The junkie relaxed his grip on Dom's throat but not enough for Rossi to do anything meaningful. He wanted no mistakes while he was this close to the barrel of a pistol. He took a shallow breath.

'You all heard him,' he shouted in a strangled voice.. 'No one fires, no one, and someone stop these Spanish bastards from doing anything stupid.' A female voice rang out speaking in fluent Spanish, translating his instructions. Annabelle. Now where the hell had she come from he wondered? The junkies grip strengthened again.

'That you Annabelle?' Gilmour smiled wickedly as he continued walking. 'Come to see your boyfriend get what he deserves for trying to set me up, have you?' He stopped about four metres away from Rossi, gun held steady in his hand.

The metal of the damaged gate made a grinding noise as Annabelle held it in her two hands and shook it hard in frustration. 'You're a bastard Ian. You always have been. Even growing up it was all about you.'

Gilmour glanced towards her while keeping his gun firmly pointed at Dom. 'Aw darlin', didn't know you were the jealous type! But see, me being the oldest, well – that was how it was always going to be. Our parents were old fashioned that way. They just liked me more than you.'

Dom laughed. 'In your dreams Ian. The only person that's ever liked you is you.' There was the sound of a gunshot, and a bullet thudded into the grass between Dom's feet. The junkie jumped.

'For fucks sake Mr Gilmour!'

He ignored him. 'You know Rossi, I've just about had enough of you,' Gilmour spat through clenched teeth. 'First you ruin my chances of hitting the big time by killing Barrera, then you frame me for that, then I find out my entire fucking extended family is involved in helping you take over my organisation.' He shook his head and a grim smile spread across his face.

'Well I'm afraid it ain't going to happen Dom boy. I'd liked to have dished out some of what that nutter Carlos had in store for me, but needs must.'

'Ian, shoot me and Billy and Marti are not going to be happy bunnies. In fact, I doubt you'll live long enough to get ten yards along that road. Dom watched Gilmour warily. Maybe there was still time. Maybe there was a way.

'What if I can help you get away Ian? You must know Carlos is gunning for you, and without help there's nowhere in the world you'll be able to run to. Nowhere you can stay safe.'

'Right, and all I have to do is put down my gun and we'll all be pals. I know, you can build us all a big campfire and we'll sit around it singing Kum-By-Ya and having a natter about the old days. Forget it Dom. In fact, I've had enough of this.'

Gilmour moved his gun slightly to better his aim. The drug addict loosened his grip and stepped to the side, not wanting Gilmour's bullet to hit him as it tore through Dom's body. His pistol was still trained directly at him though. Rossi closed his eyes, waiting on the shot to tear parts of his body to shreds. There was the bang of a pistol, then a loud double blast as if from a shotgun, but surprisingly no pain. He slowly opened his eyes. Ian Gilmour lay before him on his back, arms outstretched, the gun he'd been holding nowhere in sight. Rossi glanced to his side. The junkie who had threatened him was lying crumpled on the grass, red blood black in the gloom staining the ground. A weary sigh from the tree line caused Dom to spin on his heels. He saw Miguel, half slumped against a tree for support. Dom realised he must have crawled after him and then seen what was going down. As he began to move towards Orejuela, the Colombian waved him back.

'I am fine Domenico. Check Gilmour.'

Rossi turned back and began to walk towards where his adversary had fallen. There was a fist sized hole in his chest where the pellets had penetrated his lungs and blood bubbled from the deep wound. Gilmour coughed. A spray of crimson came from his mouth and trickled down the side of his chin.

Dom looked at him feeling – well, feeling nothing. Ian had started this, but Dom had survived it. He took no pride in that. His business had been disrupted and he had done some things he would have thought himself incapable of a few short weeks before. Looking down he saw Gilmour trying to say something. He knelt closer to him.

'Who?' he wheezed. 'Who?'

Dom turned and looked at Annabelle. Standing beside her, behind the ruined gates holding a shotgun was Angela Phillips. She had gotten her revenge for Charlie Easdon, for her father, for herself and for all of them. Turning back, he stood up and watched as the light went out in Ian Gilmour's eyes. His head fell to one side and he stopped moving as his final breath gurgled from his throat and the hole in his chest.

At last it was over.

THIRTY ONE

'How is he?' Dom asked Gabby as he stood over the unconscious figure of Orejuela. She sat on the edge of the bed. The bullet was a through and through. The exit wound was ragged, but Gabby and Annabelle had cleaned it up and found no metal fragments left behind. Annabelle stood by Dom's side, her arm draped through his, as if holding him for support.

'He'll be fine. The wound looks clean. The bullet nicked his collar bone so he was in a lot of pain, but a half bottle of Glenmorangie and a few codeine tablets sorted that out. He's been out for nearly two hours, but when he comes back round I'll let you know.'

'Thanks Gabby. You did well.' Dom placed a hand on her shoulder.

'Yeh, Doctor to the Mob, that's me,' she smiled weakly.

Dom and Annabelle left the bedroom where Orejuela was being cared for. As they walked into the hallway, Annabelle turned to Dom.

'What now?' she asked him, the weariness evident in her voice. 'I mean what do we do with my brother's body.'

They stopped walking and Dom's expression took on a faraway, thoughtful look. Despite all the bullets fired, all the mayhem caused, the only four people to have been hit were Miguel, Archie Todd, Sandy the junkie and Ian Gilmour. Todd, the junkie and Gilmour were dead. The remaining disparate group of *soldiers* had fled back to Glasgow and Dom doubted any of them would be too concerned about Gilmour's fate once they found out. Some of Miguel's men had wanted to follow them, but Annabelle had quickly calmed them down and outlined the difficulty of getting rid of that many bodies in a small place like Scotland. This wasn't Columbia. There was no jungle to bury them in. He turned and looked at her, a pained expression on his face as he knew how much his words would hurt.

'I'm sorry, but they all have to disappear. If you try and have him buried properly? Well, you can imagine the questions that will raise.'

She looked sad. 'I know,' she agreed. 'I don't care what you do with the others, but despite everything Ian is my brother. It would have been nice to have buried him with some dignity.'

Rossi shook his head. 'Billy and Marti will deal with the bodies. Tomorrow I want you and the girls to head back to Glasgow. Meet up with Tony Smith. Bring him up to speed on what's been happening. Don't mention anything about Ian being set up for Barrera's murder. If he asks, and he probably will, just tell him what we rehearsed; that Ian wanted to work with Los Malvados instead of the Barrera's and took Antonio out to prove his worth to them. Somehow I don't think Tony will care too much who he works for as long as the money keeps flowing. Then tell him I'll speak with him in the next few days and explain the new reality to him. If he doesn't like it.......' Dom shrugged.'

Annabelle nodded and started walking again. 'What about O'Boyle? What do I tell him if he asks Tony or me about the coke deal?'

'If O'Boyle contacts you, tell him that as far as you're concerned, the deal is still live and that Ian's replacement will be in touch with him in the next few weeks.'

She smiled. 'And that would be you!'

'That would be me,' Dom agreed. 'Provided you're still happy with the arrangement?'

'Rossi, I want nothing to do with this crazy business ever again. I've had enough excitement over the last few days to last me a lifetime, so you're welcome to it.'

He nodded. 'Good, your heart needs to be in this game.'

She looked at him grimly. 'Except it isn't really a game Dom, is it?'

Rossi could think of nothing he could to ease any pain she was feeling over the death of her brother, so he simply shook his head.

They walked down the stairs. Dom had asked Annabelle to get Miguel's men to help clear the place up. They were working on the front side of the house. Every room there had been peppered with bullets. There were no intact panes of glass left in any of the windows. In some rooms there were no windows. People were sweeping and clearing on every floor. Dom didn't think Miguel's hired hands were too happy about it, but they would stay here until Miguel was fit enough to travel, so they may as well be of some use. Later, when things settled down, Dom would get a renovation organised, but first, there was the no small task of trying to collect the spent bullets and shell casing lying around. Miguel's men were piling up what they could find ready to bury in a deep hole he would have them dig later in the back garden. Then there were the bodies. The two disused farms lying adjacent to his estate had old septic tanks. They had been drained years before and Marti suggested the bodies be dismembered and disposed of in one or both of these. It wasn't the worst idea, Dom had thought, and later he would arrange to have them filled with concrete, as a safety precaution if anyone asked. But that was tomorrow's problem. The three bodies were in the basement of the House, wrapped in old tarpaulins.

Annabelle saw Angela tearfully trying to help sweep up some broken glass, her Uncles murder of Charlie Easdon still raw, and her murder of her Uncle preying on her. She slipped her arm from Dom's and walked over to her daughter, wrapping her in a hug as the girl sobbed on her shoulder. Dom yawned as he watched them. No one had slept last night. There was too much adrenaline in the air and in their systems. They had done some clearing up, drank some tea and coffee laced with whisky and tried not to think too much about what they had just been through. Truth be told, the entire incident had taken little more than twenty minutes to play out. When the shooting started, events had moved quickly. Now, Dom just wanted to leave and get back to Glasgow, but he also wanted to talk again with Miguel. He needed to find out more about Carlos and what had happened to him after they had dropped him at the safe house. As far as Dom knew he was still there. It had only been a week, so the Spanish police had not stood down their search for him. The TV and online news confirmed that. Finding a route for him back to Colombia would need to be put on hold until things had calmed down. He might even need to spend two weeks cooped up in one of his own semi submersibles, sharing a bucket with the crew to return safely to South America.

Dom had contacted Miguel the day after the fiasco in Mijas, but their conversation had been brief. It was limited to Dom asking if there was any way Miguel could help him at Torridon, as he knew Gilmour would probably come with a small army. To his surprise Miguel had said he could. The Villa in Mijas had not been in his name. In fact he had travelled into Spain under a false name so getting over to Scotland would not be an issue as the Spanish police were not suspicious of him. He would also get some of his men from Amsterdam to come across, and he had contacts in England where he could access the weapons they would need. Impressed, Dom detailed what he wanted him to do. Come to Torridon. Camp out near his Estate in the Highlands, wait, and then, when Dom contacted him, provide the backup he knew he would need. And he had done it all. But now he was lying upstairs in pain from a bullet he had taken doing just that. Rossi swore he would make it up to him in any way he could. He walked on down the main hallway of the House and found Billy and Marti in the kitchen, sitting at a table quietly drinking tea with Cassie. Dom leant against the door frame, folded his arms and smiled at the scene.

'See you've found your two grand-dads then Cassie.'

Cassie had her back to him, but he could sense her smile. 'That's right Rossi, at least these two will look after me and not get me shot to death or nabbed by the Spanish police.'

'Touche,' he replied. He nodded to Billy and Marti. 'Shouldn't you two be out there helping clear up or something.'

Billy glanced up at him. 'We're the gaffer's boss. Too old to work.'

'But we have the experience,' Marti grunted.

Rossi walked over and sat down beside Cassie in the one spare chair. Billy slid a cup across the table to him and lifted the teapot, pouring him a drink.

'Bit stewed,' he said unapologetically, 'but then you know where the kettle is.'

Dom began to laugh. They all looked at him, but he didn't stop until there were tears running down his cheeks.

'Bloody hell. I should be doing stand up,' Billy smiled at Cassie.

'I think its hysterics Billy.'

Dom's laughter eventually subsided. 'I'm sorry,' he choked. 'It's been a long few weeks.' He sat back in the chair, picked up the cup and took a sip of the by now lukewarm black liquid. 'You all know I never wanted to put any of you through this, and I'm sorry if it's caused you any pain.'

After a few seconds, Cassie reached over and placed a hand on Dom's arm. 'Oh fuck it,' she said quietly. Turning in her seat, she reached up to Dom's head, grabbed the sides with both hands, pulled it closer to hers and planted a long, wet kiss on his lips. Dom sat there eyes wide, shock on his face. Billy and Marti smirked.

Eventually she let him go, turned around and folded her arms. After a few seconds, she reached up and wiped her mouth with the back of her hand. This time it was Billy and Marti that began to laugh.

'Well, well, well. Something you two aren't telling us?' he heard a voice from behind him.

Dom recovered from what Cassie had just done and turned to see Annabelle and Gabby standing in the doorway, a stony look on both of their faces.

'It,.....it isn't what you think,' Dom stammered.

'No!' Annabelle replied 'Then why don't you elaborate please? I'd love to hear your explanation.'

They both stood there for a few more seconds before they too dissolved into laughter.

Dom's head swivelled, looking at them all. Then he too smiled and burst out laughing again, together with Billy and Marti. Cassie stood up and walked over to Gabby. She held out her arms and the two of them embraced.

Bloody hell he thought, it was good to be alive.

READ ON FOR A SAMPLE FROM THE NEXT BOOK IN THE

Rossi Trilogy

Past Sins

Due out in 2022

PROLOGUE

The man's black leather shoes splashed through puddles as he walked along the red ash cemetery path that meandered between the gravestones of black marble and mottled granite. He knew where he was going. He could walk the path blindfolded. You wandered through the old Victorian graveyard with its lichen and moss covered monuments speckled and damp with soft summer rain. Then you kept on, up the slight incline to the large monumental wooden cross in the centre of the cemetery, the one commemorating all the priests of the Diocese who had died. He recalled that many years ago some young man had hung himself from the crossbeam. A protest against the priest who had abused him years before, they had said. Next, turn left onto the new tarmac path, then head for the carved statue of a football player kicking a ball atop a marble pedestal above the grave of another young man killed in car crash. Too much youth here, he often mused. After this, you took the gently sloping tarmac of the path into where the new lairs had been created, except even these were now full. Death never stopped, just like Scottish rain he often thought.

A few drops of a returning summer shower began to settle on the shoulders of his brown jacket. He opened the small umbrella he carried and hiding beneath it kept walking to the far side of the cemetery, close to the random rubble boundary wall. As he approached his destination, another figure stood in front of a lair with her back to him. Although there was a chill in the air, she was clad in a sleeveless black blouse and wore a long, black a-line skirt. A white bag hung on her right shoulder. Above her, a red umbrella kept the soft rain at bay. She mimicked a Flanders poppy of remembrance. She turned her head slightly as she heard his footsteps come towards her, but didn't look all the way as she knew who it was. As he reached her side, he simply stood with her, looking down at the black polished marble of the headstone. What little writing there was, etched into the glassy surface, was picked out in bright gold paint. It said simply;

A Loving Brother
Taken too soon by violence
We will never forget
And a Mother
Safe with him once more

There were no names. No mention of who they were, how old they had been. There was space aplenty though to add these details later. For that's what they had both decided all those years ago; wait until the bastard who had murdered their brother had been dealt with. Only then would they complete the wording on the headstone. Only then would they and their brother find some kind of solace, and their mother some comfort. But after more than thirty years, they had still not found a way to achieve this. Not that is, until now. The legal route had not been for them. That would take too long with no guarantees, and it would have been too impersonal. No, their now dead mother had made them promise years before that they would make his brother's killer pay in the cruellest possible way. And that was what they both intended to do.

'You're late,' his sister eventually chided him.

The man knew he should have been here at eleven o'clock, the exact time they had interred his older brother's coffin, but business had held him up. He glanced at the Hublot on his left wrist. It was only eight minutes past the hour.

'It isn't always easy planning your own day when you work for someone you hate.'

She grunted faint acknowledgement. 'You've been there for a while now. Are we still going forward with what we talked about last time?'

He nodded. 'Yes,' he said. 'But it's all been about finding the right opportunity. The contacts I've made are very interested in setting up a presence in this country. They seem happy with the plan I suggested and they're willing to help with bodies on the ground.'

'Alright, I won't ask anymore, but if there is anything else I can do, then let me know.'

'I will. Just keep working where you are, keep your eyes open and let me know when he comes to see her. I still think she's our best bet, and I get on well with her. If what I have in mind comes to fruition, then it's better if you stay out of things until the end, and if it all goes tits up I'll be a dead man walking and I don't want you incriminated.'

She turned to the side and looked at her brother. 'We're both in this together, that's the promise we made to our mother before she died.' She indicated towards the headstone. 'Yes, he was a bit of a prick, but he was harmless and his murder sucked the life from her. The only solace we can give them from beyond the grave is to destroy the cold blooded bastard that put him there. So if I have to go down with you then I will.'

The man let out a sigh. His sister was younger than him by five years and he had been younger than his dead brother by the same margin. Now, here they were, both middle aged, both single, both driven by a promise made years ago to a vital, vibrant woman destroyed before their eyes. He had nearly given up on the quest many times. The way and the means had never presented themselves to him, despite the fact he had immersed himself in the same world as the killer. But then things had changed. Takeovers had happened. People had *'passed on.'* He had proven his worth and been retained. Then, with only a little effort on his part, he had found himself at the heart of the killer's enterprise.

And as a vital part of that heart, one of the functioning valves, he knew it would be easy to orchestrate its failure. He was trusted after all. No one doubted his loyalty.

By now the rain had stopped. He closed his umbrella and shook the drops from the fabric. 'I can handle this sis. He'll only find out it's me right at the end, just before I put a bullet in his head.' Water dripped down his trouser leg, and he waved the umbrella around again, throwing off more drips, some of them splashing onto the black marble.

She reached out and grabbed hold of his arm tightly, fingers curling into a claw trying to rip through the fabric of his jacket. 'I need to be there. I need to see it happen, to spit my venom at him.' Her piercing dark eyes skewered him leaving no room for doubt.

He nodded. 'I'll make sure of it.'

Lowering and closing her own umbrella, she slipped an arm through his and turned once more to look at the grave and the headstone with its strangely incomplete wording.

'Perhaps next year we can finish this. Next year we can let the world know exactly who lies here.'

He patted her arm linked through his. She didn't know it, but by this time next year he intended to be the one running things. But to do that he would need to take them all out and despite what he had said to her, he knew he would need her help to ensure that happened. Then he would begin to build his own legacy with the help of the people he had lined up. Removing her arm gently from his, he walked across the newly mown grass towards the black marble headstone. He transferred the umbrella to his left hand, kissed the index and middle fingers of his right hand, then bent down and placed them gently on the wet stone. 'Then my brother, I'll build a monument to you. To what you could have been. To what our mother thought you were.'

He felt a hand on his back and his sister crouched down at his side, a tissue in her hand, wiping away some of the rain and dirt staining the headstone.

'Amen to that,' she whispered.

CHAPTER ONE

Detective Constable Hunter McGowan yawned - again. It was three thirty in the morning of July eighth, or was it the ninth? Definitely the ninth he decided. He was sure the sun had rolled over into another day. A sliver of bright light broke through between the cloudless sky and the North Sea, calm for once at the start of another nineteen hours of daylight. This was Hunter's third night on call as Duty Officer, which meant he could sleep until disturbed, or as per last night, fall into his now more usual alcohol induced haze. Headquartered at Lerwick on the Shetland Islands, it was unusual to have the CID woken and dragged out of their beds at this hour, but he supposed he shouldn't complain. The previous forty eight had been quiet, his sleep unbroken, his dreams obscured by the whisky. Speaking of which, he hoped no one got near enough to smell his breath. He popped another fruit pastel. Mints were too much of a giveaway. Not a good idea to be breathalysed by one of his underlings.

He had woken up groggy, poured himself into a pair of jeans, grabbed a not too rumpled white shirt and found a pair of black trainers under a chair. Running his fingers through his almost shoulder length brown hair, he then travelled the 3 miles or so in his old Model 3 Tesla down to the quayside. His brown leather bomber jacket helped insulate his bones from the early morning chill of the harbour air, but he shivered nonetheless. The boat he was headed for was surrounded by blue and white police tape. A couple of constables stood guard in front of it, chatting quietly to each other; a male and a female the man unashamedly chatting up the girl. Hunter smiled. She was gay so McGowan knew it was a futile effort. He noticed the sergeant who had called him standing some way off, puffing contentedly on a cigarette. Hunter walked along the quayside continuing past the boat that would eventually become his main source of interest, nodding to the two equally tired looking officers. Scenes of Crime had not yet arrived and until they did, the vessel was off limits to everyone, himself included, although he imagined the Sergeant had already been inside.

'Well Halcrow,' he asked, walking closer. 'What pathetic excuse have you come up with for dragging me out of my pit at this ungodly hour?' He knew full well though, it had to be serious.

Sergeant Ewan Halcrow turned and looked at McGowan as he approached. 'You know, sometimes I just fancy having a wee chat with someone who has a modicum of intelligence, unlike those two plods down there.' He flicked his half smoked filter tip into the harbour and walked to meet McGowan. 'But then I remember it's you on call and realise I can't have everything.'

McGowan wondered how he could afford the smokes at nearly thirty quid a packet, but each to their own. 'So, what do we have then?' He waited as Halcrow, pulling one of his monthly, week long night shifts, walked to meet him. They stopped about 20 metres away from the yacht.

It was a meeting of opposites. Hunter was in his late twenties, banished, as he saw it, to the bald hair follicle of Scotland for no apparent reason he could fathom. Just one of Police Scotland's indecipherable foibles. A six foot tall Aberdonian with sandy hair, he was turning from the physique of his rugby playing youth into practice mode for early middle age. After two years on the island, his introduction by Halcrow to the community nightlife had allowed him to indulge his taste for beer and whisky, items he was beginning to consume in almost industrial quantities when off duty. Such was life. Halcrow was what McGowan would be in thirty years if he kept practising. Bald, overweight, red faced, hollow legged. A sergeant at peace with his lot and an island native to boot. He and the fifty five year old had somehow hit it off father son style. Plus, Halcrow's knowledge of the islands and their people had proven invaluable on the learning curve for an incomer.

The Sergeant took a breath. 'Looks like a stabbing. On the yacht. Victim is a black male. Mid thirties. One stab wound to the chest and another to the throat. Not a cut to the throat that I could see, but an actual stab wound. He bled out fairly quickly so no need for the medics, just the Doctor to certify death.'

'Black?' McGowan was surprised. 'Not an ethnic minority we have much of up here, is it?'

The Sergeant shrugged. 'He probably came in on the yacht. Caribbean perhaps?'

'Have you been onboard?'

The Sergeant nodded in the affirmative. 'The Harbour Master dug up a pair of bolt cutters for me.'

'Bolt cutters?' McGowan asked quizzically.

'Aye. The hatch to the cabin had been padlocked closed from the outside. Chained with a padlock'

'Okay, interesting. We'll need to arrange a PM at Lerwick General for the IC3. I'll put in a call to the PF in the morning so they can arrange for the pathologist.' He looked around the still almost deserted quayside. 'Who found the body?'

'The Harbour Master,' Halcrow told him. He opened his notebook, an old fashioned paper one in lieu of the now compulsory tablet. Hunter raised an eyebrow.

'Don't worry, I'll input onto the system later.' He glanced at McGowan's, hands stuffed deep in the pockets of his leather jacket. 'Anyway, where's yours?'

Hunter went slightly red. In his haste to leave he had forgotten it, a cardinal sin. Just as well he had a good memory, plus access to everyone else's notes. 'Just get on with it,' he mumbled.

Halcrow shook his head then glanced down. 'The yacht was logged as arriving at its berth around ten o'clock last night by the Harbour Master. A bit late but not unusual. The Captain didn't report in, so the Harbour Master wandered over about eleven, but the boat was in darkness and appeared empty. He figured whoever was on board had buggered off to the pub and decided he would get to it sometime in the morning then continued doing his checks. About an hour later though, he was coming back past it again and this time there were some cabin lights on. The hatch was secured with a padlock. He knocked, not expecting an answer, and wasn't disappointed, but he managed to look through a gap in the curtains covering a window. That was when he saw our John Doe lying in the cabin. He called us, we called you, and that's it.'

'Any witnesses?'

'Give me a break boss. We'll do the canvas in the morning. But there haven't been any reports of a disturbance from anyone. Everything was in darkness until we arrived and noised the place up.'

The sound of a vehicle pulling up further back drew their attention. 'Good, SOCO has turned up,' McGowan yawned. 'I'll let them get their wee white tent set up and then grab a *Noddy Suit* and go and have a gander at our victim. In the meantime,' he turned back to Halcrow, 'head over to the Harbour Masters office. Find out what you can from the CCTV and ask them for a copy. Make sure they check and keep any recording from the last few days as well.' Halcrow raised a questioning eyebrow at this. 'Just in case whoever did it has been checking out the harbour recently.'

'Okay, will do. Oh, and boss!'

McGowan looked at Halcrow expectantly.

'Just as well you'll be wearing a mask. Don't breathe on anyone.' He smiled and walked off.

Hunter shook his head. He knew Ewan was only half joking - he hoped. It had been him after all who had introduced him to the Island nightlife. At twenty nine, what he couldn't get used to though was being called boss by a Police Sergeant on the cusp of retirement who outranked his constable status. That *was* strange.

McGowan walked back along the quayside towards where the SOCO'S were emptying their van to embark on what looked like a camping trip. They would tent over the gangway to the yacht deck and use this as their initial base; their sterile zone. He wondered who was on duty tonight, but as there were only two senior Scenes of Crimes Managers on the Island, it would be either Maria Maldini or Stanley Tate. He grinned to himself as he saw Maria step from around the vehicle, already kitted out in her white paper suit but with the hood still down. In Hunters eyes, she was, to be polite, simply fucking gorgeous. Unfortunately Hunter knew that in her eyes, he was simply a pain in the arse constantly annoying her by asking her out.

As he walked over she spotted him and rolled her eyes heavenwards. 'Remind me to check which shifts you're pulling in future so I can avoid them.' Grabbing a large pilot's case, she walked past him then stopped. 'Well, come on. It's your crime scene I presume.'

He fell into step beside her as they walked to the boat. She was thirty two, hailed from Largs was still single. Hunter thought the five foot ten inch, alabaster skinned, belying her Italian Heritage, dark haired women beside him, was the best thing on the island. Even the loose fitting paper suit did little to hide her curves. But she was intellectually brilliant. A first class scientist with a mind honed like Toledo steel. And unless he saved her from drowning or some other catastrophe, he doubted they would ever be together.

'Well, what do we have then?' she asked him, all business.

'One victim, two stab wounds. Halcrow is the only one who has been on board and we're waiting on the Doctor to come and certify time of death. His DNA and fingerprints are on file for elimination.'

'Whose?'

'Halcrows.'

She nodded. 'Right, once we get the tent set up, you can climb into a suit and overshoes and we can start.'

Twenty five minutes later they were ready, including overshoes, hoods, gloves and masks. The Doctor had arrived and she too was kitted up ready to go on board. Hunter had met Doctor Caroline Ash a couple of times before. She was his GP as well as moonlighting for the police, with a cruel acerbic wit he liked.

Hunter led the way up the short gangplank, across the deck toward the hatch and down the short set of stairs into the cabin. It was nothing special. From his little knowledge of sailing, McGowan guessed this was an ocean going yacht. It was certainly large enough and rigged for sea travel. On the uncarpeted, timber floor in front of him was the body of the unfortunate victim. Male, mid thirties, ebony black, dressed in a blue shirt, a pair of jeans and wearing deck shoes and no socks. His eyes were open, a look of mild surprise frozen on his countenance. A red, coagulating puddle extended from around his midriff and spilled across the deck. McGowan walked in and stood to the side, allowing Maldini and the Doctor to enter. As the others went to work, he stood in one corner and looked around the cabin. Nothing appeared out of place. There were no signs of a struggle indicating the victim may have known his attacker, or attackers. The cabin itself was small, too small Hunter felt. His father had been an architect and Hunter had spent a few summers on building sites, so he had an inkling about measurement. The dimensions seemed all wrong.

He waited and watched in silence together with Maldini, as the Doctor examined the victim. The rest of the SOCO team stood outside, but they were already working, taking fingerprints and photographing the deck and the hatch covers. After about fifteen minutes Doctor Ash stood up and stretched. McGowan waited.

'Well?' he asked her.

The sixty year old GP turned and looked at him. 'Well he's definitely dead.'

He knew she was smirking behind the mask.

'Going by the amount of blood pooling around the floor near his abdomen, the cause of death is a single stab wound up underneath the sternum, missing the ribs and straight into the heart. Very professional. Not done in the heat of the moment'

'What about the stab wound to the throat?'

She shook her head. 'Well it certainly didn't help.' Again, a masked, hidden smile. 'But probably post mortem. Very little blood from that location. Time of death was around midnight, give or take fifteen minutes.'

'That ties in with the Harbour Masters statement to Halcrow. You say professional. A hit?'

She shrugged. 'You're the detective. I'm simply giving you the facts. I'll get a copy of my full Death Certificate to you in the morning. In the meantime,' she turned towards Maria and handed her a slip of paper. 'You can use this to call the undertakers when you're ready for the body removal. All yours now,' she said before leaving.

Hunter watched as some more SOCO's entered and began doing whatever it was they did. He stepped forward past the body, careful not to stand in any fluids and stopped when he reached the bulkhead. Something about the cabin was still troubling him. It was too cramped, even before five people had squeezed inside. He glanced out of a porthole and noted a location on the quayside as a marker. Turning, he went back outside into the sterile tent and removed his overshoes, placing them in an evidence bin so they could be examined later in case they had picked up anything by accident. Walking off the boat, he turned left, moved to where the cabin started and then began pacing off. When he reached the reference point he had noted from inside the cabin, he discovered he was still nearly four metres short of the bow. There appeared no obvious reason why. Glancing towards the deck he saw no sign of a hatch indicating the presence of a storage compartment.

Wearing clean overshoes, he returned to the boat and squeezed past the other people working there. He tapped the bulkhead, unsure what he was looking for. It was metal, which was unusual and rang with a hollow note. He stepped back a pace and ran his eyes over it. It didn't look factory fitted. The gaps around the perimeter were slightly too wide and they didn't appear to have been sealed properly. Someone had just run a bead of clear mastic around the joint.

'Maria,' he said turning toward Maldini. 'Do you have a boroscope?'

'What. The piece of kit we use to see inside small cavities? I think so. Why?'

'I have a feeling there might be something hidden behind this bulkhead.' He tapped it with his knuckles. 'Any chance you can drill a hole it so we can have a look.'

She nodded all business then called to someone on deck to get the necessary equipment. 'What are you thinking?' she asked, stepping around the body and wandering over.

'I'm thinking our guy here was killed for some reason, and probably by someone who knew him. And the reason,' he pointed, 'might be lurking behind this.' He rapped the bulkhead again.

Ten minutes later a metal drill bit had eaten a 10mm diameter hole in the middle of the wall. The boroscope snake, connected to a portable monitor was threaded through the hole, it's led light on full. The operating tech wiggled it around to get some sense of bearing, but Hunter had already seen enough. He'd been correct. The space they were looking into was filled with tight, plastic wrapped packages. And if his suspicions were correct, it had to be cocaine.

'Bloody hell. That's a lot of cling film. Good work Sherlock,' Maldini said to him. 'Well deduced.'

He smiled at her compliment although she could only really see the crinkle of his eyes. 'I'll leave you to the rest of it and go and track down Halcrow and the CCTV. Let me know if you find anything else of interest.' He turned away, then stopped and looked back. 'Please,' he finished, but she had already begun talking with one of her colleagues. Ah well, he sighed, perhaps a murder scene wasn't the best place to do any flirting.

After divesting himself of the *Noddy Suit*, he walked around the quayside and accessed the Harbour Masters office with his

ID Badge. He found Halcrow sitting in a room staring at a monitor with nothing on it and with someone who wasn't the Harbour Master next to him. He was drinking coffee and doing nothing much else. He looked around as McGowan entered.

'Any joy?' Hunter asked him, his tone making it clear he thought Halcrow should be doing something a bit more active than just getting edgy on caffeine.

'Maybe. Jimmy here's the tech. He's been whizzing around his recordings and has come up with a few things.'

McGowan looked at the youngster. Jimmy was very young he noted, like, school boy young. Perhaps it was a summer job. He was nervous and it showed.

'Okay Jimmy, show me what you've found.'

'Eh, aye, right. Give me a second.'

'No rush son.'

Five minutes later Hunter was about to tell him he shouldn't take that too literally, when a video popped up on the screen.

'I was able to find these two guys who I didn't recognise coming into the harbour two days ago and then spotted them again tonight, arriving then leaving about fifteen minutes later.'

McGowan shrugged. 'Well just because *you* don't recognise them, doesn't mean they're our boys, does it?'

Jimmy squirmed a little and appeared to become even more nervous. Halcrow butted in, looking at Hunter, stern faced.

'What he means boss, is that they were really careful. They kept their mushes well hidden from the camera. They had their hoods up at all times, even though it wasn't raining when they visited last night or before.'

McGowan nodded. 'Okay. Good work Jimmy. How many sightings of them did you make?'

The young man seemed to relax a little. 'Only those two. I can keep looking for you if you like?' He was more enthusiastic now.

'That would be great Jimmy,' McGowan replied. 'Keep at it. Oh, and what time were they here last night?'

'The time stamp says they arrived at eleven forty and the

system caught them leaving again at eleven fifty five.'

'And did you see which boat they went to?' Hunter tried to keep his hopes in check.

Jimmy shook his head. 'It doesn't cover that side fully I'm afraid.' He looked between the two of them. 'Budget cuts.'

'But it was the same side where the boat we are interested in is berthed?'

The boy nodded.

'That's good, Jimmy. Give Sergeant Halcrow a copy on a memory stick of everything you have. I'll get some of our tech people over later today to do a formal backup.' He turned to Halcrow. 'Ewan, get onto the council street camera team. I want to know if their system picked up their faces or at the least, where they went.'

Halcrow nodded. 'It'll be later today boss. They are all tucked up sound asleep just now.'

'Can I have a quick word outside?'

The sergeant stood up and followed McGowan into a small corridor.

'I – we found something on the boat, hidden behind a false bulkhead.'

'Coke.'

'How.....?'

He shrugged. 'Stands to reason. Dead black guy, sea going yacht. They were probably coming back to get the gear later, until our eagle eyed harbour master got curious and spoiled it for them.'

McGowan smiled. 'Fine, Hercule, just get me the CCTV for the morning so I have something to show Ronaldson.'

'No problem boss. I'll push young Jimmy for it.'

'Good. Oh and Ewan?'

'Yes boss?'

'For fucks sake stop calling me boss. You're making me feel like an old man.'

Halcrow grinned. 'If the cap fits.'

McGowan blew out a sigh and left. He trudged back to the

yacht, got himself kitted out again, and walked on board. Maria Maldini was leaning over the body at the victims head. Hunter couldn't see what she was up to, but as he was looking at the fabric stretched taut across her backside, he didn't really care. After a few seconds though, she spoiled his inappropriate thoughts, and straightened up letting out a sigh. The young SOCO photographer who had been next to her did the same, without the sigh.

Did you find anything?' he asked her.

Maldini turned around to face him, a pair of silver tweezers in her right hand. There was something gripped in them and she held it out towards him.

'What is it?' he asked.

'Not sure. I was looking for fibres around his mouth when the torchlight caught something further back. I've just pulled it from the back of his throat, near the cut.'

'May I?'

She nodded. 'Let's take it outside to the evidence table and get a better look.'

The SOCO photographer was snapping away at what was held in the tweezers. Hunter waited and when he had finished, Maria dropped the item into her gloved palm. It looked like a piece of wrapped paper. Not crumpled, but folded up, close to its general maximum of seven.

They went on deck, Hunter leading the way, and entered the tent. Maldini got an evidence bag and laid the folded paper on top of it. She gently used the tweezers to coax it open, until it eventually lay as flat as she could get it. It was coated in a thin layer of saliva flecked with watery blood.

'What? Was he trying to swallow it? To hide it from someone?' he asked her.

'Maybe, but given the neat way it has been folded, I'm not so sure. There are no bite marks on it so it wasn't being chewed, just some saliva staining.'

'You mean it could have been forced in there?'

Maldini made a face. 'Forced may be too strong a word if it

was post mortem. I think whoever placed it there wanted us to think our IC3 was trying to get rid of evidence.'

'Or perhaps they knew with your scientific brain, you would find it anyway. Besides, even if he had swallowed it, the post mortem would have picked it up in the stomach contents. So it could be a plant.'

Maldini shrugged. 'Possibly.'

'Okay. Anything written on it?'

'See for yourself, but first.......' She nodded to the Crime Scene Photographer who walked over and took some more photographs of the exhibit. When he had finished, Hunter came closer, took out his mobile phone and snapped some images himself. He looked up at the SOCO photographer with his large, full frame mirrorless Nikon Z10 and just knew he was smirking behind the mask. Then he examined what she had discovered. It looked like the torn out page from a lined notebook. Nothing special. Just ordinary High Street, newsagents stationery. However, written in black ink on the bleached white bleached eighty gram per square metre paper was a single word followed by an eleven digit mobile phone number. McGowan had no idea who the number belonged to. He also didn't recognise the word. Well he did, but it appeared to be just a name, probably a surname.

It simply said 'Rossi.'

So who or what thought Hunter is Rossi? And what did the Rossi have to do with a dead black sailor found on board a drug smuggling yacht in the Shetland Islands of Scotland?